I0675539

TAKE MY *Breath* AWAY

The Breathe Series: Book One

WENDY L. WILSON

Take My Breath Away
Copyright © 2015 by Wendy L. Wilson

All Rights Reserved

No part of this publication may be reproduced, distributed, or trans-
mitted in any form or by any means, including photocopying, re-
cording, or other electronic or mechanical methods, without the prior
written permission of the publisher, except in the case of brief quota-
tions embodied in critical reviews and certain other noncommercial
uses permitted by copyright law.

This book is a work of fiction. Names, places, characters and inci-
dents are a product of the author's imagination and are used ficti-
tiously. Any resemblance to actual persons living or dead, events, or
locations is entirely coincidental.
Printed in the United States of America

ISBN: 978–0-9962379–0-1

Cover Design by *Cover to Cover Designs,* www.covertocoverdesigns.
com
Cover Photo by *MH Photography*/Female Cover Model, https://
www.facebook.com/pages/MHPhotography-stock-and-custom-pho-
tos/575584915823179
Male Cover Model, *Julio Elving,* https://www.facebook.com/Jepmod-
el
Author Photo by *Ashleigh Pettis*
Editor, *Jeremy Thompson*
Formatting by *Champagne Formats*

Dedicated to the ones that take my breath away . . .

To my husband and two wild little boys:

You support me, motivate me and encourage me every day of my life to be a better person, to believe in myself and to always strive for more. I love you and truly could not have done this without all three of you by my side.

Also,

In Memory of my Daddy.

I know you have always watched over me and every breathtaking moment of my life.
I love you, dad.

Hit by a truck

I PRY MY EYES OPEN and squint from the blinding sunlight streaming in through my bedroom window. Instantly an aching sensation in my head reminds me of yesterday's events. I feel like I've been hit by a truck. No, it's as if a massive construction crane went for a joy ride and ran me down. Not just once either. Nope, it plowed me down, turned around and did it again. I suspect it considered taking another pass at me, but missed the chance when I ran away to save myself. Even though I physically feel crushed and beat down, it is nothing compared to the cracked, broken and shattered remains of my heart.

I flip onto my stomach and let my body sink into the mattress as I grasp onto my feather-down pillow. The softness of it against my skin lends a false sense of comfort as I pull it tightly to my chest. Hoping a little sunshine will improve my mood, I peer out the window at the head of my bed. Last night's torrential downpour seems to be letting up to a steady drizzle and the sun barely peeks out from behind the clouds. *If I see a rainbow, I may have to scream.*

Being careful not to jostle around and make my pounding headache any worse, I sit up gradually then reach over to the nightstand for my phone. I power it up and quickly notice twelve missed calls and eight missed texts. Unfortunately, they are all from Kyle, with the exception of one that came in this morning from Bethany. As my hand hovers over the word delete, I sigh and let the details of the day before replay in my mind.

The bus ride back from the state track meet was complete pandemonium.

Throw in the excitement of last night's graduation, a landslide win today and our last high school meet ever and you get a seriously amped up bunch.

In the four years since Kyle joined the track team, our school has dominated the sport. School records have been broken, and we have managed to head to state every year. He wiped out the competition and made it look so easy; if it wasn't for sweat dripping from every inch of his lean body, you would think he put no effort into winning at all. He would glide around the field as if he was on skates and was never passed by another runner.

I snuggle up close to him in the back seat of the bus while he bounces around telling jokes with his teammates. The other cheerleaders are all seated in random spots and join in on the celebration. Kyle whoops and hollers with the others before he settles down beside me as we pull into the school parking lot.

He looks at me with his deep chocolate eyes while he traces circles across my outer thigh. "We're here, gorgeous."

I lift my chin to meet his gaze as he gives me the smile that stops most girls in their tracks.

"Wake up," he whispers against my cheek.

"I'm not asleep," I giggle.

The bus jolts to a stop and we both stand to file out with the crowd. I shuffle along behind him as he says something to his friend Chris and then follows it up with a high five. Still on his heels, we exit the bus and all disperse to our separate vehicles but not before Kyle announces, "Party at my house, tonight!"

After a quick peck on the lips, I jump in my car and steer out of the school parking lot for possibly the last time.

I race home at record speed and leap up the stairs, skipping every other one on the way to my room. Halfway there I hear hushed tones coming from my parent's room. I sneak up to the cracked door and peer inside planning to eavesdrop.

My mother and father embrace each other as Mom's sobs fill the air. I immediately assume the worst when I see Mom's puffy face. The last time I saw that hopeless look on her face, we were headed down a long road of chemo treatments, lab work and doctors visits. I push the door open and pray they will fill me in.

"Mom, Dad, what's wrong?" They both look at me while my mother tries to recompose herself.

I cross the room and wrap my arms around Dad's neck, collapsing down between my parents with tears stinging my eyes. Dad hugs me tightly and comforts me in the same way that he did last time we crossed this bridge.

When he was initially diagnosed with cancer two summers ago, our family's world was turned upside down, yet Dad always managed to keep his head up. Even when he was too weak to lift his arms and too sick to hold any food down, he still continued to reassure us that everything would be fine. He kept a smile on his face and a positive frame of mind the whole way and by that following spring there was no trace of cancer in his body.

I have no idea how I would ever live without Dad and I never want to find out.

"Honey, we are going to keep our faith," Mom says, shaking me out of my thoughts.

I blink my eyes and let a few more tears slip down my cheek.

Mom clears her throat and begins to explain the gravity of the situation. "Sweetie, your father had a biopsy done this morning. We don't know anything yet and may not hear back for another week so we cannot assume the worst. Let's just pray for the best results and believe that everything will be alright." She takes a deep breath and I can tell she is trying to convince herself just as much as me. "You caught me at a weak moment, that's all. My mind was getting carried away and I was thinking the worst." She pulls me into a hug with a small unconvincing smile.

I seal my eyes closed and focus on regaining some amount of calmness. Opening my eyes back up, I see both of my parents staring at me with pained expressions. I know the last thing they want to do is worry me.

Dad keeps his arm firmly grasped behind me and pats my knee with the other hand. "How did the meet go, anyway?"

His swift attempt at changing the subject makes me smile. I know the conversation is closed and to not talk about it until we know more.

My parents have always reminded us to never dwell on a problem unless there is a tangible reason to worry. Even in times like this, that same level of faith applies. It's how my parents raised me. *Smile instead of cry and focus on the positive,* I repeat in my head to reassure myself.

"Dad, you're changing the subject," I point out, knowing this is Dad's way of keeping his mind off of it.

He nods his head with a soft chuckle.

"It went fine," is the only response I can get out.

Mom lifts off from the edge of the bed where she is sitting with me sandwiched between them. She walks to the doorway, straightening her crumpled up slacks and smoothing stray hairs back into her barrette. When she shifts her body towards me, I see her bloodshot eyes and know that this was more than just a weak moment. She is scared. The edges of her mouth lift into a hint of a smile as she also shifts the topic to today's track meet.

"I assume Kyle wiped out the competition as usual?" She asks with a soft smile that tells me she is putting on her brave face.

I tip my head forward to confirm and loosen my grip on Daddy.

As much as I want to fall onto the floor in a blubbery mess, I know it won't help matters so I swipe my arm across my face and dry my eyes. *There's nothing to worry about. Everything will be alright,* I silently tell myself.

Dad joins Mom at the doorway, but turns to ask me one last question before leaving the room. "Are you and Kyle going out tonight?"

They know my Friday and Saturday nights usually consist of being out with him, but the last thing I feel like right now is being around a bunch of drunken jocks, so I lie. "Actually, we don't have plans tonight. Besides, I'm in the middle of a good book so I think I'll hang out in my room and finish it." I plaster on my best I'm-doing-just-fine smile and my parents nod their understanding.

After I am safe and sound behind the closed door of my room, I shoot Kyle a text.

Me: I'm so sorry, but I can't make it tonight. I'll miss you. Call me tomorrow. <3 U

As soon as I hit send, his name lights up my phone. He is not going to let me off very easily.

"Hello." I don't even have to try to sound upset, because I definitely am.

"Hey, babe." My heartbeat picks up at the sound of his voice and I know this will not be easy. "Why can't you come? I really need you here," he begs.

I really don't want to get into the particulars right now so I just come up with a bland explanation, hoping he will understand.

"My parents already made plans for us tonight as a family. Now, I'll feel bad if I leave," I say, knowing this will not satisfy his urgency to have me there tonight, so I go a bit further in my explanation. "Besides, I really don't feel that wonderful at the moment. I think I got too much sun today." It's not the complete truth, but it is true. I'm nauseous from Dad's news.

There is a stretch of silence and I grit my teeth to keep from relenting. If he doesn't speak up soon I know I'm going to hop in my car and speed over there.

"Ok, but I'll miss you. I was hoping you could stay the night," he says as I hear him muffle the phone and holler something out to Chris. His best friend must be there helping him get ready for the party. *Great, I feel guilty for lying.*

A text message sounds in my ear and I know it must be Bethany, my best friend. *Wonderful!* I forgot I had made plans to go with her tonight. *Let's see how many people I can let down in one evening.*

Kyle's firm tone comes back on the line. I'm half a minute away from telling him I will be there in fifteen, but he lets me off the hook. "Ok babe. I have to go because people are starting to get here. Get some sleep and feel better. I'll call you tomorrow. Love you."

"Love you too, and I really am sorry," I tell him right before hitting end on my phone.

Once I'm off, I click on my messages icon and read Bethany's text.

Bethany: You just about ready to head to the party, chicka??

I blow out a loud sigh after reading her text message. Here I go again.

Me: I'm gonna pass, girl! Sorry! I don't feel good. I think I got too much sun today. Have fun and drink a beer for me.

As soon as I hit send, I grit my teeth while waiting for her reply.

Bethany: Bummer! Now I'm going to be all alone! I guess I'll forgive you this time, but call me tomorrow! Maybe we can go shopping if I'm not too hung over. Lol! BTW, you suck for standing me up!:P

At least she isn't giving me too much grief for bailing on her. I laugh knowing Bethany's intention at most parties is to find a guy to hook up with for the night. She won't be alone for long, so I don't feel too bad.

Me: You mean if you're home and not crashed with some random guy somewhere at the party! LOL!!

I giggle, remembering some of the stories she has told me about her weekends.

Bethany has always been a bit more outgoing than me in that department. By our sophomore year she had already lost her virginity. I, however, had tried to hold onto my virtue as long as possible more out of fear of the unknown rather than being responsible. I made Kyle wait until our nine month anniversary. He never pressured me and always pointed out that he was fine with waiting, but secretly I think it was killing him.

Bethany: You know it, girl! Call me tomorrow and I'll fill you in on my night!! LOL ;)

Me: Will do! Have fun and B careful!! <3

I lay my phone down on the nightstand beside the bed and kick my sandals off to get comfortable. *I might as well stay true to one thing I said I was going to do tonight.* With that, I roll onto my stomach and grab the book I just started reading last night. This will, by far, engage my mind better than partying with a bunch of classmates that I tried my best to avoid my entire high school existence. I can get lost in a good book. It will at least let me escape my reality for a while.

Minutes soon turn into hours and before I know it five hours have passed.

My parents have since said their good nights and I've changed into my PJs. I've also indulged in a bowl of ice cream and enjoyed a couple drunken texts from Bethany.

I put my book down and glance over at the clock when I hear the door downstairs slam shut. It's 10:46 so that must be my older sister, Abby, coming home.

Sitting up, I raise my arms to stretch just as she cracks open the door to my room.

"Don't tell me you're reading on a Saturday night," she states more than asks in a distracted tone that tells me she is trying to keep her mind busy as well.

She stands with her hands on her hips and her golden hair hangs loose around her face.

Abby and I had never been close until a couple of summers ago. Hearing such dark news about Dad woke our family up to how short life can be and since then, we have all been very tight knit.

Her petite frame glides over to my bed then she not so gracefully plops down to her knees on the hardwood floor. Clearly needing some sense of security herself, she reaches out to grab a fuzzy aqua throw pillow that I flung to the bottom of the bed earlier and hugs it to her chest.

"So, I guess you decided to stay home tonight after hearing Dad's news?"

I draw my eyebrows together, knowing her heart holds the same fear as mine. No doubt she is trying her best to cope with this, just like me.

"Yeah," I suck in a deep breath.

She is going to force me out of my hiding spot. She above all knows I am in fact hiding, afraid to leave the house for even a second. The reason she knows this is because she did the same thing a couple of summers ago. Back then, I pushed and pushed until she joined me in silly mind-consuming adventures. Before long, I had her helping me plant flowers in the front yard, building a birdhouse with Dad, shopping with Mom and many other excursions that ultimately drew us all closer.

Abby heaves out a loud breath and jumps to her feet. She darts to my closet in a blink of an eye and swings the door open. Rifling through it, she shoves outfit after outfit to the side to examine the next.

"What are you doing?" I ask as I stand up and walk over to see what's going on.

She twists around to face me so fast that her body creates a small breeze that flips my long blonde hair into my face. I spit out the small hairs that land in my mouth while she shoves a black halter top and white skirt in my line of sight. Leaning away from her, I giggle as she shimmies her hips and shakes the outfit to add a dramatic effect to her actions.

"Get out of those jammies and get all sexified. We're going to a party." Her eyes light up and her face glosses over with a huge smile.

I know she is talking about Kyle's party and there is no reason for me to even argue. Besides, I know that look. She will drag me there if she has to.

Grabbing the outfit, I laugh as I point to my black toeless wedge sandals at the base of my closet. She obeys my silent request, handing them to me and then jets out to change herself.

I quickly wiggle out of my tank top and shorts and slip on the outfit my sister so carefully selected. Smoothing the soft, felt tip edge of my pink lip gloss over my lips, I spruce myself up just a bit and finish up by swiping some mascara across my ridiculously long eyelashes. I love my sister. Here, I was prepared to mope all night and she pulls me out of my slump. She always seems to know what I need before I do.

Kyle's house is in the same subdivision as ours. It is located four blocks down from our house on a private cul-de-sac. Giving that the news forecasted rain this evening, we choose to drive and immediately notice flickering lights behind the house and hear the loud thuds of bass coming from the inside as we drive up. There are tons of cars haphazardly parked along the circle drive and filling his driveway.

Abby parks up from his house so we won't be blamed for blocking anyone in later.

Heading for the house, thunder booms in the sky, warning us that the weatherman did in fact get this one right. *Great!* Fat raindrops begin to fall from the sky pelting us as we race to the shelter of the covered front porch. People yell in the back yard as the sky opens up into a downpour.

Abby rolls her eyes and shakes her head, obviously flustered that the rain has put a damper on the half hour effort she put into her hair and makeup. Honestly, I really don't care. I've always been a "less is more" type of girl.

As soon as we are inside, Abby jets off with a couple of her friends. I swear the entire senior class is here plus a few from the class before us, which is Abby's graduating class. The place is still packed at this late of an hour, so after about fifteen minutes of looking for Kyle I resign myself to asking around.

I ask a couple people that are clearly too drunk to form words and decide to go with the hand gesture I get from a drunk girl that looks ready to pass out on the staircase. She points up the stairs. *He must have escaped to his bedroom to sleep it off.*

He has never handled alcohol well. Four to five beers and he is flat on his ass.

I bite my lip as I climb the stairs, excited to see him. His door is shut, but I pass on knocking. I'd rather go for the full element of surprise since he isn't expecting me.

Opening the door, my heart climbs up into my throat as the dark room fills with a familiar sound and a strong salty smell of sweat. I take two steps towards his bed and see his body shifting under the sheets. His heavy breaths and grunts tell me he must be taking care of himself out of frustration that I am not here.

Then I hear a noise that puts my emotions on high alert. A female voice calls out, "Oh, Kyle," into the darkness just as he moans. I stand there in shock, unable to move, unable to speak, unable to breathe. A loud cry escapes my throat along with the breath I had been holding. I throw my hand over my mouth and back away from the bed just as he turns his head.

"Oh shit . . . no, no, no!" he yells as he jumps to his feet, bare-naked.

My eyes look over him just as I hear the girl scream and throw the covers over her face and body. I have no idea who she is and I don't care.

He reaches for what I assume are his jeans and starts tugging them on.

"Alyssa, baby . . . let me explain," he pleads as I turn and rush out of his room.

I can't think or even manage to understand what just happened.

Racing down the stairs and through the party like I'm being chased by a vicious dog that's foaming at the mouth, I shove people out of my way with Kyle quickly closing in behind me.

"Alyssa just wait!" he yells out while clumsily trying to tug on a pair of skinny jeans that look two sizes too small.

My face heats up with embarrassment as I notice several people pointing and laughing with their phones held up to take pictures of the drama that is unfolding between us. I continue my descent out the door into the pouring rain hoping to spare myself any confrontations of what I just witnessed.

I run as fast as my legs will carry me, racing nearly two blocks past where we parked and until my lungs are burning and screaming for air. I'm breathing hard and soaked from the rain when Kyle catches up to me. Clamping his arms around my waist, he stops me dead in my tracks, pressing his bare chest against my back.

"Please, please don't go! Hear me out, please!"

I can hear the regret in his voice, but I can't feel anything but emptiness and pain.

"Alyssa, baby . . . you weren't supposed to be here!" he pleads with me, squeezing me so tight that I can feel his heart hammering in his chest.

Those words make my blood turn to molten lava and I tear myself from his grasp. I swing around with my hand raised, fully intending on slapping him. He grabs my wrist before it strikes his face and he pulls me into him once again. I fight to get away, not wanting to be anywhere near him.

How dare he say I wasn't supposed to be here?! So if I'm not here, it's ok for him to screw around? My eyes widen as I think about all the parties I have missed, and this could be exactly how those nights ended for him as well.

I lean forward feeling vomit rise into the back of my throat. *I hope*

I throw up all over him!

"Alyssa, please, please! She meant nothing. Nothing!" he says to me, sounding as if he should be on his knees begging. "I love you, Alyssa! Please, don't leave!" he insists as his wet chest rises and falls so quickly that I think he may hyperventilate.

I swallow the bile in my throat and force back all the tears I have been holding in from this day. Looking into his big brown eyes that I have looked upon so many times in the last year, I manage to form only one complete sentence before my sister drives up.

"It's over, Kyle!"

There is no need to say more. There is no explanation that will be good enough, and there is no way I will ever believe he loved me.

Kyle's hands drop to his side and his eyes widen. I take advantage of the moment to slip into the car with Abby.

"You asshole!" Abby screams out the window in a deafening tone before peeling out.

I look in the rearview mirror and see Kyle fall to his knees, dropping his face into his hands.

When we get home, Abby helps me to my room, changes me into my PJs and tucks me within the security of my fluffy comforter. Sliding onto my bed beside me, she lays her back against the headboard with careful mothering movements and then slips her legs beneath my head.

My body feels numb and my heart is empty, yet my cries echo in the room as she runs her fingers through my hair and turns off my phone after it continues to ring over and over.

As I closed my eyes, the images and sounds from Kyle's room repeated in my mind and I knew that I was going to be hit by that truck over and over again, mowing me down until nothing was left.

Girl's getaway

A GAINST MY BETTER JUDGMENT, I finish listening and reading every one of Kyle's messages. Although I should feel absolutely nothing for him after what he did, the sound of his choked up voice begging for my forgiveness brings tears to my eyes. After the first few messages, I really should stop listening instead of inflicting more pain upon myself, but I don't. After I listen to the last one, I decide to text Bethany a generic message rather than calling her and rehashing last nights' events.

Me: Gonna have to pass on shopping today. Bad night last night . . . we'll talk about it some other time. Ttyl! :)

Exhausted, I stagger to my dresser and examine my reflection in the large oval mirror hanging on the wall. *I even look like I was hit by a truck.* I slump my shoulders and fall backwards onto my bed. *Screw the brave face.* I prefer to wallow in my misery.

Right then, the reason to put on a happy face walks into my room: my dad. I take one look at him and decide if he is strong enough to make it through what life has thrown at him, then who am I to give up.

Dad flashes me a sympathetic smile, and I know Abby must have filled him in on what transpired the evening before; I'm just hoping she didn't share all the details. I didn't have to tell her much; she came to the correct conclusion of what happened due to Kyle's half-clothed body and the apologies he kept yelling out.

Not to mention, after getting online this morning, I quickly saw every social media site plastered with Kyle sporting a pair of faded wash skinny jeans with rhinestone stars on the thighs chasing me through the party. It seems that my entire class knows about what happened by now. Even though I got a bit of gratification from seeing Kyle humiliated, seeing the pictures and the fact that he was wearing some girl's jeans still stung a bit. Here he thought he would sneak around behind my back and in his haste he couldn't even manage to grab the correct pants. *Genius!*

Dad sits down on the edge of the bed and wraps his arm firmly around my shoulders. He always seems to be the one comforting me when I should be comforting him.

"I hear you and Kyle broke up?"

I nod as tears well up in my eyes. *I will not cry, I will not cry,* I chant to myself over and over.

"Listen, I understand if you don't want to talk about it, but I'm here if you need to."

I look up at him and see that he is looking straight ahead, almost like he is lost in his own world. Knowing he needs the support more than I do, I snuggle up closer to him.

He looks down at me and goes on. "You know, sweetie, your life is going to be full of unexpected moments. There will be heartaches, joys, lots of laughter, I hope; some may make you question why you should even try and then others will absolutely take your breath away." My father pulls me against his side even harder upon saying these words. "But no matter the moment or the situation you are faced with in life, make sure you always hold your head up and live life to the fullest. When you are dealt a lousy hand of cards, don't just play that hand, rearrange them, move them around and make the most of that hand."

I scrunch up my eyebrows a little confused by his words and Dad lets out a laugh.

"Sometimes you just have to look beyond the present and learn to move forward. Enjoy life." He kisses the top of my head and adds, "Alyssa, one of my greatest joys in life has been watching my three beautiful baby girls grow into the intelligent, gorgeous young women you all are today. I truly could not be prouder of who you have become. You, sweetie, have given me more moments that have taken my breath away than I could have ever hoped for or dreamt of having in a lifetime. You and your sisters and your mom have made my life full. And someday, someone is going to come along and you will know what those breath-taking moments feel like. You will know it without a doubt. You may question it at times, but you will know."

Dad beams at me with the widest smile I think I have ever seen on his face.

"Daddy . . ." I hear my voice squeak out barely above a whisper. "How do you know?"

I look back up at him and he raises his eyebrows in question.

"How do you know when someone really loves you? Because I thought . . ." My voice fades off and I look down into my lap so he doesn't see me cry.

"Honey . . ." he smiles, "Oh honey, you will know." He laughs.

I remain silent, tossing his words around in my head. *I thought Kyle did love me. I thought we loved each other.*

My father continues on with his words of wisdom. "Someday, some guy will look at you just as you are right now and he will say to you, you are the most beautiful girl I have ever seen." Dad laughs louder and I see a twinkle in his eyes like he knows something I don't. The joy in his eyes brings a smile to my face as well.

When I look across from us at the mirror above my dresser, I can see why Dad is laughing. My hair is a tangled mess. I have mascara smeared under my eyes and down my cheeks, plus my eyes are puffy and swollen from crying. *Yeah, sure! Real beautiful, Dad!* I spit out a loud giggle as he goes on.

"Someday, a guy won't think twice about doing truly horrendous things to make you happy."

This makes me and Dad both break into a fit of laughter as he ruffles up my hair adding " . . . like cleaning the hair out of the sink drain because you complain about it getting clogged up or killing a spider when you squeal and scream like a mass murderer just broke in or when you . . ."

Dad and I are now laughing hysterically.

"Ok, Ok . . . I get it," I say and then hug Dad with all the love I have in my heart to give.

Dad whispers into my hair as he squeezes me tightly, "I love you so much, honey."

Someone clears their throat in the doorway and we loosen our bear hug to look up. Mom and Abby smile as Abby runs over to the edge of the bed and crashes into us, knocking us over into a monstrous hug. Although she nearly knocks the breath right out of me, I still laugh uncontrollably. *Who needs Kyle? I have my family; I freaking love them all.*

After we finish up our laugh-fest, Mom informs us that there is a batch of brownies in the oven, especially for me. *That's right, brownies for breakfast!!* According to her, brownies cure all heartbreaks and I definitely can attest to the fact that they do help.

"Well, I tell you what, girls. We are going to make this a wonderful summer," Dad declares as he shoves himself off the bed and heads over to stand by Mom.

Mom's face lights up as Dad puts his arm around her shoulders and then turns to face us. Abby and I remain curled up on the bed, side by side.

"In fact, your mom and I decided to live on the edge for once." They both laugh, but I stay quiet, wondering what they could possibly be referring to.

Live on the edge; this is definitely not the time for Dad to be living on the edge.

Clearly reading the alarm that must be written on my face, Mom stifles a laugh and then quickly adds, "Oh stop worrying you two. Your father just means that we have booked a trip." She looks over at Dad and they smile as if they are having an unspoken conversation. "We're going to the beach and we'll be gone for a week and a half. We've never went away by ourselves, at least not since you girls were born, so we figured no time like the present."

The weight that was tugging at my shoulders after the words "live on the edge" eases up and my heart is filled with relief. *A vacation, I can handle that.*

"That's great. You both deserve to do something like that," Abby says as she stands up. "I'm leaving tomorrow, too. Remember, I'm going out to the lake for a week with Piper and the girls?"

All eyes turn to me and I shiver from the thought of how low I may stoop if I am left here alone. I have visions of myself moping around, un-showered, teeth un-brushed and cramming brownies down my throat the whole time.

They all share a look of concern as I stare at them deep in thought. I force a smile on my face, absolutely refusing to beg any of them to stay. Mom opens her mouth to speak but Abby beats her to it.

"You should come with us, Alyssa."

I giggle at her enthusiasm while bouncing off the bed and then trailing down the stairs.

"Oh my gosh, Alyssa, you will have so much fun. You remember the cabin that Piper's parents own down at the lake? You know the one that I spent a couple of weeks at, a few years back?"

I slide my hand along the smooth surface of the banister listening to Abby go on and on about why I should join her. Once I round the corner into the kitchen, my hunger is awakened by the sweet, sugary, chocolaty smell of warm brownies that are perfectly positioned in the center of the dining table. The smell attacks my nostrils and pulls me toward the table like a magnet.

We both sit as Abby continues, "Well . . ." she says in a peppy tone, "We decided since we're all young . . ." her voice lowers a bit as if she has a secret and she glances over to our parents to see if they are listening in on us. " . . . totally single and hot, we will just have a blast without worrying about relationships and all that crap."

Dad slips his hand over Abby's shoulder grabbing a brownie and sinking his teeth into it. Chewing his large bite, he mutters out of the corner of his mouth, "beautiful not hot, sweetie . . ." he tips his head to Abby. "Don't degrade yourself. And I agree. You should go. You both are too young to worry about relationships. Be young and have fun."

He starts heading out of the kitchen and then turns to add with raised eyebrows. " . . . But not *too* much fun!" He smiles and then heads upstairs to start packing for his trip.

Mom giggles and follows behind him, mouthing, "You *are* hot . . ." She smiles at us both then turns and says loud enough for Dad to hear, "And have *lots* and *lots* of fun, girls!"

She winks and I hear Dad yell from the top of the stairs, "I heard that!"

Abby rolls her eyes and we both laugh.

My sister goes on and on while we polish off a whole batch of brownies with a full glass of milk each. "So there was all this drama that happened several years back and we both swore off ever going to the lake again, but . . ." she draws out her last word with a mischievous look in her eyes, " . . . according to Piper's dad, the whole east side of the lake is vacated up to the Fourth of July."

I nod my head, curious where this is going while I gulp down the last of my ice cold milk.

"Apparently, there is a construction crew . . ." Abby blatantly licks her lips as she mentions those words and goes on, " . . . doing renovations on all the cabins. So yeah, Piper and I figured we could get drunk, go skinny dipping at night and flirt shamelessly with some hot construction guys," my sister whispers with an evil laugh.

I'm not sure whether to be excited, nervous, or scared. Leaning back in my chair, I try to process all that has been proposed. *I don't think I will be indulging in skinny dipping with a group of girls. Flirting with guys doesn't top my list of fun things to do at this point either, but having some drinks and a good time, that sounds like a plan.*

"Ok, I'll go." I'm strangely excited with my decision, yet somewhat worried. I know her group of friends can get pretty wild. "No pressuring me though or giving me crap for not joining in on anything that makes me uncomfortable. Deal?"

"Deal . . . now go get your ass packed. This is gonna be a girl's getaway to remember," she winks and then darts out of the kitchen and upstairs.

I inhale a deep breath and squeeze my eyes shut. *I really hope she's right.*

Trouble

A FTER SEVERAL STOPS AND A four-hour drive later, we pull up in Piper's Dad's van. As soon as the side door opens, I hop out and stretch my arms above my head hoping to soothe my aching, stiff back. The entire trip here I sat scrunched up in the back seat with two other girls. My sister lucked out and rode shotgun the whole way. My lips dip down into a frown as she gets out and gives me an amused grin. She knows I'm cranky after that drive.

"*Oh. my. God . . .* This is going to be trouble," Piper spews in an angry tone and then hides behind the van.

"Oh, shit," my sister calls out before joining her.

They carry on in whispered tones, looking over at a neighboring cabin only a short distance away with a crew of guys working on the roof. From the frowns on their faces, I'm guessing something about the construction crew has them worried.

Swinging my neck around, I immediately notice several vehicles parked in the small gravel lot. I lift my hand above my eyes to shield them from the sunlight and take in the view. Ripples of water stretch out in front of us for what appears to be miles past a large man-made sandy beach. Boat engines sound off in the distance, but where we are seems peaceful and fairly quiet.

A loud banging infiltrates my tranquil thoughts and I whirl my head around. Immediately I see what must have Abby and Piper so riled up. Crouching on the rooftop are four guys all without shirts and showing off perfectly sculpted abs and golden tans. They look to be around our group's age and definitely do not look like a professional construction crew. As the other girls in our group set their eyes on them, all four of the guys take note and stop what they are doing. One of the guys stands tall on the roof and lets out a high-pitched whistle, while the others laugh.

A door slams a few feet away from our van and I turn my head. A fifth guy that looks like he should be doing underwear ads for a magazine, stands in front of a pickup truck clutching a water jug in one hand and swiping his other arm across his forehead. My eyes instinctively wander down his bare chest to his loose fitted jeans that hang low on his hips and then back up. His dark brown hair sticks out from beneath a white baseball cap that is positioned backwards on his head. As he tips the jug back to take a drink, I cannot pull my eyes away from the sight of his biceps flexing and abs tightening with every swallow. I gulp down a breath and hear giggling around me.

"I think Alyssa sees something she likes," my sister calls out with a loud laugh.

Her words echo in my ears and I just know that god-like creature slurping down water had to have heard.

I swing my eyes back over to the tanned perfection standing only a short distance away. Lowering the jug into the back of the truck, he makes eye contact with me and the corners of his mouth rise into a crooked smirk. After what seems like an eternity of being caught in his web, he finally flashes me a full smile before returning to the roof with his friends.

A couple of other guys join in on the cat calls while we gather our bags and head to our cabin. I roll my eyes listening to some of the girls giggling like little teeny boppers at their first boy band concert. *Oh yeah, this week is definitely going to be trouble.*

Inside, I take a deep breath at the realization of how up in my business this week may be. The cabin is a nice size but looks as if the furniture has been crammed to one side, but what truly has me stressed is the row of cots that line the back wall. *What is this, boot camp?* From the corner of my eyes I catch my sister sliding up beside me and I blow out a huff of air.

"Ok, so we have to sleep three feet away from each other, but come on . . . we are going to have so much fun," she says in a peppy voice as her elbow digs into my side.

I roll my eyes and nudge her back. Stepping around an old, worn down, brown couch, I crane my neck back her way and flash her a full mouth of teeth before tossing my bag onto a cot. *I guess it could be worse.*

After we get settled in and explore the contents of the cabin, I pull out my swimsuit and grab my towel, fully intent on catching some rays. Most of the girls have already headed down to the beach.

Once I'm changed, I race down and stretch out on my towel with a book in hand. I promised Abby I would be social, but for today I just want to lose myself in this novel and pretend my life isn't a disaster.

My back begins to heat up under the sun and the skin on my shoulders sting as if it is on fire. As I continue to read, splashes and screams bounce me out of my thoughts and make me realize that fun is going on all around me. I am most definitely not doing as my father said. I'm not making the most of this summer and I am not living life to the fullest. *Nope, I am wallowing!*

Tossing my book onto my towel, I quickly strip off my shorts, feeling a stinging sensation over my thighs as I slide them down. I extend my leg to fling them onto the sand and spin around. Stepping off my towel, my feet instantly hit hot coals. I make a mad dash for the water, hoping to avoid scalding my feet from the searing sand.

Once I feel the relief of the water across my bare legs, I look out in the distance to see where everyone is. Crystal hangs onto a floating cooler as if it is the last lifeboat aboard a ship destined to sink. Two other girls sit along the edge of a square dock anchored out in the deeper waters while my sister, Piper, and Lanie all sip drinks and socialize. They appear to be having "lots of fun" as Mom instructed me to do. *To hell with sulking!*

My eyes lock with Abby as she extends her arms in the air to cheer me on, "Come on, Alyssa! Whoo!" she yells being extra cautious with her daiquiri.

I giggle and then dive in, vigorously paddling my arms to swim as far as possible on one single breath. The water glides along my skin, feeling cool and refreshing. My lungs burn from needing air so I know I must be close to them. With one last swift push of my arms, I raise my head above the surface. My feet quickly find the pebbly ground and I stand up only a few feet from the group. While flipping my arms to the side, the choppy water laps at my chin as I step up closer to my friends.

"I thought I'd join you." I give Abby a genuine smile as I bow my back and run my fingers over my slick, wet hair.

"It's about time," she says with a goofy grin, handing me a beer out of the floating cooler.

At the same time a dark haired girl named Skylar yells out, "Abby's sister . . . hey girl!"

I look over at her and help her out, "It's Alyssa." *I'd really rather not be referred to as "Hey Girl" all week.*

She smiles at me and then nudges her head up towards the shoreline. "Well Alyssa, that hottie you were drooling over earlier has been checking your ass out hard."

Everyone starts to laugh and I squint over to the roof of the cabin. He's knelt down beside another guy hammering down shingles, but every few moments he glances in my direction.

I look over at Skylar and shrug, trying to play off the butterflies that begin to swirl in my stomach.

"Whoo, Alyssa . . . you already have someone hot on your tail! How did I know that would happen?!" my sister yells, looking around at the other girls while nudging her thumb over her shoulder in my direction.

"Oh yeah, didn't you date Kyle Webber? He's flipping hot, too," one of the girls sitting out on the dock sunbathing shouts out. "I saw what went down at his party the other night all over my news feed! I guess he's a . . ." she starts, but Abby swipes her hand across her neck, signaling for her to shut up.

My excitement for the day fully deflates as the girl snaps her mouth closed and everyone looks over at me, clearly figuring out that this subject is off limits. I don't know this girl's name but apparently she must know all about me.

Tossing Abby my unfinished drink, I dive back into the water to head for shore. *Social time is over for me today.*

Before my head falls below the water, my sister calls out to me in a regretful tone, "Alyssa, come on . . . don't leave."

For now, I think lying in the sand with my book is a much safer place. I definitely do not want to rehash the details of my breakup with a group of girls I barely know.

Late into the afternoon, after I am sun-burnt and half of our group is loopy from all the alcohol, we head in for dinner. Dragging myself to my cot, I pounce down and unwrap a peanut butter protein bar while most of the girls rummage through the kitchen for random snacks.

"Hey, what would you guys think about going down for a moon-light swim?" Skylar wags her brows and sticks her tongue between her teeth.

Laughter sounds throughout the cabin and everyone chimes in.

"Whoooo! Skinny dipping, ladies?" Lanie adds.

"Maybe the group next door will join us," a redhead points out excitedly from the kitchen table.

"No! Definitely not!" Piper looks up from the couch.

They all laugh and carry on, making plans for a midnight swim while downing wine coolers.

After wadding up my empty bar wrapper, I fling it to the night-stand and walk across the cold wood floor. *Joy! Girls gone wild here I come,* I think to myself as I grab another margarita.

I'm going to need to catch up so I can join in on all of the goofy giggling and comments that make them sound like they are a bunch of junior high girls at their first sleepover. So far they cannot make it five minutes without some sexual reference that brings on a whole new lev-el of giggles, complete with the comment "Oh my gosh, I just peed my pants." Then their laughter kicks up to an even higher notch.

I glance at the clock above the wood stove in the living area and see that it is nearly 11:30. *Showtime!* After swallowing the contents of my margarita, I pull the fridge door open and grab two more drinks.

"Let's go, girls!" Piper hollers as she opens the front door.

Trailing behind Abby, I make my way out the door and down to the lake, not altogether excited about how my first day here has gone.

Grass tickles the edges of my feet as I twist off the top of one of my drinks and cram the other in the front pocket of my shorts. We walk a little further as I take a large guzzle and finally feel my feet sink into sand and mush between my toes.

"Ok, so you don't have to join us if you don't want to," Abby whispers.

Squeals and screams ring in my ears as a couple of the girls drop their bikinis and rush into the water without a second thought. The rest, including my sister, look around to make sure we are alone.

"Yeah, I think I might take a little walk." I raise my hand and point down the shoreline away from the cabins.

"Ok, drink up and come join us if you feel up to it later." Abby giggles and then turns her back to me as her top hits the ground. "Aaaagh, it's so cold!"

I nod my head and start to walk in the opposite direction; my head already light and fuzzy with the beginnings of a buzz.

I've only been gone for about five minutes and have managed to get maybe ten yards from the beach when male voices sound out in the distance. My eyes widen as I realize they are getting closer to where all of my friends are so carelessly swimming in the buff.

With my drink gripped in my hand, I run through a wooded area with only moonlight to guide my way. I keep my mind concentrated on my feet slamming against the hard ground one after another until suddenly my whole body smashes right into a brick wall. Wham! A heavy weight crashes face first into me and my feet come right off the ground, landing me in a pillowy patch of sand and grass. I hold my drink upright and wiggle it to make sure it didn't spill. *Yep, I am definitely tipsy if I am only concerned with whether my drink survived the fall instead of the fact that I am being crushed by something or, wait, someone.*

"Are you ok?" a deep voice whispers against my cheek.

His head cocks back and his body raises up to slightly hover above me, braced by two muscular arms. Still studying him, I wobble my drink down into the sand beside us so I can keep all of my focus on my current situation.

Looking up, I take note of the shaggy brown hair sticking out around a baseball cap and the butterflies start. I can barely see his face but I can make out the same crooked grin that I admired earlier. My eyes also zoom in to a small dimple that forms on his right cheek. I can't make out the color of his eyes due to the lack of light, but I can see that he has a strong square jaw and his muscles are . . . *Oh God, I have my hands on his chest.*

As if he just read my mind, he laughs and waves his hand in front of my face to snap me out of my daze. "Did I knock you out or knock the breath out of you?"

I shake my head, reeling from the sensation of his hard body against mine. *Why is he still laying on me?*

"No . . . I mean yes," I croak out nervously.

"I did knock you out?" he snickers.

"No! No, you didn't knock me out."

He looks at me and I realize how awkward this has become with us still lying here, yet in a strange way I'm enjoying it.

"Dude, are you doing her already?" a male voice shouts out from a few yards away.

"Way to go, Judd!" another voice bellows out.

All of the girls laugh as Abby roots me on, "Go for it, Alyssa," as if I am having sex right here on the beach. *Well, she is obviously already trashed.*

He mumbles something under his breath that sounds like "piss off" as he rises up to his hands and knees and then stands to help me up.

"Sorry, my friends stumbled upon a discovery and were getting a bit too frisky for my taste. I figured I would head in the opposite direction," he states as he points his thumb over his shoulder towards the beach and his very excited friends.

After hoots, hollers and discarded clothing rain through the air, a mass of guys run into the water, igniting loud giggles from the girls and telling me that this has definitely turned into the wild and crazy week my sister had in mind.

I nod my head in understanding, considering I was down the shore trying to escape the craziness myself. Taking his hand, he pulls me to my feet. The contact of his hand to mine immediately sends a shiver through my body. His hands are rough and it feels as though he has bandages on several of his fingers. Now standing beside him, I look up and realize he is nearly a whole head taller than me.

His lips curve into a smile and a crazy flutter soars through my stomach.

"You wanna join me?" He tips his head to the side to study my face.

What the heck. After quickly bending over to fetch my drink and the other that apparently was tossed from my pocket, I hold the unopened one between us. "Here . . ." I smile as he looks at my gift, " . . .

a peace offering for our collision."

Nodding his head with a chuckle, he gently grabs the drink from my hand and twists the cap off, taking a huge swig. I gracefully hold my drink up in a Cheers gesture and join him.

"I'm Judd by the way." My heart spins and speeds up in my chest like I'm on a thrill ride of a lifetime as we turn in the opposite direction of the beach to head off alone.

I giggle and then break out into a full laugh, contemplating whether this is nerves or the alcohol. Judd laughs with me, probably figuring I may be a little loony.

"I'm Alyssa," I say, trying to catch my breath from laughing. "I'm sorry. I think I am getting a bit tipsy. I'm trying to keep up with the level of crazy that I am surrounded by this week."

Judd leans his head to the side and looks at me with a gorgeous smile as we walk further down the beach.

"So, I've never seen you out here. Have you been here before?" he asks as we walk along, sharing tid-bits of information about one another.

I look over at him nervously with butterflies swirling through my stomach every time we make eye contact. "Actually, my parents used to bring me and my sisters out here when we were little, but gosh . . . it's been at least fifteen years since I've been here." Feeling fidgety, I grasp my bottle in both of my hands, twisting them back and forth until the label is wrinkled and loose. "What about you?"

"You know, I'm not sure if I came here when I was little, but I've been coming out here regularly for a few years now." He swings his free hand between us and I get the feeling he may be just as nervous as me. "This summer I'm giving my best friend a hand on some renovations. His grandfather owns the land and the cabins over here." He pauses and flashes me a small smile while pointing to a clearing ahead. "Well except for the cabin you're staying in."

Before long, I notice the sounds from the beach have faded away and it's now just the two of us in a secluded grassy area down from the cabins. There are trees all around us and although I should be freaked out by being alone with a strange guy out in the woods, I am oddly comfortable around him. Settling ourselves on the ground a few feet from the water, we stare out at the moon's reflection and carry on idle conversation.

"Do you go to school out this way?" I ask, trying not to be obvious about wondering how old he is. *He looks like he is my age.*

"Nahh," he tosses back another swig of his drink and then places his hands back to his side.

I cannot help but glance down at the hand he places between us. Excitement bolts through me at how close our hands are and I have to resist the urge of scooting mine towards his.

"I actually live about five hours away in Rosemore. I graduated from there just last month," he states.

I gasp out at what a small world it is. "That's crazy. I actually graduated from Fairview High last week," I laugh, knowing that our schools are huge rivals.

He chuckles, "Did you ever go to any of the Fairview-Rosemore football games?"

"I went to every single one," I tell him and watch as his eyebrows rise in surprise. "I was a cheerleader, so I cheered at all the football games. What about you?"

"I played. I was the quarterback," he states in a proud tone. "Wow! I'm sure we crossed paths a time or two." He flashes me an easy smile while taking another drink.

"I'm sure we did," I say, looking over at him. *How on earth did I not notice him?* I guess my mind was preoccupied with watching Kyle at the time; *crazy that they played each other.* "So are you going to the local college in Rosemore?"

"No," he answered quickly, looking a bit relieved with his answer. "I have a scholarship to play out in California, so the end of July I will be headed to UCLA."

We fall silent for a moment, but I don't miss the fact that he stares over at me with a small smile touching his lips. I feel as though my nerves have woven my tongue to the roof of my mouth. Even if I could speak, I would probably stumble all over my words and say something stupid. *God, he makes me nervous . . . in a good way, though!*

"What about you?" His words break the hushed calmness of our little secluded shoreline.

Leaning to the side, he playfully bumps his shoulder into mine, sending ripples of goose bumps to crop up over the entire surface of my body.

"Do you have any plans for the future?" he goes on with a gorgeous smile that completely has me wound up.

"I got accepted to Purdue. I leave in August," I tell him. *Of course I would meet someone out here that is going all the way across the country from me.*

"I see. Do you know your major yet?"

I laugh and toss my now empty drink to the side, slowly sliding my hand to the ground to support myself as I lean back, gazing out at the water. Judd shifts and once again I notice his hand getting closer to mine, which is making me giddy.

"You know, I have no idea," I spit out a laugh, looking over and seeing that he has been watching me the whole time with an unreadable expression that truly has me about to melt into a puddle.

We talk on and on, throwing pebbles and spears of grass into the water with only the sounds of peace and seclusion surrounding us.

Judd tips his drink back one last time and lowers his hand back down. What was at first a good foot or so of space separating us, has now become only a few inches with our hands sunk into the dirt and stones between us. I continue to catch him inching his fingers towards mine and my heart skips a beat each time, knowing it has to be intentional.

Our conversation flows with such ease that I find myself sneaking glances in his direction while he talks. I watch his lips move and can't help but imagine what it would be like to kiss him.

Further up the shore, we hear nearby shouts that sound like our names. Judd rises to his feet and reaches out to help me up.

"I think we better go before our friends call out the rescue dogs," he says as I hesitantly let go of his hand after I am on my feet.

His hands land on my hips to steady me as I stumble. "Whoa, I think the alcohol is catching up with you," he points out with an easy smile that sets my heart racing.

I lean into him to catch my bearings, only planning to stay there for a second, but the warmth of his body completely captivates me. I breathe in and catch a soapy scent that tells me he must have just showered. Moving my head a little closer, my chest expands as I take another deep breath and revel in the fragrance of his skin.

He quietly laughs and I know he must notice me clinging to him. His hands brush along the contours of my hips up to my waist, but instead of pushing me away he pulls me in closer.

"You want me to help you back to the cabin?" he asks in a concerned tone.

I pull back just enough to look at him, not wanting to completely break our contact. "I was just dizzy. I think the alcohol rushed to my head," I mutter, shaking my head and giving him a shy smile.

He stares down at me and I really wish it was daytime so I could see his eyes.

"I like your smile." I hear him gulp and watch as he grazes his teeth across his bottom lip.

A shiver travels down my spine just as I let out a calming breath to unwind the ball of nerves forming in my stomach. His hands remain at my waist and I don't dare move any further away.

He leans towards me to whisper into my ear, "Are you cold?"

"No," I barely get out.

He pulls his face back a few inches and I stare up at his lips, fantasizing of how they would feel against mine. One of his hands leaves my waist, but I quickly feel it curled beneath my chin to lift my gaze up to meet his. The soft caress of his fingertips tickle my jawline as his deep husky voice whispers "Alyssa," as if it's a secret.

There is a question in his voice but all I can get out is a quiet, "Mmhuh . . ."

He slowly takes a step forward and leans in closer to my face, his lips only millimeters from mine. His breath moves across my lips as he quietly asks, "Can I kiss you?"

I don't even answer, my body just reacts. I close the small distance between us and mold my lips against his. His lips open slightly as his warm, wet tongue grazes my bottom lip. Urging my mouth open wider, he deepens the kiss, allowing us full access to taste and explore.

My legs are wobbly, my body tingles and my heart is pounding so hard that I cannot think straight. I feel like I am floating on a cloud, flying like a bird, dancing with the stars in the sky.

I run my hands along the strong contours of Judd's chest, resting them where I can feel a steady thumping that matches my own hammering heartbeat.

"Oh shit, I'm sorry," an unknown voice speaks up from behind us.

I pull away first, looking around Judd's muscular frame. He turns to look over his shoulders, but keeps his hands at my waist.

"I didn't mean to interrupt, man. We were just worried."

Judd shifts around, fumbling his hand around until it settles on mine. Grasping it in his own, he laces his fingers through mine and a burst of excitement blazes through me, causing my toes to curl, my skin to tingle and my head to spin.

"Sure you didn't . . ." He and the other guy laugh in unison. "We?" Judd asks and then I hear a cough a little ways behind the guy.

It's just a shadow but I know it's my sister.

"It's just me," Abby replies, confirming my assumption.

If only I could see her; I am sure she has an "I told you so" grin plastered on her face.

"We were just talking," I quickly explain, hoping to steer off any gossip that may already be circulating.

The other guy laughs harder and I hear my sister mumble, "Looked like it," barely loud enough for me to hear.

I immediately look down at my feet, embarrassed of the audience we more than likely had while we were swept away in a kiss. *And oh wow, what a kiss!*

The guy clears his throat, bringing all of our attention his way.

"Oh . . . Alyssa, this is Evan, my best friend," Judd politely points out.

"Hey. I'd ask how it's going, but . . . you know," Evan jokes and my face immediately heats up.

Luckily, Abby jumps in to steer away any further embarrassment directed towards Judd and I, "Hi, Judd. I'm Abby, Alyssa's older and very protective sister."

Her arms rise over her chest and I just have to roll my eyes at her attempt of intimidation.

Judd and Evan both chuckle.

"Maybe we should head back," Evan suggests, "We have an early morning."

We let them take the lead as we head back to the cabin, arriving at mine first.

No sooner than the front door is in site, Abby races for it. "Night guys, I'm hitting the hay. See you in a bit, Alyssa." She gives me a sneaky glance and swiftly heads inside.

Evan walks ahead, pacing in a circle between our cabins as he waits for Judd. I am sure he is hoping to get details on what we were doing out in the woods for so long just like I am expecting to get grilled by Abby as soon as I step inside. *Wow, I can only imagine the talk already going around. I really don't care though.*

As I nervously step side to side, I look at Judd, wishing there were more hours in the night. "Well, this is me," I whisper, slowly sliding my hand from his grasp. "Good night." *I really don't want to let go!*

He tightens his hold on my hand and pulls me into him in one quick motion. His arms fully wrap around my back. *Please let him kiss me again.*

His cheek brushes against mine as his alluring voice speaks into my ear, "Can I see you again?" He leans away and looks into my eyes as if the answer is waiting there for him. "I work down at the shower house all day tomorrow, but I would really love to see you when I get through."

"I'd like that," I say quietly, trying to contain the squeals and giggles that are going off inside of me.

His mouth breaks wide open into a huge grin and he leans into me for a quick peck on the lips. Before I can say another word, he pulls away and softly says, "Good night."

Hesitantly turning away, he jogs to his friend and gives me one last glance.

I watch them fade into the darkness along the pathway that runs in front of the cabins with a silly grin painted on my face before stumbling up two remaining stairs to head inside. *Time to defuse the gossip. Piper was way off when she said this trip was going to be trouble. I have a feeling this may very well end up being the most amazing week ever.*

Not TOO much Fun

A SHARP SOUND SHATTERS ME out of my blissful dream of Judd. Peeling my eyes open, I spring upward in my cot with the sheet still clasped in my hands. Gasps and squeals fill the air and I look in the direction of the noise.

"Good grief, Piper. Are you trying to give me a heart attack?" one of the girls calls out.

"Butter fingers," Skylar says sarcastically.

"I think she had too much booze last night." Jessie tilts her head back and brings her hand to her mouth as if she has an imaginary drink.

Giggling breaks out around the kitchen table where I see most of the girls drinking coffee and cramming pastries in their mouths. Piper is kneeling on the floor between the table and sink, sweeping up what looks to be a broken plate.

"Good morning, sunshine," my sister calls out in an overly chipper voice.

Sucking in a monstrous breath of air, the corners of my mouth inch up into a huge smile.

Last night when I came inside, a handful of the girls, including my sister, Piper and a girl with bright red hair were awake and loaded with questions. Still grinning ear to ear from the heart-pounding kiss I experienced with Judd, I quickly cleared up their assumptions of me making out in the woods all night. *Holy crap, did that really happen?*

The past two days have been so surreal; I swear I am living in

31

some kind of alternate universe watching where my life currently is or where it could be, depending on my choices. If that is the case I choose door number two, kissing Judd. One evening of getting to know him and now I cannot wait to see him again.

"Alyssa, are you going to stay in bed dreaming about lover-boy all day or are you going to join us at the beach?" My sister's playful tone and the quiet snickers that fill the room, tell me that Piper and Abby must have shared the details of my night with all the others.

"Good job, Alyssa, that one is yummy," Lanie moans.

"No doubt, I would have been all over that in a flat second. Screw the kissing," Red chimes in.

"Well I think you were sparking your own fires out by the boat dock, Jessie," Piper teases the red head.

I make a mental note of Red's name, fling my sheet to the bottom of my cot and swing my legs over the edge. Stretching my arms high up in the air, an exaggerated yawn escapes my mouth. *Coffee, I need coffee.* Just as that thought enters my mind, Abby sashays across the room in a white and pink polka dot bikini with a large coffee cup in hand.

I drop my arms into my lap and look at her with a big smile. "Thank ya, Abbs."

After I grab the cup, I bring it to my mouth and let the steam moisten my skin as I breathe in the strong hazelnut aroma. I gulp down several swallows, thankful that it isn't too hot.

Abby stays in front of me with her hands on her narrow hips.

"So, are you going to join us?" she says while sliding her pedicured, tan feet across the floor to bump into my unpainted, neglected toes.

Ha . . . she is fishing for information. She beams with pride, looking at me as if this is a path she personally chose. It's no secret that she knows how Judd affected me, plus she witnessed us sucking face firsthand, so she definitely knows that he lit my fire.

I shake my head, having absolutely no intention of joining the girls today. *No way, when I know where he is going to be!*

She crosses her arms and smiles. "Ok, soooo . . ." she pesters me with a grin nearly as huge as mine.

The sound of birds chirping outside of the cabin alerts me to the fact that it has suddenly become eerily quiet. Craning my neck to see around Abby, several heads snap in the opposite direction. Abby and I share a look and then laugh realizing she is not the only one interested in my plans for the day. It feels like this cabin is full of a bunch of junior high girls with their first crushes. The crazy thing is I'm acting like one, too.

Turning our attention back to each other, Abby squats down in front of me.

I bite my lip hard and twist my hands together in a nervous manner. "I was thinking maybe . . ."

Abby nods with excitement in her eyes, letting me know I have her full attention.

" . . . I might go down to the shower house and see how Judd's work is going, because we didn't set a time for meeting up. So if I'm not here and he's not there, then we may miss each other. So I thought . . ." I stutter, trying to make excuses why I am ready to abandon a day hanging with the girls.

Abby laughs and puts her hand up to stop me from my ramblings. Pursing her lips, she stares at me with an intensity in her eyes that I've only seen a few times. A warm laugh slips out of her and she pats my knee before standing back up.

"Don't sweat it. Have fun Lyssi-bee."

Oh no, she's breaking out Dad's nickname for me. This is getting a little too mushy for my taste.

After placing my coffee mug on the floor, I spring off the bed and plant my feet on the ground beside her. Playfully bumping my hip into hers, I unintentionally bump her harder than I meant to. I remain frozen, unable to judge her reaction as she stumbles and lands flat on her ass. She glares up at me and I know I'm in trouble.

"You're getting it now," she says with a sly grin as she pushes back up to her feet with cat-like reflexes.

We both race into the kitchen and my lungs feel as though they may explode from laughing so hard. Abby's full weight tackles me to the floor and she starts in on the tickling. Nostalgia washes over me as the room fills with laughing, yelling and cheering. A couple of girls even lend her a hand and get in on the mayhem by holding me down. *Yep, I was right . . . A bunch of junior high girls.*

Once the onslaught of tickling diminishes, I excitedly head back to my cot so I can change into a bikini while the others discuss plans for the week.

"Piper, don't forget . . . we need to run to town to get food for the bonfire with the guys tonight," Abby calls out from the living room.

I snap my head in Piper's direction, and see her still standing in the kitchen by the sink.

"I say we get a little sunshine and head to the store after lunch," she shrugs.

"Sounds good to me," Abby smiles and then looks toward me. "Hey Alyssa, you want to ditch your plans and come join us?" she says with a bit of a smirk and a wink of her eye.

My eyes widen not wanting to discuss out loud what my plans are, even though half of the girls more than likely already gained knowledge of my agenda when they were eavesdropping. I shake my head and lower my eyes in a warning to Abby. *Shut it!*

"Wait, isn't Judd Tristan's younger brother?" Crystal asks and I honestly haven't got a clue.

My ears perk up with the mention of Judd's name and now I fully intend on following along with their conversation.

"No, I thought Mitch was," Jessie corrects her.

Piper throws her hands onto her hips as if someone has all of a sudden hit a chord. "No, Mitch is Evan's brother and a total loser," she says in a spiteful tone and then starts muttering something under her breath that I can barely hear. The only word I make out is Evan's name and it doesn't sound like she's saying anything nice.

"Now isn't Mitch the one you used to date, Abby?" Lanie looks at my sister. "Yeah, that's who you lost your . . ."

Hhhmmmm . . . so that's the Mitch. I remember the name from a couple of summers back and her marathon phone calls with Piper, talking about him. That was the year she came back all heartbroken and then we found out Dad had cancer.

Abby shoots her a glare and Skylar sympathetically swoops in to redirect the conversation back to who is who, "Tristan is Judd's older brother, I'm pretty sure."

"Good grief, did you see him drop his drawers? Holy hell! Give me some of that," Jessie cries out while distorting her face into a look of awe.

Crystal screams out and points to Jessie, "Oh. My. God. I know! It was dark out but there was no hiding that appendage! I think my eyes bugged out of my head."

"Oh girl, we were all looking at that!" Skylar adds.

"All I can say is stay away from Tristan and Mitch. They are straight up players and sleazebags," Abby says in a motherly tone, like she is ready to issue us all chastity belts.

This brings on a whole new round of laughter from everyone, myself included.

"Yeah, Abby, because we definitely don't want that; two guys that are looking for nothing more than a roll in the sack with a group of girls that came out for a fun, no strings attached week. Yep, we'll keep our distance!" Jessie rolls her eyes and we all laugh hysterically at her sarcasm.

Abby waves her hand in the air and abandons her efforts of convincing the girls that some of the guys are bad news.

Once the hysteria dies down, the girls retreat to the beach while I finish getting ready. I adjust the triangles of my black and white zebra print bikini to position them equally over each of my breasts then grab my brush to run it through my thick blonde locks. Puckering my lips, I smear on a thin coat of lip gloss and decide to forgo the mascara or blush. My baby blue eyes are already framed by long dark eyelashes and sometimes mascara seems like overkill.

Standing back, I look into the full length mirror hanging on the wall of the tiny bathroom. I take in the entire view so I know just what Judd will see. Luckily, the scorching red sunburn I received yesterday has paled, giving my usual porcelain skin tone a soft bronzy glow. My flat stomach shows off a belly button piercing that I got last summer with both of my sisters, and the slight heel of my sandals make my legs look sexy and toned.

I giddily bounce on the balls of my feet in anticipation of seeing Judd and then turn to put my toiletries back in my bag.

Uneasiness rises within me as I wonder if he will be bothered by my surprise visit. With that thought, Dad's words replay in my mind, *"Be young, don't worry about relationships and have fun!"* I nod my head deciding to take a chance, however, immediately knowing I fully plan to disobey my father's last words, "Not *too* much fun."

Sorry Dad, but I have been cheated on, lied to and deceived. I deserve to move past that and have a whole LOT of fun! Definitely TOO much is in order for this week and Judd is just the one to show it to me!

I freaking love paint

COMING OUT OF THE CABIN I suck in a breath of fresh air letting the sweet woodsy fragrance fill my lungs. My mind feels lighter than it did two days ago and everything around me looks brighter. Nervously twirling a strand of hair around my finger, I make my way to the shower house. It sits at the edge of the lake with a long dock stretched to the side of it. At the end it juts out to each side with an awning, a gas pump in the center and a couple of hitches for boats. A small building called The Snack Shack sits to the opposite side of the shower house. As I race onto the dock, a large door with a white and blue multi-gender sign on it comes into view.

For the most part, the cabins are equipped with bathrooms that provide a toilet and sink but as far as showers are concerned, you have to come here or stink during your stay.

Several of us swung by for showers yesterday between our lake outing and the midnight fun but this place in no way, shape or form made me feel clean. Inside, it had a high pitched ceiling covered in spider webs and mud dauber nests. The beamed wood ceilings came down and surrounded you in a dark wood that made it look gloomy and dull. The shower floors were caked in crud, the shower heads looked corroded with calcium build up and the mirrors over the sinks were all cracked. It is in bad need of a good make-over to say the least. The smell of mildew and mold attacked my nostrils as soon as I walked in, plus the shower stalls had old tattered shower curtains that made it most definitely not ideal as a multi-gender shower house. Given the lack of privacy, we took turns standing guard at the door while the rest of us rinsed off.

Leaning back with all my weight, I tug on the huge, solid wood door and step inside. I immediately suck in a quivery breath at the sight of Judd. He stands in front of a sink steadying a large mirror with both hands. Once again he is shirtless and his back muscles shift and flex with beads of sweat dripping down his spine. My mind gets so foggy that I swear I can hear the sound of the sweat gliding down his perfectly tanned and toned back. Running my tongue over my top lip, I close my eyes and imagine my hand running over the contours of his skin.

His smooth, deep voice pulls me out of my daydream. "Give me a minute and I can leave if you need privacy."

He doesn't turn around so he has no idea it is me. Continuing in his efforts of pulling the mirror to eye level, he focuses on cradling it into a newly affixed fern shaped brass bracket.

I stand there in silence, not wanting to startle him with my voice and make him drop the mirror. My eyes wander over the room, silently taking inventory of all the work that has been done since yesterday. *What in the heck time did he get up?* A strong chemical odor stings my nostrils and has me looking from the newly painted white walls and scrubbed sinks. A ladder stands in front of the shower stalls with new white shower curtains draped over it and a tray of paint, a wet paint brush and roller sit at its base.

A gasp has me snapping my head back to look at him. He still holds the mirror up with one side secure in the bracket and a screw driver in his other hand, ready to fasten it down. Although instead of focusing on the mirror, his attention is fully on my reflection staring back at him.

His mouth slowly stretches up into an adorable smile; highlighting the dimple in his right cheek and all I can think is *did I really kiss those lips?*

My eyes focus in on his eyes and I can finally make out that they look to be hazel or a light brown. With no windows in the shower house, it is still too hard to make out.

"Hey . . ." he breathes out without even the slightest waver of his smile.

My heart does summersaults as I reply, "Hey back."

The mirror shifts and he directs his attention back to resituating the weight of the glass. I jet over to his side and pull the screwdriver out of his hand without thinking. He balances the mirror in front of him and looks over at me with a skeptical look in his eyes. I smile and place the screwdriver into the screw holding the bottom bracket to the wall.

"I'll screw, you hold the mirror," I shrug my shoulders and glance at him through the corner of my eyes.

His eyebrows rise in surprise and he flashes me a heart-melting grin as he settles the corner of the mirror completely into the bracket.

After we get the mirror fully affixed to the wall, Judd brushes his hands together to dust them off and then swipes his forearm across his forehead.

"Thanks," he says as he grabs the same jug he held onto yesterday.

Of course, as he tips his head back to take a drink, his body is no less hypnotizing as it was the day before. He places it back down on the bench in the first shower stall and then looks at me.

"I guess I should have had some help for some of this . . ." He motions around the room, eyeing the mirrors. " . . . But I was too eager to get it done so I could come see you."

He looks directly into my eyes when he says this, completely fearless of how I may read into that simple comment. Here he admits to that while I am trying to play down the fact that I was going crazy, wanting to see him again after our kiss last night.

"That's why I came down here. I figured I would see if you needed help," I playfully smile at him with slow even breaths, hoping to calm my pounding heart.

Keeping his eyes on me, he slowly glances down the length of my body to take in my apparel. His eyes find their way back up to my face and his lips curl into a smile.

"Nice work outfit." His smile deepens and he runs his tongue across his bottom lip before adding. "I'm not sure I'll get much done besides admiring my co-worker if you help, though." His soft laugh causes a crazy fluttering sensation to dance in my stomach. "But I definitely would choose your company and this view . . ." he says while looking up and down my body, " . . . over any of the guys, any day!"

His smile lights up and he takes a step forward towards me.

My heart hammers in my chest and I wobble back and forth on the sides of my feet. As much as I want to step forward and be closer to him, I refrain from moving.

Instead I ask, "So what do we do next?"

He shakes his head as if he was expecting me to say or do something differently. We both laugh and then get busy finishing up the shower house side by side.

While Judd scales the ladder and attaches three huge dropdown fans, I stay on the ground and hand him tools. In between handing things up, I decide to scrub down the shower floors and shower heads.

Judd was quite troubled with finding me a job to help him with so I took it upon myself to slip on some elbow length gloves and start cleaning the stalls.

"You know, you really don't have to do that," his voice sounds strained as if it pains him to see me getting ready to dig my hands into shower grime.

"I know that has to be disgusting. You don't seem like the squeamish type but if that grosses you out then stop doing it. I'd rather you not leave, plus this doesn't exactly seem fair to you considering I am getting paid to get my hands dirty," he points out.

Moving down onto my hands and knees, I look up at him, "I'm not going to leave," I assure him, "and it really doesn't bother me much."

Lowering one of the older fans down off the ladder, Judd stops and smiles that gorgeous smile, completely captivating me.

After that, we get serious about our work, each of us vigorous in our own tasks.

I love that I keep catching him staring down at me. A couple of times, I found him leaning his head to the side admiring my ass. He would quickly make out as if he was examining the fan, but then a few minutes later I would catch him staring again. One particular time, I thought he might fall off the ladder, but after mumbling a few curse words under his breath, he regained his balance. I could not help but giggle to myself at how distracted I was making him. After that I made a point of bowing my back and sticking my ass in the air even more. That definitely got his attention.

Besides, I checked my butt out in the mirror earlier and it isn't bad. It's got a nice heart shape to it with a little more meat than some girls but my narrow waist and D cup chest seem to even it out. I might as well flaunt it if he wants to look. *Who am I to deny him an enjoyable view while he works? After all he's working hard! He deserves it!* I laugh to myself, proud of the newfound boldness that he seems to bring out in me.

Looking up, I see him screwing in the last large palm leaf shaped fan blade. I am on the last of the five shower stalls as well. Surely we are in the home stretch, although he had said something about additional painting that needed to be done.

Stepping down from the ladder, he takes a couple more gulps of water and then hands the jug my way. *Don't mind if I do.* I take the jug and put it to my mouth imagining the feel of his lips on mine again. The cool water glides down my throat, instantly granting my sweaty body some relief from the heat. After a couple of gulps I set it back down.

"I still need to paint the floors."

I frown at his words puzzled at why someone would want to paint a floor. He chuckles at my expression, sending swirls of flutters through my belly.

"I know, weird, huh? I think he wants to lighten it up. Not to mention, anything is better than this blood red color it is painted now," he points down to the ground and like a magnet my eyes follow.

The gravitational pull continues as my legs immediately move forward to stand beside him as if they have a mind of their own. My arm brushes up against him as I lean over to look at the bundle of papers he is holding.

It seems that Mr. Jansen, Evan's grandfather, owns a lot more than I originally thought. Listed in bold font are eighteen cabins, three shower houses, four docks, a pavilion, two boathouses and the Snack Shack, all located on his property. Under each item is a massive list of renovations and updates to be done to each.

"Wow, this is going to take you all summer."

"Nah . . . we're over halfway done already. I think we are making good time. We should only have a little over a week's worth of work left," he assures me with a bright smile.

My head spins with the thought that I only have a week to get to know him and that he will be working the whole time. *This sucks!*

Judd turns all three fans on high speed and I breathe a sigh of relief for the added breeze. My skin feels as though it is melting from the mugginess in the air. He also wedges the door half open so the fumes don't get too over powering.

Crouching down on the floor, he pours more paint in the tray and hands me a plastic edger. Once again getting down on my hands and knees, I start to lay a thin coat around each stall while Judd rolls a good layer of paint behind me.

After over half of the floor is painted, Judd grabs the edger out of my hand and shoves it and his roller back into the paint tray. He strolls over to one of the sinks and I follow his lead as he squirts some soap in his hands from a new wall dispenser, lathers up then pulls a paper towel free to dry his hands.

"Why don't we let that side dry for fifteen minutes or so before we start the other side? Are you hungry?" he says while reaching to grab a small cooler that I saw earlier under the sink.

I nod my head, finish washing up and slowly crouch down to the floor to sit. Sleeking down onto my hip, I stretch my arm out to hold myself up and fold my legs out beside me. I glance down, making sure my stomach looks flat in this position and that my bikini is still fully covering me.

Judd settles down beside me, triggering an explosion of chills over my body as his arm sweeps against mine as he places the lunch box on the floor in front of us.

"Ok, we have slim pickings here. I was sort of in a hurry this morning and wasn't too worried about what I would eat later." He looks at me from the corner of his eyes with a small smile.

My toes curl and the fluttering in my stomach picks up at the thought that he was just as ecstatic to see me today as I was him.

"So let's see," he says while pulling out the contents of the lunch box. "We have a turkey sandwich." He raises his eyebrows and looks at me. "Mustard and cheese?"

I giggle and nod my head, "Sounds good."

He carefully tears the sandwich in half and hands one side to me with a smile. Grabbing the soft bread, I put it to my mouth and take a bite. Immediately the tanginess of the mustard mixed with the smooth texture of the cheese brings my taste buds to life and I swear this is the best sandwich I've ever tasted. *Actually, it's probably only because it is from him, but it is still amazing,* I think while sneaking a glance at Judd chomping down on his half without a care in the world. I bring the sandwich back to my mouth for another bite so I can keep from giggling.

After finishing up our sandwiches, Judd unwraps a chocolate chip granola bar and my mouth begins to water.

"Do I even need to ask?" He snickers at the expression on my face which I assume must look as though I haven't eaten in decades. *Chocolate; I do love chocolate.*

Pulling my half out of his hand, I make sure my fingers touch his and linger for a second before pulling away. I scarf the bar down, much like Judd did his sandwich and then we stand to get on with our work.

After a good hour and a half of painting and after my hands are partially coated in paint, we stand in front of the showers and examine our work. We both are barefooted now, to avoid scuffing up the paint. With each step I expect for my feet to stick to the floor but surprisingly enough the first side already feels completely dry.

"I'll be right back. I'm just going to put the ladder outside the door with a wet paint sign so nobody comes in and messes up the wet side." His biceps bulge as he hoists the ladder up into his arms and exits the shower house.

As he moves past the paint tray, he bumps it, sliding it across the floor and splashing a trail of wet paint in its path in front of me.

"Great," Judd murmurs.

I make a mental note of the mess, fully planning on cleaning it up but as he comes back into view, I am so focused on his sweaty physique that the wet paint takes a backseat in my mind.

It all happens so fast that I barely register my feet slipping out from under me as I step forward, until we are both flat on the floor, face to face once again. *I can definitely handle these falls.* His fingertips press on the back of my scalp and I realize the thud that I heard was his knuckles hitting the concrete and not my head.

I whimper and Judd looks at me wide eyed in alarm.

"Ouch . . . my butt," I squeeze my eyes shut and let out a giggle.

Surprisingly enough, nothing on me hurts, but I'm sure my ass will be bruised tomorrow.

Judd laughs. "Good gracious, we don't want that damaged," he manages out between chuckles and I know he is definitely not talking about the floor. *Yeah, he enjoyed the view earlier.*

Our laughter dies down and we lie on the floor together, Judd's body flush against mine. Our sweaty chests stick together as a very comfortable silence forms between us. My chest heaves in and out and my body trembles with a full-blown desire that I have never felt in my life. Staring into his eyes, I swear I see my feelings mirrored in his.

He lifts his hand to my cheek and warmth floods my body as he smoothes his fingers along my jaw.

My mouth waters and my body tingles as his lips move closer and closer to mine. He captures my bottom lip, softly sucking on it before coercing my mouth open. Clutching his shoulders, I pull his full weight onto me as our tongues slide together in perfect unison. Electricity pulses down both of my legs and back up, telling me I am more than turned on. He shifts and a sudden protrusion against my thigh tells me that his response to this is just as intense.

He leans back a little and gently pulls his hand out from behind my head. Thick masses of blonde hair stick to his hand.

His eyes open wide as he looks down at me in alarm. "Shit! Your hair!! There's paint in it!"

He raises himself off of my body with his other arm and straddles my hips with both my legs between his knees. Gently, he removes the sticky hairs from his hand careful to not rip them out of my head. Small slivers of pain pierce the back of my head as a hair or two is pulled from my scalp, but I'm too focused on the extinguishing of the fire that had ignited between us rather than the mess. At this point I would gladly roll around in a mud pit, a bucket of paint or even a pool of chocolate pudding if it meant having his hard body back against me.

He looks down at me with an easy smile that highlights his dimple and my heart speeds up. I haven't moved. I'm still lying on the freshly painted floor and I haven't said a word. I've assessed the situation and I know I am breathing. My breaths are a little harder and heavier than they should be, but I am breathing. *And I really don't give a damn about the paint.*

No one has ever made me feel this way and yet I barely know this amazingly perfect looking guy that is now moving down toward my lips. *Yes!* I close my eyes but he barely brushes his lips against mine for a slow, soft kiss before removing them way too soon. *No!*

He remains on his knees, with his face leaned down and his forearms around the top of my head like he is protecting me from a falling object.

His mouth moves to my ear and I hear him softly whisper, "You're beautiful." Pulling back, he looks into my eyes and examines my reaction.

I suck in a breath and hold it while he moves back to my ear.

His breath dances across my neck as he says, "We have paint all over us. Do you want me to help you clean up?" in a deep tone that makes my body tingle.

I raise my eyebrows in surprise. *I'm not sure what getting me cleaned up entails, but I like the sound of it.*

Standing up, my legs wobble and shake as I hold my arms out to the side and inspect the damage. *I am a mess!* Pale gray paint is smeared around my torso and I can already feel the tightness of it drying across my back and arms. I brush my hands into my hair and instantly my fingers find sticky globs of paint binding my golden locks together. Huffing out a laugh, I look at Judd and can tell he is holding in a fit of laughter from the way he pushes his lips together, emphasizing his dimple even more. I can't hold back any longer. Laughing hysterically, I realize I have laughed more in the past two days than I think I have in an entire year.

Judd wipes at his eyes with the back of his hand to remove tears that are building up from laughing so hard. His warm hand slides over mine and he clears his throat to compose himself.

Pulling me towards the back shower stall, he leads me in and turns the water on full blast. He steps aside, sweeping his hand in front of him.

"Get in and I'll help wash the paint out of your hair," he says in a deeper tone as his chest rises and falls with an intensity that tells me the thought of me in the shower is affecting him greatly.

I nervously look down at my swimsuit and he chuckles.

"Just shower with it on, unless you want to strip down." The corner of his mouth crooks up and he wiggles his eyebrows up and down.

I do exactly as he says and keep it on. I move forward into the shower letting the soothing water cascade over my body. He takes in the sight of me in the shower, breathing harder than he was before as he steps forward to get in. *I can't believe I'm doing this,* but then I go and surprise myself even more.

"Wait!" I shout out before I can stop myself.

He stops mid-step and draws his brows up in confusion. I'm sure he thinks I am about to reject him.

"What about your jeans?" I question, realizing his work clothes would be soaked when we leave; at least I have a suit on.

He lifts his eyes wide for a moment then lowers them to look at his own attire.

"Should you maybe, take them off or change . . ." I stutter around as he moves his hands down to the snap of his jeans without hesitation or apprehension.

Now I'm the one breathing heavily. I draw in a sharp breath and look down hoping he doesn't have anything else on underneath. *Wait . . . What! Good gosh! I have turned into a sex-crazed horny teenager overnight. What is wrong with me?!* I quickly move that thought aside and continue to watch him.

His hands flip the snap open and then he quietly whispers, "Are you sure you're ok with this?"

I can hear the pleading in his voice as if he is praying for me to tell him to continue.

His hand is on his zipper and I can see the waistband of boxer briefs peeking up barely out of his jeans. *Well crap!!*

I nod my head, letting him know it will not make me uncomfortable at all. I hear metal slide over metal as he inches his zipper down and then slowly shakes his jeans off of each leg while glancing up at me periodically. My mouth gapes open once he has his pants off and he stands there in fitted black boxer briefs.

Thank you for spilled messes that need to be cleaned up because right now. I. FREAKING. LOVE. PAINT!!

$\cdots\cdots\cdots!$

*O*H DEAR LORD! AS IF I wasn't panting heavily enough, I see that he is seriously turned on. My mouth is on the floor; I know it is, but I cannot look away. *Hopefully slobber isn't running out of it.*

He lets out a quiet snicker after taking in my expression and bows his head as if he is embarrassed. Moving in behind me, his chest sweeps across my back and a shiver rolls through me. Snapping my mouth shut, I turn to face him and let the warm water shower down my back.

Large drops mist down his chest creating a small stream over his body. As the water rains over his lower region and soaks his briefs, every detail hidden under the fabric is perfectly outlined. *Wow!* My breath catches in my throat; I am speechless.

My stomach tenses up as his warm hands slide around my waist to pull me closer.

Resting my cheek against his firm chest, I close my eyes and sigh, savoring every second of this. I'm trying my best to hide the exhilaration that his touch is creating within me, but as his hand trails from my waist to my neck, I shiver again. This reaction seems to be becoming a habit and, honestly, I really like it.

His hand moves into my hair and with gentle strokes of his fingertips, he massages through it to remove the paint.

Still pressing my face against him, I open my eyes back up to get a close-up view of his perfection. I quickly zone in on a tiny stream gliding down his chest, only centimeters from my mouth. I part my lips and barely nudge my chin forward so I can feel its wetness. The way the water glistens on his skin has my mouth yearning for a drink. Allowing my lips to softly brush against his body, I dart my tongue out for a split second to taste his skin. I feel him shudder as his hands fall from my hair.

In a matter of seconds, strong hands cup my ass and my feet leave the ground. My heart drums up into my throat as he presses me up against the wall. Full streams flow over his shoulder and create a warm pool of water where our bodies are crushed together.

His mouth attacks mine as my inner voice screams out, *"Yes, yes, yes!!"* While coercing my mouth open with his tongue, his hand grips the skin of my ass tighter. The other slowly slides up my rib cage coming to rest under the weight of my breast, and I'm dying for him to move it up further.

Tilting my hips forward, I feel myself throbbing from the intense feeling of his erection against me. The need inside of me builds and builds as I grind into him and feel him do the same.

What has come over me? My mind is swirling with so many thoughts and emotions, yet I don't want to stop this. Half of me fears what he may think while the other half wants to scream out for more. However, right now how much I want him outweighs all sane and rational thoughts about whether this is a good idea or not.

A quiet whimper slips out of my mouth and he breaks contact with our lips to look directly into my eyes. My mouth stays open pulling in breath after breath as his chest rapidly rises and falls beneath my hand.

Finally, his hand inches up and slides under the fabric of my swimsuit. I bite down on my lip as chills roll through me. Barely moving his fingertips, he looks at me with a question in his eyes. I nod my head and his hand immediately slips all the way beneath the fabric of my swimsuit top.

"Ahhh!" I let out a loud moan when his hand fully cups my breast, sweeping his fingers over my nipple.

He continues to knead my right breast with soft caresses to gentle squeezes while gliding his lips down to my neck.

His moist lips follow the trail of water;

Sucking . . .

Licking . . .

Kissing . . .

Nibbling . . .

At my skin until I feel as though I may lose all sense of reality.

The fire between my legs turns into a full inferno and he is the only one that controls the flames.

As his lips dip further down, he slowly slides me higher in his grasp. My arms hold firmly to his shoulders and every single one of his muscles beneath my hands stiffen with his movements. I keep moving against him, knowing I may climax before we even get to the good stuff.

He trails kisses down to my swimsuit top and then carefully slides the fabric to the side, looking up at me for acceptance. I want to root him on . . . *Go, go, go . . .* but my mind no longer feels present.

His mouth closes in around my nipple and I feel myself reaching over the edge of ecstasy, climbing and climbing; going in a hundred different directions all at once. His wet touch grazes the back of my neck and fumbles around until my top slides between us. After muttering something under his breath, his mouth descends in on the other nipple.

There's no way there's enough oxygen in this room. I suck in a deep breath, one after another. He flicks his tongue against my tender flesh and I throw my head back, right into the wall. A light thud ringing in my ears is followed up by a dull pain in my head.

He pulls away from my chest and the sudden loss of his lips on my body has me forgetting the pain. With a small grin on his face, he gently moves his hand to the back of my head as if he is checking to see if I'm hurt. I see tenderness in his eyes for only a second before he pulls my lips to his. Slowly letting my body slide back down, I once again feel contact with the overly enthusiastic parts of his body. *Oh!*

His hard body grinds against me and a moan escapes his lips as his face crumples up into a painful yet blissful look. Frantically trailing a path to my ear and down to my neck with his warm tongue, his heavy breaths dance across my skin and make my body quake.

"Ohhh . . ." I breathe out and squeeze my eyes shut; my heart may rupture.

Our moving and grinding picks up pace until at last I'm climbing, climbing, climbing. Fireworks explode inside me, shooting zaps of electricity through my core and back to my center. I inhale and exhale deeply as Judd groans loudly and throws his head back, thrusting forward one final time. His head falls forward and nuzzles into the spot between my neck and jaw, tickling me with his heavy breaths.

After my breathing has returned to somewhat normal and I have climbed back down from the most intense experience I have ever had, I run my fingers through his wet hair. *Holy Freaking WOW! What on earth would other things be like if this was that mind blowing?*

He pulls his head back, still breathing hard, and looks at me. No words are spoken; we just smile.

His fingertips move behind my ear into my hairline and he kisses me slowly. As soon as he pulls away, his eyes shift down to my bare chest. I instinctively look to see what he sees. My bikini managed to hang on for the ride, still fastened at my back. However, the small triangles of fabric are wedged between his chest and mine now, giving him full access to look. *And oh, he does!* My eyes widen when I feel a slight twitch down low on his body.

His eyes swing back to mine and he searches my face. For what I'm not sure, maybe wondering if I regret this, but I remain quiet and dine on this amazing moment that truly took my breath away . . . !

Moving too fast

FTER A FEW MINUTES, JUDD shifts his body with me still locked in his embrace. I'm sure his arms are about ready to give out from holding me up for so long. Bowing my back, I feel a slight ache from being braced against the wall. He lowers me gradually towards the ground, now using both hands to hold my weight.

"Can you stand ok?" he whispers.

I smile and nod my head. Just to be sure, I push my toes down to barely touch the slick shower floor. *Hell, I'm not even sure my legs work anymore. They could have exploded and been swept down the drain.* Honestly, I would not have even noticed with the overpowering pleasure that was surging through my veins.

He lowers me down the rest of the way, moving his hands from my ass to my waist to support me. His touch is so soft and gentle, yet I can feel the wrinkles in his skin from us being under the water for so long. I grab my top and pull it up to cover myself with my forearm held across my chest.

"I wasn't trying to sound cocky like I just rocked your world or anything." He chuckles with a half grin and then adds, "I only asked because I nearly fell to my knees there at the end." His voice trails off and I think I see embarrassment cross over his expression.

Laughing, I put my free hand on his chest just because I know I can, plus I desperately want to continue touching him in any way.

"Well, just to be clear, you did rock my world and honestly, until my feet hit the floor, I wasn't sure if I would ever walk again."

His bit of embarrassment fades away into a bright beautiful smile that lights up his entire face as he leans in to claim my mouth once again.

Later, as I adjust my swimsuit top back across my chest, Judd tip-toes over to the next shower stall leaving his pants behind. *I'm not sure what he's doing.*

Less than a minute later, he rounds the corner. As he trails back into our stall, I pause in tying my suit around my neck to take in the fact that he is now wearing swimming trunks. *What?!* He chuckles at my reaction and shrugs his shoulders. I look at him puzzled and point to his attire.

A mischievous smile takes over his face.

"What? Did you expect for me to pause in the middle of all that and say," he raises his voice an octave for added effect, "Excuse me a moment while I go slip into my swim gear." He dips his chin forward and laughs a bit harder before continuing, "No way . . . I was not going to chance you changing your mind and high-tailing it out of the shower."

I cock my head to the side and paint on my best stern look.

"So you planned this?" I say, but cannot hold my seriousness when I see his playful smile change to concern.

Once he realizes I'm joking, he steps forward and slides between me and the wall. He softly wisps his fingertips across the skin of my shoulder and up to the base of my neck where I hold the strings to my suit. Taking them from my grasp, he quickly ties them together and rests his hands on my shoulders.

"If it was up to me, we would just keep this off. And no, I definite-ly did not plan that." I turn my head to look over my shoulder at his face as he adds with a wink, "but I really like how it all worked out. Best work day *ever.*"

He chuckles with a sexy grin as my face heats up. *Geez, I can't believe that happened but I couldn't agree more.*

As he slides his hands from my shoulders down to the curves of my waist, a whole new onslaught of goose bumps surface on my skin. He wraps his arms around my stomach and gently pulls my back against his chest into a hug. His cheek is pressed against mine and I have to close my eyes to remind myself that this is real. *How on earth did this happen?*

We stand in a tight embrace for longer than we should before the peaceful silence is broken.

"You wanna go down to the lake and swim? I think all the guys are headed down that way when they finish up. We could join them," he suggests.

A tinge of nerves takes hold at the thought of hanging with all the guys.

His arms tighten around me as he whispers right against my ear, "Honestly, it doesn't matter to me where we are. I'd just like to spend my afternoon with you."

With those words, all of my worries fly right out of the window. My eyes close as my hands move to rest on top of his.

We reluctantly break apart and decide to clean up our mess.

Coming out of the shower house we both stop mid-step when we see Evan sitting beside the door. He instantly cranes his neck to look up at us with the widest grin I think I have ever seen on a person. *Oh NO!*

Judd reaches back behind himself where I'm standing and intertwines his hand with mine. Just this small gesture causes butterflies to swarm in my belly. I love that even though we hardly know each other he seems to know what I'm feeling without me saying a word.

"Well," Evan says with a goofy ass grin on his face.

Standing to face us, he looks back and forth between Judd and me, "Did you get any of your work done or did play time come early today?"

Judd glances over his shoulder at me briefly and replies in a serious tone, "I got it all done. I've been working my ass off all day. We both have. Go in and check it out," he says in a matter-of-fact tone while pointing back to the building.

He doesn't sound mad at his friend's accusations, not even annoyed. I soon realize Judd is feeling him out to see if he actually walked in on us or overheard our cries of passion. *Oh please don't let him have walked in on us.*

Evan grabs his bare stomach and laughs hard, doubling over for added dramatics. He stands back up with a shitty grin on his face and places his hand on his friend's shoulder.

"Yeah, it sounded like you were working . . . *hard.*" He laughs even more and Judd shakes his head while sneaking a glance in my direction.

I shrug my shoulders. Ok, *he just heard us. I can live with that. I wasn't that loud . . . or was I?* Sighing from relief, I move forward to stand beside Judd.

"So you stood out here the whole time and listened in on us? Isn't that kind of perverted?" I say, raising my eyebrows to look a little bitchy.

Judd puts his hand over his mouth to stifle a laugh and Evan places his hand over his heart to act wounded by my comment.

"Hey, I'm not into that kind of shit! I assumed someone was showering while Judd was breaking for the paint to dry. I took a seat to wait for whoever to exit when all of a sudden I hear. . . ." Evan looks back and forth between me and Judd with his eyes real wide. He throws his head back and "Ohhh, Ohhh, Ahhh, Ahhh . . ." he moans loudly, mocking sounds he very likely heard only minutes ago.

"You jackass! It wasn't like that!" Judd adds with a shove to his friend that nearly sends him over the edge of the dock.

I gulp down the ten shades of red that I know I must be turning and begin to join the laughter, still gripping Judd's hand.

After a few more teasing comments from Evan, all three of us make our way up to a dilapidated shed and put away all the work materials. I carry a small crate full of painting supplies while Judd grips the ladder under one arm and a bucket of paint in the other. We pile it all into the shed, including a huge toolbox that Evan carries, and then go to The Snack Shack to meet up with the rest of the guys.

After standing on the dock outside the convenience shop for nearly twenty minutes, Evan gets fed up and runs off to find the others.

"Is everything ok?" I ask Judd as soon as Evan is out of sight.

He has been very quiet since we left the shower house and I worry that he is now regretting what happened between us.

"Yeah, I'm fine." He gives me a warm smile and tightens his grip on my hand.

Finally in the distance, I see a pack of bare-chested guys laughing, roughly shoving each other, and goofing off like typical boys. Judd squints in the distance at the group and then quickly pulls me around the side of the building.

As soon as we are perfectly concealed from all eyes, he presses me against the wall and crushes his lips to mine in a fiery kiss. He pulls away; leaving my lungs feeling oxygen deprived and levels me with a serious look.

"Ok, no . . . everything is not ok. I mean . . ." he stumbles around his words, "Am I moving too fast for you? I mean, is this too much too soon or am I scaring you off . . . *at . . . all?*"

He leans his head forward looking at me through long lashes. With all the wildness and craziness that has happened today, I just now get a chance to really look into his eyes. The sunlight shines down across his face and his hazel eyes sparkle with flecks of amber making them nearly look brown.

I place my hands on each side of his face, running my fingertips over the course bristles of stubble on his jaw as I pull him toward me.

"I don't think this could go fast enough for me," I say with absolute certainty.

I smooth my hands across both sides of his face and smile, all the while, looking into his unbelievably gorgeous eyes.

He breathes out an exaggerated sigh and crooks his mouth into a cocky grin.

"Good gosh, woman, I . . ." he pauses with an uneasy look on his face and then quickly adds, "I am crazy about you. This is all kinds of new for me. I mean, I'm not usually like this and I definitely don't move this fast . . . *ever.*"

My heart trips up with his words, feeling exactly the same way. *How is it that just a few days ago I was in a relationship with someone else? Kyle never made me feel this way!*

He pulls me against him, burying his face in my neck as I reflect on how wonderful this thing between he and I feels. When several rambunctious guys round the corner, he does not even try to pull away from our embrace.

Moving too fast? Not at all! This feels just right; it feels perfect!!

Could this be love

EVERY EYE IS ON US as the group of guys near the door to The Snack Shack.

Judd moves away a few inches and quickly grabs my hand in his as he turns to face the group.

"Guys, this is Alyssa," he announces as they get closer.

"Well, well . . . looks like you've been busy," a stocky blonde, whose name I believe is Tyler, says as he nudges Judd in the shoulder.

The rest of the group laughs and throws out a couple more teasing remarks. The heat in my face spreads like wildfire and I know it must be as red as a cherry. Judd doesn't try to defend himself against their sarcastic comments but instead turns to give me a reassuring smile before we all start to flood into the store.

"So, I guess you're keeping my brother occupied," a tall guy with chin length brown hair and bright hazel eyes says with a smirk.

Brother? This must be the infamous Tristan. That explains the similarity he shares with Judd. They look very much alike, only Judd is a couple of inches shorter.

The guy slaps Judd on the back, motioning for us to go in as he holds the door open. Judd looks nervous, but guides me in front of him.

"Don't even think about checking out her ass, Tristan," Judd spits out in a commanding tone.

I look back and his brother holds up his hands in surrender. He chuckles, barely sticking his tongue out between his teeth and I notice another similarity, dimples; only his brother has one perfectly placed on each cheek.

Once inside, they storm the shelves for food and beverages, putting a good dent in the store's supply. The guy behind the counter must be used to it, because he carries on about his business like it is completely normal for a mass of sweaty guys to clear the shelves like it is Armageddon.

Loaded up with premade hoagie sandwiches, cases of beer, beef jerky, snack cakes and soda, the guys push and shove their way back out to the dock and head for the beach.

Judd pulls my hand back into his at the same time a sweaty arm is flung across my other shoulder.

I look over to see his brother once again at our side, wiggling his eyebrows as he says, "So tell me, is your hot sister going to join us?"

I shrug my shoulders and laugh. Judd obviously doesn't find this as funny as I do. He grabs Tristan's wrist, picking his arm off of my shoulder like it is a stinky old sock that he wants to dispose of quickly. I have to giggle from his reaction. It's clear that he wants to keep the 'womanizer' as far away from me as possible.

Running down to the beach like a pack of wolves that have just been set free from captivity, I hear several whoops and hollers as all of my friends come into view. They are on the beach loading up coolers, towels, and rafts.

Mitch and Tristan lead the pack as they collide with the girls.

"Where you going?" Mitch asks as Jessie shoves a towel in her bag, a couple yards in front of me.

"Hey, you don't want to leave. Come on, the party's just getting started," Tristan joins in on the plea to get the girls to stay.

"We were calling it a day, but I guess we can stay for a while longer. What do you say girls?" Skylar motions to Abby and Piper, who are just now coming out of the water.

"I say hell yes!" Jessie hollers as she drops her bag and dashes into the water with Mitch hot on her tail.

Mitch and Tristan obviously think my friends are a 24-hour buffet that they can take full advantage of.

"Whoo! Come on, let's get wet!" Crystal splashes water at Tristan, beckoning for him to follow.

I guess with my group of friends, they haven't had to try very hard either.

We end up swimming and goofing off until the sun goes down. Judd and I try to socialize more instead of remaining in our own little intimate bubble. He cuts up with his friends while I sit on the dock cracking up at Piper's stories about summers she'd spent out here; however, I barely hear a thing that is said. My mind is too focused on all that happened earlier, and the recognition that through this entire evening, Judd's eyes keep wandering my way.

At the end of the night, we all head for our cabin, with the exception of a couple of people who have paired off to have their own fun. I notice Mitch and Crystal over by the dock having a bit too much. Jake, who I found out is Judd's younger brother, and Evan take off to do some night fishing while Tristan grabs Jessie and darts off to the woods.

Inside, everyone breaks into a serious game of strip poker; even Abby who seems to be far gone by now from the cooler full of daiquiris that she drank. Judd and I decide to forgo the game and head back outside to be alone just as several girls start to lose their tops. Tristan passes us at the door, walking ahead of an extremely pissed off looking Jessie.

Moving past us, he looks at Judd and whispers, "Next," with a sly grin on his face.

My jaw drops. *Wow! What an asshole!*

Judd grabs my hand and we race away from the drama to his pickup truck. He opens the cab and pulls out a couple blankets, a jacket and a small cooler, throwing it all in the bed of the truck. Hoisting me up over the side, he puts me down like I am precious cargo and jumps in behind me.

After spreading one blanket out and shoving another one up against the back, he lays down, pulling me in beside him. He reaches into the cooler and pulls out a beer for each of us, then extends his arm out. Automatically, I nestle against his shoulder, letting the heat from his body warm my skin.

I had figured we would go for a walk or go somewhere when he first led me to his truck, but as we lay here, I can see why he chose this destination. His truck is perfectly positioned with the tailgate facing the beach. There are no trees or cabins in our line of sight, just an open view of the sky. As the last traces of sunlight fade from the sky, countless stars peek through the darkness and light up the night.

Lying within the security of each other's arms, time stands still and it seems like days, but is more than likely just a few hours. We hear several of the guys leave the cabin to head back to their own and we even giggle when we hear far off moans coming from the water and woods.

"So what brought you out here anyways?" Judd asks as the cabin door slams shut to our right and the air fills with hushed voices and giggles.

I shift my head, making an extreme effort to touch every inch of his chest as I pull my hands up to support my chin.

"It was actually Abby's attempt to cheer me up." I can't see the expression of Judd's face, but I feel him move and notice his face falls forward so he can look at me. "I actually just got out of a year-long relationship not too long ago, so I think she was trying to get my mind off of it."

"Wow," he says as he moves his head to look back up at the stars.

I can only imagine what he is thinking.

"I walked in on him with someone else. I mean, I literally walked in on him," I add, not feeling the least bit of pain from the memory.

"That's awful," his voice is laced with compassion, yet a hint of uneasiness at the same time. "Are you over him?"

His question surprises me, because I haven't really thought about Kyle in the last few days. All I've had on my mind is Judd and how he makes me feel.

"I guess that's a rude question. What I meant, is do you think you two will get back together when you get back?"

I don't even hesitate to answer this, "Absolutely not!"

Pressing my toes to the bed of the truck, I push myself up so that I can be closer to Judd's face. "Just so you know . . . this is the best week of my life," then I place a gentle peck on his lips.

He lets out a heavy breath through his nose, closing his hands in around my body to hold my lips against his for a while longer.

As the hours tick by, our conversation flows like music, and our empty drinks have been thrown back into the cooler. The sky glimmers above us, but no matter how magnificent, I continue to take my eyes off of it to gaze up at him. He looks down at me with that playful smile on his face.

"So explain something to me," I raise my eyebrows and giggle at the not-so-subtle question I'm about to ask. "Why on earth are you single?"

He chuckles and then turns his face towards the sky. "I've never really had time for dating. I mean, yeah, there were a couple of girls I dated, but nothing serious. Nothing like a year-long relationship like you had."

"Why didn't you have time?" I ask, curious about all things Judd.

He lets out a dry laugh that sounds troublesome. "I was busy with football and I worked on the weekends at a farm with my younger brother. I was also always trying to keep my grades up, hoping I would be eligible for a scholarship eventually."

I laugh at his response. *Wow, no girls; Tristan must not have got that memo.*

"Have you always played?" I feel as though I am quizzing him, but judging from the smile on his face with each question, I don't think it is bothering him.

"Pretty much." His chest swells with a breath and the warmth of his hand melts into my skin as he slowly trails a path up and down my arm. "My dad got me, Jake and Tristan into it when we could barely walk. He played when he was in high school. He was pretty good, too. I think he hoped we would follow in his footsteps. By the time we were all in elementary school, we loved the sport, so it just kind of stuck." He stops talking, but his warm breaths dance across my ear and make my entire body tingle.

Laying my head on his shoulder, I tilt my face to look over at him. It's dark out, but I can't miss the fact that his eyes are locked on me.

I catch how he refers to his dad in the past tense, but I don't dare ask him about it. We haven't really approached the subject of my dad either and the worry that I have buried down deep this week. Judd seems to keep my mind occupied just fine, so there is no need to dive into depressing subjects.

"Ok, so what about you?" he counters.

"What about me?" I decide to tease, knowing he is checking to see how available I am.

"Why in the world does someone as amazing as you not have guys lined up to go out with her? I mean, so you broke up with the asshole that cheated on you, but why were there not a million guys swooping in to take his place?" His soft chuckles make me smile, but then I realize I have to tell him about Kyle; particularly the part where we just recently broke up.

"Well actually, it just happened the weekend I came out here."

All of a sudden, I'm nervous to talk about this. Last thing I want is for him to think I rushed into whatever is going on between the two of us. I guess it was fast, but I seriously haven't even thought about Kyle since I saw Judd.

"Did you love him?" Judd draws his eyebrows down and looks away from me.

"I . . ."I go silent not knowing how to answer that. *I thought I did, but then again he is the only boy I've ever really been with and if I loved him, wouldn't it hurt more than it does? Would I really be able to move on so quickly if it was love?*

I open my mouth to say no, but Judd quickly speaks up, "You know what? Don't answer that. You two are no longer together and you're here with me now. I think we should just focus on that."

I bite my lip at how bad this may make me sound, but I want to give him an answer. "Well, my answer is no. I don't think I would be where I am right now, feeling how I feel if that was love," I say and then quickly look to Judd to see if he is prepared to race out of the parking lot and away from me.

His arms tighten around me and he pulls me in closer, sending an electrifying sensation straight up my spine and leaving my body in a state of euphoria.

"Precisely," he says, flashing me a gorgeous, confident smile that washes all my worries away. "It's his loss, anyways," he adds and then places a quick kiss on my forehead.

We go back and forth, story after story. As we continue to talk, he looks at me through his long lashes every now and again and a fluttering stirs in my heart.

I stare back at him and silently question what this feeling is that is taking root in my very soul. *Is it too soon for me to feel this?*

Right then, Judd stops talking and gently bends to kiss the top of my forehead with his soft lips. It sends electric waves through my whole body so I close my eyes tight, breathing in and out as his lips linger. Butterflies dance in my stomach and something shifts in my heart. That's when I have to stop myself and question if I am, just maybe, falling in love.

Good news

TRICKLES OF WATER AND A sudden movement beneath my head pulls me out of my sleep the next morning. *Geez, what happened to peacefully waking up?*

"What the. . . ." Judd cries out, flinching upward.

My eyes snap open as I hear Evan's laughter fill the air.

"Hey, let me up for a second." I shift my body and sit up, feeling stiff as a board.

Judd jumps to his feet, braces his arm on the side of the truck bed and catapults himself to the ground. Evan darts off to the other side of the truck, laughing hysterically.

"Evan, I am going to beat your ass when I get ahold of you."

I look at Judd and realize the small splashes of water that hit me were nothing compared to what he got. His hair is dripping wet and the entire right side of his shirt is weighted down and sticking to his chest. Looking down to survey my own body, I see just a few splashes here and there. *Hmm, Evan must have been careful not to get me.*

"Come here!" Judd hollers while Evan runs around the back of the truck.

"Oh, don't be too mad! You know you needed that! I was doing you a favor," Evan yells from the front of the truck.

"Evan," Judd calls out as a warning.

Evan slaps his hand on the truck and howls out even louder. "I just wanted to bring a little realism to the wet dream you were . . ."

"Evan!" Judd yells even louder as he lunges for his best friend.

They take off towards the cabins, running as fast as their legs can carry them and it looks like Evan may be in trouble. I giggle, wondering how bad Judd will hurt him when he gets ahold of him. If this were Abby and me, it would end in tickle torture, but I'm thinking a good wrestling match may be in their near future.

"It was a joke . . . a joke, man!" Evan's laughter and hollers ring out in the distance.

I crack up watching Judd go after his friend as he darts away like a scared animal, all the while realizing the bugs must have feasted on me all night long. Trailing my nails across my thighs and arms, I notice swollen red welts.

A little while later, Judd and Evan make their way back to the truck where I am still snuggled up in the back on the dry side of the blanket. I hug my legs to my chest, feeling worn out and extremely itchy.

Judd gasps for air as he shoves Evan, who is still laughing. "You have to admit, it was needed." He smiles at Judd and somehow I get the feeling that Evan had reasons for the water bucket this morning.

"Yeah, thanks," Judd says as he elbows Evan and quickly glances to me with a small, embarrassed smile on his face.

Oh! Listening to their silly banter, I easily put two and two together. I take it that Evan was trying to spare his friend humiliation from publicly displaying his unintentional 'rise and shine.'

While we both frantically itch, Judd and I both come to the conclusion that while sleeping under the stars may be romantic and all, it is definitely not something you should do without a massive amount of bug spray. Scratching from head to toe, I kiss him goodbye so he can go to work.

Evan rolls his eyes and shakes his head, making fun of us. "Ok, come on before I have to hose you down again."

Giggling, I head towards my cabin, making sure to look over my shoulder as many times as possible.

The rest of the day drags by, but I keep myself occupied by hanging with the girls, playing volleyball on the beach, making a run to the store with Piper and Abby and gathering wood for the bonfire tonight.

Hammers echo in the distance and every once in a while we hear roars of laughter, but other than that you wouldn't even know there was anyone else here.

Evening comes and I am relieved to see Judd's face among all the guys as they mosey down the beach.

We all tear into the packages of hot dogs, buns, marshmallows, chocolate bars and graham crackers, ready to stuff our faces.

While we chow down, Tristan is sure to make a spectacle of eating his hot dogs as if he is trying to teach each of us girls life skills that has nothing to do with food. He also spends the entire evening harassing Abby as she makes a point of moving as far away from him as possible. To her disappointment, he stays on her heels like a lost puppy while making obscene gestures; he definitely enjoys every minute of her aggravation. It seems she and Piper are about the only girls that don't cave to his charm, and his efforts are getting pathetic.

Sunk into the sand and nuzzled back on Judd's chest in front of the fire, I look around and smile. Our groups have become great friends; most of us at least.

Piper has planted herself on Tyler's lap. He nonchalantly drops graham cracker crumbs on her chest, trying his best to nibble them off of her. Through quiet giggles and her playfully shoving at him, I get the feeling that she is getting annoyed. What I definitely cannot miss, and what I think everyone, including Piper, can see, is the heated glare that Evan is shooting her way from across the bonfire. I watch as Piper and Tyler wander off towards the guys' cabin, with Evan storming off not too long after.

Closing my eyes, I let the sounds of laughter fade away so that I can focus on one thing; the warm, strong hold that Judd has on me. His forearms tickle my sides as his hands tightly clasp at the front of my waist.

"Are you tired?" Judd's face brushes against my hair and his warm breath grazes my ear.

Keeping my eyes closed and my body completely melted against his, I nudge my chin forward to answer. Sleep tugs at my eyelids, sealing them shut as my body gets lighter and lighter until it feels as if I am floating through the air; *no, lightly bouncing.* A crunching sound rises up from below as arms hold me tightly. A clicking, then tapping similar to that of footsteps and hushed whispers softly rings in my ears. I'm half asleep, but trying desperately to wake myself so that I don't miss a moment of being with him. Prying my eyes open just enough to see him leaning over me, I suddenly realize I am no longer floating, but instead a firm, somewhat uncomfortable structure is tautly stretched beneath me and I know it is not Judd's body.

"Good night, Lyssa." I hear his voice whisper and a delicate touch brushes over my lips as my eyes and body fade into a deep slumber.

Thursday morning is a bit of a bummer when I wake up in my cot instead of snuggled up to Judd's chest. My heart drops knowing I won't see him until later. Hoping to focus on something other than the clock, I pick up my phone to call Bethany and catch up. Scrolling through my recent calls, I tap on her name and wait while the phone rings.

"Hey, girl, what on earth have you been up to? It's like you dropped off the face of the earth. Is everything ok?" Her all-too-cheerful voice immediately brings a smile to my face and pulls me out of the dumps.

"Oh yeah, I texted you before I left, that I was going to the lake with my sister. Sorry I haven't texted or called since. I guess I've been too busy having fun." I hold back a little, not wanting to tell her that I have been caught up in a tornado of feelings for a heart-pounding hot guy that makes my toes tingle every time I look at him.

"Fun, huh? That's great, considering . . ." She pauses and I know she is referring to my cheating ex.

"Yeah, that's history. I'm not going to waste my time on him anymore. So what have you been up to this week?" I ask while watching the hands on the clock above the kitchen sink slowly tick by like they are mocking me. *Come on day, move faster so I can see Judd.*

"Well, there is this guy I kind of like and I have been trying to get his attention. I'm just not sure he is ready . . ." Bethany stops talking abruptly and sighs, "You know how that goes."

Thankfully, for the rest of the phone call she stays focused on her week and asks very little about my trip. I know Bethany well enough to know that one mention of a guy I like and she will start diving into crude questions and comments that will only belittle my feelings for him. I'd rather let this thing between us blossom and see where we end up before sharing it with anyone else. *Well anyone besides the huge group of us out here this week. Luckily reception isn't the best in most places out here; otherwise, social media would have already killed that for me.*

Glancing back at the clock, I realize I have been on the phone with her for a while and we have basically talked about everything other than anything important.

"Well, I guess I better get off of here and go enjoy some sunshine," I announce, contemplating heading to the beach verses taking a nap.

Bethany sighs, "You suck. I need a tan bad; maybe I'll head to the tanning salon. Well, have fun and hopefully I'll see you soon."

"I'll call you when I get back to town. Bye."

"Bye, girl," Bethany says and then I hit end. *Now what to do?*

The boys work late, trying their best to get as much done as possible. By the time they get off, none of them are as lively as they usually are. I get to visit with Judd for a bit before calling it a night. My heart sinks and my anxiety level flares with the thought that we only have a few days left before we leave to go home.

The days on the calendar slowly get crossed off as Friday morning comes. *Two days till I leave.* As soon as my eyes and ears zone in on the dark silent room, my mouth drips down my chin into a deep frown and I probably look like a child that has just sat and watched the ice cream truck drive by. I would really rather be waking up in the back of Judd's truck, lying beside him, but instead my back aches and my hip feels like it's been pushed out of socket from being on my side in this uncomfortable cot all night.

Finally deciding to leave the solitude of my gloomy mind, I snatch up my phone and look at the time and date, halfway expecting that it is still night time. It lights up with a sweep of my thumb and I see that my restless night of sleep only held out until 4:46 this morning.

Suddenly awake and full of adrenaline, I fling my sheet over the side of the bed and hurry to the bathroom, nearly forgetting to grab my bag in my excitement.

After I am changed, I race outside and across the gravel lot to Judd's cabin. I really hope I can catch them before they head out for the day. With my chest heaving and my lungs on fire, I stop at the porch of his cabin and listen. My ears are met with the sounds of the water lapping at the shore, the crisp sounds of leaves brushing up against the other as the wind whistles through the air and then I hear what I was hoping for.

Deep voices and laughter collide with my eardrums as I quickly move to the side of the porch and out of sight. I slink up against the wall, hoping to blend in like a chameleon in a sea of grass. Several guys filter out of the house, buckling tool belts to their waists, some of them shoving food in their mouth and others yawning as if they need to go back to bed.

A tall figure in a ball cap catches my eyes in the semi dark hours of the morning and I just know it is Judd. Sneaking up from the side, a couple eyes turn my way.

"Well, well . . . looks like someone got a house call." I hear Mitch's annoying voice.

"Oh damn, baby . . . I know I'm irresistible, but can't you just wait till I get off work," Tristan says in a tone I've heard him use on my sister.

I stop and fold my arms across my chest, trying to hide the smile that's creeping onto my face.

"Hey . . ." Judd's smile is evident even though I cannot see his face from under the dark shadows of the porch awning.

"Oh, no! No, no! We've got shit to do, man. I know that tone and you are not skipping out to go play today." Evan moves in beside Judd, sounding somewhat serious, yet his tone is laced with his usual sarcasm and mischievousness.

"Damn, he's whipped already," Matt says as the rest of the guys, excluding Evan and Judd, hop off the porch and stroll away.

"Don't worry! I'll be right behind you," Judd informs his friend but Evan doesn't budge.

With his arms crossed, Evan corrects him, "Oh no! Your chick's here and I know this reunion is going to take at least an hour if I leave. Get on with the kissing and then we're headed to the work shed. Together!" He looks back and forth between me and Judd.

I laugh and hope I didn't get him in trouble.

"Whatever." Judd turns to face me with a crooked grin. "He's just kidding," he informs me.

"Nope, I'm serious. I'm not leaving." I giggle at Evan's parent-like strictness.

"Hey," Judd says, softening his voice into an affectionate tone as he turns his attention back to me, completely ignoring his friend.

My heart sails above the clouds at the sound of his voice and for an instant I forget that we have company as well. "Hey," I say, with my hand over my mouth to hide my cheesy grin.

"Oh, Jesus! Is this going to take all day?" Evan's annoyance is climbing and I can tell he is eager to get started on their work.

"Good grief! Could I have a minute? Just a minute," Judd huffs out, "and back up. Damn, do you want to join us or something?"

I laugh and then stretch up to give Judd a small peck on the lips so he can satisfy Evan's urgency to leave.

Pulling away sooner than I'd like, warmth spreads through my body as he cradles my face in his hands.

"I just wanted to say hi and tell you to have a good day," I say in a sweet tone and then kick up the volume of my voice, "Now, go hammer some crap together and get it *all* done."

Evan snickers beside us and Judd's face breaks into a huge grin. "Ok. I'll see you later?"

I nod my head and he slips one more peck in before turning to sneak away with his friend.

Evan follows along but not before turning for one last comment, "You're ok in my book, Alyssa," he says surprising me.

I watch them leave and then run off to start my boring-no-Judd day. I get back to the cabin, scarf down some cereal and prepare for some fun in the sun with the girls. They have rented jet skis from across the lake so I figure I might as well join in.

Glancing at the clock, I notice it is 9:22am; I'm so ready to get on with this day. Dressed in my lime green and white chevron print bikini, I snatch up a soft terry cloth towel and prepare to head out when Abby's shrieking voice calls to me from the back room.

"Alyssa, get in here. Mom and Dad are calling!"

My mind wastes no time telling my legs to move; run; get in there. As soon as I enter the room, I hear Mom's beautiful voice on speaker phone.

"Hey, sweetie," Mom says in her usual cheerful voice.

"Alyssa is here, too, Mom," Abby informs her with an anxious tone.

"Hey girls," Dad joins in on the conversation.

I slide down onto the back bedroom bed, which is Piper's parent's old room. Dad's voice sends my mood shooting through the roof and makes everything seem better.

"Hi Mom and Dad," I say, feeling as though I have not seen them for months.

"Hi honey." Mom clears her throat. "Are you both having a good time?"

I quickly look over to Abby and put my finger up pointing at her in a warning. No doubt she will be the first to blab about me meeting a guy, but I have loads of ammunition on her. She wouldn't want Mom and Dad to know she's been skinny dipping with several guys this week.

"We have had a blast, some of us more than others," Abby says looking directly at me with an evil smirk on her face.

"What about you guys? How's your trip going?" I ask knowing good and well that they have probably had a ball soaking up sun and drinking fruity umbrella drinks on the beach.

Mom brings us up to speed, "Actually, we are on our way to Andrea's now. We just left home."

Abby and I both share a puzzled look. With this bit of information, I am ready to throw all of my stuff in a bag, steal Piper's dad's van and race back home, but she goes on.

"Your father's doctor called and some of his tests came back inconclusive so they wanted to see him immediately so they could rerun some tests. We figured we are just going to extend our vacation and go spend some time with your sister."

My heart sinks knowing we have to wait longer to find out the results.

"Why don't you two stay a little longer? Abby, I'm sure the hospital will work with you. If you two are having fun, then there is no need for you to come home. Besides, won't it just be boring without your father and me being at home?" Mom suggests with a laugh.

Even with her attempt to lighten the subject with a joke, I still am not completely convinced.

"Mom, I don't know. I could come home and maybe talk to some of the staff at the hospital and see if those tests could be rushed through." My sister's persistent tone tells me that she is not altogether on board with waiting.

"Honey, they are rushing them through. Trust me, everything is fine, and we are very excited to stay the week with Andrea. You should have heard how ecstatic the boys were when they heard that Mama and Papa were coming to visit."

Abby and I look at each other and laugh. I can imagine my nephews' laughter at the news. I have no doubt Mom and Dad will have a ball at my sisters.

It takes a little more persuading before Abby and I relent. Pondering on it for a moment, it makes more sense to stay here where it feels like heaven everyday rather than going home and waiting. There, all I would be doing is torturing myself when there isn't necessarily anything to worry about.

"What do you think?" I ask Abby before we get off the phone.

"I'll have to call work and ok it, but it shouldn't be a problem," she pauses, her eyes wide with excitement. "Let's do it!"

"Ok then, good," Mom says in an equally thrilled tone, "Then we will see you around the sixth. That's when we will be back to the house."

"Ok Mom. Have fun. I love you both," I say to them, barely able to wait to tell Judd the news.

"Bye, love you," Abby joins in.

"Bye sweeties. Have fun. We love you," Dad says further away from the phone.

Abby hits end and we squeal and giggle, bouncing up and down on the bed like we're about to have a pillow fight. Once we find a way to contain our enthusiasm, I dart out of the room ready to go find Judd.

As I'm sliding a pair of jean shorts over my hips, Abby's enthusiastic voice calls out from the back room.

"It's set!" She sprints into the room and bounces down on Crystal's cot, directly across from mine. "My boss said it is fine. I have a lot of ETO that I need to use. Next time I am on the schedule is on the seventh." Her teeth sparkle and her eyes dance with happiness.

"Yay," I giggle, clapping my hands and bouncing on my toes. I pause in my celebration for just a moment, "Hey, are you ok with me spending so much time with Judd? I mean, I know this was supposed to be a girls' getaway and all, and here I've snuck away every chance I can to see him." I grit my teeth, hoping she says it's alright.

Much like Mom, Abby waves her hand in front of her letting me know I'm silly for asking.

"Oh Alyssa, I'm glad you're having fun regardless of whether it is with us or with that stud you have latched onto."

I roll my eyes and giggle at her choice of words.

"Just please tell me he is nothing like his brother?" Abby crosses her arms across her chest, pushing her D-cups halfway up to her chin. "He is such a man whore."

I belt out a loud laugh and slap Abby on the arm. "Abby, he is nothing like that. Trust me, you have nothing to worry about."

All week long I have seen Tristan traipsing off into the woods with a girl on his arm, only to return and leave with another. Often I wonder if half the girls I'm staying with have any self respect at all. When I hear them sharing stories, I go with the fact that they definitely don't.

"Well then, on that note, I am going to happily forgo the lake time and go find where Judd is working. I have to tell him the good news." I shimmy my hips back and forth while biting my lips.

Laughing at my giddiness, she calls out as I run to the door, "Don't do anything I wouldn't do!"

If you don't marry her, I will

HUFFING AND PUFFING, I SPRINT in the same direction as I saw them heading this morning. I remember the map that Judd had when we worked on the shower house. Drawing up the picture in my mind, I recall that he hadn't marked several cabins at the center of the property line. I suppose that is where they are working, which is a good ways down.

They are nearly finished with their work and Judd told me they will more than likely finish up a couple days before he has to leave. This made me happy knowing we will have more time together.

I cannot even think about the day when we leave. We talk about home and the future in terms of our goals, but our topic of conversation has never ventured to what is going on between us, or even the fact that we are leaving in a matter of days. That scares me. It also makes me realize my feelings for him are much deeper than I will even admit to myself.

My lungs burn about a half mile in, so I slow my pace and finally let my eyes roam the scenery. The sunlight flickers over the surface of the lake, making each ripple of water sparkle like a sea full of gems. Above the water gives way to a wide open pale blue sky with fluffs of puffy white clouds lying about. The first day I got here, this all seemed so gloomy due to my mood, but now, everything I see seems to be blanketed in beauty; everyday is magical.

I've never actually been down this far from where we are staying, but I continue on the same path that runs in front of all the cabins along the edge of the lake. I've passed about nine cabins and still no sign of any of the guys. *Where on earth are they? I have to be nearing the middle of the property line.*

My chest swells as I suck in a lungful of air, enjoying the woodsy scent of the trees and the sweetness of wildflowers. Even though the air is perfumed in an array of lovely fragrances, the temperature already seems thick and suffocating with a slight breeze that makes it tolerable. The days have been downright sweltering lately. Slap on some cooking oil and the heat will sauté you in no time, I'm sure.

Grabbing my hair off of my neck to hold it off my shoulders, tiny beads of sweat tickle my skin as they roll from my hairline down my back. A whistle calls out to my right and I turn to see Tristan and Mitch up on a roof of one of the cabins. Two more guys, including Jake, are working on the porch.

"Hell yeah, that's what we need to see to get our asses in gear." Mitch yells while Tristan eggs him on. " . . . Although, losing a bit more clothing may motivate us a little more," he says in his cocky tone, as if he is God's gift to women.

I drop my hair back down over my shoulders, feeling a bit less exposed. Sweeping my eyes over the landscape around the cabin, to the porch and over the entire building, I don't see Judd anywhere.

"Shut up, you asshole!" Jake jogs over and stops in front of me.

I've noticed in the last week that Jake seems to be on the shy side, always making himself scarce when the partying starts. Judd had mentioned that his little brother likes to keep to himself, unlike most of the other guys who came out here in hopes for a little summer action. Because of this, I haven't had the chance to talk to or get to know him yet. Luckily, he seems to be coming to my rescue now.

"Alyssa, right?" he asks in a very confident tone, which surprises me.

I nod my head and smile, looking at how he resembles Tristan more than Judd.

"He's working at the next cabin," he points in the direction I was already walking. "Come on. I'll walk with you. I need to go find out what's left to finish."

This gets my attention.

"Finish?" I question.

He smiles, most likely noting the enthusiasm in my voice.

"Yeah . . . we should be done after today." His reply makes me giddy.

I bounce on my toes and try to resist the urge to do a happy dance in view of several guys that just tried to get me to disrobe for entertainment.

"That's great! So on with the relaxing and fun for the rest of your stay?" I say excitedly.

His lips quirk to the side and he lets out a low chuckle as we walk further away from Mitch and his gang.

"Well, I am sure they will be doing plenty of that and more," he points his thumb over his shoulder behind him, "But after tonight, I'm heading home."

My heart stops for a moment, praying Judd is not leaving with him. Jake and Judd had driven out here together, so I may cry if he says they are both leaving.

"Just you or. . . ." I say as calmly as possible, but my voice cracks.

He snaps his head up to look at me, probably to make sure he doesn't have a crying lovesick girl on his hands.

A soft, sweet smile emerges on his face. "It's just me. I'm going to take Judd's truck home and he'll leave with Tristan on the fifth."

I let out a sigh and he cracks up at my reaction.

"I don't think any of us could get Judd to leave if we had to. I really think when the fifth comes they are going to have to drag him away kicking and screaming like a little girl. I'm super glad I'm not going to be here to see that," he chuckles as my heart swells with his words.

Judd doesn't want to leave either? Oh yeah, here comes my happy dance.

I look back at Jake and flash him the cheesiest smile I've ever felt.

"Lyssa!"

My heart races as soon as I hear his voice. Pulling my gaze up past Jake and away from the lake, I see Judd running towards us with an equally cheesy grin on his face. My heart skips a beat at seeing him.

"I was just escorting her away from Mitch's dirty thoughts," Jake says with his eyebrows pulled down and his lips into a tight frown.

Judd nods his head in understanding, "Thanks, man. I owe you."

Jake starts to reply when the rest of the group working on the cabin takes note of my presence.

"Oh, come on!" Evan stands on the roof of the cabin, a hammer in one hand and his other hand held out to question what I'm doing here. "Don't tell me you are ditching to go make out," he calls to Judd.

I guess this probably doesn't look good. Evan is Judd's friend, but when they are working he is also his supervisor. Looking around quickly, I decide there is only one thing to do.

Swinging around to face Judd, with my back to Evan, I quickly snatch the cordless drill out of Judd's hand.

"What are you . . ." Judd starts up in complete confusion.

I look up at him and smile, hoping he just goes with it. Turning around, I walk my way towards the cabin where Tyler, Evan, and Matt are working.

Judd mumbles something to himself, probably wondering what I am doing.

As I near the cabin, I take in how the guys are placing new boards across the framework of the new front porch. Once in place, they screw them into the boards below them.

"Nope . . . I just came to help," I say, looking up at Evan with a little sass in my tone.

When I get in front of the cabin, I hoist a board up into my arms. Jake and Judd stand back, eyes wide and mouths dropped open. The board is much heavier than I expect, but no way am I going to put it down.

Evan's mouth rises up into a full grin and he looks at Judd. "Damn, man, I like her! I'm going to have to add her to our payroll!" He quickly points his hammer in my direction as I start to lay the board down on the open porch. "But don't screw up!" With that, he goes back to hammering on shingles.

I throw the board down onto the deck frame, my arms burning from its weight. Pushing the board flush against the next one, I pick up a couple screws and start drilling them in, mocking the ones that have already been put down.

"Hell, if you don't marry her someday, I will," Jake quietly says to Judd.

I turn just in time to see Judd nodding his head to approve. His eyes light up and he grins at me.

"So, are you going to help or just stare?" I tease Judd as the rest of the guys all crack up.

Truly horrendous things

THE DAY FLIES BY WITH Evan's constant sarcastic remarks about how he is going to have to replace the porch again tomorrow due to it being water logged from Judd's drooling. It makes the work enjoyable and I cannot stop laughing.

After the work is done, most of the guys head to get cleaned up.

"Hey, you wanna go to my cabin while all the guys are gone? I can change into my trunks and then we can hit the lake," Judd says as we walk back along the path. "We can always go to the shower house later."

I jerk my gaze around to meet his.

His lips quirk into a mischievous smile and his eyebrows are drawn up as he adds, "You know . . . *alone.*"

I definitely do not miss the suggestion in his words.

We get to his cabin and I see it is identical to the one I am staying in. The only exception is they have actual beds, not cots.

"What?" I say sarcastically, pointing to his bed as Judd crosses the room to the bathroom.

He pauses and looks back at me.

"You have beds?" I say with a tad bit of jealousy. Placing my hands along my hips, I look away from the beds and level him with a firm look. "Well, I'm just going to have to sleep here," I say without even realizing how it came out.

His face breaks out into a huge smile. "I don't think I'll put up much of a fight with that request."

I drop my hands to my sides immediately, heat creeping across my face at what I just implied.

He snickers and then quickly changes the subject, "I'll be right back. I'm going to change real quick."

Pushing down the embarrassment that is pulsing through me, I lift my head to look at him and see his adorable smile before he disappears into the bathroom.

I shimmy out of my shorts, deciding to leave them here and get them later. Already in my bikini, I curl up on the bed that Judd had pulled his bag out from under. I stretch out and then pull my knees up to get comfortable. *Oh this feels good; a real mattress. That cot is definitely getting old.*

Judd comes out in black board shorts and snickers as he walks up to me lying on his bed. The mattress dips down as he climbs in behind me. He pulls me close to spoon with his cheek next to mine.

"This is probably more comfortable than those cots, huh?"

I look at him through the corner of my eyes and nod in mid-yawn.

"You want to go down to the lake or would you rather take a nap first?" Judd asks.

Swimming does sound good, but lying beside him sounds better than anything in this world. I smile and nod in agreement, wiggling my body against him. He sucks in a quick breath and I immediately feel his reaction to my movements. Turning my head to look at his face, his lips immediately find mine. I let out a whimper and open my mouth deeper so I can get the full effect of the kiss. Another whimper escapes my mouth as I close my eyes.

Judd pulls away, breathing heavily. "Do you know what that does to me?" he says, rolling his eyes in an exaggerated effort as his chest heaves in and out.

"What?" I ask, not sure whether he means when I wiggled against him.

"That little sound you make; the one you make every time we kiss." He flashes me a sexy grin and then runs his hands across my belly to hover at the waistband of my bikini.

I bite my lip, not aware that I make a sound but by the way he is breathing, I'm thinking I definitely like what it does to him. Craning my neck so that I can keep my lips sealed to his, I desperately hope to let loose of a couple more sounds that seem to wake his body up.

Slowly, his hand slips further down with his thumb barely dipping beneath the fabric of my bikini bottoms. It stays there for a minute, wisping across the tender flesh above my pelvic bone like he is gauging my reaction. My eyes are closed tightly and my mind is on a continual loop of, *keep going; keep going.* Right then he pulls away, sliding his hand down the outside of my thigh. *No, no! Put it back!*

His fingertips leisurely caress my thigh as his hand dips further down to my knee to gently pull my legs further apart. Knowing exactly what he wants, I scoot my leg over his, giving him complete access.

His lips roam the back of my neck as his hand makes a slow descent to its original destination, inching up my inner thigh,

Closer . . .

Closer . . .

Closer . . .

I let out a strangled breath that I didn't know I was holding as his hand smoothes over the front of my thigh and slides up my hip back to my waist. *Well now he's just torturing me.*

I turn my head slightly to look at him. My eyes lock with his intense stare for only a second before his mouth returns to my neck, teasing the spot behind my ear with soft, wet sweeps of his tongue.

"Ahhh . . ." a whimper moves across my lips as his hand creeps below my waist. *I am so ready to feel him touch me.*

He slides his fingers to the area of my body that is aching for him and I let out a thunderous moan that I swear could wake the dead. From the corner of my eyes, I see him smile against my neck as his finger teases me with soft gentle strokes. *I swear I may come unglued.*

He pulls his mouth up to my ear and his breath tickles me. "Is this ok? I'm not hurting you, am I?" he says with such tenderness.

Biting down hard on my lip, I try to keep from screaming from the sensation. I shake my head and take several quick breaths.

His lips move down to the back of my neck and he plants slow wet kisses around to my ear. All the while I am whirling and spinning from the shockwaves his fingers are causing to course through my body. He repositions his fingers and begins to tease my most sensitive spot. This sends me plummeting off the cliff, freefalling into pure bliss.

It takes more than a minute or two for my breathing to return to normal. Once my heart has steadied, I twist my neck to look into his eyes and shift my hips, folding my body into his.

His hand immediately clamps onto my hips to stop me, "Easy," he says in a pained voice as he nudges me away from his lower body.

My mouth drops as I realize exactly what this whole moment did to him, and he has no relief from it. I roll around onto my other side to face him and place my hand on his chest. Looking down, I can't help but giggle from the tent that has suddenly emerged on his trunks. He laughs with me, dropping his head back in embarrassment. Guilt washes over me for being on the receiving end of things.

"Judd," I whisper in a shaky voice, a little hesitant to suggest what I'm thinking.

I place my hand on his lower abs and continue to drop them lower. "Do you want me to . . . ?"

He shakes his head and grabs my hand, pulling it away from its current destination.

Placing a kiss on my knuckles, he whispers, "I just wanted to make you feel good. I'll be alright." His smile doesn't waver, but I see a little pain in his eyes.

Taking one more look at his predicament, I take a deep breath and push down the guilt I feel for not returning the favor. He places my hand over his heart covering it with his own and that is how we fall asleep.

I wake up with Judd's finger tracing the curves of my arm. His hand moves over the inside of my elbow, up my arm, to my shoulder, and then back down. Soft lips pressed against my forehead pulls me out of my sleep and I open my eyes, looking over at him in complete happiness.

"Hey, beautiful," he whispers.

"Hey," I croak out. "How long did I sleep?"

The backs of his fingers glide across my cheek so carefully.

"A little over an hour," he says softly.

Smiling at him, my hands instinctively reach up to touch his gorgeous face. As soon as it makes contact, his smile grows. *I could look at him forever.*

"What do you want to do now? Go to the lake?" he suggests.

"I don't care." *I'm too lost in this moment of being wrapped in his arms.* "What do you want to do?" I return his question, leaving the ball in his court.

His chest rises with a large sigh as he says something that always makes me light up inside, "It doesn't matter to me what we do, as long as I'm with you."

My heart bursts with affection at his words. Looking around the room to keep from spilling out all the emotions he stirs within me, my eyes land on a couple of fishing poles and a tackle box sitting in the corner.

I flip my gaze back to him. "Let's go fishing."

His hand immediately stops its smooth pattern across my skin and he looks at me skeptically.

"Fishing? You fish?" he asks with a quirk of his brow.

"I can fish," I state in a neutral tone, knowing good and well that I completely suck at it.

He grins, placing his fingertips below my chin.

"Then fishing it is," he laughs then adds with a chuckle, "I'll even worm your hook for you."

He smiles so brightly, but all I can do is stare and revisit my father's words, *"The guy who falls in love with you will do truly horrendous things for you."* A warm flood of emotions fill my heart as I smile at him and remind myself once again to breathe.

Judd places a quick peck on my lips and then bounces up off the bed. He grabs me at the waist to pull me up and out of my thoughts.

After fetching the poles and the tackle box, we stroll down to the Snack Shack for some drinks, snacks and bait. He and I laugh and joke around endlessly as we make a twenty-minute hike around the path to the boat dock. Evan's grandfather keeps a fishing boat there that the guys have been using from time to time.

We walk side by side, sometimes hand in hand. Every once in a while I purposely walk ahead of him, glancing over my shoulder and shaking my ass. I try my best to look all sensual and get a rise out of him; it works. He lets out a groan and swats at it.

When he pulls me close, I shake loose and take off running. Even though I'd rather stay right there within his grasp, I run ahead to escape a possible onslaught of tickles. He darts after me only to catch me a second later. I whirl around and we laugh uncontrollably.

"I give up, I give up," I squeal as Judd tosses our stuff to the ground and pins me down.

He straddles my waist and holds my hands above my head as I giggle endlessly. Last time this happened was when Abby tickled me until I peed my pants. *Oh dear God, do not let me pee my pants in front of him!* I keep my face as neutral as possible, hoping I will give off the impression that I am immune to his tickling powers.

"Alyssa . . ." Judd stops laughing and gets a serious tone in his voice.

I look at him and my own amusement fades. "What's wrong?" I ask, kind of alarmed.

He stares deeply into my eyes with the look of a man stranded in a desert and I am the mirage he sees in the distance.

"I . . ." he whispers so softly.

My heart rises up into my throat, waiting for what I think he might say, for what I so desperately want to yell out to him when we touch. Every time we stop what we're doing and look at one another, those words come to my mind; yet they are words that I am petrified to say out loud. His eyes close as he shakes his head to clear his thoughts and I know the moment is lost.

"I just wanted to say that this is the best summer of my life." He gives me an uneasy smile and then hops up. "Come on. Let's go," he says as he helps me up and grabs our poles and food.

We settle into the fishing boat and he guides the vessel to a private area away from all the skiers, boaters and swimmers.

Once we're there, we sit back and bask in the warm glow of the sun while getting our poles ready.

"You know, I've never really asked about your family," he asks, tying an orange and yellow ball onto the line of one of the poles.

"We're very close," I say quietly, looking down at the tiny ripples that are formed each time a fish nips at the surface. "Actually, you know what . . ." I pause and glance up, feeling guilty for not telling him about my dad in the first place. My voice quivers as I go on, "There was another reason for this trip to the lake. My dad is waiting on test results to find out if his cancer has returned."

He stops what he is doing and listens to every word, remaining quiet with his eyebrows crinkled in understanding.

"A few summers ago my dad battled cancer, but he got past it. Then last week, I came home and found out that we may possibly have to relive that heartbreaking experience again. I just don't know what to do if . . ." I stop talking and stare at Judd.

For an instant, I swear I can see my pain mirrored in his eyes. He looks at me with so much compassion and empathy that no words are needed. That look alone completely comforts me. When I finish my story, he stumbles forward in the boat, rocking it to where I think we may flip. I realize he has reached his destination when he sits in front of me and squeezes my hand tightly.

"I wish I could hold you right now," he says with so much concern in his voice, "but I may flip the boat." He dips his chin down and smiles. "I promise as soon as we get to shore, I'll wrap my arms around you."

I beam back at him, because I know he will hold up to that promise.

Judd clears his throat and shifts around to grab a pole and bait. Reaching into the white foam container, he pulls out a worm and glances at me through the corner of his eyes.

I giggle, noticing that he doesn't like those little slimy creatures anymore than I do. My body shudders when he lifts the wiggly, dirty thing up to the hook. *Gross!!* His head falls back and his body shakes with laughter. He raises the worm up into my direct view and looks back and forth between me and the creepy crawler.

"You know, I only do this because I am so crazy about you, because honestly," he tips his head towards the worm while looking at me, "I think these fellas are pretty disgusting."

He softly laughs and then continues his task of driving the hook right through the worm. Scrunching up his face, he puts one on the hook of the other pole and hands it to me.

Although I have my nose crinkled up from being grossed out, what he doesn't see is my recognition of what he really meant when he said he is crazy about me.

Casting my line, I watch it glide through the air several yards out before sinking beneath the depths of the sparkling water. I smile to myself with a soothing warmth engulfing my heart. *I can't believe this amazing guy in front of me is more than willing to do something that disgusts him just because he is crazy about me.* Something tells me he meant more than that, because at this very moment, I know I'm in love with him and the way he is so willing to do truly horrendous things for me.

I'm all yours

WE STAY DOWN THE SHORE from our cabins well into the night before heading back.

Once we get to the beach, we find everyone indulging in a late night swim. Jake and Evan sit on the shore watching all the chaos unfold.

"Where have you two been off to all day?" Evan asks as we settle down into the sand beside him.

"Out fishing in your grandpa's boat," Judd replies.

"Damn, that's where all the fishing gear was? Jake and I usually skip out on these events and go night fishing, but we couldn't find the poles. Thanks to you, we've been reduced to watching your brother's naked ass gallivant around," he says, motioning out to the wild bunch in the water.

I look out at the water lit by shimmers of moonlight and see a figure up on the dock that looks like Piper with Abby's blonde hair bobbing in the water below her.

"Sorry, man, we got to it first," Judd replies with a laugh, right as I hear Abby scream.

"Oh my God, there's a snake in the water!" she cries out.

Straining my eyes back to the lake, I can barely make out a figure swimming closely behind her.

"I got your snake right here baby," Tristan's voice chimes in.

He must be continuing in his relentless pursuit to get my sister's attention.

Everyone busts up laughing, even Evan and Jake.

I stare out at Abby as she quickly splashes away from Tristan and yells out, "Tristan, that is a snake I would gladly put out of its misery."

She starts swimming for the shore while Tristan stays back by the dock to watch her.

"Oh baby, please put it out of its misery," he calls out, trying to sound sexy.

She makes it to shore, grabs her towel, stomping past us, and then turns back to the water giving Tristan the finger.

A few minutes later, Tristan climbs onto the dock in all his naked glory and dances around with a beer in hand. Unfortunately, the moonlight illuminates the light wood of the dock, leaving very little to the imagination when it comes to him. *Geez, this is what Skylar and Jessie were talking about. He has no shame,* I think trying to hold back my laughter.

"Oh good grief . . . I definitely do not want to see that," Judd says and then grabs my hand to pull me away from the x-rated scene.

"Where are you two going?" Evan calls out while laughing at Tristan.

"I thought we'd go listen to some music in my truck rather than get drained by the mosquitoes again," Judd answers in a sarcastic tone as we walk uphill towards the gravel lot where he is parked.

"Don't forget, I'm leaving in the morning. I still need your truck," Jake says while standing and brushing off his jeans.

He must not want to watch his brother out there on display either.

"Don't worry, it'll be here. I'm not sure if I'll make it back to the cabin tonight or not, so I'll leave the keys in the glove box," Judd yells back.

He opens the back cab door and I climb in. Leaning into the drivers' door, he sticks his keys in the ignition and turns it. He spends a few minutes flipping through stations on the radio before he settles on one.

Once soft music is filtering through the truck, he settles down beside me in the backseat and pulls out his phone.

"So the reason I really wanted to come out here is for this." He holds up his phone, getting into the contacts and pressing the button to add a new one. "What's your number?"

I giggle at his question. "Are you going to call me instead of coming to see me tomorrow?" I tease.

He laughs with me and shakes his head, "No, this is for when we leave, so that I can call and take you on an official date."

I stop laughing because this is a subject we haven't crossed yet. *He said he wants to take me on a date. I could scream. He wants my number.* I feel like I am thirteen again finding out from a friend that the boy that I like, likes me back.

The excitement coursing through me is about to burst out like a confetti cannon. I want to giggle, I want to hug myself, I want to throw myself onto my bed and sigh out in happiness.

Smiling from ear to ear, I happily read off my number. I even look over his shoulder the whole time to ensure that he gets every single digit correct. After it is entered into his phone, he hits the add photo button.

He then turns it towards me and says, "Smile!"

I flash him my biggest grin, displaying the exact way I feel right now. He saves the picture and gets out of his contacts.

I quickly snatch the phone out of his hand before he can put it away. This is an opportunity any girl would take advantage of. I get back into his camera and decide to take my own picture. Although his gorgeous face is burned into my mind, I'd love a picture to drool over at night.

Snuggling up next to him, I hold up the camera. He looks over at me and I snap the picture. I end up taking a million pictures on his phone and we get sillier the more I take. We make faces, kiss, laugh, press our cheeks together, try to look serious, try to look mad and so many other funny expressions.

After examining them all, my favorite ends up being the first one where he is looking at me. Before I surrender his phone back to him, I get into his text messages and send that one picture to my phone.

He tosses his phone into the front seat and pulls me onto his lap so that I am straddling him with my legs bent along the sides of his thighs. My arms instinctively wrap around his shoulders and my entire body shivers as he runs his hands up my sides.

Over the course of the last two weeks I have gathered that he loves my reaction to his touch and this time is no exception because his face lights up, highlighting his dimple. I never get sick of seeing his smile. I'm obsessed with it.

He slides his hand up to the bottom of my swimsuit top and runs his fingers along it like he is straightening it out. I look down at his hands, wishing they were just a little further up. Quickly sliding them around to my back, he pulls me in for a kiss. I stretch my body up against his and my breathing automatically picks up from our closeness. He smiles against my lips and I realize I must have made my noise that he loves so much. As if the smile wasn't enough to bring me to that conclusion, I notice a more intense reaction further down. I shift my hips towards him, wanting and needing him as close to me as possible.

I don't know what has come over me this past week. I have never wanted someone like I want Judd.

He frantically runs his hands down my back, pulling me flush against him. I settle into a rhythm of rubbing against him as his mouth moves all over my neck and chest.

"Wait, wait," Judd says breathlessly, pulling back from me just a bit but further than I care to be from him right now. "I want you, Alyssa," he whispers barely able to catch his breath, "but I want it to be special. You're special and I'm not going to just do this in a truck."

Just the fact that he admitted to wanting me makes my head dizzy with excitement. I try to smile but I cannot calm my racing heartbeat. *I really want to return to where we were.*

He takes deep, deliberate breaths and places his hands on both sides of my face so that I am looking into his eyes.

"I want to ask you something." He squeezes his eyes shut for only a second and snaps them open with a small smile on his lips. "This is going to sound like we are back in the junior high or something, but I'm not sure how you go about these sorts of things."

I laugh at his words, not at all knowing what he is going to say.

"So ummm . . ." he stutters around and looks away from my gaze. "Ok . . ."

His smile fades away and he composes himself to a serious expression. He drops his hands to my side as I remain straddling his lap.

"You are definitely over your ex, right?"

His question totally surprises me and I can tell he catches onto my shock.

He stumbles around, trying desperately to explain his reasoning for such a bizarre question. "What I mean is, you aren't going to go back home and get back together?" He pauses taking in the confusion that I am sure is still plastered across my face. "I'm only asking because we've known each other for around two weeks and you told me that you had been with him for a year. I just wanted to make sure that . . ."

I smile at the nervous little boy he has become and place my index finger on his lips to stop him from going on. As he stops talking, a smile spreads across his face beneath my fingertip, as if it had pained him to ask that in the first place. Removing my finger, I press my lips against his, right as he pulls me tight against his body, perfectly meshing us together.

I pull my head back just far enough to look into his eyes. "Judd, don't worry. I'm all yours," I assure him causing his face to break open into a wide grin.

"Ok . . . good," he says, still grinning from ear to ear. "Then here comes the junior high part."

Wait, what?! I thought the rambling of a little boy nervous about me going back to my ex was the junior high part.

He goes on with a playful gleam in his eyes. "I was curious," he pauses, takes a deep breath and lowers his voice as if he is shy, "Will you be my girlfriend?"

I don't even realize how my response may be taken when I lean my face into his chest and burst into laughter.

"Well, that didn't go as I planned," he says in a sarcastic yet playful tone.

I look up and put my hands on his cheeks. "Yes, I will! I was just confused and worried about what you were going to say. Then when you asked, I was happy and relieved so I . . ."

Judd's face lights up into a huge grin. He pulls my face closer to silence me with a kiss.

Pulling away, he adds to my surprise, "Well then don't make any plans for the Fourth of July." He winks and a giggle erupts out of me.

I calm down my giddiness and give him a sincere smile, dazzled by the swirl of emotion he brings to my heart.

"As if I would . . . like I told you, I am all yours," I whisper with complete and utter confidence.

After pulling the key out of the ignition and plugging his phone into the charger, he settles himself in an upright position in the corner of the backseat, allowing me to stretch out with the rest of the seat to myself. *I wish there was enough room for us both to snuggle up beside each other, but I'm happy as long as I am close to him.*

"Are you going to be comfortable sitting up like that all night?" I ask, worried that he is going to fall over in the middle of the night.

The soft cotton of his shirt brushes my cheek as I press the back of my head into his lap and look up at him. His eyes are closed, but the soft melody of his voice vibrates through my body as he quietly sings a song like music is still playing.

"Mmmhm," he barely hums with his head resting half on the headrest and half against the back window.

I twist my body to turn onto my side while curling my knees into my chest and bundling a handful of his shirt into my hand at his side. Wrinkles of denim scratch at my cheek as I get more comfortable and make every effort to forget where my head is currently laying. The weight of his warm hand gets heavier along my waist and his singing dies out, so I know he must be asleep.

Very few evenings since we met have we been apart. It doesn't matter where we are or how comfortable, as long as we can feel the warmth of each other close by. *I have no idea how I am going to fall asleep when I get back home.*

Before I know it, sleep carries me away as well.

The next morning, we wake up to Jake tapping on the truck window. Judd and I both jump up, startled.

After getting up and stepping out of the truck, we both twist and stretch, trying to work the kinks out of our stiff bodies. Sleeping in confined spaces like his truck is worse than getting eaten alive by bugs.

"Hey, I looked all over for you two and then finally figured I would check the truck," Jake laughs.

"Sorry about that. We just sort of fell asleep." Judd looks over to me with a sheepish, yet proud smile on his face.

"I guess I'll get going so you two can say your goodbyes." I lean into Judd and slip a quick peck on his lips and then turn to face Jake. "Be careful driving home. I guess I'll see you around," I say hesitantly, not looking back at Judd for confirmation.

I'm not sure where this will lead, but I hope being in Judd's life after this trip is in the cards.

"See ya guys," I say, waving over my shoulder and making a deliberate effort to not turn and look at Judd again.

"I'll come by your cabin after lunch and we'll go for a swim."

His words have me whirling around with an ecstatic smile. Flashing him one last look, I turn to jet back to my cabin and count down the minutes until I see him again.

With only a couple days left, we really do not want to waste any time that we could be spending together.

As soon as I cross the threshold of my cabin, I run to my cot, grab my pillow, hug it to my chest and fall back, smiling like a fool. After an elated sigh, it takes no time for all the girls to huddle around.

"Ok, spill," Abby says, sitting down on the cot beside mine.

"Oh girl, you have it bad," Lanie giggles.

I sit up, still squeezing the pillow as if it is Judd's chest.

"He is so wonderful. I just can't even explain it." I let out another sigh; all of them are eagerly watching me.

"Oh, come on. Details, we need details," Jessie huffs out as she sinks to the floor between the cots, also clutching a pillow to her chest. "You've spent practically every night with him. We need details," she adds and everyone laughs.

Details, no way! The good stuff is just for me!

"He's just amazing. He asked for my number and wants to take me on a date when we get back home. He tells me I'm beautiful all the time and the way he kisses . . ." I look up at the ceiling and am met with silence as they eat up every word I choose to share.

We giggle and squeal like it's an all night slumber party.

Later, the girls all filter out of the cabin intent on renting jet skis for the day while Abby parks herself beside me with an all-knowing smile on her face.

"Happy you came?"

She throws an arm around me and all I can do is laugh. My sister knows me so well; she knew I needed to come on this trip, and now I see that she could not have been more on the money.

"So . . ." I ignore her question and decide to pester her, knowing full well the direction I choose to go will aggravate the crap out of her. "You ever gonna give Tristan a go?"

I hold my lips tightly together, trying to contain the laugh that is bubbling to the surface of my mouth as she turns and glares at me.

"As if," she spits out with her nose crinkled, lips in a snarl and her eyes drawn down in a frown.

Standing up to join the rest of the group, she spins around, flipping her hair over her shoulder and tries her best to come off as annoyed.

We both laugh as she takes off to the door, giving me one last glance over her shoulder with a smile that tells me she knows I'm kidding. But if I didn't know better, I would think that smile meant she is considering my suggestion.

"See ya later. Try to come hang with us tonight, you and Judd both." She winks before disappearing out the door.

Once I'm alone, I grab my phone and power it up. *Ugh!* I have twenty-two missed calls from Kyle. *Ok, this is bordering on harassment, right?!* I delete all the voicemails and then swipe over to my texts. *Good grief, fifteen texts from him, too.* I delete all of them as well without giving a single one a second glance, then proceed to the message I so eagerly want to see.

I open up the photo from the unknown number and quickly add it to my contacts. J . . . U . . . D . . . D, I type with a ridiculous smile on my face.

Pulling up the picture again, I marvel at it as my heart races in my chest. In the picture I am pressed against his side with a huge smile and my eyes looking dead center into the camera. But that isn't why I love the picture so much; it is because instead of him looking at the camera and smiling, he is staring at me. He looks at me as if I am a priceless treasure that he has waited centuries to discover, like a lost child finally finding his way home or like a blind man being able to see for the first time. He looks at me like I am everything he has ever dreamed of.

I close my eyes and pull the phone to my chest, squeezing it to my heart. *I love him. I am completely and totally his.*

Fireworks

THE NEXT FEW DAYS, WE suck up every second of each other's time. Before we know it, it is the Fourth of July.

With Jake taking the truck home and with nearly no more vacant cabins due to the impending holiday weekend, we have to get creative in being alone. One night, we snuggle up on the beach and another we fall asleep on the dock of the boathouse.

After two evenings in a row of getting ate up by bugs, tonight we end up sleeping in Judd's cabin.

We had been out watching the stars and talking about everything. I love that we never run out of things to say. The level of comfort we feel with each other in such a short period of time is startling and scary, yet extremely exciting.

We drag ourselves in a little before dawn, careful not to wake the others. With heavy eyelids and sleep exhaustion tugging at every fiber of my body, I am out as soon as my head hits the pillow.

Stretching, I skim my hand across the sheets to the side of the bed and feel around, still unable to open my eyes. It is silent in the cabin so I assume everyone is still sleeping. After my hand finds no warm body beside me, I sit up and look around. Everyone is gone, but my ears pick up on the sounds of kids splashing around outside and boats speeding by in the distance. Sunlight showers in through the two front windows of the cabin as I glance around for a clock, but come up empty. *What time is it anyways and where is Judd?*

I fling the sheet off of my body and drop my feet to the floor to slip on my flip flops. Last night, I slept in a tank top and terrycloth shorts with my swimsuit so I currently have no extra clothes with me.

The cabin door creaks, pulling my attention to Judd's smiling face walking through the door.

"Did I wake you up?" he says as he crosses the room quickly to be at my side.

"No." I smile, not even caring now where he was. *I'm just glad he's here now that I'm awake.*

"I was hoping I made it back before you got up, so you could wake up in my arms."

He squats down in front of me, positioning his body between my legs with his elbows on my thighs. Looking into my eyes, he wraps his arms around my back and pulls me forward. His face lights up with an adorable grin that makes me want to smother him in kisses, so that's exactly what I do.

"Good morning," I whisper before giving him several quick pecks on the lips.

Chuckling, he corrects my assessment of time. "Morning? Lyssa, it's a little before 1:00. We slept away the morning."

Why did I waste most of our day sleeping? I pucker my lips into a pout, wishing we could have the entire summer together. He reaches up and brushes some hairs out of my face, flashing me his dimple at the same time.

"Do you know how beautiful you are?"

I crinkle my nose and run my fingers through my tangled hair, thinking how awful I must really look. He's just like my dad, completely blind to what a mess I am most of the time.

Standing up, he pulls me into his arms until my feet are off the ground and my legs are comfortably wrapped around his waist. With a small, mischievous smile, he holds me tight while slowly spinning in a circle as if we are on a merry-go-round.

"I have a surprise for us tonight." He wiggles his eyebrows and then sets me down. My arms stay firmly wrapped around him and I give him a skeptical look with my eyes squinted.

"What are you up to?"

Kissing me softly, he whispers against my lips, "I guess you'll have to wait and see."

We meet up with the gang around dinnertime at our cabin. The guys fire up one of the community BBQ grills while Abby and Piper run to town to get yummy food for us to feast on. Mitch mans the grill, going on and on about what a master griller he is in a cocky tone that makes me roll my eyes.

Once the steaks, brats and burgers are ready, we chow down. Everything is delicious. Of course I give most of the credit to Piper, who was in the house for an hour prepping it for Chef Mitch.

After taking a monstrous bite, I hold my burger up in the air and wink letting her know it's awesome. She catches my meaning and giggles, sticking her tongue out in his direction.

Shoveling in the last bite of what seems like Tristan's third burger, he steals Judd away. They return a few minutes later with two huge bags full of fireworks. The girls all squeal while the guys gather around like kids at a candy store.

Before I know it, we are all running wild doing exactly what you are told not to do on the Fourth of July, throwing firecrackers at each other.

Once the tossing turns to chasing, Judd grabs my hand and we race to a wooded area with Abby close on our heels. Pop, pop, pop echoes from every direction as Judd releases my hand and begins to pelt firecracker after firecracker at running targets. I notice he only aims at the guys and keeps me and my sister safely shielded behind him.

Tristan yells out, "Bombs Away!" and then, pop, pop, pop right at our feet.

All three of us race in three different directions with me and Abby screaming. Judd laughs hysterically at our reactions. I scramble over to the bags. *To hell with this; I am arming myself for this war.*

Abby slams into my back, breathing hard. "I saw Evan over by the beach," she warns me as a blur races by and grabs my hand.

At the same time more snapping blasts at our feet, followed by her giggles. I finally realize Judd is dragging me down towards the beach, throwing a lit firecracker over his head at someone.

"Hey, I'm behind you guys," Abby huffs out.

We stop near the water and Judd crouches down behind a stack of inner tubes.

"Over here, over here!" a voice calls out towards the gravel lot.

Pop, snap, pop, squeal. *That sounds like Mitch and Crystal.*

"Where's Evan?!" Tristan shouts.

Pop, pop, pop.

"Holy Hell!" Evan yells and a shadow runs past our hiding spot on the beach.

I slap my hand over my mouth to stifle a laugh. Abby snorts behind me and clamps her mouth shut trying to hold back, too. At this point I think we are slap happy.

"Shhh," Judd says quietly, barely able to hold back his laughter either.

Leaning over to Judd's ear, I whisper quietly as if we're on a secret mission, "What's the point of this? Is someone out if they get hit?"

A bubble of laughter rises to the surface of my mouth as Judd begins to answer.

All of a sudden I am knocked to the ground when Abby's body is lifted up and away from me. Judd and I land on the ground together, laughing hysterically. Popping and snapping sounds off all around us, but Abby's screams nearly drown it out.

"Put me down, Tristan . . . put me down now!"

"I've got a prisoner!" he shouts out, while racing towards the cabin with Abby flung over his shoulder.

Hmmm . . . that's strange. It sure doesn't look like she is putting up much of a fight.

Our firecracker war goes on for over an hour until we are all worn out.

Shortly after, Evan comes up behind us as we sit by the bank exchanging stories of our battle.

"Hey man, you ready to go? I have to start the fireworks display in thirty minutes and need to get there early to set up."

My heart rises into my throat with his words, concerned that Judd may not be able to join me for the fireworks show.

Grabbing my hand, an enormous grin emerges on his face. I haven't a clue why he has this cheesy smile on his face, but it seems to be contagious because I light up as well.

He gets up and pulls me along for the ride. "Let's go. It's time for that surprise."

Reaching his arm around my waist, he nudges me along.

I let out a laugh as Abby skips up behind me, wrapping her arms around my neck.

"Have fun Lyssi-Bee," she whispers in my ear and casts Judd a quick glance that tells me she may have been in on whatever is going on.

He places his hand across my lower back to lead me to Evan's jeep. He jumps in the passenger seat and pats his lap for me to climb up. I do as I'm instructed, filled with giddiness from the suspense.

Ten minutes later, we are on the other side of the lake where the fireworks display is going to start up. Evan pulls into the gravel lot, but instead of going straight to where the show will take place, he takes an immediate left. My confusion grows as he pulls up in front of a cabin across from the pier. Quickly shifting into park, he raises a lighter up between him and Judd.

"Bring it back out because it's the only one I have."

Judd pats my leg signaling for me to get up, "I'll be right back."

He slips inside of the cabin and I am clueless on what is going on. Looking around, nothing looks familiar and there are no hints to what this surprise is. *Does he know someone here?* Hoping for some answers, I swing my head over to Evan, but before I can open my mouth, he holds his hands up in defense.

"Hey don't look at me. I'm staying out of this. If you don't enjoy it, don't blame me," he says in utter amusement, shifting his eyes over my shoulder.

"Shut up, you ass! And here's your lighter," Judd says with an equally amused look on his face.

He grabs my hand, pulling me out of the vehicle and to his side.

"Thanks for the ride, man."

With that, Evan backs out of the driveway and heads to the dock to set up for the show.

Still holding my hand, Judd pulls me to the front door of the cabin and shoves a key in the lock. He pushes it open, flinging it back to the wall and then carefully leads me in with his hands at my hips.

As soon as he flips the lights on, I see a much more luxurious setting than the cabins we have been staying in. I glance around and to my utter relief, there is not a cot in sight. I turn to face him and smile. There is a flickering light coming from the bedroom and it finally dawns on me what is going on.

"Did you rent this?"

Judd moves forward and pulls me into his arms. Neither of us can stop smiling. He kisses me softly while guiding me backwards past the doorframe of the bedroom.

I pull away from his grasp just enough to take in the room. The bedroom is at the front of the cabin and has a large picture window that faces the lake. There below the window is a king sized bed. *Wow; a hundred times better than a cot.* Surrounding the bed, on both nightstands, on the dresser and on the chest at the foot of the bed, are tons of candles. They are all lit up making the room sparkle. I spin back around to face him and place my hand over my heart which is now beating rapidly.

"This had to cost you a fortune," I gasp out, widening my eyes in wonderment.

How on earth did he manage to rent this cabin with a lake front location on Fourth of July weekend? I can't believe he did this for me . . . for us.

"Don't worry about what it cost. You're worth more than this," he says so easily.

"But how . . ." I stutter out wanting to ask a million questions.

He pulls me closer and smiles like he has a secret that he can barely contain.

"I rented it the morning Jake left. I wanted our last night to be special, with no interruptions."

We are clear across the lake from anyone we know; no interruptions indeed! Bursting out in nervous laughter, it becomes very clear what is on the agenda for tonight and I am totally fine with that, more than fine, in fact.

Once I manage to get the ball of nerves that is swirling around in my stomach at bay, I ease myself down to the edge of the bed as he settles beside me and pulls me into his lap.

"Alyssa, don't think I expect anything. I just thought . . ."

Suddenly, all the nervousness, longing and anticipation of this moment merge into one, creating a love starved girl. *He doesn't expect anything; I do . . . I want this.*

I slam myself into him and smash my lips to his mouth for a heat-filled kiss. Smoothly moving my knees to each side of his hips, I can already feel the desire burning within us both as our lips rejoin a chorus of stroking, caressing and tasting each other.

I cannot believe he did all this for me and now he is saying we don't have to take advantage of this perfect night, this perfect place.

The fire in his body ignites as well when he grasps my hips and slides his hands up my back. Once his hands reach around my figure, his grip tightens and I am flipped onto the mattress, sinking into the bed with his body above mine.

We slowly slither ourselves to the center of the bed, our lips never breaking stride. I whimper out in delight as he runs his hand up my shirt and beneath my swimsuit, handling me as if I am a clay statue that he is carefully molding.

Figuring the fabric is in the way, I quickly pull my shirt off.

Judd's mouth works its way down my body to my stomach, kissing and licking along the path.

He trails kisses back up to my neck and reaches around to untie the drawstring around my neck. My swimsuit top makes its way down to my stomach and before long Judd's hand slips behind my back to untie the rest. I arch my back, allowing him complete access. The tee shirt that stretches across his chest suddenly seems like an unwelcome barrier between us. With a storm of need and desire brewing inside of me, I grasp the bottom of it and pull it over his head before he slides back on top of me.

As soon as my nipples graze his chest, he lets out a loud breath and kisses me harder. I open my mouth in a moan as his lips slowly descend back down to my waist. He kisses around my belly button ring while sliding the tips of his fingers into the hem of my shorts and looking to me for permission to go further.

"Is this ok?" he barely gets the words out.

I pull my bottom lip into my mouth, pressing my teeth down in an effort to calm my breaths. No reply is necessary; instead I lift my hips off the bed to help him out. A wave of excitement flickers in his eyes as he tucks his fingers beneath the waist of my shorts and swimsuit bottom. With one solid motion, he has them off, leaving behind a scorching sensation along my outer thighs from the movement.

Sitting up on his knees, his eyes scan my body slowly and then land back on my face.

"You're so beautiful," he softly says with a shaky breath.

As I lay there, vulnerable to his gaze, everything inside of me wants to cry out how much I want him.

Slowly he stretches his hands to the sides of my body and begins to slide back over me. I can hardly take a breath with all the anxiety over what I'm about to suggest. I gulp down all my hesitation and grab the snap of his shorts.

"What about you?" My voice is so unsteady that I barely recognize it.

His chest heaves in and out.

"Are you sure?" his voice is trembling nearly as much as mine.

Knowing my words will only come out in a quivering, breathy, near inaudible mumble; I drop my chin forward and take another deep breath. In one swift motion I unsnap his shorts and move on to the zipper. He looks down at my hands, then back up, as I proceed to unzip them and push them down his legs. Shifting a little, he helps me until we are both exposed at last.

We search each other's bodies for a moment before the warmth of his covers mine.

Feeling every inch of him against me ignites all the nerves in my body from my accelerated heartbeat to my quivering thighs that tighten around his hips.

Our lips cannot get enough of each other and our hands explore every ounce of skin we can reach without breaking our embrace.

Judd pulls away from my lips and I want to cry out. Opening my eyes, I look at him, aching to feel his lips back against mine. With deep, quick breaths that match my own, he draws his brows together and carefully runs his hand along the contours of my jaw.

"Alyssa, I'm in love with you."

Just like that he says it, something I have thought so many times but have been afraid to say aloud. I want to cry, I want to scream in joy, I want to bury myself in his touch and never return to the surface.

"I've wanted to tell you so many times, but I was afraid I would scare you off but I can't hold back . . ." he trails off, searching my face."I'm so in love with you. I've never felt this way about someone before and I know we've only known each other two weeks, but I can't imagine my life without you now."

A tear slips down the side of my face and I run my fingers through his hair, pulling him to me.

I place one small, soft kiss against his mouth and then whisper between his lips, "I love you, too." Like a rampant, uncontrollable river that has been waiting centuries to be unleashed, I let the words spill from my mouth and my heart begins to soar.

The corners of his mouth curve into a smile against my lips before returning to where we were.

Our bodies mesh together into one and we move in perfect harmony. He moves slowly and immediately waves of pleasure flow through my body. A deep groan rises from his chest as he gasps in and out. His hands reach under my shoulders, using them to pull forward to deepen the pleasure.

I'm not even in control of my body anymore. I wiggle against his movement, meeting each of his thrusts.

He kisses and licks at any accessible part of my skin, moving from my mouth to my jaw, behind my ear and down to my chest. His movements get faster and another groan escapes his lips. With one more deep thrust from him, I whimper loudly as he collapses with his face buried in my neck.

Overflowing with happiness, I run my hands down his back, letting my fingertips brush over every single curve of his sweaty muscles.

After his breathing is back to a semi-normal level, he lets out a small chuckle that tickles my skin. He pulls up to look at me with an expression of total embarrassment.

"I am so sorry that was so quick." He puts a hand across his face, half covering his eyes.

I giggle from his reaction and also from the nerves that are slowly unraveling inside me. His hand shakes as he lowers it away from his face, telling me he is still nervous.

"Here I wanted this to be a magical experience and I built it up so much to make it just right and then I ended up . . ." His low voice fades as he looks off to the side like he is afraid I may laugh.

I continue to run my fingers through his hair and stare at him in complete wonderment of where this perfect guy has been all my life.

"Well then you succeeded, because it was perfect," I whisper to him.

Unconvinced, he cocks one eyebrow and laughs. With a wide grin, his embarrassment starts to dissolve.

"I was really hoping it would be mind blowing for you. I even arranged for fireworks," he says with a smirk.

Following his watch, I finally glance out the window above the bed frame and notice an array of dazzling colors sizzling in the sky.

I squirm a little under him, trying to keep from laughing at his joke. He starts trailing small kisses along my jaw towards my ear again. My heart speeds up and heat spreads throughout my body.

"We could try again," I boldly suggest because I just cannot get enough of him.

"You read my mind . . ." He smiles, pulling me on top of him as he rolls onto his back.

I sit up, with my legs on either side of him and giggle as panic rises up into my throat.

"I want to look at you." His voice comes out in a low sensual whisper that sends tingles from my center down to my toes and back up again.

He slides his hands down to my hips and I rise up, letting my knees sink into the mattress.

His throat shifts as he swallows and then lowers his gaze down my body, like it's a work of art he is admiring.

Smoothing my hands over his chest, I stare back at him, a little more comfortable in my skin than I was a little bit ago, yet still hesitant.

"Umm, I've never done it like this."

He smiles and rubs his hand up and down my hips in a soft caress.

"I guess we'll figure it out together then."

His words send a rocket of excitement and thrill through me, knowing we will share this first as well.

We both nervously shift and move, stumbling to find the perfect rhythm. We stare into each other's eyes during the more intense moments and then end up laughing at our inexperience in the next instance.

Eventually when we figure it out, it is beyond magical; it's perfect.

Judd pulls himself up in a sitting position, careful to not break our tempo. I'm frantic with need and desire as electric currents build and build. He seems just as desperate as me, trying to put his mouth and hands all over my body all at once. We truly cannot get enough of each other.

Once I'm spiraling into a pool of pleasure and yelling out his name, I notice the fireworks still lighting up the night's sky.

I roll onto my back and lay quietly beside Judd as we both try to catch our breath.

"Was that better? Did you . . ." Judd asks looking at me through the corner of his eyes.

"Yes, I did." A giggle erupts from my mouth.

Right then, above our heads we see what seems to be billions of fireworks exploding in the sky all at the same time.

"Just . . . Like . . . That!" I burst out laughing, pointing out the window to the grand finale of tonight's fireworks show.

He cracks up and winks, saying, "Yeah, I planned it that way."

See you later

I WAKE UP LYING ON my side, snuggled up to Judd's chest with his arms firmly wrapped around me and our legs tangled together. He stirs and the soft caress of his fingertips on my hip send a heat wave rippling through my body.

Pulling my face away to gaze at him, I am met with sleepy hazel eyes that overflow with so much warmth and love that I have to remind myself to breathe.

"Good morning," he whispers while bending his neck to place a gentle kiss on my lips.

I worm my body closer to him and wiggle from the tingles that his kiss sends zipping through me. His eyes widen for a brief moment and then his lips rise into a playful smile.

Flipping me over so that his body is above mine, he lets out a soft laugh and I immediately become aware of his morning status.

My body lights up with desire and all I can think about is how good he made me feel last night. He presses his body in an upward motion against me causing me to close my eyes from the exhilaration as tingles of pleasure roll through me.

My skin instantly warms and my breath kicks up as he plants small wet kisses on my neck. *Oh yes, I am ready.*

Just then the cabin door flings open and Judd rips the sheet up to cover our bareness.

"Get up you two love birds. We have to fly the coop in half an hour," Evan says with a chuckle from the front room.

Judd remains pressed against me to shield me from his line of sight, while he cranes his neck to give him a dirty look. Not expecting anyone to waltz right in, we had left the bedroom door wide open.

"You jerk off! Go pester someone else!"

Evan laughs at Judd's annoyance and then we hear cabinet doors opening and closing from the kitchen.

Judd returns his attention back to me. "I am so sorry that he . . ." Judd begins but is quickly cut off.

Evan calls out from the front room, "So you guys finally did the deed! Thank God!! It's about time! Man, you have been a walking hard-on since she got here!"

Quiet chuckles bounce from word to word as he speaks leaving very little mystery behind whether he knows that he completely interrupted something.

Judd's face turns to a look of panic and embarrassment with his eyebrows lowered into a frown. His mouth is wide open in shock and I can't help but spit out a giggle while burying myself into his chest.

The floor creaks as Evan walks into the room. I look around Judd's shoulder and see him casually leaning against the doorframe with a smirk on his face, squirting something onto his finger and then licking it off. *What is that!?*

Judd grabs the pillow beside my head and launches it at his friend. Evan ducks and the pillow hits him in the shoulder.

He returns to his lazy slouch against the doorway and an even wider, more mischievous grin appears on his face as he shakes a can of whipped cream in his hand. "Nice," he quips, holding up his prize.

Where on earth did the whip cream come from?

"Holy shit, man . . . do you mind! At least let us get dressed!" Judd yells with a tint of blush to his face.

Evan laughs and very dramatically turns to walk away, holding his free hand to his chest as if Judd's words just shot a hole through his heart.

Headed towards the front door, he hollers out, "No more pounding privates! We don't have time for that! Fifteen minutes and I'm coming back in to pull you guys apart, naked or not."

I can just imagine the totally pleased expression on his face as he announces this.

When the cabin door closes, we know we only have a few minutes alone before it is time to leave our fairytale world. Judd pulls me to lie against his chest for what I feel like may be our last embrace ever. *Will we see each other again after this? Is this the end? How did this happen in such a short time?* The ache in my heart from knowing I have to say goodbye today is killing me. A tear slips from my eye and drips down my cheek.

He wipes another escaped tear from my face and whispers "Hey, this is not goodbye." He pauses, searching for the right words, "This is just I'll see you later. When you get home, you'll call me and I'll call you. I'll come see you and you'll come see me. Trust me this is just the beginning of this, not the end," he tells me as he motions his fingers between us with a warm smile.

His words give me hope, but I still know we are going in two different directions for college and distance is never a good thing.

Lifting my chin so that I am looking directly into his eyes, he goes on, "If you're worried about when we leave for college, don't be. There's no need to worry about that now."

His words remind me of what my mom always tells me: don't worry until there is something to worry about. I nod my head in understanding and give him a small kiss, wishing we could just stay under the covers, wrapped up in each other all day; all summer.

"Besides, I would travel to the moon and back if it meant I would be with you, so California to Indiana is going to be a breeze. We'll see each other, I promise."

He presses his lips hard against mine in a passion filled kiss, and then pulls away with a sigh.

"We better get some clothes on before Evan busts in and drags us out of bed. He was completely serious when he said he would." We both laugh.

Reluctantly sliding out of bed, I clutch the sheet to my chest as I look over at Judd, who is shamelessly standing and dressing under my watchful eyes. I make sure to enjoy the view and judging by his constant chuckles, he definitely knows I am admiring the scenery.

It takes less than five minutes for me to throw on my clothes and I am surprised when I see that my bag has been conveniently placed in the bathroom. *I guess my assumptions were right. Abby must have had a hand in helping Judd set up.*

We ride back to our side of the lake with me once again on Judd's lap. I sit with my back to Evan, out of fear that he may see how emotional I am. *I cannot handle any teasing right now.*

Judd keeps his hand tightly clutched around mine, squeezing it every now and again. Reveling in his warmth as I lay my head against his neck, I take long deep breaths to memorize the natural woodsy sent of his skin. His other hand grips around my waist and as we near my cabin, his hold is unyielding.

As we pull into the lot, we find everyone mingling, saying their goodbyes and some have even already left, but Tristan impatiently stands by his car with his arms folded and a scowl on his face.

"I'll see you around, I'm sure," Evan calls to me as Judd says his goodbyes to the girls.

After waving goodbye to Evan, we walk over to Tristan's small red sports car as he lowers his sunglasses and frowns at Judd.

"Glad you could make it. We have to go. I have to get to work," he spits out with a bit of a slur that automatically puts me on alert.

"Are you drunk, man?" Judd asks in an infuriated tone.

"No." He rolls his eyes and blows out an exaggerated breath. "I'm not drunk, I'm just hung over. *Get in,*" he demands.

Judd pulls me to the side. "Don't worry. I'll switch with him when we stop to gas up," he assures me. My heart feels like it may explode from pain as he whispers in my ear, "I'll call you later. I love you," and then places a gentle kiss on my lips.

Wrapping my arms around his neck, he lifts me off the ground in a huge bear hug.

"I love you, too," I cry into his ear.

I'm prepared to never let go, until Tristan clears his throat in sheer annoyance.

"Come on, Bro, there will be plenty of tail to chase at college."

Judd sits me down and spins around, bending into the car to make eye contact with his brother.

"Shut the hell up and give me a minute."

He turns back to me with sadness written across his beautiful face.

"Ignore him, Alyssa. He doesn't know anything about us. I love you and I will talk to you later today . . . Ok?"

He shrinks down to my level so that he can look me in the eyes. Pushing back the tears that are threatening to spill over, I give him one last kiss and let go, so this won't be any harder on either of us.

He steps away hesitantly, gets in and slams the door shut behind him. As soon as he reaches his arm through the open window and grasps my hand tightly, I know that this is bothering him just as much as me. My heart falls and my hand empties as Tristan pulls away and Judd's hand slips from mine.

I watch them drive off, keeping my eyes locked onto the side mirror where I can see him watching me as well.

Once they are out of sight, a deep emptiness settles in my chest and I realize not only did he leave, but he took my heart with him. Arms drape across my shoulders, squeezing my neck from behind and I automatically know it is my sister trying to offer a sense of comfort.

"Well this sucks . . . back to reality, I guess."

I manage a smile with her words and then we head into the cabin, both of us knowing what our actual reality may entail once we get home.

We end up enjoying a bit more of the day before we hit the road, three hours behind the guys. After putting my bags in the van, I go for a walk by myself, swinging by all the places that now hold a special place in my heart.

I stroll to the shower house with visions of his body against mine flickering through my mind. Then I wander down to the boathouse, over to Judd's cabin and back over to the wooded area where he and I spent our first night talking and getting to know each other. I know I will hear from him later, but I have to commit every moment we spent together to my memory before I leave this place.

Abby was right when she said I would have the time of my life on this trip.

Once I have memorized every location and time spent there, I make my way up to the van. Looking around one last time, I repeat to myself, "I'll see you later" with a small smile on my face to mask the fear I really feel in my heart.

Disconnected

THE RIDE BACK FROM THE lake is less than desirable to say the least. We were all exhausted and cranky. Mix that with six hung over girls, plus me feeling completely heartbroken and that equals a disastrous trip home.

Little by little, the van empties out as we drop off all the girls. Once we make it to our subdivision, it is only Piper, Abby and me. After waving goodbye to Piper as she drops us off, we drag ourselves up to our bedrooms to crash.

My eyes open at the crack of dawn the next day. As soon as I see light showering through my window, I panic. Judd was supposed to call me when he got home and I must have slept through it. In full-on-freak-out mode, I bolt up out of bed and snatch up my phone. Excitement and anxiety surges through my veins with the thought of speaking to him, but my heart quickly falls when I see that there are no missed calls. *Why hasn't he called me?*

They had to leave out early because Tristan had something going on, but Judd had mentioned that he didn't have much to do between now and him leaving for California in two weeks.

Completely confused and a little worried, I scroll through my texts and recent calls just to make sure, but I find nothing. Glancing at the clock, I take in the fact that it is only 7:21 in the morning. *Maybe I should wait till later to call him in case he is still sleeping.* Judd was always up at the crack of dawn, but I'm sure he was just as tired as I was when he got home; he may have zonked out.

The morning hours drag by and with each passing minute my anxiety level grows. Not only am I antsy to hear from him, but my parents are coming home this evening and I am very nervous to hear about Dad's test results.

Three and a half hours later, I cannot wait any longer. I don't care if he is dog tired and wanting to sleep till noon, I am waking him up. Besides, hearing his sleepy voice in my ear will bring back sweet memories of waking up next to him these past two weeks. I pull up his name in my contacts and hit dial. My heart drums into my throat as I place it to my ear, expecting to hear it ring, but instead it goes straight to voicemail. I hang up and don't leave a message. Last thing I want to be is one of those girls stalking their boyfriend and continuously leaving message after message. *He'll call me as soon as he has a chance.*

Morning soon turns into afternoon and I start to get nervous. Not wanting to seem too needy and fill his phone up with missed calls, I call him only one more time.

Kyle drove me absolutely nuts the last few weeks with his relentlessness. Plus after thirty messages or so, it really bordered on pathetic. He did owe me an apology, but that could be done in one phone call. Instead he was determined to explain his motives for cheating. I didn't care for an explanation anymore, so I ended up deleting all of the messages.

By night fall, I am on the verge of tears. *Could I have misunderstood him? Maybe he meant he was going to call me as soon as he got back from California. But that was two weeks away. No, he didn't mean that. He said we would see each other. Oh, why am I freaking out; it's been a day!*

My parents get back after dinner. They seem to be in good spirits carrying on about how much fun they had with my nephews, but Abby and I finally pry them off the subject of the trip to ask the questions that have been weighing on our minds.

"Ok, so did you get the test results back yet?" Abby asks nervously as I chew on my thumb nail, anxiously awaiting their answer.

"Actually we have been on pins and needles waiting to hear, but honestly we haven't heard anything. We have another appointment scheduled for tomorrow, so we're going to speak to the doctor then and hopefully find out more," Mom explains.

On top of my already wound up nerves, this makes me feel as though I could puke. No way am I going to sleep tonight and of course, I don't.

The next day goes by in a crawl with me staring at my phone for nearly half of it. I should be focused on Dad's appointment, but I cannot get my mind off of Judd. I guess, in a way, I now understand why Kyle filled my phone up with calls and texts, because honestly the obvious time that passes, the more panic stricken I become. I literally want to call him every half an hour until he picks up, thinking that the endless ringing will send a telepathic signal to his brain telling him that he should call me. Considering, that is pretty obsessive, I resist the urge until mid afternoon.

By then I am going insane with questions, worry and confusion. I dial his number, but this time a disconnected message rings in my ear.

You have reached a number that is no longer in service. . . .

What?! No way! Something has to be wrong.
Sitting on the edge of my bed, I hold the phone on my lap looking at it like I can will it to ring somehow. Screw worrying about appearing clingy. I dial it again.

You have reached a number that is no longer . . .

Slamming my finger down on the end button, I toss my phone to the floor with fear and heartache boiling in my veins. I want very badly to chuck it against the wall, but if it's broke he'll never be able to call. My eyes start to blur and a stabbing pain throbs in my heart. *I don't understand. Wait . . . what if . . .*

I yank my phone back up off the floor and scroll over the text I sent from Judd's phone the night we took pictures. *Damn, it's the same number.* My heart drops when I realize that there's no chance I was dialing the wrong number all along.

Tumbling through my mind, I struggle to think of anything that could cause his phone to be disconnected or his lack of calling, because the obvious is not an option. His voicemail was an automated voice so maybe it is still possible that I have the wrong number.

I never had my phone with me at the lake, so maybe someone screwed with it. It was always in my bag under my cot so anyone could have tampered with it and changed the number as a gag. Plus this getaway was filled with pranks and gags on everyone. There were so many times when I would return to the cabin only to find a pile of condom packages scattered across my cot. Everyone thought that joke was appropriate since Judd and I were always sneaking around. Little did they know that we were not slumming around like everyone else; I had fallen in love with him and he had fallen in love with me.

Anger takes root inside of me, propelling me down the hall and straight into Abby's room.

"Did you mess with my phone?" I put it bluntly so that there can be no mistake in my annoyance.

Abby is slouched across her bed writing in her journal. My angry words definitely get her attention as she slams the book closed.

"What are you talking about and why are you barging into my room yelling at me," she spits out, quickly sitting up and crossing her arms over her chest.

"Answer me," I warn her. "Did you mess with my phone?"

Her face goes from confusion to just plain pissed off. "What!? Why would I have messed with your phone?"

My eyes glaze over with tears and my hand trembles as I hold the phone out in front of me.

"Wait, Alyssa, back up and explain to me what is going on. What's wrong?" she says, but this time I hear the concern in her voice.

It isn't a usual thing for us to fight. It used to be, but the last two years we only lean on each other, help each other and always talk about things, rather than lash out.

Meeting me halfway across her room, she throws her arms around me, knowing more than anything that I just need a hug. My arms stay slack at my side, completely paralyzed from the ache in my heart.

"Come here. Sit down and tell me what's going on."

Leading me over to her vanity bench, I lower myself onto the cushioned seat while she sits cross legged on the floor in front of me. Much like an ice cream cone clumsily clutched in a toddlers hand on a hot summer day, I slide over the edge of the bench, slowly melting to the floor to join her.

Hugging my knees, I begin to explain, "He didn't call me. He said he would call me, but he didn't so then I called and there wasn't an answer. So, I called again and now there is a disconnected message. How could that be? I don't understand," I ramble on.

Before I even finish my sentence, tears are streaming down my face and I am struggling for breaths.

"Ok . . . calm down." Abby reaches over and places her hand on my knee to let me know it will be alright. "First, tell me why you are getting so worked up."

I look at her in shock. *Did she not hear anything I said?*

"Because, he hasn't called, Abby," I bark out and take a deep breath. "And now his phone is disconnected."

Abby's eyes widen at my snippy tone and angry glare.

"Oh my gosh, Alyssa. All of us hooked up but I don't think the rest of us are waiting by the phone. I mean it has been two days since you saw him. Give the guy some space."

Her words offer no sense of comfort and only further my anxiety and hurt. Right now, I would like nothing more than to hurl my phone at her head.

Hook-up!? Is that what my own sister thinks I did this past week . . . Hook-up? Really?!

I lower my eyebrows into a frown that could probably send most people running, but my sister just looks at me with a bored look. She lets out a loud sigh and shifts her expression to understanding.

"Oh no, Alyssa, so you have feelings for him? I mean, I could tell you liked him a lot but I figured with you just breaking up with Kyle that you were just playing the field. You know, having fun like the rest of us. No strings attached . . ."

She stops talking and looks at me. I must be drawing flies because my mouth hangs wide open.

"Seriously Abby, how well do you know me? You thought I was just messing around; having fun? Did you not see me crying when he drove away?"

My tears dry, but my mind swirls with frustration and hurt. Most of all, I can't stop thinking that if she thought that, did Judd think that as well?

"I know you, but hey, I'm not the 'no strings attached' type of girl either and I had a little fun while we were there."

The wheels turning in my head instantly come to a screeching halt. *Ok, my interest is piqued.*

"Wait . . . when . . . who?" I am in utter shock, really kind of puzzled and completely forgetting the situation at hand for a moment. "I never saw you with anyone. The only time I saw you leave with anyone is during the firecracker war when Tristan . . ."

My mouth falls open again and I think I may have just put two and two together. Abby looks at me guiltily and giggles.

"No! Really? Tristan?!" I shout a little louder than I should, fully absorbing this distraction.

"Well, I had to see what all the hype was about. Besides, I had a little too much to drink and he was looking pretty damn hot."

My eyes are truly about to pop out of my head.

"And soooo?" I ask trying to deter to a more light-hearted subject.

Abby puts her hands up to stop my train of thought.

"Oh well, I didn't get that far. We just kind of played around and kissed."

I let out a small sincere laugh, completely forgetting for the moment what our original conversation was about.

"And sooo?" I ask again, curious if all the hype, as she calls it, is true.

"Oh yeah, he is definitely smooth. Well actually, we both had way too much to drink, but oh yeah . . . there were definite fireworks. Crazy thing was when it ended and he just kind of ran off."

Her reference to fireworks makes me think of Judd and I shake my head. *I cannot believe she messed around with Judd's brother; that's weird.*

"Ok, enough about my escapades. Let's dig into this whole issue you're having," she emphasizes the word issue like I am being melodramatic. "Alyssa, men are slime balls. You know this. Hell, you dated one for a year."

Cocking my head back in disbelief that she is grouping Judd into this category, a surge of fury grips my heart and nearly has me screaming. *First off, not all men are. There are select individuals like Kyle that make poor decisions and give the rest a bad rep, but I would have to disagree with her statement. Plus, who uses that word anyways?*

"I mean as much as Judd seemed like a nice guy, he was probably having fun and messing around before he leaves for college."

A deep stabbing pain pierces my heart when I think back to the comment that Tristan made before they left, *"There will be plenty of tail for you to chase at college." I'm ill; there's no way.*

I know I didn't imagine the sincerity in his voice when he told me he loved me. *She needs to stop right here because I have had it with the speculations and theories.*

"Abby, it wasn't like that!"

She interrupts me and goes on with her 'men are slime balls' rant.

"He is an 18 year old male. Plus, he is Tristan's brother. Come on, that boy probably knows player moves like nobody's business, thanks to his brother."

My level of frustration over this conversation has peaked.

It's my turn to rant! "No, it wasn't like that, Abby!"

She starts to speak again, but I stop her. *She doesn't know how we were; nobody does.*

"There were several times that we could have gone further than we did but he was the one that put on the brakes, not me. If he is such a player why did he wait till the day before we left to have sex with me? Answer me that? And why did he tell me he was falling in love with me?" My voice has kicked up a notch, but Abby's remains steady and calm.

"I don't know the answer to that because *I . . . am . . . not . . . a . . . guy.* I don't know how they think. I mean he seemed like he was really into you, but so does Tristan when he is trying to get a girl in bed. I don't know, but tell me this . . ."

I'm about to walk out of the room and end this conversation but curiosity burns in the pit of my stomach at what she wants to know.

After shrugging my shoulders, she goes on, "Ok, so what happened after he said he loved you?"

"I said I love you back," I stutter, not sure where she is going with this.

Figuring this revelation will surprise her, I cross my arms and eagerly await her response, but she has no reaction to my confession. Instead, she stays on course to convince me that the best two weeks of my life was just fun.

With a slow nod of her head and a sympathetic expression like she knows something I don't, she questions me further, "Yeah, and then . . ."

Bile rises into the back of my throat as the light bulb finally comes on in my head. *It's not true. He didn't play me; we fell in love. I know we did. I know what I felt.*

"Then we had sex," I say slowly, with a lump in my throat and a deep pain in my barren chest from where my heart used to be.

Abby's smile softens to pity and I want to plead with her that it is not true.

He meant what he said! The heartache must be written on my face because Abby instantly pulls me into a fierce hug.

"I didn't know you fell in love with him, Lyssi-bee. I thought you were just having fun." She pulls away from me, keeping her arms on my shoulders. "For the record, the way he looked at you, it had me pretty fooled, too. I would have guessed you two were hopelessly in love. Just give it some time; he could still call, you know. Besides, I may be way off base here. Like I said, it has only been two days."

Her words should cause a whole new wave of hope to surge through me, but in the end I am left hearing the echoes of the disconnected message in my mind over and over;

. . . *you have reached a number that is no longer in service.*

Someone to lean on

AFTER ABBY AND I TALKED, I found myself hiding in my bedroom, shut out from the world.

Dad's tests came back inconclusive, showing a rise in his white blood cell count, but the mass in his lungs ended up being non-cancerous. More tests are being run to see what is causing his white blood cells to be out of whack. The news about the mass is a relief, but we all know Dad is not out of the woods yet. Actually, we are terrified. That unsettled knowledge combined with the turmoil I feel over Judd is making me a real downer to be around.

Bethany took me out shopping yesterday, assuming I was down in the dumps waiting to hear about Dad's results. Although that is mostly true, the whole situation with Judd has thrown me for a loop. Shopping was meant to lighten my mood, but instead it only reminded of how my summer has gone so far after her endless line of questions about Kyle and me. He had called and called and even came by two days ago, but fortunately I had managed to avoid that run in. Every time the phone rang, my heart would jump into my throat, hoping it was Judd.

Curled into a ball on the couch, I clutch the remote control in my hand, but still have yet to hit the power button. With my parents gone for more testing and Abby at work, the quiet is about to drive me insane, but focusing on anything right now has proven to be impossible. Not to mention, I know all that will be on this time of the day is soap operas with someone confessing their undying love for someone else. I just think that is all bullshit at this point in my life.

Stretching my legs out and flipping onto my back, I pull the plush afghan that I have draped over my body, up to my neck. The soft fuzzy fabric grazes my skin and immediately makes me think of Judd's soft tender touch. *Damn it!*

Looking at my phone, I stare down at the photo icon on my main screen with my finger ticking towards it. *Don't do it, Alyssa! Don't do it,* but I am weak. I click on the icon and pull up the last image I have saved in my album. In the picture, he looks over at me with what I thought was love in his eyes, and I have a smile that could rival a bride's on her wedding day. Running my finger across the screen, I close my eyes and imagine I am touching the contours of his face.

My heart thuds loudly and tears threaten to spill over as I long to touch his skin. I would swear my heart had left my body when he drove away that day if it weren't for this horrible pain in my chest every time I think about him.

It has only been four days since we left the lake. Although I know Abby could be right and he may still call, something inside of me has given up on thinking he will. My phone chirps and vibrates in my hand, drawing my head down to see who it is.

Abby: Hey sis! Please tell me you are not moping around in your pj's today?! :P

Chuckling because she knows me so well, I look down at my attire. Not only am I still in my PJs, I haven't showered or even brushed my teeth. *Yeah, I'm a mess! All I need now is a batch of brownies!*

Me: How'd you guess?

Abby: Well, pull it together because I just ran into Mom and Dad and they are on their way home. They looked super stressed! I just got off work, so I'm headed that way, too. I know you have a lot on your mind and I don't want to be a downer, but I think we should be prepared. I hope I'm wrong! I'll see you in a little bit! LUV U!!

Me: K LUV U 2!

Fear rises within me as I gulp down my instinct to panic and call upon as much courage as I may need. With a deep breath, I push all thoughts of Judd to the back of my mind so I can focus on Dad and fly up the stairs to get cleaned up.

Less than fifteen minutes later, I am showered, changed and about to lose my mind with worry. I drudge back downstairs with the weight of the world on my shoulders and prepare for the possibility of bad news, but as my feet hit the floor the sounds of an engine in the driveway has my mind on alert.

My dread elevates when I swing my eyes to the clock and realize that there is no way they could have made it home in this little time. The hospital is nearly half an hour away. *How bad is the news if they rushed home that fast?*

Without another thought, I scramble to the door and fling it open. As soon as I see the face in front of me, I wish that I had thought to look out the peep hole first. *Perfect timing! How dare he show up at my house, now of all times!*

Kyle stands before me with a subtle smile. He lowers his fist that I assume was set to knock on my door and quickly stuffs both hands in his pockets. His deep brown eyes stare at me with a look of sadness in them.

I really don't want to deal with this now; ever, actually. A person can only handle so much at one time and I am definitely reaching my limit.

Immediately on the defense, I fold my arms across my chest and look down to make sure I am not showing off any cleavage. Last thing I want to do is give off the impression that I am flirting.

"What are you doing here, Kyle?" I spit out, hoping my vile mood is enough to scare him off.

If I would have known he was coming, I would have skipped brushing my teeth. My breath alone would have run him off.

He looks up at me with a pained expression and shrugs.

"I just wanted to see you. I've missed you . . . I've been calling."

My jaw drops to the ground.

"Yeah, I know and you didn't take the hint when I didn't call back?"

The glare I shoot him should be piercing enough to drill a hole through his head as I ball my fists so tightly that it may cut off the circulation in my hands.

"I left you messages. Did you even listen to any of them?"

The sorrow in his voice does nothing but fuel my anger, so without another word I toss the door closed in his face.

One step back through the doorway and I notice the door never slammed shut. Sighing, I continue walking into the living room, knowing more than likely he is behind me. Frustration and annoyance bubbles inside of me as I pounce down on the couch, carefully remaining on the edge so I can dart away, if need be.

The couch dips down and heat radiates from his body as he sits beside me.

I cannot handle this, but I don't have the strength to fight with him right now. My heart has been broken repeatedly and it may possibly be ripped wide open when my parents get home. As much as I want him to leave, I just don't have the energy to do anything about it.

He places his hand on top of mine and I flinch from his touch, wishing it was someone else's. Looking down, I immediately pull my hand away and fold my arms back over my chest.

"I'm so sorry, Alyssa, I will do anything to make it up to you."

Swallowing the tears back, I turn my head to level my gaze with his.

"Kyle, you can't make up for something like that. You hurt me and lied to me. I could never trust you again so there is nothing to fix . . . nothing!"

Raising my eyebrows, I silently pray that I am getting through to him. *We are over!*

"Babe, I love you . . . you know I love you. I screwed up . . . I know I screwed up. I got drunk and wanted you there so bad and then I was just so drunk I didn't realize what I . . . ."

Holding my hand up, I stop him from talking, unwilling to listen to him call me babe anymore or any of the details of his deceit.

"Kyle, please, I can't handle this right now. Besides, I'm actually seeing someone else," I say calmly even though I am fuming.

He chokes out a gasp as soon as my response is out in the open.

"Met someone? What?! We only broke up a couple weeks ago! How the hell did you meet someone?"

The sorrow that was in his voice before has left and turned into exasperation.

Opening my mouth to answer, the words quickly leave me.

Yeah, I met someone, but it was only a summer fling for him; fun with no strings attached like Abby said. You can't really define seeing someone as one person waiting for them to call and the other going to the drastic extent of disconnecting their phone to keep that person from calling.

The pain in my chest returns and I don't even know how to answer him. In fact, I shouldn't have to answer. Bottom line, my heart belongs to someone else.

"It's none of your business, Kyle! I told you we are over. I love someone else."

That part is true; I do love Judd. I wasn't lying when I said it to him. The love I feel for him is genuine; a deeper love than I could have ever hoped for. It's the kind of love that Dad told me about; the kind that takes your breath away. If only he had felt the same.

Kyle's bitter voice snaps me back to reality, "Who did you meet and when? We've been together since the end of our junior year and you're telling me that you are dumping me for someone you just met?"

Closing my eyes, I huff out an irritated breath, fully ticked off at his words and how he is talking to me.

"No! I broke up with you because you screwed someone behind my back and I had the honor of walking in on it!" I stand up mid sentence with my fists tightly glued to my hips.

He rises up and quickly places both hands on my cheeks.

"Alyssa, wait, I am sorry. I know I screwed up, but it will never happen again. Please give me another chance. We've been together too long to throw it away. I love you and you love me; I know you do," he pleads while moving his face only a few inches from mine. "Please, babe."

My head spins and my heartbeats in an unfamiliar rhythm as if it is lost without the adjoining chorus of Judd's heartbeats beside it. All I want to do is cling to anyone for comfort, however, I know if I let Kyle put his arms around me, I will be wishing they are someone else's.

"Please," he whispers once more and then slowly touches his lips to mine.

As soon as the coolness of his body and the baby soft skin of his chin brushes against me, my heart drops into my stomach with how these are not the lips I want to be kissing.

His face flickers into my mind and I instantly push my hands to his chest to shove him away as the front door swings open.

Kyle drops his hands and moves back. Snapping my head up, I find Abby with her mouth gaped open and Mom and Dad not too far behind with equally disapproving looks on their faces.

Clearing his throat, Kyle nods his greetings, "Hey."

"Kyle," Dad says, although from the disappointed look on his face, I'd say it is clear that he knows all the details of my breakup. "Alyssa, sweetie, I would like for all of us to talk in the kitchen," Dad addresses me in a stern tone.

I nod and look over at Kyle.

"Oh, yeah, I'll just wait in your room so we can finish talking." He flashes me a smile and turns to run up the stairs.

"Ahh, I don't think . . . ." I start to tell him he needs to leave, but Abby grabs my arm.

"Worry about him later. There are more important things going on," she says with a worried look on her face.

My eyes immediately wander to Mom for some sign that everything is not as bad as I am starting to think; a smile, a wink, anything, but instead of reassurance I stare into her puffy blood shot eyes and I know the news is going to be bad.

We sit at the kitchen table for about an hour as Mom and Dad break the news that the cancer is back.

"The doctor told us that it appears that there may have been some small cells left behind and that maybe it wasn't detectable until now. They want to move forward with chemo immediately."

"Do they think it will get it all this time?" Abby asks.

"They seem very optimistic," Mom replies, still not completely answering the question.

"But have they said what the odds are of them getting it this time. I mean, it doesn't seem like they did a very good job last . . . ."Abby looks like she is seconds away from collapsing and with each word my own anxiety level picks up.

"Honey, they are taking care of it. The doctor's know what they are doing," Dad assures us, remaining positive as usual.

Mom squeezes Dad's hand as he speaks, looking at him as if she is holding back tears for his sake, as well as for ours.

"Is it small enough that they can remove it with surgery and then follow up with chemo? I mean do they know if it could spread before . . ." Abby throws out more questions while I remain quiet, listening to the chatter inside of my head, rather than their voices.

How is this happening again? Why?

Suddenly, I'm swept into a tornado of emotions I thought were left behind years ago.

Dad speaks up, bringing me back to the present, "We went over every option of treatment with the doctor. I think this is what's best." He smiles. "Girls, we've been here before and we will beat it again."

We . . . I love that in the hardest moments of our family's lives that my parents always count us as a team. That is how it should be. We will face this together.

My parents ended up laying it all out on the table, but what wasn't clarified is if the chemo was expected to work. I know as well as anyone that when it comes to cancer and treatments that there are no guarantees. What bothers me is that every time we breached that topic, they would take a u-turn from our questions.

As soon as they start discussing arrangements for getting Dad to his treatments, I know I need to make a big decision.

"Dad, I can take you anytime I have to work and then Mom can pick you up. We'll figure it out," Abby offers up.

"Wait, count me in." They all look at me, surprised.

"No, honey, you'll be at Purdue. You can't just . . ."

I cut Mom off, "There is no need to discuss it. My mind is made up. I'm staying here to help out. I can go to Rosemore this year and transfer later."

I look Mom in the eye, letting her know that I will not bend on this. No way am I going several hundred miles away when my family needs me. *School will always be there, but Dad; well I don't even want to think about that!*

After all the news is out in the open and we have discussed all sorts of changes that will need to be made due to the expenses of his more evasive treatments, I fly around the table and tackle Dad in a giant hug. He wraps one arm all the way around me, placing his chin on top of my head and his other hand on the back of my head.

"I'm sorry for the timing, Lyssi-bee," his voice cracks.

Pulling my head away, I look him in the eyes wishing I could take this burden from him.

"Daddy, don't worry about it. I can switch to Purdue my sophomore year when you are all healthy again," I tell him in a confident voice, trying my best to put hope in his heart as well as my own.

Dad gives me one last squeeze before getting up to help Mom with dinner.

"Dinner in 20 minutes, girls, and how about some brownies or chocolate cake for dessert?" She winks at us and then turns her attention to Dad.

Abby drags her feet over to my side and lets out a loud sigh. She deliberately has her back to my parents and I can see the unspoken words in her eyes. *She's just as scared as me.*

Pulling Abby in for a hug, she sniffles in my ear at the same time that another sound catches my attention, a muffled ringing coming from upstairs. *That sounds like my ring tone.* We break our hold and I look around, patting the back pocket of my shorts.

"What are you looking for?" Abby asks, wiping her fingers under her eyes to fix her eyeliner.

"My phone. I must have left it upstairs when I went up to shower earlier."

Once I remember the company that is waiting in my room, my lips crinkle into a snarl. *Over an hour down here and he still hasn't left. Great! I really cannot take this.* My body quivers with Dad's news and my heart is on the verge of crumbling.

Abby gives me a weak smile, "You better go run him off. We'll talk later."

With that, I race up to my room, clutching my hand to my heart in an attempt to hold it together. My door is cracked open and Kyle is lying in my bed with my phone tightly held in his hand which is currently pumping out music that I hadn't heard earlier.

"What are you doing with my phone? Did someone call?"

He jumps at the sound of my voice, clearly not expecting me.

"I was just seeing what kind of music you have on here. All the time we've been together and I never noticed you listened to all this sappy stuff."

He gives me a smirk that I'm sure he thinks is sexy and hits pause on the song that is playing. Crossing the room quickly, I snatch the phone out of his hand and bounce down on the bed beside him without thinking.

"Did it ring?" I ask again, pulling up all my recent calls, but there's nothing.

"No, it didn't ring. I was just listening to music waiting for you to come up. I almost fell asleep," he says in between a yawn as he stretches his arms above his head.

His shirt rises up a bit and his abs peek out from under the fabric. I glance for only a second out of the corner of my eyes, but he notices. His face lights up in delight as if I just declared that I want him back.

Shifting sideways, he faces me and starts in again, "Alyssa, take me back. I know there is still something between us. I can tell by the way you look at me."

I quickly try to extinguish his ego, "Kyle, that look you think you see is just me being thankful that you at least grabbed the correct pair of jeans this morning."

The confidence in his face falls, but he doesn't give up. His hand moves across my cheek and back into my hair, forcing me to close my eyes.

"I promise, it will never happen again, baby," he whispers right before his lips cover my mouth in a hard wet kiss that seems empty and lifeless, but I let it happen.

Unable to pull away from the numbness that penetrates every inch of my soul, I sit still with my hands firmly pressed in my lap and clutching my phone. My lips and tongue remain motionless, not giving him an ounce of passion. His mouth continues on its path with slow, soft kisses as a tear slips down my cheek.

My mind is a cyclone of emotions from the last few weeks and my heart is a crumbled, broken wreck, sinking into nothingness. Just over two weeks ago, I was smiling from ear to ear in a cap and gown, eager to start the next chapter of my life and now that future is unrecognizable.

In these past few weeks, I have managed to be stepped on, used and now crushed. I have no fight left in me. I'll save the fight for to-morrow, and the next day, and the day after that when Dad needs me, but for now I will surrender to his comfort.

He breaks away from kissing me and pulls me forward into an embrace.

"I love you, Alyssa," he whispers into my ear.

Yet, as those words are spoken, it's not his voice I hear; it's some-one else's. It's someone whose arms I wish were holding me and some-one whose lips would more than help to ease this gaping hole in my heart. But he's not here when I need him to lean on, so I decide in this moment to let him go and all the sweet memories we shared.

Ready to Party

SUMMER FLEW BY WITH US all constantly on the run. Abby, Mom and I took turns driving Dad to his treatments and stayed with him on his bad days. Andrea, my older sister; her husband and two boys sold their house and moved closer to home. That helped out so much, putting two more people in the rotation of caring for Dad.

I ended up getting a job at Rosemore Dental as a receptionist and have been working every day through the week. At first, I was hesitant knowing Judd was from there, but I figured it is a big city so the likelihood of running into each other was slim. Besides, I knew I would soon be going to college in the same city so the location of the office was more convenient than commuting each day after class.

After the first several weeks of college, Bethany raised a question that I hadn't even considered myself.

"What would you think about getting an apartment? I mean here in Rosemore, close to the college. I just got a job downtown and you work here. I figure it would be easier on both of us and save a ton of gas," she asks hesitantly.

She must be thinking I'll say no on account of not being home near my dad.

I ponder on it for a moment before offering up an answer. "I'll have to give it some thought. I've been running myself ragged back and forth, but I really need to be close to my family right now. I'll talk to Mom and see what she thinks." She steers the car back towards Fairview as I go on, "We would have to get something inexpensive. I really can't afford anything elaborate right now."

Bethany's priority would more than likely be to get some upscale apartment that would come with ridiculously high rent that I could not possibly afford.

"Think it over and let me know. It could be fun. I already looked in the paper and there is one not too far from campus that has an available unit. It's a one bedroom, one and a half bath, but it is only a couple blocks from my work, a few blocks from college and an easy walk to your work, too. It would be perfect, plus the rent includes electric, water, sewer and trash. We can look at it tomorrow after school, if you're interested."

Staring out the window in deep thought, I run over our conversation and weigh the pros and cons.

Once home, I pretty well already have myself convinced that it would be for the best, plus Mom agrees, bringing my assurance level to a 100%.

We end up getting the apartment that Bethany suggested and I am pleasantly surprised at how reasonable the rent is, yet the accommodations are comfortable and appealing to the eye. Best of all, the location allows me to walk to work and school. I take full advantage of it, mainly to give me time to clear my mind.

This week I have wound up at home more nights than not, eating dinner with my family and checking on Dad, however, for the days that I worked late, it helps to live close by.

Bethany definitely can be counted on for keeping my mind busy, trying her best to cheer me up anytime my fears start to get the best of me. When she isn't home, she is indulging in college life enough for both of us, always eagerly urging me to join in. I just haven't jumped on the party train yet, though.

Kyle lives in Rosemore as well, a couple blocks from us at some jock fraternity he pledged to. We actually see each other quite a bit and he has become someone I can truly lean on.

After unpacking the very last of my boxes, I sentimentally place a framed picture of Mom, Dad, me and my sisters on the dresser between our beds.

"Ok, so there is a party over at Kyle's fraternity tonight. You in?"

Bethany says in a chipper voice as she sits down on her bed.

We only have a small walkway between the beds and enough room for one dresser at the end beside the closet. The closeness of the beds always has me thinking about my cot back at the cabin.

"I'm really not feeling it," I tell her, knowing she is not going to let this go.

She flips onto her back and pulls her legs up to lay against the wall, forming an L shape with her body. Her shoulder length blonde hair flings out in all different directions as she tilts her head upside down to look at me.

While standing between the beds, I pry and tug at the box I have just emptied out until it is ripped apart and completely flattened.

"Oh my gosh, Alyssa, live a little. I know the situation, but you have to enjoy yourself some or you are going to go crazy. It's just one night."

Her words hit a sour chord within me and I have to hold back from yelling. The last few months my nerves have been wound so tight and my emotions have been so on edge that I fear the smallest thing could set me off.

I exhale slowly to calm myself before answering, "Actually, I was going to stay at my parent's tonight."

Bethany chuckles and rolls over onto her stomach, swinging her legs back and forth behind her.

"No, you weren't."

Squinting her eyes, she holds her finger out and points at me.

I slowly lower myself and sink into the mattress with my shoulders slumped forward while staring at my hands that are clasped together in my lap. I know I have been caught in a lie.

"You have it written down that it is Sunday night that you are going to your parent's, so don't even try to use that as an excuse." She gives me an evil smirk and I have to roll my eyes.

Why don't I carry a date book rather than the calendar on the kitchen wall? Bethany knows when I work, what time my classes are and what days or nights that I go home. I'll never get out of all these parties she insists I go to, if I keep advertising my schedule.

"Ok, you got me." I sigh and level her with a sneaky look. *She's right; Mom and Dad have been telling me the same thing.* "Fine, I'll go, but I'm not staying long. So, once I'm ready to leave, I'm leaving with or without you," I tell her and genuinely smile at her reaction.

Bethany bolts up off the bed and rushes over to the closet, throwing outfit after outfit at me in an attempt to glam me up. *Good gracious, she is just like Abby.*

Two hours later, I am outfitted in a pair of dark blue skinny jeans, a pair of black knee high boots and a black and silver fitted shirt with a lace back. She insists on doing my makeup, so I let her doll me up, but leave my hair untouched, hanging loose in thick waves down to the center of my back.

Knowing that we both will probably drink, we decide to walk the two blocks to Kyle's fraternity.

A short stroll later, we walk up to the huge blue Victorian and head up the stairs to the front porch, where several guys are sitting on the banisters, drinking. Whistles sound as soon as we near the front door.

"Ready to party?" Bethany says in an overly cheerful tone.

She shimmies her hips and takes off in front of me, batting her eyelashes and smiling at the admirers on the porch.

I follow behind her. *What have I gotten myself into?* It is only a matter of time before she falls into some corner with one of them to make out; either that or she may seek out the guy that she has been carrying on about lately. From what she has told me, she seems to be determined to sink her claws into him tonight.

Barely through the door and my body is already thumping to the same beat as the deafening music coming from the sound system.

"I'm going to work the crowd. You be ok?" Not even waiting for my answer, she is gone in two seconds flat; *figures.*

Once her body is swallowed up by the crowd, I scan my surroundings for familiar faces and come up empty. Pushing and shoving my way through a swaying mass of college students, I eventually wind up in the kitchen. I snag a cup full of beer and exit through the back door to the deck. The back yard is swarming with people as well; some dancing, some in corners getting handsy and some carrying on loud discussions.

I swing around to the side of the deck and position myself on the top stair to look out at the yard. *I don't care to mingle.* After guzzling most of my beer, I sit it down and lower my feet to the next step so that

I can lay back with a perfect view of the sky. A sliver of the moonlight shining above makes my mind flicker to a memory of Judd and me the first night we met.

I close my eyes tightly trying to will away the sharp pain in my heart. I've done a decent job of shutting him out of my thoughts, but sometimes when I'm upset or alone, his face flashes through my mind and I swear I am back in the security of his arms. I've even caught the smell of his skin as I stir in bed at night.

The truth is, even though he played me, I still miss him. I miss our easy conversations; our playful flirting and most of all, I miss the way he made me feel.

Inhaling deeply as I sit up, my chest warms and my mind gets a little fuzzy. *Yes!* I haven't touched a drop of alcohol since the lake, although the past couple months have definitely called for a drink. If I'm going to be here, I'm going to let go and de-stress with a little pick-me-up. Continuing in on my mission, I grab what's left of my drink and guzzle it. *Who cares; I just need to get drunk.* I place my cup down beside me, lean my head back and smile.

"What are you smiling about?"

Looking up, I see Kyle is scooting in behind me, his legs sliding along the edges of my hips.

"I thought you might be lonely out here all by yourself, plus, it looked like you just downed that," he says, pointing to my empty cup, "So, I brought you another one."

I laugh, already giddy from the buzz that is working its way through me.

He hands me a cup full of something strong-smelling and then sits two shot glasses, plus a bottle of liquor down beside us. I lean back and rest my head against his shoulder as I throw back my second drink.

"Easy. Slow down or I'll have to carry you home, although, you could stay here tonight." The corner of his mouth rises up into a crooked grin as he winks.

Hmm . . . no dimple. I sigh and twist around to face him.

He casually places one hand on my hip while handing me a shot with the other. I smile and toss it back as well, letting the warm liquid course down my throat and heat up my chest. Giggly and light headed from the drinks, but still aware that I shouldn't get involved with Kyle,

I gently grab his hand and move it from my hip to his leg.

He chuckles at my reaction. "I guess you need another drink, so I can take advantage of you later." He licks his bottom lip and grins.

Shaking my head, I break out into a burst of laughter from the dizziness in my head.

"Not going to happen, Kyle." I stop laughing and turn my neck to take in his expression.

His quiet chuckles dance across my ear as he places a quick kiss against my neck.

"You know, I'll never give up," he tells me for what may be the fiftieth time since this summer.

We stare at each other for a long while before I spin back around, with my back to him. I just want to have an easy night with no complications. Kyle has been there for me since my father's cancer returned and although, I know he wants more than I do; tonight I only want to feel a sense of peace and tranquility. I lean back against his chest with a deep breath and let him wrap his arms around me. With my eyes closed, I let the vibrations of the bass take hold.

After an hour passes and we have had a few too many shots, we make our way back inside. Kyle holds my hand leading me upstairs to his room, while grabbing another beer. My legs wobble beneath me and as if I'm walking on a tight wire, I have the urge to hold my arms out to my side. I'm still standing, though.

Halfway up the stairs, Bethany's voice calls out from behind me. She slams right into my back, giggling.

"Where you going, girl?!" she yells over the music.

I hiccup and giggle as Kyle tightens his grip on my hand. Leaning back against him for some sense of stability, I notice a not-so-happy glare that Bethany shoots his way as she looks around me to take in the scene.

Painting on a tipsy smile, her attention focuses back to me, "So, are you headed home soon? Because I found that guy that I have been telling you about and I think he is coming to our place. He has a friend, too." She wiggles her eyebrows up and down and Kyle's hand possessively wraps around my waist.

"She may stay here. She drank quite a bit," he informs her.

Bethany gives him an evil look and then looks at me, silently asking me if I know what I am doing.

I'm unsteady on my feet and I've had two . . . four, maybe five or seven shots, but I am totally in control. I know what I am doing.

Placing my hand on her shoulder, I touch my lips to her ear and whisper as loud as I can in the noisy room, "If you have company, just put the scarf up and I'll crash on the couch."

Bethany sticks her tongue between her teeth with a huge grin and gives me a thumbs-up as she bounces down the steps, eager to get back to her next conquest.

Once she is gone, Kyle tugs me the rest of the way up the stairs and into his bedroom. As soon as the door is closed behind us, his lips are on mine going a hundred miles an hour. I kiss him back, tasting the bitterness of beer and sweetness of whiskey on his tongue. Not a single spark ignites, and all the fireworks that once existed between us are now just useless, fizzled out duds.

He backs me up to the bed with his body flush against mine, causing me to fall back onto his pillowy-soft mattress. As he carefully eases the full weight of his body onto me, I close my eyes as our mouths move together. My heart begs for it to be someone else as my mind envisions that person touching my skin and softly kissing my lips.

Kyle's movements become more rapid as the denim of his jeans rubs hard against me, letting me know just how excited he really is.

Letting out a slow, shaky breath, I try my best to just feel and not think. *No strings attached, right? Just fun.*

His lips descend down my neck and he unexpectedly starts to push my shirt up as his tongue makes its way across my skin to my stomach. Once his hand grazes over the fabric of my bra, I gasp out loud, wanting badly to be in the moment, but not able to push Judd's face out of my mind. *I can't do this.*

Abruptly interrupting Kyle's pursuit of satisfaction, I push at his chest and clear my throat. He immediately takes the hint that this is over and slides up to look at me, thoroughly out of breath.

Once he scoots off the bed onto his knees, I sit up and stare down at him, not sure of what to say. Gently keeping his hands at my hips, he flashes me a weak smile as I affectionately run my hand across his cheek. His eyes gloss over with disappointment and although he smiles, I can tell I've hurt him.

"I'm sorry. I can't," I barely say above a whisper.

He gets up, still breathing heavily and moves over beside me on the bed. Grabbing my hand, he places a small kiss on the back of my knuckles.

"It's ok. I'll wait." His smile is gloomy and it is no secret that he feels frustrated, but I can't go through with this if my heart is not in it. "Will you stay the night?" he asks, quietly.

I shake my head, knowing it would only further his torment if I slept beside him all night long.

"Then can I walk you home?" he asks in such a sweet tone that I can't refuse.

Nodding my head, I answer him, "I'd like that," feeling thankful for his understanding, because I have truly had all I can handle for one night.

I have a lot of bouncing back to do before I am ready to party.

The guy around campus

THE NEXT MORNING I WAKE up with a pounding headache, a mouth full of cotton and uncomfortably sprawled out on the couch. *Maybe I should roll over and sleep the day away.*

Twisting onto my back slowly, my eyes make contact with Bethany's plush purple scarf tied around the bedroom door knob. She must have already had her fun before I got home last night, because normally her late night activities could wake the dead. The sounds of the bathroom door opening and closing a few times through the night had me stirring, but other than that it had been fairly quiet. *Thank goodness.* A tap on the door, at this point, may crack my skull wide open the way it is hurting.

Reaching over to the coffee table, I automatically grab my phone and notice three missed messages.

Kyle: Hey gorgeous! Text me when you wake up. I want to talk to you about last night. I hope I didn't come on too strong, it's just I miss you! The bbq is at 1:00, so if I don't hear from you, I'll swing by.

Letting out a long-winded sigh, I remember the barbeque party at Kyle's frat house that he asked me to go to last week. All the guys are bringing dates, so of course he asked me to come. I reluctantly said yes, feeling obligated to help him out as much as he had helped my family out since Dad had got sick again. I owe him a date at least, if not more. He has been working around the clock to gain my trust back since this summer and I'll have to admit, even though my heart isn't 100% on board, he is gaining ground.

Getting out of Kyle's message, I scroll to a text from my sister this morning.

Abby: Hey Lyssi-B! Mom was hoping you could come over for dinner tonight? I think Andrea will be here and I'm off work, too. They thought doing the whole family thing would be nice. :P Call me and let me know. <3 U!

A lump forms in my throat and I wonder why Mom and Dad would want me to come over tonight when I am staying the night tomorrow night. I don't work or have class on Monday so I planned on spending that day with Dad. Abby plays it off as nothing, but I am not convinced. I'll have to call her on my way over to Kyle's.

My final message is from Bethany, stamped from 11:51 last night. She must have sent it to me before she left the party.

Bethany: OMG! Have you seen this guy? Holy crap, he is hot! I am so getting into his pants tonight! If the rest of his anatomy works as good as his lips, it's gonna be a long night!! OMG!! I'll try to find you before I leave but if I don't; you're booted to the couch tonight! Scarf will be up!! Luv u chicka!

She must really like this one. Usually she isn't this persistent with guys. They pretty much come to her, but as she puts it, this one has been playing hard to get for a while. He must have finally given in or maybe he was drunk out of his mind like everyone else at the party. I laugh out loud thinking about how Bethany has taken living college life to a whole new level.

Glancing at the clock, I'm instantly alert and in a hurry. *Great . . . it's noon, already. Kyle will be here in an hour. I need to get changed and freshened up.*

With extreme effort to not jog my already pounding head, I sit up and make my way into the bathroom, fully intent on getting ready, but make a b-line for the aspirin first. To minimize the noise level, I decide to throw on my clothes from last night after I'm showered up. I need some fresh clothes out of my room, but I don't want to wake Bethany and her guest. I'll grab a clean shirt before I leave.

After spritzing a bit of body spray on my chest, I slip back into my smoke and beer reeked shirt from last night's party. I'm hoping in the amount of time it takes me to retrieve a clean shirt from my dresser that the perfume will serve as a barrier to keep me from smelling like I slept in a gutter. For a moment, I consider darting in my bedroom in my towel or bra, but with my luck, the guy would wake up and think that Bethany has decided to surprise him with double the fun. *Not going to happen!*

As soon as I dab on a little more makeup, I quietly exit the bathroom. The scarf is still hanging from the door knob, so no such luck in Bethany waking up early and bringing me a shirt.

Quietly turning the door knob, I inch it open and peek inside to make sure there are no early morning activities going on. Two pair of bare legs lie twisted up in the sheets, completely motionless.

Even though our floor is pretty solid and noise-proof, I tip toe across the carpeted floor, careful to dodge the landmine of clothes between our beds. On my side of the room it is nice and tidy with a clean made up bed, clothes all tucked away in the dresser or closet, shoes lined up under my bed and only a clock and lamp on my nightstand. However, on Bethany's side, the sheets are always thrown to the bottom of the bed, outfit after outfit scattered all over the floor and several empty 320z soda cups line her nightstand.

I live with an absolute slob, but our differences kind of balance us out. She is wild and crazy where I am reserved and serious most of the time. She is messy where I am organized; she's a partier and she is most definitely into jumping from bed to bed with guys, while I believe in commitment and love.

Placing my hand over my mouth to hide my grin from no one in particular, I look down at her all nuzzled up to the back of a tan, muscular guy. *Oh my!*

My foot hits the base of the dresser, signifying that I have reached my destination. Not paying a bit of attention, I reach into my drawer and finger through a pile of soft shirts. Craning my neck to take in all of this guy's body, I let my eyes roam over his sculpted abs, the V along his hips that dip below the sheet and his bulky biceps. He is scrunched up on his side with the pillow clutched in his hand and held over his head. *I wonder what his face looks like.*

Now I understand her being so determined with this one. He definitely has the body, that's for sure. *I've only seen one other body that is this perfect. Good gosh, I really need to get him off my mind; I'm seeing him in everything.*

Swinging my head around to pay attention to what I am pulling out of my drawer, I squat down and yank a couple shirts out before settling on a sheer black long sleeve shirt with a bright pink tank to layer underneath it.

As I nudge the drawer closed, ever so gently, I stand back up and look back at them, hoping to not make a sound. Ogling the guy's body a little longer, I notice a deep scar that runs along his shoulder and another along his ribcage. He also has a tattoo on the inside of his bicep that runs parallel to the scar. It's a large infinity sign with swirls and patterns around it. Straining my eyes to see the rest of it, I barely make out the words "breathe" scripted at the center.

A small thud makes me whirl around to the dresser to see that my family picture fell over when I was trying to shut the drawer. *Dammit!*

Behind me, I hear the crinkling of fabric and the creaking of the mattress. *Great, I woke them!*

"I'm so sorry. I didn't mean to wake . . ." I say as I spin around so that I can make a quick exit.

All of a sudden, my eyes collide with deep hazel eyes staring at me from beneath the pillow. My mouth drops open and my stomach churns. I can't move; I can barely breathe.

My chest contracts with short, quick spurts of breath that make me feel as though I may hyperventilate.

With wide eyes, he throws the pillow to the side and rises onto his elbows.

As I grip my hands to my stomach in hopes that I don't hurl, my eyes shift back and forth between him and Bethany, finally registering all that has transpired. Neither of us makes a move and I can barely think. If only I could make my legs work, I would run.

Becoming aware of the image that is set before me, he looks down at the sheet hanging across the middle of his body, glances over at Bethany, who is sleeping soundly and looks back at me as his facial expression shifts to shock then sadness.

"Lyssa?" he says in a raspy voice. "What are you doing here? I thought . . ."

I instantly throw my hand in the air to urge him to stop talking and potentially saying anything that might crush my heart any more than it already is. I don't want to hear anything he has to say; I don't even want to look at him, I can't look at him. *Why is he here? Why isn't he in California? And how the hell did he wind up in bed with my best friend?*

Finally finding my voice as my eyes well up with tears, there is only one thing I can think to say; something I don't intend to stick around to hear the answer to.

"Did you tell her you're in love with her, too?" I say in an icy tone and then bolt out the door.

"Wait a minute! Where do you get off being mad at me?" his muffled voice hollers out from the other room as I rush across the living room and hastily pull the front door open.

"What! You can dish it out but you can't take it!" His voice is louder as he remains hot on my trail.

Why is he pissed at me? Once I pass over the threshold of the apartment building, I glance back over my shoulder. In mid-run through the hallway in front of my apartment, Judd angrily tugs his jeans on while keeping his eyes locked on me the whole time. *Dammit!*

"Go back in and enjoy your slumber party!" I yell out and then realize I forgot my keys and purse. *Shit!*

My eyes blur over as I fly out of the complex. I'll jog to Kyle's house and come back for my keys later. Luckily, I held onto the clean shirt I swiped from my dresser, however, that is a decision that I'll forever regret. Completely neck deep in thoughts and wondering *"why me,"* I run as fast as my legs will carry me down the sidewalk and to the parking lot. Looking back for only a split second, I find him not far behind.

"Lyssa, wait! Let me talk to you!" he yells.

I snap my head back around so I can watch where I'm going and unexpectedly collide with Kyle.

"Whoa." He grabs my waist and pushes me back at arm's length to observe the situation. "You ok?" Kyle asks in a tender voice as he faces me with his hand pressed against my cheek.

I look at Kyle for a moment, but my eyes are drawn over my shoulder to Judd. He halts not far behind me in a defensive stance. Kyle's eyes sweep from him to me at first before he turns his full attention back to Judd.

Fumbling his hand, Kyle clasps mine in a protective hold and pulls me in behind him. Judd's eyes sweep down to our joined hands and his eyes widen. A tinge of guilt rises within me at how this must look to him, but then again, what do I have to feel bad about?

As Judd and Kyle continue their stand-off in complete silence, I realize just how bad this situation is. I never told anyone about Judd; not Bethany and certainly not Kyle. Those two weeks were something I kept locked inside my heart; a memory I visited but never talked about out loud, not to anyone except Abby.

"Is there a problem here?" Kyle's voice booms, making me jump.

His grip on my hand tightens and I look at Judd. His eyebrows lower and his expression takes on the look of an attack dog prepared to defend what is his. Judd opens his mouth to speak and I know it isn't going to be anything good. He is pissed, for what I have no idea, but I can see the anger in his eyes.

I have to get this under control . . . fast! I suck in a deep breath and pull Kyle back by the arm so that I am leaning against him.

"It's ok, he's one of Bethany's overnighters and I accidentally walked in on them. They were more than likely so busy last night that she failed to mention that she has a roommate," I bite out, glaring at Judd.

The snarl on his face gives way to shock and confusion at my words, but I don't give him time to say anything.

"Let's go," I say, pulling Kyle with me towards his truck.

Swinging my eyes back one more time to make sure this isn't a very exaggerated nightmare rather than my super sucky reality, I see the 'guy around campus' that Bethany had gone on and on about is standing motionless in front of my apartment, glaring at me and Kyle.

Barely staying afloat

"SO, WHO WAS THAT?" KYLE starts rifling out questions on the short ride to his fraternity house.

"I told you. He stayed the night with Bethany," I answer him, not at all lying, but still holding back who Judd is to me.

"Yeah, you said that, but he sure looked at you like you meant something to him." Kyle's eye flick over to me before returning to the road. "He looked at you kind of like I look at you."

Staring over at him, I am a little startled by how on track he is. It's no big deal if he knows Judd's the guy I fell in love with, after all we were broken up. I also could care less if Kyle hates him for it, because right now I am pretty much to that point myself, but regardless, I still don't want to discuss him with Kyle.

"He woke up and there I was, in the bedroom at the foot of the bed. He was probably freaked out. I think waking up to someone standing over your bed must have shocked him a little." I gulp down the nausea that floods my body with the memory.

No, I definitely have no intention of discussing those two amazing weeks with anyone. Last thing I want is for someone to belittle what I thought we had and make me feel even more like a fool than I already do. I've beaten myself up enough for my lack of judgment.

"Ok, if that's all you say it was, then I'll drop it," he says with a shrug of his shoulders, "I'm just glad I came when I did."

Walking into the frat house, Kyle grabs us both a beer from the fridge while I slip into the bathroom to change my shirt. Once we step onto the deck in the back, I see girls all clustered around chit chatting and carrying on while the guys seem to be glued to a rather serious game of quarters. Two guys stand by the grill, flipping burgers and other couples are off in their own world, drinking and getting frisky already. *Good grief, don't they ever take a break from the partying?*

Standing idle beside Kyle, I watch as he flips a coin onto a card table they have set up. I haven't touched my beer; *I probably should just down it. I need one worse than I did last night.* Right now, I need a whole arsenal of liquor to drown out the images that keep floating through my head. *Is this roller coaster ride that I have been on, ever going to come to a stop, because it is turning out to be a ride from hell!*

Taking a deep breath, I stare into space and listen to the screaming voice in my head. My thoughts are so loud that they drown out all the laughing, hollers and fun that is happening around me.

What did he mean I can dish it out but I can't take it? What was that suppose to mean? What, because I was standing with Kyle? No, he said that before Kyle showed up. Maybe he saw him in the distance, before I did. Not to mention, what on earth was he doing there? Shouldn't he be in California now? I run everything he shouted at me through my mind over and over.

As the minutes pass by, Kyle must sense my apprehension to join in on the festivities.

"Hey, come with me," he says, grabbing my hand.

Pulling me along behind him, we make our way across the deck, through the back door and up to his bedroom. *This again!* I've just about had enough of seeing the inside of anyone's bedroom, even my own.

His room is quite a hazard, much like Bethany's. After wading through a mess of football gear and clothes that are strung across the floor, I pounce onto his disheveled bed as he shuts the door and locks it. I huff out a loud sigh and fear what he wants to talk about or whether he expects to talk at all. Luckily, Kyle doesn't bring up the subject of the shirtless brute that was set on attack mode earlier.

"Alyssa, I just wanted to say sorry for last night. I'm a guy and I'm clearly still attracted to you. It's just hard to control myself around you some days. I'll respect how you feel and keep it casual unless you tell me different," he says with a warm, sincere smile.

His confession surprises me and washes away all the concern I have over Kyle's feelings for me. He's never made it a secret that he wants me back, but sometimes it does get uncomfortable when he gets desperate.

"By the way, how is your Dad? Have you heard anything more about his prognosis?" His question warms my heart and reminds me why I had been in love with him in the first place.

"He's getting weaker, but still being Dad. You know, nothing gets him down, really. We haven't heard anything else. I just keep hoping it's a horrible dream."

My hands lay slack in my lap, as I look intently at them, wishing with all my heart that I could change everything that has happened with a snap of my fingers. The bed springs creak beneath me as Kyle's sits beside me and slides his hand over mine.

"Let me know if there is anything I can do." The tenderness in his tone causes me to look up and into his eyes.

I smile, hoping to relay just a bit of appreciation for him thinking of my dad. "I will. Thanks, Kyle," my voice shakes out at the thought of Dad's situation.

With a deep breath, I work on gathering my wits before this morning's events and all other emotions I've so carefully hidden, come crashing down on me.

"Do you mind if I hang out in here for a minute and maybe borrow your phone? I need to text Abby back. I'm not supposed to go home until tomorrow, but I think I may head that way here in a bit. Maybe they will have some good news." Even saying those words out loud does nothing to shake loose the pit in my stomach.

Honestly, I'm nervous about why my parents want me to come tonight instead of tomorrow, when I had planned. However, given the situation, I am relieved to have an excuse not to go back to my apartment for the night. I really do not want to be face to face with Bethany right now. Sure, she doesn't know about any of this and technically she hasn't done anything wrong, but I still don't want to see her. Just the thought that he touched her and they . . . *Oh God, I think I may puke!*

My phone vibrates in my back pocket and I remember that I put it there after I got dressed. *Great!! Of all the things to remember!* I failed to get my money, my purse or even my keys, but of course, I remembered the one thing that keeps me in direct contact with the people I don't want to talk to right now.

"Ummm . . . never mind." *I swear I am an absolute basket case lately.* "I guess I have my phone after all."

Kyle nods with a smirk as I lean up and slide my phone out of my pocket to see it lit up with Bethany's name. In an attempt to make her go away, I squeeze my eyes shut and focus on happy thoughts; anything, but none come to mind.

Kyle laughs, causing me to open my eyes and look up at him. He's staring down at my phone.

"You don't want to talk to her, huh?" He chuckles a little louder and then mumbles, "I don't blame you."

Another vibration from my phone alerts me to the fact that she is not going to give up. Judd must have told her about us. *Wonderful! Just wonderful!*

"Ah . . . Kyle, I need to take this."

He smiles, kisses my forehead and then steps out of his room to give me some privacy.

I gulp down the panic that is rising up in me and hit accept.

"Hello," my voice trembles, so I take a deep breath and wait for her to start yelling.

"Girl, what was that all about this morning? I woke up to yelling and then saw that hot guy I brought home last night was chasing you out the door," she laughs.

Maybe she doesn't know anything, so I decide to tell the truth; part of it, anyways, "Oh, well I needed a clean shirt and I accidently woke him. I was embarrassed and ran off to avoid any kind of confrontation. I think he was just confused about who I was or something. I don't know for sure. Did he end up coming back inside?"

I'm not sure why I ask, because I really don't want to know.

"Of course he did. I was waiting for him in bed. Can you blame him?" She giggles, sending a shiver down my spine.

I would like nothing more than to reach through the phone and wring her neck. My hand grips the phone harder and I just know my finger prints will be embedded in the silicone case.

"So did you stop running long enough to get a good look at him?"

She laughs loudly. "Did I tell you he was hot or what!? I think I could dine on him for weeks. Last night he . . ."

I start coughing loudly hoping I choke so I can be put out of my misery. *I cannot take anymore!*

"Hey, I really have to go. Kyle is waiting for me downstairs and then I think I am going to go home when I leave here," I say, trying to fight the urge to hang up and end the call right there.

"Ok, no problem, I'm tired anyways. I think I was up all night. Can you believe that he . . ." I cut her off before she can say more than I care to hear.

Good gracious, can she not take a hint?

"Really, Bethany, I need to go," I shout out a little louder and snappier than I should. "I'm tired too and I really want to get on the road soon."

"Sure. We'll talk when you get here," she joyfully announces.

Her assumption that I will be coming home makes me want to laugh. *Yeah right. No way am I going back to the apartment today.*

"Actually I was just planning on leaving from here and heading straight to Fairview." I want to shout out, *"HA . . . in your face,"* but then I hear her giggle and I know I am missing something. Not to mention, I don't think I've ever realized how much her laugh annoys me until now.

"Well, have fun with that, girl, because news flash, your keys and purse are sitting here on the coffee table right in front of me."

Shoot! I forgot about that! My car is there too; so much for a quick getaway.

"Oh yeah, well, I guess I'll have to swing by there first. Are you going to be home all day?" *Please say no, please say no.*

"Yeppers . . . all day. I might take a nap for a bit. I'll see you later."

Cringing at the cheerfulness in her voice, I hit end. I need a truck load of strength right now, because I am bound to lose it.

After shooting Abby a quick text that I am coming home a day earlier, I end up staying at Kyle's for a half hour longer before he drives me the two blocks back to my apartment. I should have walked to prolong the wait, but I'm kind of hoping that Bethany has dozed off by now, hopefully in the bedroom. *I'll just slip in, grab my purse and keys, and rush back out undetected. Screw getting a clean pair of clothes;*

I've been rocking most of this outfit for two days straight, so what is one more day. Wearing clean clothes is overrated anyway!

Dreading the thought that she may be in the living room, I drag myself to our door and step inside to of course, find Bethany comfortably lounging on the couch watching TV, wide awake. Her blonde hair is all tangled up and makeup is smeared under her eyes. *I hope Judd saw her looking like hell this morning.*

Forcing up my most sincere smile, but knowing it is weak, I hesitantly walk into the apartment as if there is an explosive waiting to be disarmed. My eyes stay on my purse, sitting on the edge of our glass top coffee table, which is directly in front of her. *Would it be weird if I dart in, grab it and take off? I could plead insanity. In fact, I should be insane by now so it will not be far from the truth.*

"Ok, girl, fess up," Bethany's words startle me as she lays her feet on the coffee table, folds her arms and gives me a sneaky grin.

"Aaaaa . . ." I'm at a loss for words.

My mouth hangs open and she bursts out laughing.

"I know, right, he is so freaking hot. I knew you checked him out." Her eyes twinkle like she just saw a dessert that she has been dreaming about for months; one which I would love nothing more than to snatch out of her hands and gobble down in front of her.

"You can tell me. I don't mind you giving him a look over, but hands off," she laughs harder, pointing at me in a scolding manner.

Her shrill laugh is like fingernails down a chalk board and I want so badly to say the same thing to her; *keep your hands off.*

"I'm just joking. I know you wouldn't go there. Ok, so really, what did you two talk about? He was in a ridiculously foul mood when he came back for his shirt."

After her assumption that I wouldn't go there, which normally I wouldn't, I completely try to zone her out, but the last thing she says peaks my interest.

I decide to ignore her question and counter one back, "He came back for his shirt? He didn't stay?"

I'm sure my question sounds absurd considering, of course, he would come back for his shirt.

Bethany smiles like an evil witch that just did away with her nemesis.

Looking up at the ceiling, she playfully sings, "Well . . ." drawing out the word.

I swear I am going to choke her.

"Yes, he came back for his shirt and then we talked for a bit. I'm seeing him again this Wednesday," she goes on, making my heart plummet.

She is seeing him? He is dating her even though he knows she is my roommate? I want to cry; I want to puke. I just want this pain to go away, because I am barely holding my head above water.

"Where is he taking you on Wednesday?" I say in a defeated tone.

Bethany gets up, strides into the kitchen and dips her head into the fridge.

"He's not taking me anywhere, but I am taking him to your birthday party. You didn't forget, did you?" She stands back up and snaps her head in my direction. "Oh my gosh, you did!"

My mouth is agape and for the first time in years, I wish I was not turning a year older. Most eighteen year olds are thrilled to watch the hands of time turn and inch closer towards that magical age of twenty-one, but I would really rather just skip it this year. Besides, all I really would like for my birthday is to hear that Dad is healthy and healed; not a party.

"I didn't forget. I already told you a party is the last thing I feel like, plus why would he want to come to a party for someone he doesn't know?" I lie. I'm really just fishing for details of whether he hinted around about knowing me.

Instead of waiting for an answer, I stride into my bedroom, deliberately stomping like I am a two year old in the middle of a tantrum. Reaching under my bed, I pull out a bag and toss it onto my comforter so I can pack.

"Well duh, he isn't coming for you. He is coming so I can hang on him and hopefully bring him home again and . . ."

Lalalalalalalala . . . I am not going to listen to her. I need to get out of here. Screw the clothes!

"And since you are going to your parent's house on your actual birthday, it's the only day we could do it. Come on, Alyssa, I already have it planned," she stands in the doorway of our bedroom, puckering her lips into a pout and begging me to agree.

Technically the party isn't for me; it's just a simple excuse to have a party.

"Fine . . . I'll be there. I guess I have to be, since it is a party for me." I roll my eyes and give her a strained smile.

Not paying particular attention to what she's saying anymore, I cram this and that into my bag and fling it over my shoulder, eager to leave. *I'm out of here!*

The silence is deafening on the drive home and all I envision is him lying next to her. Blinking my eyes rapidly in an effort to chase away all thoughts of whether he touched her like he touched me, my hand flies up to switch on the radio. After flipping through station after station in hopes that the music will soothe my overactive imagination, I soon make the discovery that every song ever written seems to have something to do with love, breaking up, relationships or cheating. *Just perfect!* I punch the knob to turn it off and let out a blood curdling scream that I'm sure makes me look like a complete nut-job to the fellow drivers.

My phone! I quickly grab my purse out of the passenger seat, drop it in my lap and swim my hand through a sea of useless possessions while keeping my eyes on the road. As soon as my hand makes contact with the smooth slick surface of it, I rip it out feeling extremely grateful that I have an entire playlist of happy songs. While sitting idle at a stop light, I plug my phone into the stereo adaptor and flip into my music file to find some upbeat tunes.

Fast-paced music pours out and vibrates through the car immediately. I soak it up and let it fill my soul, praying it changes my mood. It doesn't help much, but I get through it.

Finally pulling into the driveway, my heart swells with gratefulness that I am home. This is where I belong; with my family, the ones that truly love me, the ones that hold me up when I am falling, the ones that help me out when I am barely afloat.

I would not change a thing

MY FEET HIT THE HARDWOOD floor of the living room and I am immediately greeted with the aroma of bacon frying and fresh biscuits coming out of the oven. *I love being home.*

Abby rushes down the stairs at the same time that Mom rounds the corner of the kitchen. I throw my arms around Mom's neck and instantly feel comforted.

Looking over her shoulder to the kitchen and then back behind me to the living room, I question, "Where's Dad?"

She smiles and tips her head over to the spare bedroom across from the dining room. I look at her quizzically as Abby throws her arms around my shoulder to crush me in a huge hug.

"He's getting too weak to go up and down the stairs, so Mom and Dad moved down here to make it easier. He'll talk to you later," Abby says with a disheartened smile.

Mom looks at me with a gloomy expression and motions me to come in the kitchen with her. My heart fills with panic and I look to the spare room, remembering how drained and frail Dad had looked last week.

"I'm going to go visit with Daddy first," I say with my heart already halfway to the doorway.

Abby grabs my arm, nudging me towards the kitchen as mom gently suggests that I wait.

"Honey, just wait, he needs the rest. He will be awake soon enough and will join us." Mom gives me a reassuring smile, so I take her advice and force my legs to move into the next room.

We carry on with small talk until dinner is ready. Mom has always outdone herself with cooking and baking. She goes all out for dinner, treating us to big meals like an Italian night, complete with pasta, pizza and homemade garlic bread.

Tonight, her specialty happens to be my favorite: breakfast, with eggs, biscuits and gravy, sausage, pancakes and bacon. I know she is overcompensating to keep our minds off the obvious, but it makes her happy and she is an awesome cook.

Honestly, I did not inherit that gene; instead I got Dad's fascination with tinkering in the garage.

Since I was little, Abby and Andrea would cluster around Mom while she was busy cranking out cookies, cakes and pies in the kitchen. I, on the other hand, would follow Dad out to his workshop. He'd give me spare pieces of wood, nails and a hammer and I would be hard at it creating and building all sorts of projects. Most of the time it ended up being a tower of scrap wood nailed together, but it meant spending time with Dad, so I loved it.

Dinner is quiet, as if we are afraid to speak. It's not very often that we sit at this table without Dad.

Finally, Abby decides to break the ice in true sisterly fashion, "Ok, spill your guts. You have man-problems. Let's talk about them."

My mouth drops to the table and I look from her to Mom. *Is she kidding me?*

Mom presses her lips together trying to suppress a smile.

"Oh come on! Do you want me to leave?" Mom asks with a laugh that makes her sound like she is a teenager gushing about boys with her best friends.

Laughing to myself, I admit, "No, it's just not something I can really talk to you about."

Feeling a little ashamed that I said I can't talk to her about some things, my eyes dart down to my hands in an effort to not look her in the eyes.

She blows out an exaggerated breath and slaps her hands to her forehead.

"Oh please, I thought the same thing about my parents at your age. Honey, I've had 3 children. I know all about the birds and the bees so don't think there is anything you can't talk to me about," she informs us in a proud tone.

Both Abby's and my mouth are hanging open.

"What? You think your father and I didn't have fun, too? This one time, your Dad and I . . ."

Whoa! I have to stop her right there!

"Mom!" Abby and I both shout out in unison.

"Ok, I get it, but still . . ." I add, but Mom holds her hand out in an impatient gesture like I'm not listening.

I surrender all efforts of explaining why I can't discuss boy drama with her and smile.

"Ok, you sure you want to hear this?" I ask, stunning myself that I am going to have the nerve to talk about this with Mom.

She nods her head.

"You have to start from the beginning, Alyssa. Tell her all about the lake this summer," Abby throws in there, making me feel nauseous with nervousness.

With my palms sweating and my body wracked with anxiety about sharing intimate details with someone else, I tell her everything from the beginning and travel down a beautiful road of how I fell in love with Judd.

My heart speeds up at the memory of us lying under the stars in the back of his truck and I giggle when I tell her about him asking me to be his girlfriend. There are some details I choose to keep to myself, but I spill nearly everything, even the fact that we slept together the last night at the lake.

". . . . So then he just never called me, ever. He just up and vanished." My heart squeezes as I hear myself say the last part.

Mom's expression doesn't change and she never tries to interrupt me, so I go on, "Oh and he even got his phone disconnected."

I press my hands against the hard surface of the kitchen table as though I can brace myself for the next piece of the puzzle I will share with them.

"Ok, so what is the new information that you said you needed to tell me?" Abby asks referring to my text I sent her from Kyle's room earlier today.

I inhale a deep calming breath and silently chant to myself, *stay calm and don't cry.*

"Well, last night Bethany brought some mystery guy home with her, so I . . ."

"Holy crap, NO WAY!!" Abby shouts out before I can finish.

She slams her hands against the kitchen table with wide eyes. I'm glad she figured out the obvious, because I'm not sure I can say it out loud. Nodding my head, I fold my arms across my chest as if they can protect my heart from any further damage.

"No freaking way!" Abby sounds as crazed as I feel. "How? I mean, did he know you lived there? Oh. My. God. Did they . . ." Abby clips her blatant thoughts off as I squeeze my eyes shut, to keep from crying.

Upon opening my eyes, I see my mom and sister both staring at me. As much as I need support for how hurt I am, I'm silently hoping Mom doesn't look down on Judd as a bad guy. He pretty much is a slime ball, I suppose, and I should hate him for how he used me, but to hear someone else bash him will probably hurt more.

As usual when I least expect it, Mom surprises me.

"Oh, honey . . ." She reaches across the table and squeezes my hand. "It sounds like you really developed some strong feelings for him."

I stare at her; *that's all she took from that.*

"I think that is beside the point, Mom," Abby chimes in.

Mom holds her finger up to signal that she is not finished talking. "When you love someone you have to fight for them."

"Yeah, but . . ." I start, but Mom raises her eyebrows into a stern expression and keeps her finger held up in front of her.

"What I heard you say is that he ran after you, that he was mad and that he kept arguing. To me, a person would not display any of those emotions if there were not feelings there. Why would someone bother to fight, argue or get mad at someone they didn't care for? When you love someone, you fight with them, you get mad at them and you say hurtful things when you know you shouldn't. It's not all butterflies and rainbows or unicorns or whatever you kids say these days." Mom waves her hand in the air and then gets up to clear the table.

"What's not all rainbows and unicorns?" Dad voice fills the room.

"Is that how that phrase goes?" Mom jokes with him as she rushes to the stove and fixes Dad a plate.

Her speech comes out of nowhere and leaves me a little stunned, but right now I'm too excited to see Dad. I scoot my chair out and race over to hug him.

"Alyssa fell in love this summer and now she has a major dilemma," Abby brings him up to speed even after I flash her a dirty look. "She met a guy out at the lake and now he just might be seeing Bethany," she adds.

I clear my throat and make an extreme effort to change the subject. *What a blabbermouth.* I definitely do not want to dive into this with Dad, too.

"Well, if this boy knows what's good for him, he'll come to his senses," Dad says, looking over at me as Mom places a plate of food on the table.

Abby and I look at each other and smile at Dad's words.

A few minutes later and after a nice save from mom, we all sit at the table discussing Mom's fall garden rather than my love life. The sound of metal scraping against ceramic has me looking over at Dad while he pushes food around on his plate. I put my hand on his arm and feel nothing but bones. He looks over and offers a small smile and I notice the deep, dark shadows under his eyes and the way his shirt hangs around his neck like he's wearing someone else's clothes. His once salt and pepper, short hair is now replaced by a shiny bald head which he keeps hidden under ball caps.

Once Dad has given up his attempts of eating, Mom clears the table and they decide to let us in on why they wanted us all together tonight rather than tomorrow.

Dad clears his throat and sits up, looking ghostly pale.

"Honey, I can tell them," Mom's quivering voice has alarms screeching in my head. *This is not good.*

Mom takes a shaky breath, closes her eyes and then opens them back up, looking as though she has gained a sense of strength and fortitude. "Your father's body is not responding to the treatments. The doctors say it would be best to discontinue the chemo at this point." Her throat wobbles as she closes her eyes, trying to obtain courage to go on, "He had more tests run this week and the cancer has spread." Mom keeps a steady voice while she delivers the news.

Looking at Dad, I see the same confident smile he always displays as he clutches Mom's hand in his own. My heart crumbles into a million pieces leaving me gasping for air.

"What, that's it?"

Abby trips over her words and sniffles beside me, but I can't see her face through my tear-hazed eyes. Reaching my hand under the table in an extreme effort to find comfort, I grab onto her hand and hold it tightly. *I can't breathe; I'm suffocating! Please, don't take my dad!*

"Don't you worry, sweetie. I haven't thrown in the towel," Dad tries to direct our minds away from the obvious, but mine is already spiraling uncontrollably.

Abby's quivering hand has an unbearable grip on mine, but I welcome it; somehow it holds me up and diverts the pain away from my heart.

Dad's weak voice bounces me back into the present, "Your mother and I have discussed this several times. We knew this was a possible outcome, but we wanted to wait until we knew for sure before talking to you girls. I know this is scary . . . I have to admit that I have a little trouble with it, but bottom line, I am still here. There is no need to mourn me before I'm gone."

Dad leans over to run his thumb beneath my eyes to swipe away a tear and then stretches over one more seat to do the same to Abby. We both look at him and I know Abby sees the same thing I do.

This is our hero; the man we measure all men up to; our rock; the only man that will ever love us completely and unconditionally.

Dad has saved me from nightmares.

He's danced with me in the living room.

He taught me how to hold a hammer without slamming it over my thumb.

He has dried my tears when I've cried and he has always been here for me, no matter what.

He is asking me to be strong, but how can I be when I know that someday I will have to live without him? When someday I will have to say goodbye?

Dad smiles brightly as I look up and run through a thousand words in my mind that I wish I could say to him. My chest shudders and vibrates as I gulp down a deep reassuring breath that lets me know I can still breathe.

Dad hugs Abby and me while softly assuring us both, "This is by no means goodbye. This is just another reason to live life to the fullest."

His words grip my heart, penetrating the deepest corners of it.

"I learned a long time ago that life is a gift that we should never take for granted," he adds happily.

Leaning back in his chair, he slumps over toward the table and I can tell how exhausting this conversation is for him, but he goes on, "I've been looking at this diagnosis as a blessing. So many people don't get warnings when their time is coming. They don't get this extra time to hold their loved ones close. They never even get a chance to say goodbye and truly know that their family knew just how much they love and cherish them."

Dad looks over to Mom with a smile. She smiles back through the river of tears trickling down her cheeks.

Looking back at us, he goes on with his mouth curved up into a warm smile, "This is a gift and I am so grateful for it."

After we have all shed several tears and wrapped ourselves up in each others' loving embrace, Mom and Dad head to bed. I watch as they slowly walk away, Dad's arm loosely wrapped around Mom's waist while she hugs to him as if he is her lifeline.

Trailing behind Abby, my feet seem to be on auto-pilot carrying me from one step to the next until we are both in her bed, curled up under the covers. I pull her feather down comforter up to my neck as I huddle up to Abby's side. The light from her bathroom shines into her bedroom, illuminating her face as she stares up to the ceiling.

"Do you remember when we were little and we'd go sledding with Dad down that big hill?" I giggle at the memory and allow just one small tear to escape.

Making sure to stay near each other all night long, we stay up half the night sharing stories. Every once in a while a quiet falls between us and I can't help but wonder if she is thinking what I am? *God chose the two most perfect parents for us. Sick or not sick, I would not change a thing. I love my family and I will love them all until the day I die.*

I'll find you

THE NEXT MORNING, I GET up well before Abby and sneak downstairs for a cup of coffee. At the foot of the stairs, I hear dishes clanging together and I know Mom is up. As I round the corner, her worn out expression and mellow smile has me racing across the room so that I can pull her into a fierce hug. She clings to me and blows out a serene breath before breaking away from our hold.

"Excuse me. I'm going to work out back in the yard until your Dad wakes up. I poured you a cup already." She points over her shoulder to the counter with a subtle grin.

Grabbing my steaming cup of coffee, I quietly slip out the front door and slide onto the porch swing, pulling my knees to my chest.

A minute later, the door opens behind me and Dad steps out with a cup of coffee in hand, obviously with the same plan as me. His loveable smile causes my heart to explode with love for him and my own smile grows the longer I look at him. The vise on my heart tightens when I think about how brave he is. His charcoal gray jogging suit hangs loosely on his body and his navy blue baseball cap that is turned backwards takes me back to the night I met Judd. I don't know why I think of him, but I do. I even wish I could feel his arms around me to ease this pain.

Dad takes a seat and slides his arm to rest on the back of the swing. "What are you thinking about, Lyssi-bee?"

Looking into Dad's eyes, there are so many questions that whirl through my head that I desperately want to ask; so many things I want to say to him. My lip trembles as I open my mouth to speak. Dad's smile deepens and he rubs his hand across my back.

"Let's talk. I know you have questions. Ask me."

My hands start to shake and I know I am going to cry. Bending forward, I quickly place my coffee on the ground and shiver from the loss of its warmth. A profound sigh sneaks up my throat and out my mouth as I snuggle to his side and draw upon just a little of Dad's optimism. This is where I feel brave; this is where I gather my strength. His warm arm engulfs me and we sway in the swing, side by side.

Finally working up the nerve to ask some questions, I bring up the thing that I am the most afraid to know, but I ask anyways.

"How long? Do they know?"

He lets out a small sigh as if he knew this was the question I would ask. While keeping his eyes locked on the front yard, he pulls me in tighter and begins to tell me all the delicate details that I never thought I would have the courage to hear.

"It's spreading fast, sweetie. The doctor said I could have as much as two to three months at the most, but they are not sure how the quality will be with me refusing the medication as well."

I sit up straight, startled at this news. "You stopped the medicine, too?"

"Honey, they were just taking from the life I had left. They were making me weaker, but not making me better. I want to live. If it means the length of my life is shorter, but the quality is better, then wouldn't I want that more?"

Leaning forward, he places his elbows on his knees and clasps his hands between them.

"Suppose if I had two days off to spend with you, but I chose to go out to the garage alone while you stayed in the house to watch TV. But on the flip side, what if I had only one day off and we went hiking, fishing, we laughed, we talked and we spent the whole day together . . . which would you choose?"

I don't answer; I understand and he knows which one I would choose, but I'd rather not say out loud that I would choose one less day.

Getting more comfortable, he leans back and places his arm around me as we go back and forth, with Dad answering every question from,

"Are you scared?" to "What do you think happens when you die?" Through it all, he never gives pause, always offering up an answer that leaves me with hope and that fills me with peace, because that is what Dad does. He always makes the bad seem good.

"So, what about this guy you met this summer?"

His question comes out of left field and I stumble around to find an answer. He laughs at my expression because I must look dumbfounded.

"Well, his name is Judd."

Dad nods his head like he is approving of the name or agreeing with something that I don't remember saying.

"We went fishing this summer. He even wormed my hook for me," I say without even realizing how that phrase could be misconstrued if I was talking to anyone other than Dad.

Dad's face lights up into a huge grin and he dips his head down with a quiet chuckle, slowly nodding his head.

I have no idea what I said that is funny, but his smile is contagious and I plaster one on as well.

"Truly horrendous things. You better keep your eye on that one." He laughs and I laugh with him, thinking back at how I thought about those same words that day.

Looking into his eyes, I think for a brief moment how this could be the last conversation like this that he and I share. *Live life to the fullest and leave no words unspoken!* That will be my motto for the rest of my life. So, I go for it. I'm going to leave nothing unsaid; no matter how much it hurts to say it.

"Daddy, I'm going to miss you."

As the dam breaks, I throw my arms around his neck and hug him like this is the last time. He wraps his arms all the way around me and runs his hand down the back of my head.

"I don't think I can breathe if you are gone. I'll be lost without you, Daddy."

I want to beg him to stay, but I know it is not in our control. Dad pulls me back to look into my eyes and holds my face steady in his hands.

"Oh Lyssi-Bee, that will be one of those breathtaking moments I told you about. When you feel like you can't breathe, it's only because you love me so much. I took your breath away."

He kisses my forehead and continues to encourage me.

"And you will never be lost because I will come find you. Just because you cannot see me doesn't mean I'm gone. I'll still be here. I'll always find you when you are lost."

My chest heaves up and down, feeling as though the air is being sucked right out of my lungs.

"But what if you can't find me? I want to be able to see you. I want to know you are there. I don't want you to leave me, Daddy."

Racked with fear and sobbing uncontrollably, I know in my heart I need to stay strong for him, but I can't.

Dad brushes his hand through my hair, remaining calm and collected as he softly laughs.

"Alyssa, I promise you . . . if I can't find you, I will send someone who can. I will be there. You may just have to look a little harder to see me. I will be there in every breathtaking moment of your life. I will watch your laughter, your tears, your joys and your heartaches. I will be here every day for the rest of your life, I promise."

We stay on the porch together until Abby wanders out. Looking over at Dad, no words are needed to know that he needs to have this same talk with her, so I make myself scarce.

The day goes by fast and we make the most of it. Andrea swings by to join us for dinner and not long after she walks in, Dad pulls her aside as well. Abby and I watch as they disappear outside for what we assume is their talk. All in all, it ended up being a long emotional day for us, but by the end of the night we all curled up on the couch with some popcorn to watch a movie as a family, just like old times.

Amidst all the heartache and defeat that we all are feeling through the day, we still have each other. Dad made me realize, we will always have each other regardless of our path in life. If you love someone, nothing will ever keep you apart, not even death. You will always find them.

Still want to run to him

TUESDAY MORNING, I HEAD BACK early, stopping by the apartment briefly before I head to class. Luckily, a text from Bethany yesterday told me she is going to Fairview and will not be there. I'm relieved, because I'm not all together comfortable around her right now. Even though, technically she didn't do anything wrong, in my eyes it still feels like she has betrayed me. I have no right to feel this way, given the fact that I never told her about Judd, but it still hurts.

As soon as I step inside, I notice a couple of empty soda cups, a dirty plate and a small white box in the center of the coffee table. *I love how Bethany leaves her trash sitting around for me to pick up.* I curl up my lip, more disgusted by her sloppiness than normal.

After flinging my bag and purse onto the couch, I scoop up the plate in one hand, wedge the two half empty sodas between my arm and waist, and then pick up the foam container in my free hand.

Her side of the room is also slowly trickling into the living room with several shirts and socks thrown on the floor.

"What a slob," I mumble under my breath as I place the dish in the sink and turn to throw the other stuff in the trash.

After tossing the two drinks in, I notice the container is weighted down like it still has something inside. I flip open the box and immediately snap my hand over my mouth with a gasp. *This is not for Bethany.* My breathing comes at an accelerated rate and my heart begins to flutter as I stare down at its contents. Lying in this small white Styrofoam container is a gooey brownie with creamy fudge dripping down the sides and a bright red firecracker stuck in its center.

My mind races with memories of Judd and me out on the lake fishing and how I told him about the huge batch of brownies Mom made me to soften the blow of my breakup and Dad's pending test results. He cracked up when I explained Mom's logic of how chocolate cures all ailments.

I poke my finger on the edge of the brownie, letting my fingertip dig into the soft slab of chocolate. Pinching my thumb to my index finger, I grab a small chunk and allow myself one taste. Closing my eyes, I let the smooth rich flavor dance on my tongue as I take a step back towards the kitchen table. I open my eyes back up, sink into the chair and toss the container on the table in front of me as if the contents were a creepy insect rather that a mouth watering dessert.

Minutes click by as I stare at the firecracker and analyze what on earth it means. *When did he leave this here? Why would he leave it here? And does Bethany know now, otherwise how did it end up here?* My mind whirls with questions, all of which I know I may never get the answers for. Slowly, I pick up the firecracker as if it may explode at any second. Holding it between my finger tips, I roll it back and forth studying it while nostalgia floods my heart and head with sweet memories.

I close my eyes and envision the snapping and cracking of fireworks all around me. Pop, pop, pop. Laughter rings from every direction and my hand suddenly warms as if it is tightly woven with his.

Gripping the firecracker to my heart, my mind drifts further into the night to how his hands ran over the contours of my body as if I was a precious gem. His green eyes emerge in my mind and his whispers fill my head. "I'm falling in love with you," and "This is not goodbye," echo through me as if he is standing in this very room. Shaking my head, I push the memories and the feelings that they stir within me to the back of my mind.

Letting the firecracker slip through my fingertips back into the small box, I hastily clasp it shut and storm over to the trashcan, with a grip that is sure to leave dents in the container. I move my foot to the opening lever, fully intent on throwing it away, but pause as my head and heart stage a war of what to do. My grip is uncompromising; it's as if it is glued to my fingers. *Throw it away. He's just screwing with you.*

Realizing that my stroll down memory lane caused me more time than I had to spare, plus the fact that my mind was not going to win, I toss it onto the counter as roughly as I can, hoping by force I can rid myself of some of the confusion it caused me.

I'll just throw it away later.

Jetting through the apartment, I throw on a pair of jeans, a t-shirt and sneakers, throw my hair up in a clip and scoop up my bag. Before exiting the house, I glance over to the Styrofoam box calling to me from the counter and decide one more bite won't hurt. *Maybe I'll just bring it with me and throw it in a trashcan on campus.*

By the time I pull up to class, the container is empty and my tummy is rumbling a chorus of appreciation.

My two morning classes creep by at a snail's pace, but finally the professor releases us and I head back to my car. Halfway to the parking lot, my phone chimes in my bag and I dig inside to retrieve it. As soon as I get it out, my heart crashes into my stomach and all the happiness the chocolaty goodness brought me vanishes. My legs stop working and I stand on the sidewalk, staring down at Judd's name.

I never had the heart to delete his contact or our picture, but considering his phone number was disconnected last time I tried it, I didn't think it would ever appear on my phone again. With shaky hands, I pull up the message.

Judd: Hey, this is Judd. I doubt you still have my number in your phone, but I figured I would give it a shot anyways. I think we should talk, plus I wanted to see if you got my gift?

I take a deep breath to slow the surge of anger racing through me while rapidly blinking my eyes as if it may disappear. It's bad enough that I caught him in bed with my roommate, but now I find out that he actually still has my number. He never chose to use it when it mattered, but he has it. Maybe he has a folder of contacts on his phone entitled 'booty calls.'

On top of that, he has the audacity to say we need to talk. *Talk?! Really! I have nothing to say to him.* He played me and I was gullible enough to fall for it. Now, I find out he has moved on to the next girl;

end of story.

After hastily shoving my phone back in my bag, I continue on my path across campus, focusing on the way the sun shimmers off the sidewalk and how the soft, lush blanket of green summer grass is slowly fading to a dull brown the closer we inch into autumn. My eyes swim over the landscape, looking for anything to concentrate on other than him, but as I turn the corner of the Music and Arts building, my phone chimes again. Coming to a sudden stop, I place the weight of my bag against my abdomen, let out a frustrated sigh and dig my phone out again. *Another text from Judd.*

"I hear nothing from you for four months and now you're stalking me," I mumble under my breath to absolutely no one, but myself.

Judd: Ignoring me! Really!? The least you could do is talk to me!

Every muscle in my body tenses as I grip my phone so hard that it may break. Looking around for a stone or a stick or anything that I can throw to release some of my frustration, I throw my phone back in my bag, fully prepared to stomp on it. *The least I could do is talk to him?!?* I don't owe him anything, least of all any form of communication, considering he severed that when he didn't call me.

"So, I take it you don't want to talk to me?" The sound of his voice is a lightning bolt shooting straight through my heart, crippling me and rendering me immobile.

Slowly, my body begins to work as I lift my head and lock eyes with him. All the anger that I was feeling only seconds ago evaporates and I begin to quake. He stands only two to three feet in front of me with one hand in his loose fitted faded jeans. His eyebrows are lowered into a frown and he is not smiling. This is not a look I am used to seeing on him.

Knowing I cannot surrender to the warm and fuzzy feeling that he usually stirs in my heart, I automatically go on the defense and fold my arms across my chest. *If he looks pissed, then I should be pissed and I definitely have nothing to say to him! My lips are sealed! He can just walk away! God, he looks good! No . . . focus, Alyssa, focus!*

His eyebrows lift in question and he looks irritated.

"You really aren't going to talk to me, after everything that happened between us this summer." His voice sounds desperate, yet livid at the same time.

However, my anger level just shot straight through the roof with him bringing up what we shared. *To hell with not talking!*

"What we shared?! Are you kidding me, as if that meant anything to you. I mean really . . . how many notches have you put in your belt since I last saw you?!"

Blood races through my veins as I struggle to keep from raising my voice and drawing attention to us.

"What is that suppose to mean? And why on earth would you think it didn't mean anything. I never . . ."

As if there wasn't enough tension in the air, Bethany walks up with an all too cheerful expression on her face and completely cuts off our conversation.

"Hey guys, what's up?"

She looks from Judd to me with a scrunched up face. *Great, she must have caught part of our conversation.*

"Did I interrupt something?" Bethany swings one hand onto her hip like she's striking a pose and side steps to move closer to Judd.

Looking directly at him, it occurs to me that I have no idea how to explain to her what was going on between us. Judd's frown deepens, but I see that his attention is set on Bethany. My heart sinks.

"Were you guys discussing your initial meeting or something else?" She is not going to let this go.

Going with her idea, I give a generic explanation, "Yeah, I was just apologizing for busting in on you two, the other morning."

Bethany's eyes light up and she glances at Judd.

He takes a step back to add distance to us all. No doubt this has got to be awkward, being faced with two girls he has slept with, one of which knows what a player he is. *I hope this is torturous for him!*

"Well it sure looked like a heated discussion," she adds with a giggle.

Judd's eyes shift to mine and he makes absolutely no effort to hide it from her.

Forcing myself to smile, I raise my chin and nip this situation in the butt, "No, not at all, but hey, I really need to go. I have to be at work in an hour, so I'll talk to you later, Bethany." I wave my hand towards my roommate and then spin around to walk away from them both.

My heart feels like it has been trampled on. If that wasn't enough to send me spiraling off a cliff, I make the mistake of turning back for one more look at him. That quick look does me in and sends me sprinting for my car. Judd's once-love-filled eyes are directly on me as Bethany stretches up onto her toes in what looks like an attempt to kiss him. *I can't watch.*

I get to my car and nearly rip the door off the hinges to get inside. I clutch the steering wheel and press my forehead against it. So far, I've managed to hold the tears back all morning, but I can't anymore. My eyes sting and my breaths come in fast gasps. *This is too much! This is all too much!*

I need to be focused on Dad, not a two week summer fling that I took way too serious. *Why does he want to hurt me more? What could we possibly have to talk about?* I squeeze my eyes closed as tight as I can, allowing my heart to numb from the pain. The thing that kills me the most and what makes me want to kick myself, is that even after all that has happened between us; after all the hurt he has caused me, I still wanted to run into his arms when I saw him.

Happy Birthday

WITH THREE MID-MORNING CLASSES AND work, the next day goes by in a rush. Luckily, I don't have any run-ins with Judd.

Once I hit the door to the apartment, all that is on my mind is soaking in a long, hot and relaxing bubble bath, with not a single care in the world.

I strip down slowly, too tired to move faster than a crawl. Sinking into the steamy water, I wave my arms around and cover my body with the soapy froth. As I slouch down further with my chin barely grazing the surface, I close my eyes and clear my mind. Tiny fizzes and pops lick at my skin as the bubbles start to dissolve.

When my eyes start to get heavy and my back starts to slowly slide down the slippery tub, dipping my mouth beneath the water, I decide it's time to either get out or stop relaxing, so I don't fall asleep.

Pivoting my body to the side, I lazily fold my arms along the cold edge of the bathtub and reach for my phone so I can call Mom. *I need to check on Dad.*

"Hello," her voice warms my soul and makes me feel a sense of comfort that I haven't felt in the last two days.

"Hi, Mom. What are you up to? How is Dad?"

"We just ate a bit ago so your Dad and I are getting ready to dive into a game of dice."

I laugh as images of previous game nights with my parents dance in my head. Mom gets so competitive and of course, Dad armed with that information, always conveniently loses. It's really quite humorous watching her strut around and brag about her win while Dad sits back and smiles. He would do just about anything to bring a smile to her face.

"That sounds like fun. Wish I was there. Is Abby out?"

I'm curious if my sister will swing by the party tonight. A part of me really wants her here for moral support.

"I told her to go out tonight. Seems like you girls have sacrificed so much of your time in the last few months and it really isn't fair to you. You need to enjoy your lives, too."

Her words surprise me. *Doesn't she know that she and Dad are our lives? We would be nothing without them.*

"Mom, we want to be there. We do it because we love you both so much and we never look at it as a sacrifice," I quickly correct her assumptions.

Mom laughs and I can almost see her waving her hand in the air as if I have embarrassed her.

"Oh honey, I know. Besides, this is a win-win for all of us. Your dad and I get a date night alone and you girls get to go enjoy yourselves."

On that note, I think it's time to wrap up this conversation. I don't want to hear about my parents alone time, although it is cute that she refers to it as a date night.

"I guess I will let you go then, so you and Dad can enjoy your date," I giggle into Mom's ear.

"Have fun at your party. Are you still coming home on Friday?" Mom says as I hear Bethany call out from the other side of the door.

"Hurry up, girl! It's almost party time!" I snarl my lip at the sound of her voice.

I'm dreading tonight for three reasons.

Number one, Judd will be there!

Number two, Judd will be there with Bethany!

Number three, Judd will be there!

If I had to add a number four to the list, it would be because my life is a disaster and the last thing I want to do is party. I intend to just suck it up for one night, though.

"Yeah, Mom, I'll be there Friday. I have to go get ready. I love you. Give Dad a big hug and kiss for me."

"I love you, sweetie!" Dad hollers out in the background.

His voice makes my heart thud in my chest and I wish so desperately that I could wrap my arms around his neck.

"Bye Honey. I love you. No matter what, make sure you have fun tonight." Her soothing tone lets me know it's ok to relax and have fun for one night.

"I will," I half-lie, "I love you both, too." I just hope I'm able to enjoy my evening. I'm afraid that one look at Judd with my best friend, may send me screaming back home or have me collapsing into a blubbery mess.

Once I'm out of the bath, I squeeze into a navy blue mid thigh length fitted dress, buckle a brown belt around my waist and then slip on a pair of brown boots. Usually, I would go for a simple hoody and jeans, but it is my birthday party so I might as well look the part. Plus, I want to look good so Judd can see exactly what he is missing.

After plastering on more makeup than I would normally wear, I prance out into the living room for Bethany's approval. Once I step out of the steam filled room, I am stunned into silence. Judd sits casually on the couch, typing on his phone.

The thought crosses my mind for a second to flee, but he jumps to his feet before I can even take a step. His eyes slowly move from my feet to my face, taking in every inch of my body the same way he did Fourth of July night. I wrap my arms around my waist in an effort to contain my nervousness and to hide how naked his gaze makes me feel.

"Wow," he whispers in such a low tone that I can barely make out his words. "You look beautiful."

The look in his eyes is a replica of the expression he cast when he said that he was in love with me. My heart leaps into my throat. I want to question him and ask him why he led me on, but instead, my lips are cemented shut and all I can do is watch him.

Staring directly into his eyes, he levels me with an equally intense stare as I remain completely motionless; silent and trembling from the familiarity. The drumming of my heart and the quiver of my breath is the only sound in the room until our spell is broken.

"It's all set," Bethany says, rubbing her hands together as she en-

169

ters the room. "Oooo . . . you look hot, girl," she adds with a glimmer in her eyes.

Judd clears his throat and walks past her to the door with a look of annoyance on his face. *What did I do now?*

Bethany strides over to me, linking her arm with mine as if we are preparing to skip to the party together. As she pulls me past Judd, I force my eyes dead ahead. The click of the door closing and the subtle sounds of an extra pair of shoes hitting the floor, tells me that he is right behind us as we make our way out of the apartment complex.

Remaining arm in arm with Bethany, we walk across the parking lot to the community center, my skin tingling from his watchful eyes the whole way.

The building is jam packed with only a handful of people I know. *Geez, did Bethany invite the entire campus?* Only when my body gets swallowed up by the mass and I don't see Judd anywhere around, am I grateful for the crowd.

Abby and Piper find their way over to me, laughing and giggling with drinks already in hand. Abby hands me a shot and I gladly gulp it down, hoping the fiery liquid will erase all the thoughts swirling in my head.

A couple hours later, all my worries are washed away, I'm floating on air and have a smile that could give a clown a run for his money. I have probably had one too many shots, but Abby, Piper and several other people are knee deep in a game of quarters and taking me along for the ride.

While giggling and laughing from how bad I suck at this game, I tip another shot back and look past Abby, immediately finding Judd in the distance leaning against a wall, studying me. *Well shit, that's sobering!*

I look away quickly.

"I'm going to the bathroom," I mumble out with a hiccup.

"Well, don't be gone too long, because I have a surprise for you," Bethany calls out, sounding pretty blitzed herself.

I nod my head and stand up on jiggly legs that don't seem like they are getting the correct orders from my brain to hold me up. Teetering back and forth, I grab for the table as Abby bursts out laughing beside me.

"Oh, sis . . . you're hammered."

I put my hand over my mouth to hold back a sudden case of giggles, but it's too late. Bending at the waist and clutching my arms around my belly, I laugh so hard my body shakes and my abs are on fire. Although, my head is fuzzy and my vision is distorted, I can't remember the last time I had so much fun. Well, actually I can, but I choose to forget that for tonight.

Through blurred vision, I stagger to the bathroom with my eyes focused on not falling, but still glancing around periodically to make sure Judd is nowhere near.

I stumble into the restroom and make my way into the stall, losing my balance a couple times and nearly falling in. After flushing the toilet, I stammer to the sink and stare into the mirror. My face is plastered with makeup that I usually don't wear, my hair sticks out in a frizzy mess and my dress clings to my curves. I laugh to myself at how silly I am being.

"Good grief, Alyssa, move on. He has," I mumble, looking at the reflection of my glassy, bloodshot eyes.

Walking out, my feet continue to find speed bumps in the floor until I collide with the one person I am trying to avoid.

"Whoa! You ok?" Judd's fingertips slide around my waist, igniting a blast of goose bumps to blaze over my skin.

I rock backwards as his hands hold tight, steadying me, and I can't help but think of a time before; a time when he held me up.

With my hands on his chest, I close my eyes and try to regain some sense of stability. My eyes sweep upward from his strong, solid chest that had been my pillow night after night, and land on his face only inches away from mine. Nervousness churns in my stomach as my attention is averted to his lips. His tongue swipes across his bottom lip, leaving a trail of glistening moisture and an ache in my heart.

"I'm fine," I whisper as I ball my hands into fists and push off from him.

With this amount of alcohol in my system and the way his touch affects me, it's probably best if I keep my distance. There for a minute, I was prepared to lunge at him and swallow his face whole.

Clearly uncomfortable himself, Judd shoves his hands into his back pockets and looks at me as if I've wounded him.

"Alyssa, can we go outside and talk?" he asks me in a steady tone, but the tremble in his voice tells me that his heart may be pounding just as loudly as mine.

I start to give in and respond to the fluttering in my stomach when Bethany comes up behind us.

"Just the two I was looking for," she says in a sugary tone that is going to give me a toothache by the end of the night. *Does she time her interruptions or does she just have a sick sense for when he and I are talking?*

She puts her arm around my shoulder and pulls me in for a we're-drunk-and-besties kind of hug that I am not feeling at the moment.

"Ok, so I keep catching you two talking like you've known each other forever. So, spill! What are ya'll chatting about all the time?"

Judd's head cocks to one side and a small smile pulls at the corner of his lips. I know he is wondering if the alcohol will make me offer an explanation of our encounters, but I am sobering up as the minutes stretch by, especially with him so close. *Why hasn't he told her he knows me? I guess it may mess with his game; that's probably what he wants to talk to me about.*

So I decide to go with something general, "We were just discussing school and fall season football. You know, since him and Kyle both play."

Bethany breaks out in a fit of laughter, spraying beer out of her mouth.

"Wow! Why are you talking about school when you should be partying?" she cackles and then turns her sights on Judd. "You play football?"

I'm not sure if Bethany notices or not, but I don't miss the fact that Judd's eyes don't leave me.

"No . . . I don't play. I used to play." His answer comes in a cool and collected tone.

It's such a simple answer, but it causes my head to swim with questions. *Football meant so much to him. He had a full ride scholarship to UCLA. He talked about going pro someday; what had changed in such a short amount of time?* I wish I had the nerve to ask him why he never went to California. Every time I see him, I am so overcome with emotion that I forget all the questions I should be asking.

Judd keeps his expression serious and pinned on me, but the time to interrogate him disappears when the emcee announces that everyone needs to head to the parking lot.

Bethany grabs my arm and tugs me out the door, squealing and giggling, "Wait until you see your surprise! You're going to love it!"

As soon as we are out in front of the building, Bethany motions to the sky. I look up into complete darkness, searching. The earth feels as though it is spinning beneath me, but I keep my eyes glued to the black sky thinking maybe a comet or falling star may bleed into my vision soon.

All at once, bursts of color start exploding in the sky, then another and another
and another.

My heart falls into my stomach and I am immediately sober. Everyone is cheering and whooping and hollering around me. Bethany is jumping up and down like she is cheering at a winning game. A hand slides around my forearm and gently tugs at me, but I can't look away from the sky to respond.

"Alyssa, are you ok?" My sister's voice confirms who has a hold on me, more than likely offering me comfort over a thrilling event that is causing irrevocable damage to my heart.

"Do you like? It was Judd's suggestion. He had a whole bag of them left over from the fourth and since one of Kyle's frat brothers has an uncle on the police force, we got permission for a grand finale for your birthday bash!" Bethany yells above the noise.

My eyes widen when she says he suggested this.

"Oh shit!" The concern in Abby's voice tells me that I'm not the only one that understands the gravity of this situation.

I look a couple bodies away and see Judd. He isn't looking up to the sky like everyone else. His dark brown eyebrows knit together above his piercing eyes with a look I can barely describe. He doesn't look mad. It doesn't even look like he is on some mission to destroy my world. His face is etched in sadness and remorse, but underneath it all, I see what looks like a glimmer of hope.

With my eyes still on him, I draw in a calming breath and hope above all to gain some understanding of what is going on. Neither of our gazes waiver as the sparkles blast above. We are transfixed on each other and for an instant it is just him and I standing there, face to face. We are alone in a cabin, his body above mine as he whispers "I'm in love with you," but instead of saying those words, his lips part and he mouths "Happy birthday."

I want to say so much, but instead I offer a small smile and turn to excuse myself as the last of the fireworks light up the sky.

All is revealed

THURSDAY MORNING COMES WAY TOO soon and I know my back to back afternoon classes following my morning shift at work will leave me drained and exhausted. I'm grateful for a busy day to keep my mind occupied, but what I am not happy about is yet another pounding headache from staying out too late and drinking way more than I should have.

At this rate, I may become an alcoholic. I shouldn't indulge like that at all. If something would happen to Dad and I was intoxicated, I would never forgive myself for not being lucid.

My last class lets out at 4:15 and I am starving. Thursdays are jam packed for me so I hardly have time to eat. I usually shove a protein bar or something in my bag, but this morning my head was not screwed on straight so I left the apartment unprepared. Unfortunately, a stale donut from the break room at work was all that was left to tide me over for the day.

Inside my apartment, I throw my keys on the counter and fling the fridge open. Peering inside, I realize how much I have slacked on the upkeep around here lately. A nearly empty box of pizza, a jug of milk that has barely a swig in it and a few condiments stare back at me as my stomach growls. Gritting my teeth, I slam the fridge door and pull open the cabinets above the stove, hoping for something edible.

My phone rings from the counter, so I quickly abandon my search and drag myself across the room to see Bethany's name on the screen.

I might as well pick up. If I'm lucky, maybe she is going through a drive-thru on her way home. I'd kill for a burger right now.

"Hello."

"Hey girl, you out of class?"

She knows my schedule is hectic on Thursdays, which is why my party was thrown two days before my actual birthday. Usually, on Thursdays when my feet hit the door I am in my PJs and out for the night. Plus, given the fact that the community center is booked tonight and I will be at my parent's house tomorrow night, Wednesday worked out much better.

"Yeah, I just got home about ten minutes ago. Where are you?" Chattering and the clanking of cups and plates sound in the background, sending all my dreams of a cheeseburger, fries and shake landing in my lap, right out the window.

"I'm at work tonight, remember? I traded shifts so I could get off last night for your party."

Bethany works as a server at a bar and grill downtown, about four blocks away. "I was in such a hurry, I forgot my purse. Can you bring it down real quick?"

I sigh completely annoyed that I have to get back out.

"Ok, but you owe me. I am tired, cranky and starving," I snap out, pretending to be a little bit more irritated than I actually am by her request.

"Well then you're in luck, because I just so happen to know a place where you can score some good food. My treat when you get here?"

Music to my ears! My stomach growls in approval. "Ok, see you in a bit."

I promptly grab my purse along with Bethany's and head out the door. The parking lot of our complex is filling up quickly from whatever party is going on at the community center tonight. Bass booms even with the doors closed, so it must be well under way. If I leave, I bet I will have one hell of a time getting my spot back when I return, so I opt to walk.

Ten minutes and a short walk later, I slide into a barstool, toss Bethany's purse across the counter, and slam my hands to the hard surface of the bar, ready to eat. She nudges a plate of fries and a burger in front of me, sending my mouth into a salivating frenzy. I waste no time digging in.

I'm a quarter of the way from finishing my food and about to bust out of my jeans when Bethany brings up the dreaded subject of Judd. Of course, I can't get through a day without hearing about him. I stuff more food in my mouth so the sound of my chewing will drown her out, but then her words catch my attention.

" . . . so I am determined to get in that boys pants this weekend."

The last thing I want to hear about is her getting Judd in bed, but her words totally have me thinking that maybe she hasn't yet.

With that in mind, I decide to be bold, "So wait, do you mean you haven't slept with him?"

She raises her eyebrows and smiles like a school girl. *Oh great! Maybe I don't want to know the answer to this.*

"Oh well, yeah, we've slept . . . together." My heart drops, but then she goes on, "he slept and I slept . . . in the same bed . . . but unfortunately, that's it," she laughs while looking down at the bar as she wipes it off.

Relief washes over me as I run her words back through my mind just to make sure I heard her right. I'm not sure why this revelation makes me so happy; it doesn't change anything between him and I, but just that tidbit of information has my insides swarming with giddiness and makes me want to break out in song and dance.

"You never let me finish telling you about that night. He was so drunk. One of his friends was trying to hook us up, saying how he needed to get over his ex or something or other. Anyways, his friend helped him up to our apartment and then left. I managed to get most of his clothes off . . ."

This is when I should tune her out, but I keep listening, hoping to hear better news.

"I was so into him and ready for the night of my life and he yells that he is going to puke. So I spent most of the night fetching the trash can, glasses of water, aspirin and a washcloth from the bathroom. It would have made more sense for him to just sleep in the bathroom, but in the end he never did get sick."

And there is the good news I was hoping to hear. What would have made it better is if he would have actually vomited when she was pulling him out of his clothes.

"So I guess this ex did a number on him or something, because he is completely and totally emotionally unavailable. I mean, usually that doesn't bother me, but he says he would rather us just be friends. I don't intend on giving up though," Bethany says with a gleam in her eyes while she licks her lips.

I shove another fry in my mouth to keep from snarling at her.

"I think I am going to give him a call tomorrow night and see if he will come over. Then, I can . . ."

She goes on and on about her plans to break him down while I polish off the remainder of my plate and tune her out.

What ex? Maybe he got back together with someone from his past and that is why he never called. No, that couldn't be it. He said he focused too much on football and work to get involved with anyone in high school. Could it be possible that he didn't play me at all, but rather met someone when he returned home?

My mind is going a hundred miles an hour with scenarios and speculations. Any one of those would explain his lack of calling and the fact that he seems absolutely hell bent on getting my attention now. *Maybe he feels bad for not contacting me and feels the need to explain himself.* I push that out of my head for now and focus on heading back home.

As soon as I drag myself into the apartment, I shed my clothes and fling them over my head one by one on my trail to the bathroom. I adjust the temp before turning on the shower, carefully sticking my fingers under the spray of water to test it against my skin. A quick chill runs through me so I turn the hot water nozzle to heat it up.

Once my tired feet land on the wet shower floor, I let out a relaxing sigh and let the water soak over me, gently unraveling each knot in my body one by one.

I'm washing the last of the conditioner out of my hair when the bathroom door clicks open and then shut. My eyes widen in fear as I scan my surroundings, moving from the soap to my razor in search for an available weapon. *Bethany isn't supposed to get off till 1:00 in the morning, so who the hell is that?*

"Hello," my shaky, stuttering voice echoes in the small room as I grab a shampoo bottle and envision myself catapulting it at the intruder's head. "Bethany, is that you?" My voice comes out in a screech.

"No, it's me," Judd's smooth voice calls out in the same room as me.

What the hell! I rip the shower curtain to the side, careful to pull it against my body for cover.

"What the hell are you doing in here?!" I shriek in absolute shock.

He nonchalantly leans up against the counter, his arms folded across his chest and one foot swung on top of the other, in a lazy stance. Meanwhile, water is dripping down my body as I cling to the curtain to shield me from the grin that forms on his face and has me about to jump out of my skin.

"Well, I figured if I wanted to talk to you, my best bet was to catch you in a compromised position like this . . . that way you can't run." His lips quirk up as if he is trying to hold back laughter.

"Like hell I can't! I can leave if I want to!" I snap back, fully ready to storm out.

He smiles and pulls the bathroom door open slowly. "Really? Ok, leave then."

A blast of cool air sweeps across me and has goose bumps spreading over my legs and arms. Then again maybe it isn't the air at all.

His face breaks open into a full blown smirk as he waves his hand in front of him. I look down at my naked soaking wet body, covered by a thin sheet of vinyl and second guess my escape plan. *Ok, so maybe I won't bolt!* I clutch the curtain for dear life and level him with a firm glare.

"How did you get in here anyway?" I demand.

Judd keeps the grin painted on his face as he swings the door shut and casually leans one hand on the sink behind him and shoves the other in his pocket.

"I used a key Bethany loaned me."

Pulling his hand out of his pocket, he dangles it by his finger between us like a ball of yarn luring a cat into a trap, and of course, I take the bait. *What, now he has a key to our apartment?!*

I reach out and swipe my hand to grab it and nearly slip out from under the security of my shower curtain. Judd kicks his head back and snickers, clearly finding my reaction amusing.

"Why do you have a key and why are you in my bathroom? Do you mind?" I say sarcastically, trying to calm my nerves so he doesn't see how uneasy I am in his presence.

He lays the key on the counter behind him and then looks straight at me.

"I left my hat here and when I came to get it, I decided to leave you the brownie." He shrugs his shoulders after he reveals this tidbit of information.

I'm confused and curious and it must show on my face.

"I wanted you to know I still cared and that I still thought about you, even if it was too late," he reluctantly says in a much lower tone.

I stand up taller and feel that familiar flutter in my heart that only Judd can invoke within me.

"Why?" I breathe out in a barely audible whisper, and then raise my voice an octave, "Why? When all you did was play me? What . . . was Bethany not enough? Did you want . . . ?"

I stop talking, remembering what Bethany had told me about the ex he was not over. Then I take in the scowl on Judd's face. His body shifts and I can tell I hit a nerve.

"What the hell are you talking about? Played you? I never played you!" He steps forward only a foot away from me and clinches his fists to his side. "Lyssa, I told you I was in love with you. How do you figure I played you? It felt more like I was the one that was played! How do you think it felt to know I was just some summer rebound for you until you got back home to your boyfriend?"

My eyes widen and I let go of the curtain, pointing at his face.

"Wait just a minute! Rebound?! Kyle and I were over when I met you! Why would you think you were a rebound?!" My puzzlement starts to quickly flow into anger as this conversation moves forward.

Judd's eyes widen and he pushes my finger out of his face.

"I don't think that. I know I was!" His voice kicks up a notch and my adrenaline level rises as he goes on, "How long did you wait to go back to him? Was it the day you got back home or the next?"

I fold my arms across my bare chest, not even caring that I am standing in front of him stark ass naked.

"What!!" I spit out. "I never went back to him! Where did you get that idea! Just because he came to my apartment the night I saw you with Bethany! News flash, we ended almost three months ago when my life was falling apart and you were nowhere around! Did you expect me to sit around and wait for you to call this whole time?" My voice has elevated to a full out shrill.

Judd's face distorts to astonishment and this time he points his finger at me. "Don't give me that shit! When I called you, the guy that answered said he was your boyfriend. That was only four days after we left the lake. Four days!" he roars out with more venom than I have ever seen, yet my anger level muddles out as soon as he utters the words "when I called."

He called?

"You called?"

Judd lowers his finger and his expression softens.

"Yeah, I called. Four days after we left and a guy answered the phone saying he was your boyfriend and asking me who *I was*."

I look down at the bathroom floor and my mind races. *Four days . . . four days! What was going on four days after . . . ?* My mind comes to a dead stop and I stare directly at him.

"Four days after I got home, my dad told me his cancer was back," I breathe out in an unfamiliar voice with a million different emotions crashing down on me and burying me alive.

Judd's facial expression relaxes into a look of understanding and concern.

"I'm sorry, Lyssa. Bethany told me about your Dad. That's why I left the brownie the next day. I remembered you telling me that your mom made them when you were upset. I just figured it might make you smile and maybe . . ." His voice trails off and despite the fact that he brings up Bethany's name; my heartbeat speeds up at his compassion.

I can't believe he remembers that little detail from when we went fishing together.

That day, I had finally let my guard down and told him everything about my father's battle with cancer along with the tests that were weighing so heavily on my family's shoulders.

That day, I had made my mind up to completely trust him, open my heart and let him in.

That day, I fell in love.

He clears his throat and his tone is laced with sorrow. "I am sorry to hear about that and I wish I had gotten the chance to be there for you, but why . . ."

I decide to interrupt him. Something still isn't adding up. He called? He said he called that day.

"You said you called?"

He nods his head.

"But I never saw your number on my phone. And what guy?! There wasn't anyone that could have . . ." I stop midsentence as an image of Kyle sitting on my bed, holding my phone emerges in my mind.

Oh no! Kyle had my phone and I swore I had heard it ring when I was downstairs.

"I called from Evan's phone. Mine was crushed so I had to borrow his to call. I called as soon as I got out of surgery and was awake enough to think," he says weakly, looking me in the eyes.

Surgery? I struggle to breathe as I tumble his words around in my head.

He dips his chin down and steps forward to close some of the space between us. I can't look away from him. *I don't understand.*

"Lyssa," he pauses and a pained expression sweeps across his face. "Tristan and I had a wreck about an hour out from the lake. I was in the hospital for three weeks. I couldn't call you right away, because I was in and out of surgery, plus I wasn't even conscious. When I finally was able to, I called. I wanted you there so bad. You're all I've thought about."

My heart snaps in two and my eyes fill with water. The shower is still pounding against my side but the tears streaming down my face rival its current.

"I didn't know. I wish I would have known. Oh God . . . you were hurt!?" I half ask, half tell myself, trying to overcome the utter shock that is engulfing me.

My bottom lip trembles as I bite down on it and look at him through foggy eyes, feeling completely ashamed of thinking he was playing me all while he was laid up in a hospital bed. My mind rewinds to the morning I first saw him again; to the deep scars and marks that lined his shoulder and rib cage. In my selfishness, I hadn't even questioned them or the tattoo.

My body shudders with remorse as Judd reaches a hand up to brush away a tear slipping down my cheek. As soon as his soft touch grazes my skin, every ill feeling, every bit of anger and sadness I felt over him dissolves.

His brows are pulled together and his eyes sparkle with tenderness and devotion; with the same look I had seen so many times before. Pressing my cheek into his hand, I close my eyes and revel in his soft, gentle touch that I have missed for so long.

Still needing to explain some things, I open my eyes and meet his stare.

"I didn't know. And that day . . . it must have been Kyle. He came over to try and get me back, but I told him I had met someone and then my dad came home." I halt my rambling to catch my breath and I can see understanding in his eyes. "Dad needed to speak with us and I couldn't get rid of him. He waited for me and he must have answered my phone and felt threatened when he heard your voice. I promise you, I never . . ."

Judd's fingertips softly trace the edge of my face down to my lips, letting me know that he needs no further explanations.

"I get it. I believe you."

His lips curve up into a delicate smile and his warm hand runs back along my jaw into my wet hair as he steps forward to be closer. I grab the curtain, still not caring that I am bare but suddenly feeling light headed and dizzy from the rise of emotion within my heart. This whole situation got so heated and out of control over a misunderstanding and lack of information.

Judd's Adam's apple bobs as I hear him swallow. He straightens up his stance so that our bodies are only inches apart and separated only by the ledge of the tub. He drops his hand from my hair, both his arms dangling motionless at his sides. My body aches for his touch, but neither of us move.

"Do you still love me?" he asks quietly, yet I'm already prepared to shout out the answer for everyone to hear.

I don't even hesitate, "Yes! I love you!" I've never felt more strongly about anything else in my life.

Now that all is revealed, all the tension and confusion between us melts and it is like no time has passed. I look at him, knowing he still owns my heart. Judd's face lights up and he closes the remainder of distance between us.

Making up for lost time

OUR BODIES COLLIDE TOGETHER AND slam against the shower wall as water cascades over both of us. Water quickly seeps into every inch of Judd's jeans and long sleeve shirt, but he doesn't break away for even a moment. His hands dig into the flesh of my hips in a gentle, yet firm grip that has us both panting and our chests rising and falling rapidly against one another.

Whimpering at the sudden rush of electricity coursing through my body, I welcome his lips as they devour mine with so much fire and passion it could ignite a billion fireworks. A groan rumbles from his chest as his strong arms lock around my silhouette.

My hands are all over him all at once, reaching under the drenched fabric so I can touch his skin. I run my hands up his back into his hair, slowly wrapping my arms around his shoulders in an effort to get closer. Gripping my thighs in his hands, he swoops me off the ground and guides my legs around his hips.

After sliding one hand up the length of my leg, his hand squeezes at the skin of my ass as he presses me into the wall, locking us together.

His lips find their way from my mouth, to my jaw and down to the tender areas of my neck. I swallow gulps of air, trying to catch my breath, yet it is the sweetest feeling in the world. Tiny sucking noises have me shivering with desire as the wetness of his mouth glides across my neck back up to my mouth.

His other hand that is pressed to my back, supporting me, works its way up to my hairline. He pulls his face back just enough to look into my eyes.

"I love you, Alyssa. I couldn't stop thinking about you these past months. I missed you so much," he breathlessly says against my lips.

I can't form a single syllable!

A whimper escapes my lips at his words and that's about all the response I'm capable of giving at this point.

He pulls us away from the wall, still holding me in his arms and with his lips still attached to mine, he strains to reach down. The corner of my eyes catch him as he fumbles with the faucet to turn the water off and then steps over the ledge of the tub. Miraculously, nothing has slowed our hunger for each other. Once he has me pulled tighter into his arms with his hands braced at my ass, he stumbles through the bathroom and out the doorway. He never breaks our connection, keeping his lips firmly planted on mine while continuing on his path to my room. My arms hold so tight to him that I shudder from the pressure or maybe from wanting him so bad.

Once we fall onto my mattress, he quickly peels his wet shirt off and tosses it to the side. He kisses me down my neck and I see him struggling to fling off his shoe with the other foot. He looks at me frustrated; almost embarrassed.

"Hold on. Just one second," he says with a self-conscious smile that highlights his dimple.

Standing quickly, he kicks his shoes off in one swift motion, then proceeds to battle with his soaking wet jeans, tugging and shifting his hips.

I'm so nervous, so excited and so happy that it's making me giddy with anticipation. A loud giggle vibrates through my chest and out my mouth right as Judd peels them off completely.

Looking at me with a slight grin, he slides his body back over mine, sending tingles of excitement through me.

He places his face in my neck, tickling my skin with his breaths as he chuckles. I laugh at his reaction as he pulls his head up to look into my eyes. His face reflects all the love I feel in my heart. My eyes snap down to his lips as he smiles and laughs; I can't stop staring. *God, I missed his smile. I missed that adorable dimple.*

"And here you thought I was a player. I can't even manage to be smooth with you."

A bubble of laughter bursts from my mouth and I squish my head back into the soft pillow as visions of our first time surface in my mind. *He was so embarrassed that time and now he gets stuck in his wet jeans!*

I softly kiss his lips and speak from my heart, "You're smooth enough for me." He is everything.

My hand runs along the slight stubble of his jaw, over his cheek and around the slight dip from his dimple as he smiles. I circle my fingertip causing it to deepen and then his lips are back on mine.

We don't hold back and this time, there is no waiting for the perfect moment or ideal place. He is here and we love each other; it doesn't get any more perfect than that.

Our bodies move in a perfect rhythm with one another. What started out as desperation and need turns into tenderness and passion.

He handles me so carefully, keeping his movement slow and steady. His mouth roams my skin licking and tasting like a man that has been starved for months. I run my hands over his skin, letting my fingertips memorize the curves of every muscle, the rigidness of each scar along his rib cage and then down to the v's in his hips.

I continue my path up and down his body, listening to his breath pick up with every touch. His hands and lips work their own magic as sensations build and build inside me, making my thighs quiver and my stomach swirl and tighten.

Right as I am spinning out of control, he whispers into my ear through heavy breaths, "I love you."

"Juuuuddd," I call out in a breathy whimper as bolts of electricity shoot through my body, making my center pulsate and my breathing come in quick spurts.

His muscles tense and his movements slow as a deep moan escapes his lips. He collapses against my neck and tenderly kisses my skin between breaths. My fingers wisp through each lock of his thick brown hair as I try to calm the passion that is still ignited within me. *I can't get enough of him. I want more of him; I need more of him!* My chest expands in a deep deliberate breath and then I slowly let it out.

Judd slides down to rest his chin on my chest as he stares at me with contentment in his eyes and a sweet smile. My heart swells and my eyes water with so much happiness that another tear escapes.

"Hey, don't cry. I'm here now," he whispers so gently.

He knows I'm not sad; he knows exactly what I am feeling, because he is feeling it, too.

"I thought I had lost you forever." My voice cracks as it dawns on me that all the pain and hurt from losing him is behind us.

He scoots his body up so that he is hovering above me and looking into my eyes.

"You never lost me. Didn't I tell you that it wasn't goodbye forever?"

I smile, remembering his words the morning that he left.

We hold each other for a long while, lost in the reality that we are together again. *I still can't believe it.* Not even a minute is allowed to pass by before he is whispering "I love you" or "I missed you" and each time, my heart melts a little more.

Finally, I slip something on, gather his heavy wet clothes into my arms and run them to the dryer down the hall.

Once I'm out of Judd's sight, my feet tread carpet like it is on fire so that I don't miss more than a second with him. When I return, his bare body is still lying comfortably in my bed with a smile on his face and the sheet strategically placed, making me want to rip it off. My hand inches up to my opposite forearm and I pinch a small amount of skin between my fingertips just to make sure this is not a dream. Hooking his finger in front of him, he wiggles his eyebrows playfully, beckoning me back to bed.

My knees sink into the mattress as I crawl in beside him and then decide to bring up the tough subjects that will need to be talked about. As I lean my body across his chest, I carefully run my hand over the deep scar on his rib cage that I had seen the other morning along with the one on his shoulder.

"What happened?"

He shivers from my touch and his face changes to a serious expression.

"Tristan was in a foul mood and we ended up getting into a heated discussion. He got distracted for a minute and rounded a corner too fast. We flipped and I was thrown from the car."

My body shudders when he says the word 'flip' and my adrenaline races when I imagine the pain he must have experienced. *I wasn't there with him; I should have been there with him.*

"I was in and out of it for the first couple days. I came to after three days and multiple surgeries, but I was too exhausted to even think until the next day. It felt like I had every injury under the sun, including a piece of metal that had lodged itself only a hair away from puncturing my lungs." Judd looks at me and smiles, running his hand across my cheek as my eyes once again begin to tear up. "It was bad, but it could have always been worse; I'm alive."

As if my heart wasn't flying enough from the exhilaration of this night, those few words completely sweep me away and make me fall deeper in love with him. *It could have been worse! That's something Dad would say.*

At that moment, a bold thought enters my mind and I refuse to ignore it, "I am going home tomorrow. Would you come with me?"

Judd wiggles around beneath me nervously with a huge grin on his face. He suddenly flips me over and presses his hard body against mine, with a devilish smile on his face.

"Are you asking me to meet your parents?"

I laugh. "I guess I am," I tease back. "I guess it's kind of sudden to ask you that, but I think they would really like you."

His fingers lightly stroke my cheek as he searches my face from my eyes to my lips and back up again, as if he is committing every detail to memory.

"Not really. You know, it wasn't really the physical part of our relationship that I missed as much as the way we talk. How we can talk all day and never run out of things to say. It's so easy being with you; so right; like my life has never been without you. I love when you talk about your parents and sisters. So meeting your family doesn't feel sudden to me at all. It actually feels like I already know them."

His slow caress along my face and honesty sends shivers through my body. All I can do is stare into his beautiful hazel eyes. His seriousness fades to a playful grin as he shifts a little above me to get comfortable.

"So my answer is yes. I will definitely come with you to your parents."

His answer has my heart bouncing with happiness as I throw my arms around him and squish him in an over-powering hug.

He laughs and counters my hug with a slow, warm kiss that sends electric surges straight down to my toes.

We hold each other and talk half the night away from his car wreck to Dad's sickness. When I ask about Tristan, worried that he was injured in the car wreck as well, Judd explains how he himself doesn't know much about the details of Tristan's injuries and then he quickly diverts the conversation.

Once we get to the topic of Dad's news this past week, he holds me close with assurances that I will not face this alone. Caught up in thinking about my father, I tell Judd story after story and he listens to every word.

As the seriousness of our conversation starts to wind down, he runs his hand over my cheek to catch a few fallen tears and gives me a look that says just how much he loves me. I have no doubt that he will be here for me and that has me finally being able to come up for air.

Somehow the topic changes to when we met and my somber mood quickly changes.

". . . . I almost dropped the mirror when I saw you in that bikini. I really shouldn't have been doing all that work alone, but I wanted to get it done and go see you," he admits, making me giggle from the memory. "Oh and when you were cleaning the shower stalls . . . Geez!" His eyes dance with excitement as he pulls me closer.

My stomach bounces with laughter and butterflies. *He never had me fooled; I knew he was enjoying the view.*

"Oh, I know." I press my lips together to stifle the huge smile that is itching at the corners of my mouth. "I think I was about to pass out the first day I saw you. Here, I step out of the van and there you are . . . no shirt, all sweaty and flexing." I roll my eyes dramatically and let out an exaggerated breath.

"I was not flexing," Judd laughs and moves in, snug against me.

"Oh, you were in my mind. Then my mind proceeded to strip you down one layer at a time."

Covering my mouth with my hand, I burst with laughter while Judd stares at me. His eyes flood with adoration and love, as a small smile ticks at his lips.

"Hey, Happy Birthday," Judd softly says before laying a peck at the corner of my mouth.

"Thank you, but my birthday isn't until tomorrow," I correct him between laughs as I lean my head sideways to look at the clock on my nightstand. "Holy crap!" I flinch and look at Judd a bit alarmed.

It's after midnight.

Judd leans back to a sitting position.

"What's wrong?"

Of all the things we discussed tonight we never breached the subject of Bethany. She will have a conniption fit if she sees us together, considering she doesn't know that I already knew Judd.

"Well . . . it's just that . . . Bethany really likes you." I look at him, trying to think of a way to explain this.

She is my best friend and to her this would be an act of betrayal.

"Yeah and so? I love you, not her. I've never been with her. . . . *ever.*"

I sigh, not quite sure I can clarify how this may look to her. "I know you do and I love you, too, but she is really into you and since I never told her I knew you, it will seem like I made a move on her boyfriend."

Judd's eyes widen in surprise.

"I was never going out with her. I told her I just wanted to be friends and that is all she's ever been; a friend. Besides, technically you're still my girlfriend, because we never officially broke up." He smiles with the last line and my heart skips a beat before getting back to the topic at hand.

"No, no . . . I know that. She told me that, but she was still dead set on getting with you."

Judd shakes his head.

"Maybe we should just tell her about us and this summer," he suggests and although I agree with him totally, part of me is selfish and just wants this perfect night to remain ours without her drama; and there will be drama once she finds out, no matter the reasoning.

"I agree and I will, but for now, I don't think she should come home and find us together. Either way, it will hurt her, plus I think seeing us lying in bed together would be a bad way to break this to anyone."

Judd's eyes narrow in confusion as if I said something that caught him off guard. "You want me to just leave?"

I take in a deep breath and quickly divert him from that thought.

"No, I mean, maybe we could go somewhere else . . . together."

His mouth crooks to the side in a sly grin and then he stands up, grabbing my hand to pull me up.

"Let's go stay at my apartment. We can leave for your parents in the morning and then tell her later."

I smile and give him a quick kiss before running off to get his clothes from the dryer.

Once I am back, Judd throws them on, looking eager to get to his apartment. "Do you need to pack for your parents?"

"Shoot, yeah, I almost forgot." I bolt over to my dresser and point to my bed. "Can you grab my bag from under the bed?" My stress level is elevating as the clock ticks closer to 1:00am, so I throw random clothes in my bag as fast as possible.

As I shove a pair of flannel PJ's on top, his warm arms snake around my waist and he pushes my hair away from my neck, tickling me with his breaths.

"I don't think you'll need those for tonight."

My pulse rate kicks up with that comment as he slings my bag over his shoulder and leads me away from the dresser by the hand.

We rush down to the parking lot where he has parked out in front of the building and I scan the lot nervously.

When he opens the door of his truck, my mind instantly diverts to the last time I was in here with him. It was the night he asked me to be his girlfriend. My body tingles as I climb in with him right behind me. Before he puts the key in the ignition, he flips the center console up and instructs me to sit right beside him by slapping the seat. I happily obey and scoot over with the warmth of his body immediately heating me up like a furnace.

He must feel the energy passing between us as well. Out of nowhere, Judd pulls me closer and his mouth closes in on mine, his tongue softly caressing my own.

We stay wrapped up together, heat building in my core as he pulls me into his lap between him and the steering wheel. My hands find his face and I kiss him wildly, lit up with the same frenzy I always have when I'm with him. I move my hips towards him, instantly feeling the excitement within him. I want him and I don't even want to wait. His hands run down my back and our bodies melt together.

A headlight flashes into the truck and douses the blazing fire between us. We both look over to see cars spilling out of the parking lot. The party at the community center must be over.

Judd breaks the silence, "We better go before she gets home. Besides, I'd rather have you to myself rather than putting on a show for everyone that passes by."

Unable to help myself, I brush my lips against his one last time before scooting to my side of the seat. From the corner of my eyes, a shadow in the doorway of the apartment complex catches my attention. I snap my head back around sure that I will see Bethany, but only see an empty door frame. Shaking my head, I push away the thoughts of her finding out about my summer this way while Judd puts the truck in gear and drives away.

It's a short drive from my apartment to his. The whole way, I lay my head against his shoulder, breathing in the intoxicating smell of his skin. Like magnets, his fingers naturally slide between mine and he keeps a firm grip the entire way. My eyes watch the road briefly before they turn back to his face, allowing me to marvel at the fact that he is right here beside me at last. I only wish I could erase the last several months that we were apart.

Keeping my eyes glued to his face, I study all his perfect features: from his sharp jaw and the slight shadow of stubble on his chin, to his long eyelashes that surround his flawless hazel eyes up to his soft brown hair that is just long enough for me to comb my fingers through. His lips curve into a gorgeous smile, highlighting the dimple in his right cheek and I know he can tell I am watching him. *I missed that dimple.*

Judd slides the truck into park, we scurry out and up the stairs to his door in record time.

Before we even make it inside, he pins me against the door with his body. His lips attack my mouth with a longing and need so strong that I can barely contain myself. After fumbling with the keys, he gets the door open and in one swift movement he has me up in his arms. I'm not paying attention to anything except him; the way his hands hold me steady, the caress of his tongue against mine, the way his heart drums in his chest and the sound of his rapid breaths.

My back falls onto something soft and Judd rises back up, pulling his shirt over his head. He looks at me with a playful gleam in his eyes. His fingers slowly ease down to the snap of his jeans and he wiggles his eyebrows up and down.

I giggle and sit up, hoping for a show. He nods his head, clearly reading my mind and then proceeds to shove his shoes and jeans off. My eyes follow a path down his chest to his chiseled abs, on to the deep v along the edge of his hips and then to the obvious sign that he is just as hot and bothered as I am. This is definitely a sight I could get used to. I slowly trail my eyes back up his body and return my gaze to his.

His mouth quirks to the side as he points to me, motioning his finger up and down. "Your turn."

I burst out laughing.

Bouncing up onto my feet in the center of the bed, I crisscross my arms to grab the hem of my shirt. I take a deep breath and see Judd do the same. His smile is gone and he stares at my hands in anticipation. Wanting to make this show as entertaining as possible, I sway my hips side to side, slowly pulling my shirt up and pausing every so often to prolong his torture.

Once the shirt is over my head, I throw it to the side. My hands immediately go to the front clasp on my bra and his eyes lower into a sexy glare. I take two steps towards him, trying not to get my feet tangled in the sheets as I move and continue to sway to the silent music playing in my head.

Judd places his hands at my waist and looks up at me as I drop my bra to my feet. I have every intention to continue my seductive dance for him, but his fingers move to unfasten my jeans before I can. The rough denim brushes over my thighs as he slides them off and then gently nudges me backwards to lie on the bed.

Like fire burning out of control, goose bumps spread over my skin as his fingers hook under the edges of my panties. As if they have a mind of their own, my hips rise off the bed allowing him to glide them down my legs.

Finally, after ditching his boxers, his warm body covers me in an instant and has me hungry for his touch. Trailing a path down my neck and over the entire length of my body, his moist lips taste every inch of my exposed skin while his hands work their own magic. Mocking his actions, I glide my fingers up his back feeling each dip and curve of his muscles, but unable to touch him enough to quench my desire. He leans up and looks at me.

"I love you," he whispers right as the door flies open.

"Hey man, are you asleep? I need to talk . . ."

Judd pulls the sheet up and over our bodies within seconds.

"Damn it, Evan! Could you knock?" Judd hisses over his shoulder.

My face is buried under the pile of sheets, but cool air on my legs tells me that he may not have gotten us fully covered.

"Hey, it's about time. Hell, I thought you were going to join a monastery and take a vow of celibacy. Good to see you're finally moving on."

Evan's words do something to my heart, knowing that this whole time I have weighed so heavily on Judd's mind. I push the sheet down to my chin and peek out, letting my presence be known. Evan's eyes widen and a full blown smile spreads across his face. He raises his eyebrows and looks from Judd to me and then back.

"Well, cool . . . you got her. Way to go." He looks back at me and drops his smile. "I was just kidding about the whole moving on comment," he says while comfortably leaning back against the wall.

For a minute, I think he is going to just come right in and have a seat.

"Get out, Evan!" Judd yells waving his hand back behind him and this time he sounds completely serious.

"Oh yeah, I guess you guys are busy, huh?"

I nod my head, nearly unable to suppress my laughter as Evan continues to get under Judd's skin.

"Yes, we are! Would you leave?" Judd blows out a frustrated breath but then he suddenly looks like he may laugh.

"No problem." Evan gets the door halfway shut and then slips his head back inside. We both look up at him and I can't stop myself from giggling. "So, are you guys going to be making lots of noise?"

I squeeze my eyes shut remembering how Evan got to experience our noise level first hand back at the shower house at the Lake.

"Yes, we are! Leave!" Judd hollers with a smirk on his face.

"Ok, I'll go take a drive for an hour or so. You guys have fun; go nuts, get crazy," Evan says, shaking his fist in the air like he is rooting us on.

Finally, he shuts the door and Judd swings his gaze around to me. He shakes his head and laughs.

"Oh yeah, I forgot to tell you that Evan is my roommate."

I laugh along with him. "Well, it just wouldn't be normal if he wasn't included in this reunion," I laugh harder as Judd's face shifts to a mischievous grin.

"Are you staying the night?" he says in a husky tone.

"I don't have my car with me so I guess I'm your hostage for the night," I tease, knowing very well that there is nowhere else I would rather be.

Judd leans in and starts placing slow, intimate kisses from my neck to the corner of my mouth as he says, "Then, he is going to be real disappointed when he gets back in an hour, because I don't plan to let you get any sleep tonight."

I laugh between breathless kisses, because I know it's the truth.

Tonight, I am fully prepared to make up for lost time.

Home for the weekend

AFTER AN EVENTFUL NIGHT FILLED with breathless kisses, whispers of love, heart stopping pleasure and definitely no sleep, Judd wakes me in the best way ever.

Not even ten minutes after I catch my breath from the amazing things that he can do with his tongue, he whisks me away to the shower. Although I think Judd would prefer to spend the day glued to each other under the spray of the water, we eventually get cleaned up and get on our way to my parent's house.

On the trip there, I sit as close to him as I possibly can while he grips my hand, rubbing tiny gentle circles into my skin with his thumb. We both sneak goofy grins at each other and I shiver every time his dimple appears on his cheek. *I missed the sight of that.*

How did I survive this long without him? I swear there is a direct link from him to my happiness. The last few months I felt like I was going through the motions; just passing one day to the next. Now, I feel alive; on fire; like I am a bird soaring above the clouds.

He squeezes my hand and smiles over at me, his green eyes sparkling with love and I know he feels the same thing I do.

As we merge onto the interstate, I decide to send Abby a quick text.

**Me: Hey Abs! I'm on my way but I am bringing company . . .
. . . .**

I grip the phone in my hand, anxious to hear back from her, because I know she will more than likely want an explanation.

Abby: ?????

I sigh when she instantly texts me back. *Do I just say his name or do I go into details of what happened?* Last I told her, he was with Bethany; at least that is what I had thought.

Me: I'm bringing Judd.

I decide to go with a more shocking confession of my guest and just lay it all out there. Gritting my teeth, I watch the phone feeling as though time is moving in slow motion.

Abby: WTH! Are you joking!?

Bringing Judd home to meet my parents, at first, seemed like a crazy move and I have actually been nervous since the idea spilled out of my mouth, but the closer we get, the more excited I am.

Me: Ok, calm down! He and I finally talked and it was all a big misunderstanding. I'll talk to you later about it but please, just be happy for me. I love him and always have, you know that!

Abby: I know you love him and I trust your judgment, but even if it is ok between you 2 now . . . isn't it kind of sudden bringing him home? I mean with everything going on, do you think it is a good idea?

I don't even have to think about the reasons I want him to come home. I want my dad to meet him sooner rather than later; while he is still himself. There is no way for me to know where this thing between Judd and I will lead, but I do know that I am absolutely freaking crazy in love with him and I truly believe he is head over heels for me, too. So, if there is a chance that this is my forever, I want him to know my dad.

Me: That's the point, Abby. I want him to meet Dad. I really do! Honestly, the whole thing was a big misunderstanding that will take me forever to explain, but I really want him with me. We've already missed so much time. Be happy for me! Please. :)

Abby: I am happy for you, Lyssi-B!! And I get it! I think Mom and Dad will love him. I love you and I am so glad you found each other again! I can't wait to hear the details!

Me: Yay!! I love you! Well get ready, we'll be there in less than 20 minutes. Tell Mom and Dad. C u in a bit!!

Abby: Lol! I will! <3 U

Nineteen minutes later, my parents greet Judd with open arms, but Abby still seems a bit skeptical. *I really should fill her in.*

After catching her snippy tone when she greets him, I quickly pull her aside to explain things. "Abby, it was a big misunderstanding. He was in a wreck this summer and wasn't able to call." Her eyes widen with my words as I go on, "Then when he did call, Kyle intervened . . ." I stop talking and raise my eyebrows, peering over Abby's shoulder to see Judd speaking to my parents.

Holy crap . . . I abandoned him before I even introduced him. I cannot believe I did that!

Right then, I lock eyes with Mom as she squeezes Judd in a tight hug that I am sure has him about to run for the hills. As she hugs him, she gives me a not so casual wink of approval.

Blush creeps up and burns my cheeks when I become conscious of all that I shared with her last weekend. I quickly cover my face with my hands to steer off the embarrassment. *Oh Dear Lord! I told her some very personal things about our relationship. I even went into detail of how spellbound I was by his abs and toned arms when I first saw him.*

"Alyssa," Abby calls breaking me out of my mortifying trance. "Was Tristan hurt, too?"

Her question catches me off guard, but then I look over at Mom practically flagging me down with a secondary grin and a thumbs-up that tells me that she approves and is more than likely remembering my story word for word now. *Oh great!* Let's hope she didn't share all that with Dad.

Abby waves me off laughing as I watch Dad give Judd a firm hand shake and then lean forward to say something to him. I cannot make out the words but from Judd's intense stare and sudden stillness, it looks as if it makes him a little uneasy. As soon as it dawns on me to worry, they both break into a smile. Dad closes the introduction with a firm hug that surprises me and brings a wide grin to Judd's face.

My guess is that it has been a while since he has had a parent wrap their arms around him, but I could be wrong. The topic of Judd's parents seems touchy and a little closed off so we have yet to discuss that; I'm hoping eventually he will open up and talk about it. I'd be lying if I said I wasn't extremely curious, though. Whatever the issue is with his parents, it's a shame. They have one hell of a son that they should be proud of.

It's nearly dinnertime and we are all gathered in the kitchen. Dad seems somewhat weak, but is still managing to get around.

"Do you need some help, Mom?" I ask at the doorway of the kitchen with Judd holding my hand tightly.

"No, sweetie. You and Judd take a load off. We have it taken care of," Mom answers back then turns her attention to Dad, who is working his way to the back patio door.

"I've got the grill going already, honey," Mom calls out as Dad unlocks the back sliding door. "I was just going to throw the steaks on there while the rolls and casserole cook in the oven."

"I can do it." Dad smiles, turning to go around the breakfast bar.

Abby stands at the stove with Mom, greasing a pan for the potato casserole while Judd and I sit at the kitchen table. We soak up each other's company and watch as Dad grabs the back of each barstool for support. I look past Dad, assuming he is headed to grab the plate of steaks on the counter, but right when I'm about to open my mouth and dart out of my seat to help, Judd beats me to it.

"I can get those." He rounds the bar and pulls the plate into his hands along with a bag of corn on the cob. "Do these get grilled, too?"

I settle myself back in my chair, watching as Judd so effortlessly fits right in with my family.

"I was just going to boil them. Are they good grilled? I've never made them that way," Mom asks as she pauses in her stirring to wipe her hands on a towel.

"Oh yeah, Tristan . . . ahh, my brother, makes them like that all the time. You just grill them up husk and all." He looks at my mom with excitement in his eyes, like a kid learning to ride a bike for the first time.

Glancing over to Dad who is still resting behind one of the bar stools, he adds, "I'll come out and help you with the meat and we can grill these up, too."

Dad smiles and then they both stroll out to the backyard. Judd flashes me a huge grin as he turns to slide the door closed. *I'm so glad I asked him to come.*

After the door is shut, I move a couple chairs over so that I have a perfect view of the back patio. My heart fills with so much warmth as I watch Judd and my dad together. After Judd gets everything piled on, he takes a seat with my dad at the outdoor dining table.

Abby comes up behind me and leans down to wrap her arms around the back of my shoulders.

"Aren't you afraid Daddy is going to scare him off with 'the talk'?" She laughs and I roll my eyes.

A loud laugh comes from Mom's direction and we both turn to look at what has her so tickled.

"Oh girls, you don't have to worry about that. He already breached that topic when he asked him if he was going to need his shot gun." She laughs harder and my mouth drops open from shock.

"Is that what he said to him when we first got here?"

I knew Dad had said something that brought a certain level of concern to Judd's face earlier but it was quickly snuffed out and Dad had laughed. *He must have been teasing him.* Mom notices my look of terror and laughs even harder.

"Oh relax," she scolds me in a playful tone. "Once he saw how alarmed Judd was, he told him he was kidding."

I let out a breath I didn't know I was holding and look back out the patio door to Dad and him. *Maybe I should worry.* Dad may be even more protective now that he knows he won't be able to take care of me forever. I cringe at that thought, but then the ache in my heart fades away when I see him and Judd talking and carrying on.

"I wouldn't worry about him threatening a shot gun. I would worry about him approaching the topic of the birds and the bees with Judd. How embarrassing would that be?" Abby adds and then walks over to Mom, who has a devious smile on her face.

I look between her and all that is going on outside, not 100% sure I shouldn't crash their good time and break up any humiliating subjects they may gravitate towards.

"Don't worry about that either," Mom says.

Abby laughs and looks at me. I'm sure my eyes are about to pop out of my head.

"Calm down," Mom insists, "Your Dad and I trust you."

She levels me with a serious expression and with that one look I fear that instead of Judd having to endure this topic, it seems that my conversation is veering in that exact vicinity. *Just great.*

"We trust you and besides you're nineteen. You're an adult and we believe that you are fully capable of making wise decisions."

I sigh, relieved that this conversation took a turn before it reached a mortifying point.

But then in true Mom fashion, she decides to go there, "You are using some type of birth control, right?"

She raises her eyebrows with a small smile touching the delicate features of her face.

I look past her and see Abby bent at the waist, silently laughing with her arms clutching her stomach. *Oh she thinks this is funny, does she?!*

"Of course, Mom, Abby took me to the clinic when I was fifteen to get on birth control. She didn't want to get on the pill without someone else, so she took her *little sister* along for the ride."

All amusement drains from Abby's face as she stands up straight with her mouth drawn open.

Once Mom turns to glare at her, I stick my tongue out at my sister with a small gratifying smile tugging at the corners of my lips.

"Not what I was expecting but ok then," Mom says in an exasperated tone while scowling at Abby.

I hold my laughter in, although, I want to roar from the look on Abby's face. *How's that for shock value?*

"I don't exactly approve of the ages you chose to make these decisions, but either way you both are adults now," Mom says, looking between Abby and I.

My stomach hurts from trying not to laugh. Abby crosses her eyes and sticks her own tongue out when Mom looks back at me. I can't hold it in any longer and we all break out into a fit of laughter, Mom included.

The glass door slides open and Judd and Dad step inside, looking around at the disorder unfolding in the kitchen.

"What's so funny?" Dad says on a chuckle.

I grit my teeth, silently pleading that Mom does not answer. *Mortification does not even touch what I would feel discussing birth control methods with my dad.*

After discarding the plate piled high with steaks and corn onto the counter, Judd steps in behind me and places his hand on the small of my back. I lean back in an effort to get as close as possible. Just this little contact is like paddle boards to my heart, sending it into a frenzy of heavy thuds and drums deep in my chest.

We all sit down for dinner and listen as Judd and Dad brag about their skills on the grill. They get along and cut up just like two high school friends that ran into each other after years of being apart. Our conversations flow from one topic to the next and after hearing Judd's deep voice joined in, I realize my parents treat him as if he is just another member of our family.

It doesn't take long for the evening to tick by.

"Well I guess we are going to hit the hay," Dad announces, standing to give me a hug.

I kiss Dad good night and try to hide my own yawn. I'm exhausted and depleted of all energy, but even as fatigue claws its way into my body, I have to smile at the reasons behind it.

Mom nudges Judd and I up the stairs towards my room after we all exit the kitchen.

"I'll be to bed in a minute. I'm just going to help them get settled." Mom tells Dad as we make our way up the stairs. *Wonderful, are we in for a lecture about no sex under their roof?*

Once we get to the top of the stairwell, Mom leads me by the elbow to their old room and opens the door.

Looking around, I am stunned to see that the room has been transformed into a cozy guest room that you would expect to find in a quaint Bed and Breakfast somewhere. All the details that she has put into it, tells me that she has been trying to keep her mind occupied and it makes my heart ache.

In complete awe, I walk in with Judd a little ways behind me and Mom. As my hand runs over the raised stitching of the embroidered comforter, I smile at all the hard work and effort that Mom put into making it. I had seen her working on each piece of this quilt through the summer while sitting with Dad. She carefully stitched tiny petals and leaves on each flower and quilted a beautiful lattice design between each block.

My eyes wander the room and take in the hand sewn curtains on the window, the crocheted lace runner hanging across the center of the dresser and then at last, my eyes fall on the wrought iron corner shelf. It displays a rickety wooden birdhouse Dad, Abby and I made when he was first diagnosed with cancer. It was a trial before we made the one that now adorns the corner of the front yard.

The next shelf down holds a clay ashtray that Abby made Dad back in grade school even though no one in our family has ever smoked. My eyes continue its search down each level of the shelf and I see a wooden box Andrea made Dad for Father's Day when she must have been about twelve.

Then on the last shelf sits a small tower of four blocks of wood messily screwed and nailed together then colored on with crayon. On the edge of each block are all of our names.

That was the first masterpiece I ever worked on with Dad in the garage. I was only five so he helped me swing the hammer and hold the screw gun. I had been so proud of putting those scraps together that I insisted on putting my name on the very top block and showing it off to my sisters.

Later that night, Abby had taken it from me and wrote her name on another one of the blocks. I was so upset that she had ruined my artwork, but Dad had settled the fight by calling Andrea out of her room, giving her a crayon and instructing her to write her name on the next block.

He had told me that it signified the way our family had been built and then he turned the tower around to face him, scribbling something on the bottom block with absolute determination in his eyes. Flipping it back around, he pointed to the bottom block where he had neatly wrote 'Alex loves Angela.'

"First it was just your Mom and I, but as the years went by we added more blocks until we were a family." I recall his words and then hear my tiny, squeaky voice reply back, "Daddy, I want you to have my tower since you started it, but promise you'll keep it forever," just like it was yesterday his voice rings in my ears, "I promise." My eyes glaze over with emotion.

"Mom, it's beautiful. You did such a good job decorating it." I gulp down the emotion that is overwhelming me and point to the shelf.

Mom beams with pride as she looks in the same direction.

"I can't believe he kept all of these," I say to her as she gives me a quick hug.

"Of course, he kept them. He cherishes anything you girls give to him. He is as sentimental as they come. He still has the boutonniere I gave him for our very first high school dance." She smiles so brightly, looking off in the distance as if revisiting a lovely memory.

She clears her throat and turns to Judd, who uncomfortably shifts from foot to foot as if he is intruding in on a private moment. She reaches her hand out, grabbing his arm and pulls him closer to us.

"Ok, so here's the deal."

Oh no, this is it. She is going to embarrass me.

"So, I know you two probably stay at each other's apartments and all. I'm not so old that I don't remember being your age, but . . ." I look over at Judd and grit my teeth and he just responds with a nervous grin. " . . . I would like you two to stay in separate rooms while you are in our house."

I look at Mom and nod in agreement. *That wasn't so bad after all.*

Mom gives Judd a huge hug and then kisses my cheek. She heads to the door, but then spins to face us at the last minute.

"So . . . no hanky-panky while you're under this roof."

Wow and she really went there again. She's on a roll.

My mouth is hanging open and I am sure Judd's jaw has dropped to the floor as well, only I'm too self-conscious to look.

Mom laughs at our reactions, turns and grabs the door to close it.

For a moment, I am confused at this. The no hanky-panky speech is not jiving with the fact that she is about to leave two horny nineteen year olds in a room behind a closed door.

Pausing before stepping out, she adds, "Now visit as long as you want before lights out, but no funny business." She covers her mouth to hide a giggle before going on, "But, if by chance, you two would lose track of time and fall asleep in the same room, it would just be our little secret. Night, kiddos."

Mom gives us a playful wink.

"Ahh . . . good night," Judd quietly stutters in a baffled tone.

Yep, I think she definitely remembers being my age. I sigh as the door clicks shut.

The night gets away from us and just like Mom had suggested *or warned,* we do lose track of time and we do wind up falling asleep together, wrapped in each other's arms. Thankfully, sleep deprivation keeps us from breaking Mom's rule. We crash for the night and sleep clear into late Saturday morning.

I wake up before Judd and slither out from beneath his arms. As soon as I move, he clutches for me but then settles back into a blissful sleep, embracing the comforter in his arms as if it were me.

Sitting on the edge of the bed, I take a minute to admire the way his dark brown hair flips up around his ears; the way his dark eyelashes rest on his cheeks, and the way his breathing comes at a steady tempo that I could listen to for the rest of my life.

He lowers his eyebrows into a painful expression and I can't help but wonder what he is dreaming of. I stay by his side for a few more moments, marveling at his perfection and eventually make my way downstairs.

I spend most of the morning with Dad while Abby and Mom play around with new recipes in the kitchen. Dad appears to be doing well, although I quickly notice that his energy is depleting so much faster than it was last week.

Shortly after lunch, Dad exhaustedly disappears into his room for a nap. Sneaking in his room afterwards, I lie beside him and watch as he breathes in and out, already in a deep sleep.

A bit later the sound of fabric rustling in the doorway catches my attention. With my feet hoisted up on the bed alongside Dad and my back wedged against the hard wooden headboard, I pivot my neck and see Judd casually leaning against the doorway, arms folded with an unreadable look on his face.

The sight of him instantly makes me smile. Turning my body back to Dad, I press a small peck of my lips to his forehead and then quietly slip off the bed to join Judd.

As soon as we are out of the room, his arms encircle me and he places a passionate kiss against my lips, making me weak in the knees and my head dizzy.

"I love watching you with your Dad," he whispers in my ear as he pulls his head back to look at me.

Over his shoulder, I catch a glimpse of Abby walking up, rolling her eyes.

"Get a room," she says sarcastically on her way out the door.

I spit out a giggle and roll my eyes back as Judd laughs, pulling away from our embrace only a fraction. *Good, because I want him close every second.*

"I'm headed over to Piper's for a bit. I'll be back later. Will you guys still be here?"

I nod my head as she snatches up her purse and darts out the door.

After a perfect day of hanging out with my parents, a trip to the store with a fun layover in the ball field parking lot and after showing him stacks of pictures of me as a kid; we disappear to my bedroom to be alone.

"So, will you ever be able to play again?" I ask Judd as he lies on my bed with his hands clasped behind his head.

Sitting with my legs wound together like a pretzel beside him, I run my hand over his stomach and feel his muscles tense up beneath his shirt. He smiles, watching me with utter fascination.

"No, my shoulder injury ended that. It's actually a pretty common injury for football players, but given the extent of mine, the doctor said I should never play again."

My heart hurts knowing that he lost something he loved so much. Wanting to be close to him in any way possible, I slip my hand under his shirt and move in a slow caress up to his rib cage. The heat from his skin radiates through my own, creating goose bumps and the hair to rise on my arms.

As my hand grazes his shoulder, he adds in a low tone, "It actually still hurts. If I pick something up too sudden there's a jolt of pain."

I grit my teeth thinking of how many times in the last forty-eight hours that I have crawled up his body as if I am a rambunctious child climbing a tree.

"You know, even if it wasn't for my shoulder, I still would not have made it to California in time for this season's opening game, let alone training." He sits up suddenly, pulling my hand out from under his shirt in the process. "You better stop that or we're going to have to leave your parent's house and take a road trip back to my apartment this time." Laughing, he folds his legs in to sit like me.

Sitting the opposite direction, he rests one arm along my leg and brings the other hand to my face. His soft touch across my cheek has me closing my eyes and pressing my face into his hand, yearning for him. *I love the way he touches me.*

"Either way . . . if it hadn't been for that wreck I would be clear across the country and would have never found you." I instantly flutter my eyes open as he goes on, "If football is the sacrifice I had to make to be with you, then I will gladly take that trade."

With his words, I throw myself forward into his embrace with a kiss that says everything that I don't have words for. I melt into him, his arms holding tightly around my body.

As I bury my face into his chest, my eyes zone in on the tattoo that I've never thought to ask about, which is peeking out from beneath his shirt sleeve. I worm my arm up between us, to trace my fingers over the black ink and intricate details. Judd pulls away, letting me have room to inspect it. He doesn't offer up any information; he just stares at my face as I look, still keeping his hands at my back.

"When did you get this?" I never noticed it before so I know it had to have been this summer.

"When I got the brace off my arm." He looks down at his arm with a troubled look in his eyes, before glancing back at me. "It seemed fitting at the time." He smiles, drawing me closer, but closing the subject.

We spend most of the afternoon talking, moving from topic to topic and learning much more about each other. I figure out quickly that the matter of his mom's passing is somewhat off limits by the way he deters the conversation, so I make sure to steer away from that, knowing he will tell me when he is ready.

Later, my sister Andrea stops by along with her husband and kids. My nephews chase Judd around like he is a big kid and he is totally enamored with them. They flip and fall all over each other in the back yard while my sisters and I clean up after dinner.

That night, we respect my parent's wishes and retreat to separate rooms to sleep.

I toss and turn, feeling empty without his warm body beside me.

After nearly an hour of lying without him, the hinges on my door let out a quiet popping sound that I have become accustomed to. I sit up in a hurry, excitement coursing through me. Judd stands in the doorway, fully clothed and drenched in the soft glow of the moonlight.

A couple strides and he is by my side, covering my body with his own. He kisses me deeply and then slides to my side with his arms tightly securing me against him. *This is where I belong; in his arms.*

It doesn't take long before we both drift off into a peaceful sleep; our slow steady breaths sinking into one. In those few moments before sleep captures me, all I can think about is how perfect this day was and how thankful I am for bringing him home for the weekend to meet my parents.

Breaking the news

S UNDAY GOES BY IN A flash and then we are back in route to
Rosemore.

"So, where to?" Judd asks a few minutes out from the city.
"Your apartment or mine, because I'm not letting you out of my sight,
yet." He sneaks a quick smile in my direction that makes my toes tingle
and pulse race.

"Mine," I say with no hesitation. *I want complete privacy with him
while I can have it.*

Casting me a skeptical, concerned look before steering the truck
onto the exit ramp, Judd questions my answer, "You sure? I know Evan
can be intrusive but he won't be sleeping across from us. I'm not sure
. . ."

Excitement bubbles into my chest and I quickly cut him off, "No,
no, no . . . I don't mind Evan at all." I burst out laughing and add, "That
is, if he stays out of the room while we're in bed, but no . . ." I take a
breath, realizing I forgot to tell him about the text I got the other night.
"Bethany actually texted me and said she is staying at her parents until
Tuesday so we should be good until then."

Judd's face lights up and he takes the very next right that leads to
my apartment.

"That works for me. I can run home in the morning for clothes.
After that, we can go to my apartment and take it day by day, but we
are not staying in separate places. That has gone on for far too long."

His eyes widen as he says the last part of the sentence. *I know exactly what he means. I don't want to be without him for another second either.*

I slide over on the seat and snuggle as closely as I can to him, curling my arms around his right bicep.

"Staying at my apartment gives us more time to stay in bed since we are closer to class, you know?"

He squirms beside me with his dimple dipping deep into his cheek as he flashes me a huge grin.

After throwing the truck in park, we hop out and make the small trek across the lot to my door.

"So have you decided when you are going to tell Bethany?" His question comes out of nowhere, but I know it needs to be discussed.

"I'm just going to wait, at least until later this week." Feeling uneasy about bringing up the next part, my mouth instantly feels dry and my heart thuds hard in my chest. "I also need to tell Kyle."

His jaw tenses and he stares past me as we come to the door to my apartment.

Fumbling around in my purse for my keys, I look dead ahead at him trying to gauge whether I've upset him.

"We are only friends and I don't owe him an explanation, but I just want him to know . . ." I jab my keys into the door, looking away from Judd as I go on, " . . . I want him to know that I am with you. I already told him I fell in love with someone else, but he needs to know why things will be different now."

As soon as we both step into the living room, I throw down my stuff and move over to the couch. Judd follows me and we both sit a little further from each other and a little less comfortable than I would like us to be.

With his elbows on his knees and his forehead hung into his hands, he lets out a defeated sigh and I immediately know how deeply this is bothering him.

"Hey . . ." my hand molds to his and he immediately looks into my eyes. "I love you. I am yours, you know that, right?"

Judd gives me a weak smile and then moves closer to me, pulling my face to his. "Promise?"

"I promise . . . I love only you," I whisper, inching closer to his mouth like I am being drawn in.

His lips meet mine and with that one single kiss, everything is fine.

Breathlessly pulling away, Judd looks me in the eyes.

"Ok, then do whatever you need to do. I don't exactly trust your ex, considering he lied and cost me my entire summer with you, but I trust you."

In the end, we both agreed to ride out the week enjoying each other and wait to break the news later. We know it will set off a whirl wind of drama and right now we want to revel in each other's company and not worry about anyone else's hurt feelings. It may be selfish, but I have to admit that I just want Judd all to myself.

Only a couple days back together and it feels as though not a moment has passed since this summer. I'm not sure if I will ever again be able to sleep without feeling the heat of his body next to mine.

We move like magnets through the night; I move and Judd rolls with me, never breaking our contact. The slightest brush of his skin sends jolts of electricity through my body, curling my toes and making my body hum.

Monday morning comes way too soon and we barely have enough time to get ready. We compared our schedules and they coincide pretty well on Mondays, however Tuesday will leave us little time to see each other.

Judd decides to go back to his apartment for a fresh pair of clothes and a shower, but first, gives me a long kiss goodbye while I fight the urge of dragging him back to bed.

I get cleaned up in a frenzy hoping that if I hurry that maybe he will be back faster. The mornings are getting chillier so I decide on a v-neck chenille leopard print sweater with leggings and my boots. I have to work at noon so I have to ditch my sweatshirt and yoga pants for something a little dressier. After racing into the bathroom, I dab on a little makeup, run a brush through my hair and am ready to go.

As soon as the front door opens and Judd walks in, my day is already perfect. Walking out of the bathroom, I move my eyes from his head to his toes, marveling over how gorgeous he is. He stands there with a slight grin on his face, in snug jeans, a long sleeve shirt and sneakers. He knows I'm ogling him, but by the way his eyes sweep over me, I can tell he is doing the same.

"I can't get used to seeing you in clothes and not a swim suit," he says in a low, seductive tone as he buries his face into my hair. "You smell so good."

Oh goodness. I really wish we didn't have classes this morning. I laugh, knowing he would be completely happy skipping class and staying in bed all day. I force myself to pull him out of the door and down to his truck so we can start our day, all the while knowing I will be counting down the hours until we are at each other's side again.

The day creeps by slower than any day I've ever known, but finally I'm off work.

Exiting the back door of the dentist's office, I find Judd waiting for me in his truck, vigorously hitting buttons on his phone. By the disturbed look on his face, my guess would be that he is texting Tristan. He didn't tell me much about the situation between him and his brother, but from what I gathered, Tristan seems to be dealing with a lot after the wreck and it has been weighing heavily on Judd's mind.

Hurrying over to the truck, my heart jumps into my throat with excitement. *I can't wait to be in his arms.* I hop up into his window, leaning over the door with my feet dangling beneath me to plant a quick kiss on his cheek. He snaps his head up to attention, abandoning his phone in his lap and instantly captures my face in his hands for a more intimate kiss.

With Bethany being out of town for one more night, we head back to my apartment for the night with a brief layover at Judd's place for some extra clothes.

An hour later, we are vegged out on the couch in each other's arms, talking and goofing off. Of course, that doesn't last long.

At a little past 7:00 we end up cuddling in bed, completely mesmerized with each other and enjoying a rare comfortable silence. My head nuzzles against his chest, filling my mind with the sounds of his heartbeat while his hand traces a path from my shoulders to my lower back over and over again. I tilt my head to look up at him and can't believe this is my life. *How did I get so lucky to find him exactly when I needed him most?*

He reaches his hand behind his head to support his neck, lifting up to study my face. "What are you thinking about?" His low, soothing tone sends goose bumps coursing over the surface of my skin.

"I was just thinking how crazy it is that one of the happiest times of my life came at one of the saddest times of my life. You know meeting you but then probably losing . . ." I trail off unable to say the words.

Judd moves his hand to my face, softly running his fingers across my cheek. "Have you ever thought that maybe it is happening that way for a reason; kind of balancing the scale?"

I stare into his eyes as he continues gentle strokes across my skin. His eyes are filled with compassion and understanding and I only wish I knew how he lost his mom. *I wonder if she had cancer or a progressive sickness like my dad. Did he go through what I am going through?*

"Sometimes the loss of a loved one can drive a person insane with grief. I know you are strong but maybe this is just a way to help you cope. Maybe fate intervened at the perfect time, so you wouldn't have to face this alone."

I pull myself up to a sitting position and Judd does the same. After grabbing my hand in his, he places both our hands flat on his chest. Spreading my hand out one finger at a time, I feel the warmth of his skin and silent, rhythmic thuds of his heart while he carefully outlines each of my fingers with soft strokes of his thumb.

"How did you handle it?" I know I may be intruding on a painful memory of his; one he may not be ready to share, but I really need to know.

He stops moving, lacing his fingers through mine and pulling them down onto his lap. A heavy sigh moves over his lips as he studies our joined hands like they may lend him strength and courage to discuss this further.

"I didn't, really." The pain in his voice is evident and I immediately regret asking.

"I just went from one day to the next; moving on because I had to," he pauses and looks up at me, " . . . until I met you. That was the first time I felt real happiness since she passed away. I didn't remember what truly laughing was until you came along." Looking back down, a gentle heartfelt smile touches his lips. "Sure, Evan could always manage to make me laugh but you . . . with you . . . I really laugh. With you, I see a happy future for the first time in my life." Judd looks up to my ceiling, trying to conceal his emotion, but I can tell this is difficult for him.

He pauses, regains his composure and goes on, "You know, I think your dad is more worried about how everyone he loves will be affected by all this, rather than scared of what will happen to him. I think he has made peace with it. I think he is grateful for the time he has had. He knows there is no promise as to how long each of our lives are going to be or how each of our ends will come, but he knows he has lived the best he could. And I truly believe he is ok with that. He just worries about if you all will be able to let him go when the time comes."

My eyes swim with tears and my breath catches in my throat as I struggle to take in air. Judd pulls me closer; his arms blanketing me with comfort, but I lean back wanting to look at him. I am completely amazed that he summed up my dad so wonderfully after only knowing him for such a short time.

"You learned all that from one weekend with my dad?" I say in utter disbelief and wonder.

"Well, I have to admit. You have some pretty awesome parents and your dad is one of a kind. I wish my . . ." he stops talking mid-sentence and places a small kiss to my forehead. "He loves you so much."

My heart flutters as he pulls me against him.

His lips seal over mine and he slowly rolls me onto my back, engulfing my body with his. Sucking and licking at my lower lip first, his moist lips gently work their way down to my jaw.

My head falls back against the soft pillow, allowing him unlimited access to my neck. Everything feels so right when he is near. His hands lightly graze under my sweater, lifting it inch by inch until it is pulled over my head.

He unhooks the front clasp of my bra and places small soft kisses along my shoulders as he slides the straps down. His hard chest lands back against my body and his lips are back on me.

"I love you, Alyssa," he says into my mouth as I fight to control my breathing.

I open my mouth to whisper my heart back to him, but the slamming of the front door has every nerve in my body on high alert.

Judd and I jump up in a flash, my eyes wide in alarm. He tears my bra and sweater up off the floor and tosses them to me, clearly aware of my concern.

My eyes scan the room while I try to assess the situation.

"I'm not climbing out the window. If that's what you're thinking, you can forget about it." He gives me a crooked grin, obviously thinking I am searching for an escape route.

I cover my mouth to keep from laughing not wanting to make any noise that will alert our company to our presence.

As soon as I am dressed, I shoot over to the door with Judd by my side, firmly holding my trembling hand. I feel as if I'm about to board a plane that is destined to crash.

"I guess it's time you talk to her. You want me to wait in here or come out with you?"

I take a deep breath and bounce onto my tiptoes, leaning into him. "No, I better do this alone. She is going to freak as it is, but if she sees you here she's liable to tackle me," I whisper into his ear.

Honestly, I have no idea what her reaction is going to be. I know she was hell bent on getting Judd in the sack only a few days ago, but I'm not sure how deep her feelings ran for him. Either way, walking in and finding us curled up together in bed is not the way to approach this. She is going to be pissed, so I have to explain the situation so she understands that there was something between Judd and me prior to her setting her sights on him. I may have to answer for the fact that I never told my best friend about my summer romance though.

I shut the door behind me and see a not so happy looking Bethany standing in the kitchen with her arms crossed. *Great!!* I take in the scene and realize Judd's shoes are kicked off by the front door, his keys and wallet are lying on the counter, an empty pizza box is abandoned on the coffee table and I am very sure that I look like I have been rolling around in bed; which I have and I think she knows that.

Her eyes fill with tears and my heart drops into my stomach.

"Bethany, we need to talk." I raise my hand out in front of me as if I'm dealing with a wild animal that is hell bent on attacking me.

She throws her hands up on her hips and snarls at me. "You're damn right you need to explain. How could you do this to me? Why?" Teardrops spill from her eyes as she folds her arms across her chest.

"First off, I need to explain wh. . . . ."

Before I can get a full sentence in, Bethany's shrill voice cuts me off, "I thought you were my friend! How could you?!"

"If you would calm down and let me explain I would tell you," I counter, still maintaining a calm and steady voice.

"Explain, yeah, you need to explain, now! Tell me why I come home Thursday night and swear I see my best friend in front of the apartment making out with the guy I like? So, then I decide to go back to Fairview for the weekend and I drive by your house and see his truck. I figured you would come back here and I had to see for myself."

Her expression deepens to a defiant look, with her eyebrows drawn up and her lips in a straight line. *Wait . . . she knew this entire weekend about me and Judd. So why the text saying she was coming home Tuesday night. Unless . . .*

"So you deliberately told me you were coming home Tuesday, hoping you would catch us together? That seems a little manipulative." I'm a little taken aback by her method of finding out what was going on between Judd and me. *Why wouldn't she have just asked me?*

"You're damn right I did! I had to since you were so determined to sneak around behind my back, knowing the whole time that I liked him. So that's why I kept catching you two in conversations with each other. Wow, Alyssa . . . you sure had me fooled!" Her pissed off tone gives way to sadness.

"Bethany, just sit down for a minute and let me explain. First off, I wasn't sneaking around and I would have never . . . *never* gotten involved with someone you like." She laughs and glares at me as if I have hit a nerve. "Just sit, please. I need to tell you some things I should have told you this summer."

Finally, Bethany calms down enough to sit and I instantly get busy telling her all about my two weeks with Judd and how we already knew each other prior to her newfound crush. I try to rationalize why I didn't tell her any of this, but I feel there is just no way to clear that up. *Yes, she is my best friend and usually best friends share everything, but those two weeks were special to me and when it came to an end, I just wanted to remember it as this beautiful thing without anyone demeaning it.*

She watches me and listens the whole time, keeping a defensive stance.

"Is he in the bedroom right now?" she asks, visibly hurt by the whole ordeal.

"Yes," I mumble, feeling guilty for hurting her, but then on the other hand, happy that it is all out at last. "I'm so sorry I didn't tell you any of this, Bethany. After everything with Kyle, I just didn't want to feel like a naïve fool for trusting another guy and then, the other night when we figured it all out . . . well, it just happened so fast and I wanted to tell you in person and well . . ."

Bethany sighs and holds her hand up to stop me from talking. "It's fine! I'm fine!" Yet, the animosity in her tone says the opposite of her words.

She gets up and walks into the kitchen and opens the fridge door, never looking me in the eye. *I know she is upset, hurt and pissed off!*

"It's stupid for him to hide in there! Just tell him to come out," she says in an icy tone, with a hateful look in my direction.

"He's not hiding. I told him to wait till . . ."

She cuts me off again, casting me another unpleasant glare.

"You should have told me, but just don't flaunt it in my face!"

I open my mouth to defend myself, but stop when I hear Judd walk into the room. He doesn't look happy as he walks up, pulling me close to his side. *I think this is what she meant by not flaunting it.*

I grit my teeth as Judd speaks, defending me, "Bethany, I was always straight forward with you. I told you I was not over my ex and Alyssa was who I was talking about. I just didn't want to discuss anything with anyone until I understood myself, what had happened between us."

Bethany stiffens, glancing down at Judd's arm that is protectively clasped around my waist and then turns her malice on him, but then her voice softens when she speaks.

"Be honest, did you use me to get close to her?"

I look at him with guilt clamping down on my conscience for him being in this position, but Judd's demeanor never waivers. He keeps a firm look in his eyes and confidence in his voice when he answers her.

"No, because I told you from that very first day that I was only interested in being friends with you and I never gave you any indication that that would change. You were the one that was always texting and calling me to come over, not the other way around. The only thing either of us is guilty of is not being honest about knowing each other, but I am in no way sorry for being with her now."

I stare over at Bethany, afraid of what her reaction will be. Surprisingly, instead of lashing out, she relaxes her posture and seems to cool down.

"Ok, well then, that is that and now we all know. I will just forgive and forget and move on. I can do that." She nods her head and keeps her eyes on Judd.

He smiles with a shrug of his shoulders and then looks over to me. I'm a little confused by how easily she gave in after Judd's speech, but I'm not going to push the issue any further.

"If it would make you more comfortable, I can go to his apartment tonight if you don't want me around."

Bethany gives me a half-hearted smile, "For now, that might be a good idea," she says while looking directly at Judd. "I would prefer to just try and process this all by myself." She looks over to me and continues, "I heard everything you said and I know I have no right to be upset, but I can't help but feel a little betrayed."

I open my mouth to reiterate the details of how Judd was actually my boyfriend, but yet I had the pleasure of walking in and seeing him in bed with her. Instead, I stop when his hand slides into mine.

Clearing my throat, I decide to close the subject and humor her wishes. I grab a few things and we head out to his truck to go to his apartment.

The next day, I decide to explain it all to Kyle as well. Considering he was part of the misunderstanding and now that I have all the information, I should be furious with him, but for some strange reason, I'm not. I have no room in my heart for anger right now. If my father's situation has taught me anything, it is to live life with no regrets and to be grateful for each day regardless of the circumstances.

After talking to him between classes, I get it all out in the open. He quickly apologizes then confesses that he still loves me, which makes me feel relieved that Judd did not accompany me. Understanding that he felt threatened and determined to get me back, I accept his apologies; we hug and part ways. All in all, breaking the news to them both went differently than I expected, but I am so glad it is behind me.

Keeping secrets

IT TAKES NO TIME AT all for Bethany to become her normal feisty, happy go lucky self again. Within a week, we are all comfortable enough to hang out and according to her, she even has her eye on a new guy.

Even though Bethany is over Judd and the tension between me and her has vanished, I still sense a little friction on his end. He's always on edge when she is around and absolutely uncomfortable if he is faced with even a minute alone with her, but I continue to reassure him that I am not bothered by them being friends.

It's a week from Halloween so Bethany had the idea to throw a small costume party at the community center on Saturday however, that ended up being booked. Plus, Kyle's fraternity is having some kind of senior meeting tomorrow night and since Bethany wants to hit downtown the following weekend on the actual holiday, all dressed up, we ended up planning the get together at our apartment. Luckily, our place will not hold that many bodies, so when she says a small party, this time I trust it.

Since the party is tomorrow night, Judd, Bethany and I plan a shopping trip to get costumes. Judd isn't excited about tagging along, but he agrees to for the sake of watching me try on naughty outfits. What he doesn't know, is that I'm more of a plush-bunny-costume kind of girl rather than a French maid or a slutty nurse.

Wow! I could handle seeing him in one of these hunky gladiator costumes though, I think as I stand in the costume shop filing through aisle after aisle. My heart kicks up a notch as I envision Judd's face and body in place of the model on the package in my hands.

Bethany and I both have an armful to tote into the dressing room, so I casually slip one of the gladiator costumes into my pile along with a women's Roman Empress costume when Judd isn't looking. I slide into the dressing room while he takes a seat on the chase lounge outside my room. Bethany giggles in the room beside me and I know she must have one of her outfits on already.

After throwing on my first one, I fling the curtain aside and step out for Judd's approval. Casually shifting my hip to one side, I slap my hand to my waist and strike my sexiest pose to show off my fuzzy kitten costume complete with fluffy ears and a long tail.

Judd bends at the waist and busts up laughing. "You're kidding, right?"

Biting my lip, I keep a straight face, trying not to laugh, but end up cracking up.

After a quick run over to Bethany's room to give her a thumbs-up on her Biker Chick get up, I race back into my dressing room to put on my next ensemble. I slip on my last details and then jump out in front of Judd with a huge smile plastered on my face.

Judd's head falls back and he groans. Looking back up to me with a smirk on his face, he blinks his eyes several times to focus on my outfit. No doubt the huge polka dots on these bright blue bell bottom pants and this tight rainbow striped shirt that I'm wearing with thick red suspenders, is giving him double vision. I squeeze the big, red nose I have plastered on my face to make a honking noise and chuckle along with him.

"Definitely not," he says, holding his stomach from laughing so hard.

I check in on Bethany a couple more times before she decides on an extremely short Vampire Vixen costume.

Judd's laughter dies down the more I try on. When I step out in the 20's flapper dress with a tight headband and feather holding back my long wavy hair, he raises his eyebrows in surprise. It's not as short as the empress costume that I will try on last, but it is getting close to his liking.

With a shake and shimmy of my hips as I back my way into the dressing room, the tassels swing around and Judd flashes me a wide smile.

After two more costumes, I step out in my short Empress costume with my roman sandals laced up to my knees, a cream colored sling top pushing my boobs up to my chin and a gold fabric belt attached right under my breasts. I add thick gold arm bands, a delicate gold crown and a low hanging medallion necklace last. Throwing one arm up on the frame of the door, I thrust my opposite hip out for effect. Judd's face lights up and he lets out a whistle.

"That's the one," he winks.

Pulling my other hand out from behind my back, I giggle with the men's costume casually dangling from my finger.

As he looks down, his expression changes to panic.

"No way, I am not wearing that unless it is late at night and we are doing role play or some shit like that."

I close my eyes tightly and laugh out loud. Seductively swaying my body as I inch back into the room, I bat my eyelashes and crook my finger for him to follow. He happily accepts my challenge, nearly knocking the chaise to the ground as he bolts up.

He ends up trying it on and "Wow," is all I can say. He refuses to wear it to the costume party but I end up buying it anyway since it matches the one I chose. *I'm always up for the role play idea.*

After dinner, we head back to my apartment so I can get some clothes for the next two days. Dad seems to be getting weaker and weaker as the days go by and so we thought it would be best if either both, or at least one of us, stay sober the night of the party. We also plan on coming back to his apartment afterward rather than crashing with a house full of passed out drunks. Evan's father is apparently back in town and he is spending the weekend at the lake with him and his brother, so that leaves Judd's apartment completely private and free from anyone walking in on us like Evan always manages to do. At first, I thought maybe Evan might be a bit of a pervert, but then I just figured out that he gets a massive kick out of messing with his best friend.

As soon as we return from our shopping adventure, I rush into my room and throw a couple outfits in my bag and then run into the bathroom to throw together the makeup I will need for my Halloween getup. I toss a couple extra toiletries that I can keep at his place into my bag and then step out into the living room.

Judd flies up off the couch where Bethany is sitting and darts to my side in only a few steps. He has a disturbed look on his face and holds his hand over his mouth. Looking at me, he grabs the bag quickly.

"You ready?"

His reaction and jumpiness has me puzzled. I look past him to Bethany sitting lazily on the couch. She waves her hand with a wide smile.

"You guys have fun. See you tomorrow night."

I wave bye and without a word, Judd pulls me out the door, no doubt in a hurry to be alone.

An uncomfortable silence falls over us on the drive to his place.

"Is everything ok?" I ask, feeling a surge of confusion on what could be bothering him after such a fun day.

"Mmhum," he answers back; more like reacts.

His answer is so instantaneous to my question and so vague that I can't help but feel as though there is something he is not telling me. *Maybe he is just tired or maybe his shoulder is bothering him. Could Bethany have said something that aggravated him? I know he is not that crazy about her. He's never hidden that fact.* I toss around ideas the whole drive until we finally pull into his parking lot.

He shuts off the engine and leans over to give me a long, seductive kiss. We linger there for a while until we are both panting and ready to be in his bed. He tosses the door to his truck open, hops out onto the pavement and then turns to throw me over his shoulder.

I scream and giggle uncontrollably all the way up the stairs to his door.

Once inside, he sprints into his bedroom and flips me onto the bed in front of him. My back sinks into his soft navy blue comforter as he slowly slides on top of me. Gliding my hand down his back and inside the back of his shirt to feel the warmth of his skin, I look into his eyes that sparkle with excitement. His hand softly grazes my cheek as he reaches up and brushes away strands of hair from my forehead.

"I love you so much, Alyssa," he says right before crushing his lips to mine.

I gasp out, "I love you . . ." and pull him closer, melting into his arms. We hastily rip our clothes off of one another until we are both bare and eager for more.

Judd's mouth moves down my silhouette, pressing wet kisses down the inside of my thigh while making me tremble with gentle strokes of his fingers.

"Judd . . ." I call out, licking my lips with a need to taste his skin and kiss his lips.

I gently tug at his hair, letting him know how badly I need him closer, as close as we can be.

He slides his body back up over me and rolls us so that I am straddling him. With his hands firmly, yet gently holding my hips, he helps to lift and guide me down, slowly. At last, we join as one and the electricity that instantly pulsates through me has my mind spinning.

My hands pinch and squeeze into fists against his chest as tingling sensations rise up into the pit of my stomach.

His hands grasp my waist as he lets out deep moans, opening his mouth to suck in breath after breath.

I throw my head back, climbing higher and higher as he moves at a slow, steady pace.

Running the length of my torso, his hands smooth over the skin of my rib cage and up to cup my breasts. When his thumb delicately brushes across my nipple, I flip my head forward and call out his name as over powering currents race through my body.

Flipping me onto my back without missing a beat, he moves against me until he is out of breath and collapsing onto me.

As the pulses of pleasure begin to slow, I run my fingers through the back of Judd's hair and smile; I smile one of those silly-OMG-completely-satisfied-and-I-so-want-to-do-that-again-smiles. Then I breath out the most content breathe I've ever felt in my life.

Judd looks at me like he just ran a marathon but shows off the same smile I have plastered on my face.

"Wow," I giggle and consider saying it again for emphasis.

He smiles wider as I rub my finger against his dimple; never able to get enough of seeing his smile.

"You're obsessed with that," he teases and I nod.

"I am, and I am absolutely, undeniably obsessed with you."

This makes his smile grow and he presses a strong kiss to my lips that leaves us both winded. We lay there for a while, basking in each other's presence before either of us is able to form words.

"So are you sure something wasn't wrong earlier? You were quiet on the drive home. I thought maybe you were mad at me or something," I say hesitantly, not wanting to ruin this perfect moment.

Judd stops his caress across my shoulder and turns to his side so that we are facing each other.

"No, why would I be mad at you?" he replies so quickly with such certainty that all the worries I had are lost.

"It's just that Bethany kind of still makes me uncomfortable." He grits his teeth and looks at me as if he fears my reaction.

I laugh, pushing at his chest as I assure him of her intentions, "She is over it all. Don't worry about her."

He stares at me with an unreadable look on his face and opens his mouth to say more, then decides not to. Closing his mouth, he presses his lips together in a straight line and squints his eyes as if he's in deep thought.

"Are you sure nothing is wrong?" I ask again, puzzled by his hesitation.

"Yeah, I mean no . . . I'm fine; nothing's wrong."

Yet, I still don't feel confident that he isn't holding something back, but I make my mind up to let it go. I'm more than likely being paranoid.

He looks up to the ceiling before continuing our conversation.

"So, how long have you two been friends?"

I roll onto my back to lie beside him, staring at the reflection of the street lights shining through his window above us.

"Since the end of our junior year. Kyle was the quarterback and pretty popular, so when he asked me out it kind of put me in the limelight. Bethany was on the cheerleading squad with me, but I usually kept to myself and didn't associate much with the other girls outside of games and practice. She approached me one day after school and said she had heard I was going out with Kyle and, after that, we became quick friends."

Judd shifts back onto his side with a quizzical look. "So before that you were never friends? Did she and Kyle ever date?"

Why the fascination with Kyle all of a sudden?

"No . . . they never dated. Why are you asking that?" I stare at Judd, looking for some clue of where this conversation is headed.

He shrugs his shoulders and pulls my hand into his, running his fingertip over each of my knuckles.

"I was just curious about how you all met. So you have basically been friends with her for only a little over a year?"

Huffing out a small laugh, I cock my head to the side and analyze each turn this conversation is taking. I assume the whole past situation with Bethany is still weighing on his mind more than he is telling me.

"I'm just curious, that's all," he pauses, clearly sensing my bewilderment in this line of questions, but then he goes on, "So you dated Kyle for a year until he cheated on you and then that's when you met me," he says it more as a statement rather than asking me, but I still shake my head.

"It doesn't bother you that you don't know who the girl was?"

This takes me by surprise and my face falls. That moment hurt me more than I care to think of, although, it worked out for the best, I don't care to revisit it.

I start to persuade him to change the subject when he opens his mouth to go on, "You said Bethany was at the same party, didn't you? Do you think she knows who he was with, possibly?"

Ok, I'm really ready to move this subject in a different direction.

"Actually it really doesn't matter to me who she was. She obviously didn't care that he had a girlfriend, but you know what? That was a good thing, because if it had not been for that girl, I would not have gone to the lake . . . ." I slide a little closer to Judd, trying to turn this warped conversation into something a little more light and playful. I start to walk my fingers up his chest, instantly feeling his muscles tense. He looks down at my hand with a sneaky smile on his face that tells me my attempt is working. " . . . and then I would have never met you."

I end the sentence with my body pressed up against him while moving in to place a slow kiss onto his mouth-watering lips. He grabs ahold of my hand on his chest and holds it there while nudging my mouth open with his tongue; deepening the kiss. *Finally.* I breathe out a triumphant sigh.

The kiss guides us back into the throws of passion and pleasure, but in the back of my mind, I still wonder why he would be concerned with such silly information. *He has always been slow to talk about painful topics in his life, plus he is usually so understanding and compassionate about pain I have went through, so why these questions? What is the point?*

Soft, moist kisses send tingles down my spine and I toss all thought out the window. *Judd is always straight forward and is not one to keep secrets so there is no need for me to worry about this. Especially not now,* I think as I let out a whimper as Judd sucks on my earlobe. *Definitely not now!*

Am I missing something

SURPRISINGLY ENOUGH, I WAKE UP bright and early on Saturday morning, ready for a jam packed day. We had promised to run several errands for Bethany to aid in her attempt to throw the best Halloween party ever. Normally we would spend the entire weekend at my parent's; however, Mom insists that we take a break to enjoy life. She worries that the constant flip-flopping back and forth and the stress of the situation is going to affect my grades. I agreed to stay away for one day, but am most definitely going to visit first thing Sunday.

Abby was also instructed to take a day off. She and Piper have decided to crash the party later tonight. Judd invited Evan, but he is busy this weekend and won't be back until Sunday.

I stretch my leg over to Judd's side, eagerly anticipating the brush of his skin on mine. However, my excitement for the day ahead takes a nose dive when I notice no legs where they should be. I open my eyes and look up expecting to see him curled up beside me, but all I find is a crumpled up pillow and an empty bed.

The soft cotton fabric sweeps over my skin as I sit up and look around the room, from his large dresser across from the bed, past his closet, over to the nightstand that sits only an arm's length away from me. On the worn out oak table beside his bed sits a single sheet of notebook paper with my name on it. My heart stammers as I eagerly grab the paper into my hands with a cheesy grin on my face.

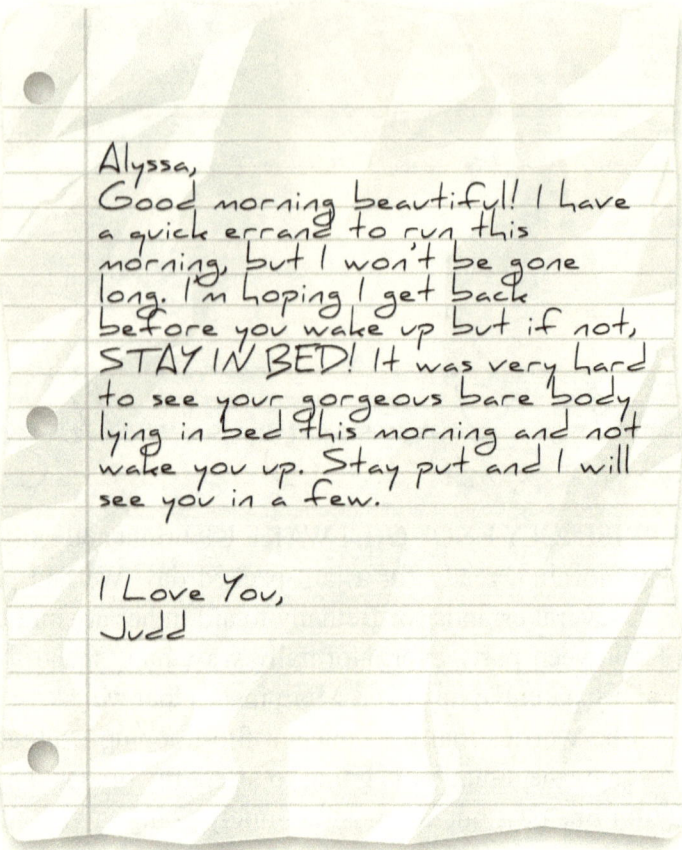

Alyssa,
Good morning beautiful! I have
a quick errand to run this
morning, but I won't be gone
long. I'm hoping I get back
before you wake up but if not,
STAY IN BED! It was very hard
to see your gorgeous bare body
lying in bed this morning and not
wake you up. Stay put and I will
see you in a few.

I Love You,
Judd

I pull the note to my chest, breathing out a content sigh. *I love him so much!*

Placing the letter down to read it again, a clicking sound from the front door has my heart climbing into my throat. I hastily toss the letter back where it was and lay back down in bed. Him *waking me up doesn't sound too bad!*

I flip onto my stomach quickly, pull the sheet up and close my eyes.

My ears pick up on a sweeping sound and then a quiet snap that tells me he just shut the door. The floor lets out a creek to let me know it is being walked on and then there is silence. I keep my eyes closed but for a second my mind starts to race with ideas of a mass murderer standing over me raising a knife in the air ready to plunge it into my back. I flinch at the thought, but dismiss it and turn my head away from the figure that I know is standing over me. My eyes remain closed the whole time.

The edge of the mattress sinks down beside me and I have to refrain from giggling. I feel like I am sweating profusely from the stress of trying to lie still. Something soft runs down the length of my back and I hear a crunching sound. I draw my eyebrows in, puzzled by what it is.

As the bed shifts, I feel heat radiating off of his body as he moves against my side. Something as soft as silk slides up my right arm at the same time that Judd's warm breath tickles my ear.

"I know you're awake."

The giddiness that was threatening to bubble to the surface erupts into laughter as I flip over and am nose to nose with Judd. His gorgeous dimple is showing and he is looking at me, completely amused.

In an attempt to wipe the silly grin off his face, I lean forward to kiss him when suddenly a handful of pale pink roses fill the gap between us. I open my mouth and look at him in awe causing his smile to widen.

"Happy one month anniversary." His words instantly have me doing a silent countdown to tally up the days.

We got back together on September 25th and Halloween is a week away. *Holy cow! It has been a whole month already?*

"Has it really been a month?" I ask trying to play down the mental guilt trip I am giving myself.

How is it that he remembered something like this but it didn't even dawn on me? I'm an ass!

I grab the flowers from his hands and stare at him in complete wonderment. With my eyes closed, I bend my neck and inhale the floral scent of the roses, letting it tickle my nostrils and nearly making me sneeze.

"They're beautiful." I smile, letting the heavy thuds of my heart inch my lips up further the longer I look at him.

"You're beautiful," Judd replies, leaning in to woo me even more with a passionate kiss.

He pulls away and flashes me a loving smile, which will never cease to melt my heart.

I look down at the flowers, feeling a little guilty that I didn't remember today was significant, let alone do something special for him.

"I can't believe it's been a month already." I bite my lip and look into his eyes. "I have to admit . . . I didn't remember."

I'm so undeserving of these lovely flowers. He shakes his head and grabs the flowers from me, placing them on the nightstand behind him.

"I can't see why. It's not like you've had anything going on." He rolls his eyes in a teasing way and pulls me against his chest. "I couldn't decide whether you were a red rose kind of woman or a mixed arrangement or what, so I went with this color." He points over his shoulder to the flowers. "It's the color of the tank top you wore the first day I ever saw you."

My heart skips a beat at the fact that he remembers what I wore that day. I bounce up onto my knees feeling the springs in the mattress as I get situated so that I can wrap my entire body around him in a gigantic hug.

"I love you so much, Judd. How did I get so lucky?"

He snickers and then tugs my chin down with his fingertips so he can look at me.

"I'm the lucky one." He plants another seductive kiss on my lips and then jumps to his feet. "Now, get changed before I decide we're not leaving this bed."

I forgo showering and throw my hair up in a clip; I'll shower before I get all gussied up in my costume later anyway. After slipping on some gray yoga pants and an oversized black hoodie, we head out the door in a rush.

"Why are you in such a hurry to get the party decorations? We have all day, you know?" I laugh as he slams the passenger door of his truck and then sprints to the driver's side.

Shutting the door behind him, he settles in behind the steering wheel, puts the key in the ignition and looks over to me with a smile.

"I was just hoping we could get everything done by noon." Raising then lowering his eyebrows in a quick, flirty motion, he adds, "I have a surprise planned for later."

Bubbling with excitement, a burst of giggles erupts from me as I try to imagine what the surprise could be.

"I can't have a clue?" I flash him my best pouty face.

"Not a chance," he snickers as he throws the truck into drive and pulls out.

"It was worth a try." I look at him through the corner of my eye and can see the amusement on his face. "Ok, then let's hurry and get this over with." I laugh as Judd heads in the direction of the Halloween shop.

Once we're inside the shop, Judd grabs a cart.

"I'm not going to be much help here, so I'll push, you shop," he says, bringing to mind that I actually have no idea what Bethany wants either.

I lead the way through the store, tossing in a spooky tunes CD, several bags of spider webs, black streamers and a witch's cauldron.

"What do you think about these?" I say as I grab several white plastic drop clothes with some tubes of fake blood. "We could put them on the floor so our carpet doesn't get all tainted up with beer." *I would like to keep my cleaning deposit.*

"Yeah, that might help, but it will probably just make more of a mess or trip people after they are drunk."

"That's true," I laugh, envisioning a bright, white monstrous mass with tentacles swallowing up my legs and dragging me to the ground for the final count.

What the heck. "I'll get them anyways. I'm sure we can use them for something," I say with a smile as I toss them in the cart.

Going through aisle after aisle, I throw in a few more over the top items and we are ready to pay then leave.

Judd cracks up as we load the bags into his truck.

"Do girls always put this much effort into an event where half the guest list will be seeing double or have blurred vision about thirty minutes into the party?" He laughs harder as he shuts the cab door.

I slide into the passenger side and sneak a look at him from the corner of my eyes. He gets in beside me and shakes his head with an amused grin on his face.

"Us guys . . . we usually just throw a keg in the middle of the floor and leave the decorating to later that night."

Heading for our next stop, he pulls out of the parking lot and glances my way with a mischievous smile.

Trying to match his enjoyment with a smartass reply, I tilt my head to the side and cross my arms with a little attitude.

"Is that so? Let me guess . . . beer towers?" He chuckles and I go on, "Well, us girls, we like things to look pretty." I raise my eyebrows, challenging him.

He looks over at me and teases me further, "Pretty? Is that what they are calling blood splattered sheets and spider webs these days?"

Unable to hold back my laughter any longer, I bend over with my hands over my face and laugh so hard I snort; in turn, making Judd crack up.

Trying to control my laughter, I point in the direction of the grocery store.

"Next order of business is munchies for the party," I get out through my giggles.

Our grocery excursion goes much like the decoration shopping with Judd continuously laughing at my selections in snack food.

"What are you looking at these for? Why don't we just grab a couple frozen pizzas and some bags of chips? Done." He chuckles with a confused look on his face when I grab several bags of cubed cheeses and meats.

I laugh with him, "What . . . Bethany wants finger foods." I look over at him trying to keep a straight face. "Oh, and I need to get toothpicks, too."

Judd bends at the waist and nearly falls on the floor from laughter. "Are you kidding me?"

By the time we reach the cash register my eyes are filled with water from laughing along with him. Judd makes an event out of drawing deep breaths in and out of his mouth to calm his hysterics, while I fan my hand in front of my face, still giggling uncontrollably.

We push the cart out to the truck, me standing on the lower bar leaning back against Judd's chest as he pushes. Butterflies swarm in my stomach as his chin rests on my shoulder.

He stops the cart beside his vehicle and slides his hands around my waist in an affectionate embrace. Taking in a deep breath, I close my eyes and shiver as Judd's lips touch just below my ear. A cool breeze sweeps across our faces and I cover his hands with mine.

"Is it weird that I think this is a perfect day so far?" I ask quietly.

He lets out a small chuckle into my neck. "It is a perfect day because we're together."

Yep! My thoughts exactly! It wouldn't matter if we were stuck in a cave or abandoned in the desert; we would still manage to find the romance in the circumstances if we were together. *Actually those situations sound pretty terrific to me.*

Clearly reading my thoughts, "Let's just blow off this party tonight and spend the whole night at my apartment in bed," he suggests, tightening his grip on me.

I worm my back against his chest and snuggle the back of my head into the crook of his neck.

Ahhh! I heave out an elated sigh, wishing badly that I hadn't promised to help Bethany with this party. *Staying in bed all afternoon and evening wrapped in Judd's arms sounds heavenly.*

I hop down off of the cart and turn to face him, puckering my lips and giving him my best puppy dog eyes.

He breathes out a chuckle and then leans down to kiss me.

"Ok, we'll go, but just so you know . . . I will be counting down the minutes till we can leave."

I give him a quick peck on the lips in return. *I'll save the in depth thank you for later.*

"We will just stay long enough to make sure everything is under control and then the rest of the night will be all ours," I assure him in my best seductive voice, letting him know that I will be counting down the minutes as well.

After loading up all the snacks, Judd drives back to my apartment while I send Bethany a quick text.

Me: Got everything. We're headed over to Kyle's to get the keg then we will head that way to drop everything off. :)

Bethany: Actually, Kyle and his friend, Hayden, already dropped off all the alcohol, so you don't have to run over there after all.

Me: That's great!! One less thing to do today! We'll be there in 10 minutes!

Plus, more time to spend with Judd, I think as I hit send.

Bethany: Sounds good! C-ya then!

We pull into the parking lot beside my car, which appears neglected after weeks of me and Judd refusing to go anywhere without one another. My car gets far better gas mileage than his big truck, but it doesn't offer the option for me to scoot as close to him as I can get while he drives.

I love to hold his hand and snuggle into the warmth of his body. I also love the way his hand lingers on my thigh until he is ready to shift into another gear. Something about that small amount of contact gets my heart thumping and my pulse racing. *Actually, I think all things Judd turn me on and fill my belly with swarms of butterflies.*

Shortly after we run all the bags into the apartment, Judd escapes back to his truck to take a call from his brother.

Standing in the doorway, I look around and am pleasantly surprised by how clean the apartment is. Bethany has on a pair of black sweat pants, a low cut white t-shirt and her hair up in a messy pony tail with fly-away hairs sticking up every which way. She is actually a mess, yet her makeup looks impeccable. *She probably wanted to make sure she looked good in case one of Kyle's roommates brought the booze over.*

I glance at the clock and then back at Bethany.

"Do you need help or will you be ok if I take off?" I ask, my face heating with guilt over wanting to skip out.

Normally, I would love to do this sort of stuff with my best friend, but it's already 11:37 and I want to see what Judd had up his sleeve. That leaves us plenty of time to do whatever he has planned, go to his apartment to get dressed and then come back to help before the party.

Bethany springs up from the end table she was dusting and lowers her brows into a scowl.

"Of course I need help!" She snaps. "Why?"

I grit my teeth and prepare for a tongue lashing. "I was just hoping I could come back later before the party and help you."

Any hope that she would let me off the hook fades as her mouth draws open and her frown deepens.

"Well, I need your help now. You can't expect me to do all of this," she whines, placing her hands on her hips.

"You won't be. We will come back an hour early and help out. Plus, I got pre-made snack platters, so half the work is already done." I beam proudly at my decision in getting those, despite Judd's arguments of buying several pizzas to throw in the oven.

"Fine, but don't get all caught up rolling around in the sheets and end up blowing me off. This is our party."

She sounds plenty annoyed, but I'm just glad she gave in so easily. It's rare when Judd and I have time to go anywhere. Usually we are so busy with school, my job, his job at Evan's grandfather's construction company and from countless trips back and forth to help with Dad, so I am not going to let a guilt trip hold me back from enjoying my afternoon with him. This is the first Saturday in the past month that we have not been vegged out on the couch at my parent's house and I intend to indulge in whatever he has planned.

"I won't skip out on you, I promise. Judd and I will both come early and help." I bounce up and down, eager to find out where this day is going to take us and hoping my excitement will redirect her irritation.

Bethany stops cleaning and walks me down to the truck where we find Judd leaning up against the driver's side door in an intense phone conversation. His eyes meet mine and he abruptly wraps up the call.

Shoving his phone into his jean pocket, he takes two strides and is at my side. His face lights up when he looks at me but then strangely falls as soon as he sees Bethany not too far behind.

"So what are you two up to that is so pressing that you can't help me?" She bluntly asks and I have half the mind to flick her in the forehead.

Wonderful! With his brows lowered and his lips etched into a frown, his aggravation is evident.

"I told her we had something planned and that we would come back early to help." I say, bringing Judd up to speed.

He smiles at me and squeezes my hand for reassurance.

"Absolutely," he says to me in a gentle tone before looking back toward Bethany. "It's been a month since we have been together so I figured I would take *my girlfriend* somewhere special this afternoon."

I flinch at the icy tone he takes with her and how he stresses the words 'my girlfriend.' Looking back and forth between the two as they level each other with a heated glare, I come to the realization that they are definitely not over the whole, 'He used me to get to you' and 'She was obsessive and stalkerish even though she knew I wasn't into her' ordeal. I clear my throat, ready to end this standoff.

"Is everything ok?" I ask Judd quietly.

"Yeah, just a bad conversation with Tristan, that's all." He smiles and then looks away.

"I'm in a foul mood, too," Bethany throws out; her glare has softened to a weepy expression. "The guy I told you I was chasing after keeps blowing me off and I'm just about done with this whole cat and mouse chase." She lifts her eyebrows and lets out a frustrated sigh.

"Ok then," I say still feeling there is something I'm missing. "Sorry to hear that. You'll just have to show him and hook up with some hot guy tonight."

She laughs and then waves us on. "I better get back to getting the apartment ready. If I get it all done, I'll shoot you a text. Have fun." With that, she turns and scurries away.

I'm a lousy friend for not sticking around to hear about the deal with this guy, but it is so seldom when we get a whole day to ourselves.

"Is everything ok? I mean, you seem a little on edge?" I ask, unable to shake this feeling as we both hop into his truck.

Judd starts up the truck and his grip tightens on the steering wheel as he answers, "Yeah, it's fine. It's just she . . ." he pauses, flashing a quick glance my way as he continues, "You know what, it's no big deal. Besides, I don't want to worry about this right now."

He smiles over at me and I, in turn, scoot across the seat to get as near to him as I can possibly sit.

The bite in his tone earlier told me I am definitely missing something, but at this point I am way too focused on him and this surprise to worry about anything else.

A date to remember

A FTER SWINGING BY ONE OF my favorite cafés, we pull into the gravel lot of a small playground. Judd throws the truck into park, turns to look at me and grabs my hands, pulling them into his lap between us. I crinkle my nose and give him a wide grin, absolutely wound up with anticipation.

"Ok, so since we haven't had a chance to go on an official date and this is the first time we have really had a day to ourselves, I wanted to take you on a real date."

He looks straight into my eyes and shows off the brightest, most gorgeous smile I've ever seen. I feel like a little girl that just got called up on stage to be sung to by her favorite rock star. As I gaze into his eyes, my heart thuds so loudly that I may melt into a puddle at any moment.

"But instead of taking you on some cliché type date like dinner and a movie, I wanted to share a part of my past with you and take you somewhere that is special to me."

I grip his hands and look around at the park. He chuckles and then opens the door, pulling me out on his side.

Once he hoists me down to stand beside him, he reaches into the back and grabs the bag he brought out of Sonny's Café earlier. I know for certain it contains food regardless of the fact that he will not reveal its contents. As soon as the creamy scent of cheddar mixed with the bold aroma of onion and broccoli hit my nose, I knew he had gotten me my favorite; Cheddar Broccoli Soup. *Lunch is definitely on the menu for this date.*

I try to hold back the giggle that tickles at my stomach from being so ecstatic. He holds the sack in one hand while nervously swinging our joined hands back and forth between us. My stomach swirls, my heart pounds up into my throat and my insides are tied in knots. You would think I am thirteen years old out with a boy alone for the first time. I am so nervous that my hands are sweating. *Oh Lord, please don't let him notice.*

My ears perk up to the rattling of the swing chains and the quiet squeak of the merry go round as the wind hits it. Walking past them and an old weathered slide, we make our way to a weedy area between two trees.

At first, I swear he is leading me to absolutely nowhere, but as he pulls me along I can make out where the grass has been worn down into a path. The earthy fragrance of autumn rises up into the wind, along with the sounds of leaves crunching beneath our feet as we wind along the make shift trail in silence. The path is narrow, so I stay close behind Judd with my fingers still laced between his.

He pushes a couple of branches to the side and steps off the path, motioning for me to go in front of him. I hesitate, afraid I may fall in a hole or run into a bear or something, but then I hear the steady stream of water and my curiosity takes ahold of me.

I step from under the canopy of branches and my mouth opens with wonder. The rustling of leaves and twigs stir from behind me as Judd's arms engulf my waist in a warm and secure embrace. He pulls me to him and lays his cheek against my head.

For once, the feeling of his warmth isn't the only thing that has me mesmerized. I glance around slowly and know I must be in some sort of fairyland. In front of me sits a beautiful body of water that is only about twelve feet around, but it is encased in what looks to be some type of cobblestone with a gorgeous fountain in the middle.

The fountain reaches up towards the sky with four tiers, each of them spilling a steady stream into the main circle of water.

I step a little closer to take in the details and see the bottom of the water shimmer as the sunlight hits it. Looking even closer, I can tell it is covered in pennies, nickels, dimes and quarters, all of them very likely waiting on a wish. But that isn't the most astonishing part of this place.

Wrapping around the fountain is a pathway that twists, turns and circles back around. It is made up of small, intricately cut stones and gems in an array of colors, creating all kinds of images. One image is of a woman cradling a baby and another is of a woman standing hand in hand with three small children.

Walking the entire perimeter of the fountain, I look over every detail of each beautiful picture. After strolling by every single one, I stop my investigation at a large slab area to the left side of the fountain, closed in by a curved bench. The image that lies before the bench is by far the largest of them all and truly the most beautiful. It displays a woman with a halo above her head, out stretched wings and her hands held up to the sky as if she is personally delivering a message to the heavens above. Along the bottom of the mural rests the letters T, J and J. I bring my hand to my mouth and swing around to look at Judd.

He is still standing at the opening of the magical place with the sack resting at his feet and studying me this whole time. My heart drums into my throat as I open my mouth to ask what I think may be on the tip of his tongue.

"Is this you and your brothers' initials?" I ask as I point down to the letters.

With a small pained smile, Judd comes over to the area with the angel and pulls me to sit at the base of the bench. I notice how he is extra careful not to step on the image of the lovely winged woman with brown hair that is the same shade as his.

We sit side by side as Judd tells me the story of this place.

"After my father left, Mom tried everything to occupy our minds so we wouldn't ask too many questions. Most weekends, we ended up playing at that playground with several other kids our age," he says, nudging his head towards the way we came.

"One day, we drove to the park, but instead of playing she told us she wanted to go for an adventure walk. She seemed pretty down so I think she needed us to take her mind off things. So we went for a hike. That ended up becoming our thing; we would venture out into the woods around this park, each time choosing a different path. Then one day we found this fountain. It was all grown up and dirty but it seemed magical to us for some reason, especially Mom. She loved that it was a wishing well, because she said we all needed to believe wishes could come true. So that is where it all started. Mom got in touch with the parks and recreation department and then gained permission to fix it up."

Judd sighs, looking around at all the artwork surrounding the fountain. He puts his hand down and runs his fingertips across the stones before he says the next words.

"Mom was really artistic. She could do anything with her hands. So she brought us here week after week with scrap pieces of craft supplies she got from work and all four of us made this."

He looks up at me and gives me a pained smile. I look down at the angel and carefully touch my hand to the stones.

"And this is her?" I question, knowing it is. He smiles so sweetly and then places his hand beside mine on the cold stones.

"My brothers and I came out here and finished this part after she died. We swore this would always be our place where we could be closer to her."

My eyes fill with tears as I watch Judd's brows crease. I look over at his face and can feel the pain in his memories like they are my own. Slowly leaning into him, I brush my hand over his sturdy shoulders which seem so fragile to me now. My hand grazes over his tensed up jawline as I press a tender kiss to his lips, hoping he can feel all the love I hold in my heart for him.

"I love you. Thank you so much for sharing this with me," I whisper against his mouth.

His lips rise into a small smile and his hand softly roams across my cheek, then up into my hair.

"I want to share everything with you . . . always." His words shoot right through my heart and I completely believe him.

Following more talk about his mother and the property that the wishing well sits on, my stomach lets out a loud roar.

"I think that is our cue to eat, not to mention, it may be getting cold by now," he laughs while nudging the sack in my direction. "I wasn't sure what you wanted so I got a little of everything. Go ahead and pull it all out."

I look at him a little puzzled because he knows exactly what I get from this café every single time, but I bite anyway and reach into the sack. First thing I pull out is a turkey and mozzarella Panini on rye with pesto sauce.

I giggle, "Yeah, sure you didn't know what I wanted." *This is only the same thing I get every single time I order from there.* I give him my best sarcastic glare by cocking my head to the side and trying to arch one eyebrow.

He kicks his head back on a laugh, "Keep digging," he says as he motions for me to empty the rest of the bag.

Reaching back in, I pull out another sandwich and I know this is his usual; Steak and Cheddar on sourdough, or a man's sandwich as Judd always puts it. I shake my head and reach in for more.

After pulling out a potato soup and the mouth-watering Broccoli cheddar soup that was attacking my nostrils earlier, I look to the bottom of the sack to grab out the napkins and spoons. There at the bottom of the bag sits a small black box with a pink satin ribbon tied around it.

I let go of the bag and slap my hand across my mouth, sucking in a shocked breath.

Is this . . .

Judd leans forward on high alert at my reaction. "Ok, don't run away, freak out, cry or any of those things girls do. It isn't what it looks like at all. It's just something I thought you should have and that I wanted you to have."

My heart climbs out of my throat and back into my chest. There for a minute, I really thought I would look up to find him down on one knee.

I lower my head and close my eyes tightly, embarrassed by my reaction. *I just know I am the shade of a stop sign.*

He opens his mouth to speak, grabbing both my hands with a stunned look in his eyes.

"Oh, shit. Are you disappointed? Now I feel bad."

I try to hide my face in my hands, but Judd holds onto them firmly, raising my face so that I will look him in the eyes.

"Let me take you on a couple more dates before we get to that point. Deal?" he says only inches away from my lips, before descending in on them.

My heart skips a beat and then pounds fiercely as his soft lips linger against mine.

He moves away just a bit and I nod my head.

"Deal," I whisper, feeling silly for hoping that he was proposing.

Judd reaches into the sack and pulls out the tiny box.

"Open it." He places it in my hand and looks me dead in the eyes with a serious expression that has me captivated. "It may not be a ring, but it is a big step for me; a step that I want to take."

I bite my lip, excited to see what it could be.

As soon as I slip the lid off, I am surprised to find a key. I pinch it between my index finger and thumb, dangling it in the air before me the same way he did the night we reunited. Judd grabs the key out of my hand and holds it up.

"This may not seem like much, but it is the key to my apartment. This is a symbol of the fact that I want you with me all the time; every day; every second; every minute; I want you by my side. This leaves no barriers between us." He presses the key back into my palm.

I squeeze my hand around the piece of metal and press my hand to my heart, filled with so much love for him.

"This is perfect. I love it. Thank you." I smile, looking around at our peaceful surroundings.

"This whole day has been perfect and keeps getting better. I don't think it is possible to ever top this first date." Judd's face lights up like a little boy proud of his accomplishments.

After we enjoy our little picnic, we end up walking hand in hand around the entire perimeter of the wishing well while Judd tells the story behind each image in the path. We end our date throwing a couple coins into the well and silently making our own wishes.

I giggle as I throw my first one in.

Please let this night go by fast so we can be alone.

Running my fingertips along the bumpy surfaces of another coin, I know I have one more wish. Closing my eyes tightly, I send one more wish out into the world before tossing it in.

Please let him be mine forever.

I open my eyes and sneak a look at him right as he tosses his last coin in. He doesn't even have his eyes closed; he stares at me with a slight smile as he flips it into the water.

"What was your wish?" Judd pesters me on our way back to his truck.

"I can't tell you that. It won't come true." *I'm not saying a word; no way do I want to chance those wishes not coming true.*

"Come on, just a clue." He flashes me his dimple and it's all I can do to not cave in.

"Nope, I can't tell you."

Walking close behind me, his firm hands slide along the contours of my waist, pulling me against his chest right as we make it to his truck.

"I'll tell you mine, if you tell me yours." The sudden warmth of his breath near my ear sends shivers through my body.

"Mmhhhuhh," I breathe out, leaning back into the security of his arms.

"Was it about me? Mine was about you."

I quickly flip around to meet his eyes with a smile across my face. His hands automatically cling to my sides as I stretch up onto my tiptoes to kiss him.

"Maybe. . . ." I say after pulling away from his lips.

Judd rolls his eyes and laughs as he opens the passenger side door for me.

On the drive back to his apartment, we tease back and forth, giggling and laughing trying to get each other to give up what was uttered in our heads before our coins dipped into the well.

We end up getting back to his apartment less than two hours before the party starts. Although this day has been beyond anything I could ever imagine for a first date, I really wish we had just a bit more time to be alone.

As soon as we are inside, it is no secret that he wishes the same. He insists we have plenty of time and makes an event of trying to get me into the bedroom. The one thing we do agree on is that we both need a shower after walking through the weeds, and since we are limited on time; why not merge it into one. *That would be the more frugal thing to do seeing as we will save time and water.* Besides, we are both more than a little addicted to taking showers together.

In no time, we are both out of our clothes and soaking wet. *So much for saving time!*

I lean my back against Judd's chest as he runs my bright pink loofah sponge over my chest and shoulders. He has the entire front of my body all lathered up, but insists that my chest needs a little further attention. *What the hell; clean away.*

Shortly after he rinses all the suds from his body and mine, my phone chirps with a new text message. On the off chance that it may be about my dad, I slip my hand out of the shower, pat it on a towel and then grab my phone off the wall shelf beside the shower.

Bethany: Already done decorating and I already have all the food out! We are ready! I'm going to get dressed and I'll see you later! Thanks for doing the running!

She also includes a picture of the apartment all set up. *Ugh!* I mentally cringe when I see the sheets tacked to the walls and splattered with streaks of fake blood and bloody hand prints. *Good grief, our apartment looks like a slaughter house or a scene from a zombie apocalypse. I guess we'll just get the carpets steam cleaned later.*

Me: The apartment looks great! Looks like there was a brutal murder that took place there! Lol! Since you don't need help, I'll probably get there just a bit before the party starts. K?

Bethany: Sounds good! C-ya then!

Judd turns off the water, breaking my trance and wraps a towel around my shoulders.

"What is it?" he asks with a hopeful tone in his voice as I resituate the towel around my body.

I giggle knowing what he is thinking, "It was Bethany letting us know that we don't have to rush."

Judd's face lights up and within seconds he has me flung over his shoulder, drips of water flinging through the air from my drenched hair.

I laugh and squirm in his arms as he fumbles with the door knob.

"We have a whole extra hour. We are damn well making good use of that time." I can hear the smile in his playful tone as his hand slaps across my bare ass.

"Ooooww," I laugh out loud as he swings the door open.

Not even one step out the door and Judd rushes backwards. A sharp slamming noise echoes in the small room as he lowers my feet to the floor, abruptly. I clasp the towel around my chest and turn to face Judd. He has his body braced against the door with his hand held over his face.

"What the hell, dude!" He yells at the door and I am beyond confused.

A loud howl reverberates from the other side of the door and I'm immediately aware that Evan was more than likely the recipient of seeing my bare ass up in the air.

My jaw hits the floor and I really hope my rear end is the only thing that was visible.

"Why the hell are you home?" Judd yells out.

Evan keeps laughing hysterically and for a moment I think we may have to go out there and do CPR.

"Evan, you better not have seen a damn thing!" Judd hollers with his forehead pressed against the door.

Finally, Evan calms his laughter enough to speak.

"Oh yeah, I definitely got an eyeful! I think my retinas are actually on fire! Either that or I might be horny! I haven't decided yet! How are you?"

Evan cracks up and a thumping sound catches my attention that I assume is him stomping his feet or fists; he is loving this.

Judd hits his fist against the door with his eyes shut tightly as if he is in pain.

"I am going to kick your ass, man! You live for this shit! Seriously, is there ever going to be a time that you don't interrupt us?"

I reach down and grab a towel for Judd while Evan defends himself between laughter.

"Hey, easy now on the accusations, I was out here all defenseless and you two come busting in here, getting all crazy like you own the place. So technically, you walked in on me this time!"

Judd shakes his head and wraps the towel around his waist.

"Wait in here till I can get you some clothes."

No problem! I'm ok with not giving Evan another eyeful.

Judd opens and then closes the door behind him and I soon hear them both laughing.

Evan is definitely a pain in the ass, but life would be pretty boring without his sense of humor and practical jokes.

Judd returns within minutes and hands me my clothes.

Fully dressed, I head out of the bathroom behind Judd and can barely make eye contact with Evan.

Of course when I do, he stays true to his teasing self by pointing to his behind and mouthing "Nice ass, Alyssa."

I turn ten shades of red, but decide to throw a little sass his way, "Hey Evan, kiss it," I silently mouth.

Evan grabs his stomach and cracks up.

"I just love her! She never puts up with my shit!" He cries out between laughter.

Judd grabs the remote on our way through the living room and tosses it at Evan to get him to shut up.

"Hey . . . What?!" Evan says innocently.

I giggle and escape to the bedroom with Judd. It doesn't take long to know that Evan's sudden company has not deterred Judd's agenda to make use of the extra hour we have.

I'm just thankful that he finally got a lock on his door a couple weeks ago.

Forty five minutes later, both of us are dressed in ear to ear grins and getting ready for the party. Judd opts to wear a long sleeve shirt and jeans, leaving the dressing up to me.

"You need some help?" he asks as I slide on my costume.

His suggestion makes my heart race, knowing full well that if we didn't have plans tonight that we would stay in bed, wrapped up in each other.

"No, go hang out with Evan while I get ready. I want my end look to be a surprise." I laugh some more, feeling like a bride about to reveal her wedding dress to her groom for the first time.

"Ok." Giving one quick peck on the lips, he turns and slips out the door.

A sudden crash from the doorway has me spinning around only to see the door shut behind him. *What on earth was that?* My ears perk up, but after quickly hearing an eruption of laughter and conversation from the next room, I get busy dousing my face with makeup in front of the dresser mirror. I double check my reflection and run through a mental check list of details before heading out to model for the guys.

Once I enter the room, Judd's mouth drops open and Evan lets out a loud whistle. Proudly, I twirl around once, careful to not let the short white empress dress fly up and show off my white lace panties. *I think Evan has got enough of a view already!*

"Holy shit, you look good," Judd says, his wide eyes saying he is ten seconds away from hauling me back in the bedroom.

"I second that, although the first view I had today even tops this outfit." Evan's comment and laughter gets an evil glare from Judd and has my face blazing in mortification.

"I'm telling you now, man . . . you better wipe that image out of your mind," Judd orders and then swings his eyes back to me.

"I'll work on that," Evan mutters under his breath. "Seriously, you're smoking in that outfit, Alyssa."

"Thanks," I tell Evan, appreciating his sincerity. "Are you joining us?" I ask after remembering that he was supposed to be out of town tonight.

"Yeah, some drama kind of got stirred up between me and my brother and I figured I would hang out here instead of going to the cabin this weekend."

Sweet memories filter through my mind at the mention of the word cabin.

"I told him he should join us." Judd looks at me hesitantly, seemingly checking to make sure I am ok with this.

"Yes, you should totally come. It's going to be a blast. You can even dress up if you want."

Evan spits out a laugh, "No thanks on the dressing up, but I will tag along."

"Sounds great. You guys ready?" I excitedly say, grabbing my purse.

They both stand and make their way to the door, Judd grabbing my hand in the process.

"Maybe you should change and save that outfit for later tonight," he whispers with a playful gleam in his eyes.

I giggle and jab my elbow into his side. He may stay pretty close to my side tonight and that is absolutely fine by me.

So far this has been the best day of my life; by far the best first date

I've ever experienced and definitely a date I will always remember.

Party for two

TWENTY MINUTES LATER WE PARK at my apartment, ready to have a blast. Just as I am opening my door, Judd reaches over and stops me.

"Lyssa, I need to talk to you. I should have told you this last night, but I didn't want to ruin the time we had alone. Plus, I know it will upset you. About Bethany . . ." I start to tense up, wondering what on earth he could sound this solemn about.

Once he brings up Bethany's name, I know he wants to talk about how uncomfortable he has been around her. *There has to be a way for my boyfriend and roommate to get along eventually.* Bethany can be super overbearing at times and quite determined when she sets her mind to it, but I know she is past it, I just wish he was.

I lean forward to stop him mid-sentence, "I know you still feel a little uneasy around her. Trust me, I can tell, but Judd, I am 100% positive she is past everything. Plus, it does not bother me anymore either. At first, I was insecure, knowing she had feelings for you and had tried to get you in bed, but then I told myself that I have you and everything else doesn't matter. So stop stressing; it is all water under the bridge." I smile and look at him with complete certainty in my eyes.

"No, that's not it. Actually she does make me uneasy, but it's because . . ."

We both flinch at a loud thud and see Evan peering in the driver's side window with an irritated look on his face. Judd ends the conversation and opens his door.

"Hey guys are we going to stay in the parking lot talking all night or are we going inside?" Evan says with a devilish grin.

On the way to my apartment door, Judd pulls me aside. "Babe, we still need to talk," he tells me quietly, "I just don't want to ruin your night."

I can tell how bad this is bothering him by the urgency in his tone, but I don't understand why this is still weighing so heavily on his mind. I really hope his level of discomfort isn't enough for him to want me to stay away from my own roommate. That thought has my stomach rolling with nerves and my body tensing up with anxiety.

I calmly place my hands on his broad shoulders then run my fingertips up his neck to his rigid jawline. The crease between his eyebrows and tightness of his jaw has me tempted to suggest that we leave and go talk, but honestly, maybe tonight can break through that bit of uneasiness that he still feels around Bethany.

"Let's just talk about it in the morning."

He nods his head with a troubled look on his face.

"Just try to have fun, ok? I promise there is nothing for you to worry about. Let's just go in and relax, mingle, laugh . . ." I giggle and wrap my arms around his neck in an effort to pull him closer.

Judd's tenseness gives way to a gentle smile as he bends to place a kiss on my lips.

" . . . and then just the two of us can escape somewhere quiet. I promise we will talk."

Judd's smile grows and his slack arms snake around my waist so that we are sealed together.

"Oh, please. Hello, I'm still here." Judd and I laugh at Evan's sarcastic tone a few feet behind us, but we keep our eyes glued to one another.

"Ok. I'm holding out for the part of that whole idea where we get to escape somewhere alone." Wiggling his eyebrows with a playful grin, for now all his worries have melted away.

It doesn't take long for our apartment to be jam-packed with numerous bodies dressed anywhere from a vampire and zombie to a fireman stripper and a French maid. There is even one guy dressed as a long neck beer bottle with a tin foil hat.

Abby and Piper finally walk in, looking like absolute knockouts.

"Holy shit," Evan mumbles, staring at Piper with a look of wonderment.

I glance back her way as she walks across the room, dressed in a tight all black cat-woman-like costume with her long dark locks in spiral curls, her eyes outlined in heavy black liner, a splash of black on the tip of her nose and three delicate lines drawn across each of her cheeks as whiskers. Her grip tightens on the black leather whip she holds in her hand as she sees Evan and for a second, I think she may break it in half.

"Great," she sarcastically mouths to Abby.

Abby nods her head and then flashes me a huge smile, rushing up to my side. She is dressed in a cute little Go-Go costume with a bright, psychedelic dress cinched at the waist with a tight belt and topped off with knee-high red boots.

As soon as they join us near the drink station in the kitchen, Piper fixes Evan with a harsh stare. He immediately pulls her to the side.

"So, what's there to drink?" Abby asks.

I point over my shoulder at the collection of alcohol that has been compiled tonight. Abby leans across the counter and quickly fills up a couple of shot glasses. She hands one to me and one to Piper.

"Let's get this party started then, girls," I laugh and indulge in one shot. *This may be my max for the night.*

"How is Dad?" I ask as Judd moves closer so he can join in on the conversation.

"He seems really good. He has a bit of a cough, but seemed in good spirits and excited about spending the evening with Mom," Abby explains.

"So where's Tristan? All these short skirts and skin tight costumes seem right up his alley." Abby looks at Judd and all amusement leaves his face.

He and Evan share a strange look before he answers. "He's been a little preoccupied lately to mess with that sort of stuff."

Judd rarely talks about Tristan and I haven't seen him since the lake. In the past month that we have been together, aside from most weekends that we spend at my parents, we have carved out time to go to some of Jake's football games and even met him for lunch a few times. Tristan, however, has kept himself scarce except for a few tense and heated calls between him and Judd.

"I heard through the grapevine that he dropped out of college. Is he transferring or just done with college all together?" Abby continues her line of questions and with each one Judd seems to get a little more uneasy.

Luckily, Piper and Evan's voices kick up a notch, distracting us all from our current conversation.

"Would you just detract your damn claws for one night? I'm here to have a good time." Evan's cool and playful personality that he usually exhibits turns harsh and spiteful as he speaks to Piper.

"Well, I really don't care to waltz down memory lane tonight!" she declares, standing with her arms folded and a hateful scowl on her face. "And FYI, I'd love to have a good time tonight, too, Evan, but should I worry about anything I say or any poor judgment I make tonight being broadcast to the world tomorrow!" she spits out.

Abby grabs Piper's arm, trying to coerce her away from the escalating situation. She finally relents and they disappear into the living room where several people are bumping and grinding to booming music.

"I'm outta here! I am not going to stay here and let her punish me for something I can't change! See ya later, Alyssa." Evan pushes his way past Judd and storms towards the door, looking back at Piper with a gloomy expression on his face.

"I'll be right back." Judd follows him out.

Kyle and Chris stroll up to the counter and go for a cup each, grabbing the keg nozzle to fill them with beer.

"Drama already?" Kyle tilts his head in the direction of Judd and Evan.

"Huh? Oh . . . no. Well, actually I'm not sure what happened." I'm sure Abby and Judd know more about the circumstances of the argument, but I'm just sorry that Evan felt he had to leave because of it.

I talk to Kyle for only a second longer, making sure to be on the opposite side of the room when Judd returns.

After making my way out to the dance floor, I huddle in between a crowd of sweaty bodies hopping to music pouring out of the speaker as I lift my arms in the air and swing my hips from side to side.

It doesn't take long before my dress is clinging to my body and beads of sweat are rolling down my back. Piper has affixed herself to Chris and Abby is cheek-to-cheek with Hayden, a guy from Kyle's fraternity.

The music winds down to a semi slower song and I decide it is best if I exit before Kyle asks me to dance. Before I can turn to leave, strong hands grip my hips and a hard chest presses against my back.

"Were you leaving before I could dance with you?" Judd whispers in my ear.

I flip around to face him and his arms naturally wrap around my waist like that is the only place they have ever belonged.

"More like, I was going to find you and drag your butt out here with me," I giggle as I clasp my hands behind his neck and start to sway with him.

"So, how much more of an appearance do we need to make before we can turn this into a private party?" My knees go weak from the thought of us being alone.

We enjoy a few more songs engulfed in each other's arms before Abby jumps in between us.

"Get your ass over here and dance with me."

The slur and giddiness in her voice is more than enough proof that she is tipsy and it is long overdue. She has basically confined herself to the house the last few weeks, helping Mom with Dad around the clock. It's a relief to see her relax and unwind.

"You dance and I'll go get us another drink." With a quick kiss, Judd darts off to the make-shift bar.

Abby and Piper quickly sandwich me between them as a fast, thumping song starts to play. I throw my arms over their shoulders and Bethany staggers over to join the group dance off.

"Make room for me."

We all laugh, singing and dancing until our feet and lungs are on fire.

A few minutes later, the song ends.

"Come on. I need another drink," Abby says as she drags me off.

Come to think of it, Judd was supposed to bring me a drink. We crowd around the counter with several other people, Abby pushing her way to the keg.

"Have you seen Judd?"

"Not since he left to get a drink. Do you want me to make you something?" Abby asks, grabbing a cup and filling it with ice.

I look around searching for Judd through the sea of faces.

"No, I think I'll pass. I think we are going to try and stay sober in case Mom needs us."

Abby stops in the middle of making a drink and turns her attention to me.

"Absolutely not, Mom told me to make sure you were having fun tonight and for none of us to worry. She's got this, Alyssa. I think we deserve to enjoy ourselves. Dad will be fine." Her smile slowly breaks through my barrier of responsibility and worry.

"Ok, but are you sure? I mean, do you think it is a good idea?" I ask with a tiny bit of hesitation.

"Yes! Party, girl! I intend on getting blitzed tonight and you should, too," she giggles, handing me a concoction she just threw together. "In fact, start with this."

I laugh and look around the kitchen, finally spotting Judd. He is parked at the kitchen table with Chris, Kyle and Hayden, all looking to be deep in conversation and by the way he is leaning forward ready to pounce on Kyle, it may be in my best interest to intervene.

I sashay my way over and slide into his lap, stopping the conversation as Judd's expression softens. He pulls me back against him with a territorial look in his eyes. Kyle shifts uneasily in his chair, watching us as Judd resumes their discussion.

"I really don't know if I should. We agreed not to drink too much tonight in case we would need to leave suddenly."

Kyle nods his head, clearly understanding his reference to "needing to leave early."

"Gotcha," he says back to Judd.

"What were you two talking about?" I ask looking back and forth between them.

Judd opens his mouth to talk, but Kyle beats him to it, "Football and then I challenged him to a game of quarters." Kyle laughs, eyeing Judd.

Abby sneaks up behind us. "Yes, we should totally play. I'm in. Come on," she hollers with a huge smile on her face while she hops to the other side of the table and lands on Hayden's lap.

Judd looks at me, clearly wondering what my plans are.

"It's ok. Abby said Dad is fine and that Mom basically ordered us to let our hair down and have fun . . . all of us. So, I guess we're in, too." I pull my cup up to my lips and take a big swallow, letting the alcohol roll down my throat.

The eight of us, Judd, me, Abby, Piper, Kyle, Hayden, Bethany and Chris, all cram ourselves around the table and listen to Kyle's instructions on how to play this particular game of quarters.

"The object of the game is to pick any part of your body and let the quarter roll off into the shot glasses. If the quarter doesn't roll, it is an automatic drink. If the quarter lands in a shot, you drink. If it doesn't roll and then falls into a shot, you have to take two shots." Kyle explains as he uses the quarter to demonstrate each action on his own body.

"However, if the quarter doesn't land on the table or in a shot glass, the person in the direction in which the coin lands has to take your shot for you." He puts the quarter to the left of him and points to me for an example.

I'm a little confused but when it comes to me, I place the quarter on the back of my hand over the table and it rolls perfectly down beside a shot of whiskey.

"No drink for you!" Kyle announces and then Judd grabs up the coin.

He places the quarter on his nose and positions his face over the group of glasses. The quarter falls flat and then bounces off into a shot glass.

"Two drinks!" Kyle calls out.

Judd slams them back and then Abby is up.

She very cleverly thrusts her chest out and lets the quarter roll into a glass off her boob.

I catch Hayden wiggling his eyebrows up and down in her direction as she seductively drinks her shot, giving him googly eyes. *Oh boy! Yeah, she is already half gone!*

The game goes round and round for quite a while and I find I am pretty good at balancing a coin. I have only had to drink a hand full of times while Abby, Judd and Bethany seem to be on a losing streak.

Little by little, everyone starts to disappear from the table and eventually the apartment seems a lot less chaotic.

By midnight, the party is winding down and most of us are well on our way to being drunk. I am still semi-sober, but have a light and fuzzy feeling gradually working its way through my system.

Judd and I sit alone at the table, grabbing up an unopened bottle of vodka.

"Ok, now for our own private game." Judd winks at me as he sets two shot glasses down between us.

I laugh, knowing the last thing we need is more to drink, but I'm curious as to what type of game he wants to play.

I raise my eyebrow in question and Judd fills me in on the details, "Ok, so we'll call this game, Truth," he chuckles, "So, we each have to think up a statement that is true about ourselves, but the catch . . . try to come up with something you may have never told me about yourself . . ." he raises his eyebrows and goes on, "If the statement you throw out is in fact something I don't know, I drink, but if it is something I do know, you drink. It's kind of a get-to-know-each-other-even-better type of game. Easy enough?"

"Kind of like truth or dare?" I ask after I hear the rules.

I think it is totally a made up game, but aren't all drinking games that way; made up when you just want a reason to drink with your friends.

"Yeah, but without the dare," he counters, "I'll go first." He smiles and starts with his first personal fact about himself, "I was so drunk when I lost my virginity that I didn't remember anything about it the next morning."

My mouth falls open and I laugh. "I knew you were drunk when you lost it, but I didn't know that you didn't remember it. So, like you didn't even know who the girl was the next day?"

He smiles as if he has just won a prize. "Ah ah . . . no questions during this game just random facts. You drink."

I tip a small shot of vodka back and then it is my turn. *Let's make this interesting.*

"I've fantasized about you on more than one occasion," I say in my best seductive tone, while leaning closer and thrusting my chest his way.

His eyes widen and he stumbles around for words, "You mean you . . . you . . ."

He stops talking, tips back a shot and slams the glass back down to the table with a huge grin on his face that brings out his dimple. *Yep, I didn't think he knew that!*

We go back and forth over and over with more facts about each other.

"Someday, I'd like to have three kids; two girls and one boy."

Definitely a drink for me.

"I told Mom all about our two weeks together at the lake."

He drinks without hesitation.

"Wait, how much did you tell her and was this before I went home with you the first time?" he asks as he refills both of our shot glasses.

"Ah ah . . . I thought there were no questions?" I throw back at him with a giggle.

Judd levels me with a stern glare and I relent, figuring I'll give him a hint.

"Well, if you want the truth, maybe you should just take another shot or . . ." I laugh as his expression turns to panic. " . . . maybe even two shots."

Immediately reading my insinuation, he tips back two more shots, probably trying to drown out the embarrassment of knowing that my mom knows the details of our sex life.

"If it makes you feel any better, the first time she met you she gave me a thumbs-up when she hugged you."

Judd's eyes get as big as saucers and he throws back another shot. I lean across the table, pressing my forehead to my arms and crack up.

"Ok, so . . ." His chest expands as he blows out a deep breath. "You were the last thing I saw when I wrecked."

My breath catches in my throat with his words and my pulse quickens.

"I had an image of you in my mind. You were sitting in that old fishing boat out on the lake. It was the day we went fishing and the sun was shining down on you while you talked about your Dad." He stops talking and looks at me with an unreadable expression.

I don't bother to drink. I did not know this, but I have no desire to drink. There are far better things that should be against my lips right now. Hopping up out of my seat, I place myself right in his lap and give him an I-Love-You-More-Than-Life-Itself kiss.

It nearly brings tears to my eyes, but then he steals my turn by adding another fact, "Do you know that the day I got out of the hospital, my first trip was to my mom's wishing well? I sat down on that bench and relived every single second of our two weeks together, too. So I guess both of our moms know everything."

After this fact is revealed I throw my arms around him. "Let's go to my bedroom. I think it's time to turn this into a party for two, don't you?"

Don't look back

L ITTLE BY LITTLE, WE HEAR everyone leaving the party as we snuggle up in my bed. It didn't take long for both of us to shed our clothes and slide between the sheets. Loads of alcohol and a few intimate moments shared while playing Judd's truth game is all it took for us both to be completely worked up and eager to feel one another. But once we are both within the comfort of my soft mattress and the warmth of our bodies molded together, sleep starts to hit Judd.

"I am so tired! I really should not have drank that much. I'm so sorry," he mumbles as his fingertips make slow careful wisps up and down my back.

The upper half of my body is draped over his chest so that I can look at him. His eyes are closed and for a moment I think he may be asleep by the way his breathing gets deeper. I shift my body to get comfortable and his grip on me tightens.

"Stay like this. I want to feel you close to me; just like this."

I laugh at how his words slur together.

"Are you talking in your sleep?" I say, keeping my voice in a hushed tone as my heart gushes with happiness.

Something about the way his eyes are closed while he talks and the way he looks so peaceful has my heart going a mile a minute.

"I'm trying to stay awake," he barely gets out and I can't help but giggle.

"You know I want to marry you some day, right?" I instantly still with his words, unable to answer. "The three kids I want someday . . . I want them with you," he adds with his eyes still closed.

He has to be talking in his sleep, but I really don't want to stop him. My heart is on the verge of exploding; overflowing with all the love that I feel for him.

A small smile touches his lips and he starts whispering more declarations of love through an alcohol induced haze.

"I want to make love to you every night . . . and I want to hold you until we both have gray hair and wrinkled skin. I want to have my arms around you when I take my last breath on this earth."

I can't take any more. I push my body up so that my chest is pressed flush against his. I cover his lips with mine and he quickly reacts. His hands come alive and engulf me. His mouth follows my lead, but soon he takes control, exploring my mouth with his tongue.

"I thought you were tired," I point out breathlessly.

"I'm not that tired," he says, flipping me over onto my back.

The shots and beer we consumed earlier did absolutely nothing to damper our passion, but instead aids in the vigor of the moment.

"I need to put the scarf on the door so nobody walks in," I tell Judd in between kisses.

"I already did," he says like it's an everyday occurrence and then continues on his mission to seduce me.

Our bodies connect and we twist and turn, taste and touch, finding our perfect tempo until we are both breathing hard and exhausted. I soon find out that alcohol seems to be an aphrodisiac for Judd. All through the early morning hours, Judd talks and makes noises in his sleep, calling out my name while his hands and body take over my own. Half the time, his eyes remain closed and he mumbles things that he has never said before; things that have me panting within minutes.

Around four in the morning and following a rather enthusiastic display of affection, Judd gets up to use the restroom that adjoins my bedroom. As I lay there trying to recover, his tall, built and bare frame drags back into the room.

"I am so tired," he says with his eyes barely open, "I think I am still drunk, too."

I giggle at his drowsy and drunken confusion as he heads in the wrong direction, turning to the right to crawl into Bethany's bed instead of mine.

"Over here," I call out softly so he can follow the sound of my voice, "You're going to fall if you don't open your eyes."

Sighing, he stretches his eyebrows open to widen his eyes and turns back towards my bed.

"You need to switch beds with her. Going back and forth between our apartments, I cannot keep this straight." He lets out a small laugh and I giggle, knowing what he means.

His head hangs down in sheer exhaustion and he drags his feet as if he is sleepwalking. Once he reaches the bed, he slides back in beside me, settles onto his back and pulls me snug against his chest. A tiny laugh moves over his lips and then his breathing gets slow and deep.

"I keep having these wild dreams about you. Then I'll feel you beside me and I can't control myself. I'm not complaining about the dreams or waking up at all hours of the night with you, but don't ever let me drink that much again," he says, his voice growing quieter and fading off as sleep begins to tug him under.

I smile, burrowing against his chest for sanctuary.

Judd remains silent and his deep, steady breaths tell me that he has finally surrendered to sleep. Dazzled by his words and the thought that he even dreams of me, I let myself drift off along with him.

A loud thump and the sound of the bedroom door sliding open wakes me to light streaming through the window. Holding my hand up over my face until my eyes adjust to the light, I peek through my fingers to see Judd still sleeping soundly.

Ok, who disobeyed the rule of the scarf? If the scarf is up, you do not come in until it comes down! At least that's Bethany's theory behind it.

I quietly giggle, thinking about how Judd thought to put it up last night without me saying a word. Abby pokes her head through the doorway and motions her hand for me to come join her. Pointing to the sheet, which is my only shield from her being blinded by my naked body; I silently let her know that I need to get dressed first.

Her eyes are horribly blood shot and her mascara is streaked down her face. I assume it is from a late night, but it still has me in a state of dread. I bolt up and throw on a sweatshirt and sweat pants, skipping my under garments.

I glance around for my phone, knowing Mom would have messaged me if something was wrong with Dad. *Damn it! I must have left it in my purse out in the living room.*

As soon as I get into the living room, my blood pressure hits the roof and my heart is about to drum out of my chest. Abby stands with the front door impatiently flung open, chewing on her thumb nail nervously.

"Grab your purse, we have to go. Dad is in the hospital," she says in a panic as soon as we reach the hall outside of my apartment.

"What! Why . . . what happened?!" My mind shuts down and I can't even think to know what to do next.

Flinging my door shut behind me, we race through the hall and out the door of my apartment building as she fills me in.

"He's ok, mom said. She sent me a text early this morning, but I must not have heard it go off. I woke up a few minutes ago and heard it ringing and that's when mom told me that she's been trying to get ahold of us. I feel awful. We should have never . . ."

"It's ok, we know now and we will get over there. What happened?" I ask as we reach my car.

Abby clears her throat before answering, "They think he has a cold or a virus or something and his immune system is too low to fight it off."

My heart aches for how scared Mom must be.

Abby looks around as if she lost something. "Do you have your keys? We have to get there, like now. I rode with Piper, but I left her a note saying I got a ride with you," she says all in one breath.

I twist around like a dog chasing its tail, desperately looking for my purse, which of course I completely forgot when I walked out.

"I have to get my keys and I will be back down. My car is unlocked. Get in and I will be right back. I'm going to wake Judd and tell him to meet us at the hospital. Is he at Rosemore General?"

"Yeah . . ." Her eyes well up with tears and her voice starts to tremble. "Alyssa, I should not have left last night. I should have stayed there."

"No, don't blame yourself. You said he was alright, right," I point out more than ask, worried sick that this is worse than either of us know, but knowing we should not blame ourselves.

"Yeah, Mom said that she doesn't think it's any more than a virus, but that they are admitting him."

"Ok, I'll be back."

I wrap my arms around my sister, hoping we can hold each other up. I am scared and she is just as distraught. In a complete frenzy, I scramble back to my apartment, throw my purse over my shoulder and turn to go wake Judd.

It's ok . . . it's ok . . . Dad's ok, my mind replays over and over.

Glancing over to the couch and sofa before I get to my bedroom door, I realize that Piper is still sawing logs, but Bethany is no longer on the couch where she was earlier.

I turn the doorknob and push my door open, about ready to jump out of my skin with worry for Dad, but suddenly my legs stop working and I am paralyzed.

My hand instantly flies across my mouth and I suck in a harsh breath of air as tears fill my eyes. Bethany's bare body lies on top of Judd's and they are both awake. He yells something and tosses her off.

It's not until that moment that it registers to me that he is in her bed. *How could this happen? I was only out of the room for twenty minutes, tops. Is he still that drunk that he could have mistaken her for me?*

My mind is swirling in fifty different directions when I finally regain my sense of hearing.

Bethany gathers a sheet over her body and instantly tries to explain what I walked in on.

"Alyssa, I'm so sorry. He got into bed with me after you . . . one thing led to another. It all happened . . . and then . . ." she pleads, her words sounding nearly foreign and clipped off from all the thoughts clouding my head.

Judd has already jumped to his feet, frantically pulling his jeans on like he's escaping a burning building. His hand snaps up towards Bethany as she rambles on.

Shaking his head, he points at her with venom in his eyes. "I did not. Don't even . . ." He looks back to me, his face altering into sadness, pity and remorse. "God no, Alyssa . . . this is not what it looks like. I did not do anything with her."

I stand there staring at him not sure what to say, what to believe. *This is déjà vu! No! This has definitely happened before!* I look back and forth between them both, not knowing what to believe. There is no denying that he was in her bed.

"Alyssa, you have to believe me, please. I was asleep and I just woke up and she was . . ."

He stops talking as I look him in the eyes and then back at my bed, silently questioning Bethany's comment about him crawling into bed with her. His brows knit together as he looks down at her bed and registers what I'm thinking. He says nothing, so I look to her for an explanation.

"What was going on? Did you two . . ."

Judd quickly defends himself, "Hell no, we did not! I would never do that to you!"

The whole time Bethany refuses to look me in the eye.

"Bethany?"

I just need verbal validation of what is already so obvious.

Judd looks down at the floor, puzzled as if he is trying to piece together what happened himself.

She finally meets my eyes and the words that come out of her mouth more than shock me; they kill me.

"I am so sorry. I didn't mean for it to happen. It just did," she speaks quietly, her voice laced with sorrow and immediately joined by Judd's angry shouts.

"You're lying! I didn't touch you!"

I've never heard such animosity in his voice, but I know what I saw.

Bethany goes on between his hollers, "As soon as you left, I came in to sleep in my bed of course, and Judd walked over and got in beside me. It wasn't like me and Kyle, he initiated this, I promise. You have to believe me."

My eyes widen in horror and I swear someone just jabbed a blunt object through my heart. *What does she mean with Kyle?*

"What are you talking about?" I say through gritted teeth.

Judd's face drops into the palms of his hands and he shakes his head back and forth as he mumbles something under his breath.

"The night you walked in on me and Kyle. I assumed you always knew. I was just jealous and we both got drunk and it just happened. That was my fault, but this time is different. He got into my bed. I thought he wanted me and so . . ."

Judd's eyes fog over with fury. "I do not want her and I did not crawl into her bed to be with her. I was half asleep and half drunk and just got into the wrong bed," he spits out, looking back at me with a snarl on his face.

I fold my arms across my chest more as an act of defense for my heart rather than anger.

"You did crawl into her bed though!" I yell as I point to Bethany's bed.

Judd shakes his head. "Yeah, but I . . ."

"He got in and I had no idea . . ." Bethany starts.

"You're a liar! I would never touch you!" he yells with such force, that his hand trembles as he holds it out and his face is red. "Alyssa, please. If you would just listen to me . . ." he continues in a gentler, pleading tone while Bethany shouts out how sorry she is.

My mind swims with thoughts of how nervous he would get around her when they would be alone. *It makes sense!*

"Have you been screwing her this whole time? Is that what was so urgent that you needed to talk to me about last night? What, you needed to get it off your chest?"

Even though I make the accusation, I don't see how it could be possible. He is always with me. He would never have the time, but it still makes me ill to even consider it. *How can this all be happening?*

"No! Why would you ask that?! You know I love you!" He yells out and steps forward.

I flinch backwards, right into the door, putting my hands out to let him know to stay back. I look back to Bethany and she looks straight into my eyes.

"We only had sex this one time. Other than that all we have done is kiss." She confesses. "He kissed me the other night after we went shopping for costumes but that's it."

A horn blares outside my bedroom window and I know it is Abby, completely in the dark and desperate to get to the hospital, but I am in shock from this new information. I let out a heavy breath and drop my mouth open; my heart has been ripped into a billion pieces today.

"No! Wait! That is not true! She's lying! I did not . . ."

Bethany quickly cuts him off, "I told him that I was the one that slept with Kyle and that I would not hurt you like that again. That's when he . . ."

"Wait a minute! I did not . . ."

I don't let him finish. *They kissed just the other night? He knew that she slept with Kyle and he kept that from me? What happened to him wanting to share everything with me? That is information he damn well should have shared!*

He opens his mouth to go on, but I have had enough of this.

"Did you kiss her? Did you know that about her and Kyle? Answer me!" I raise my voice and move forward.

"It's not like that. Please, this is all getting blown out of proportion," his voice softens to a painful, breathy whisper as he looks me in the eyes, but I don't care.

Rage boils inside of me as he accuses me of blowing this up, as if I am the one that was just caught in someone else's bed. I think I have earned the right to blow up, after all this isn't the first time I have been destroyed like this. *I can't do this right now! I have to get to the hospital!* After quickly snatching up my purse and keys from the counter, I storm out of the room with the sounds of Judd's feet thudding against the floor as he runs to catch me.

"Would you wait? This is not how it looks!"

I slam the door shut before he can make it out and race to my car, fully intent on speeding away before another hurtful word can be spoken.

Abby sits in the passenger seat with a look of shock as she takes in the scene.

I am on an endless time loop of walking in on guys that claim to love me, when they are cheating on me. *Who in the hell has this kind of luck?! This can't be real!*

I make it to my car and nearly rip the door off the hinges. *This all seems too familiar. This is the last thing I need to be dealing with now. My focus should be on my dad. It should have been completely on my dad this whole time, not some infatuation over a guy I have known for only a short while.*

After throwing my purse into Abby's lap, I start to climb in the car when strong arms grab me around the waist, stopping me in my tracks. It takes me no time at all to react to his touch. What only a few short hours ago had set my heart soaring now makes me nauseous.

"Lyssa, please let me explain. This is all wrong," he says in my ear. I whirl around to escape his hold.

"Then, explain!" I yell out loud enough for the entire neighborhood to hear. I lower my voice and begin to shake as sadness seeps into every ounce of my soul. "You were in her bed; you were naked and she was naked on top of you," I say hoarsely, trying to swallow the lump in my throat before adding the last part.

When I walked in, I had a complete front seat to it all. The sheets were off the bed and although I couldn't see his face, I could see other things that I wish I hadn't.

"I could see, Judd. You were turned on while she was on you." He shakes his head in disagreement with all the facts that I have just throw out, but I go on, even though all I want to do is run away. "She said you two kissed the other night. She said you knew about her and Kyle." I pause and look at him.

I want to believe he didn't do anything with her; I want to believe only him, but what about the other things. He never denied kissing her or knowing about Kyle and Bethany.

His expression is panic stricken as he clutches at my waist, still shaking his head in denial, but my anger level elevates with his silence.

"So please, explain all that!" I spit out with more spite than I thought I had in me.

"Alyssa, I was going to. Please, you know me. Let's just go inside and talk about this? I would never hurt you . . . I love you," he says with so much sincerity, but yet he still has not answered my questions.

Knowing this is not the time for this, I shake my body from his grasp and slide into the driver's seat.

"Save it! I refuse to be played for a fool anymore! I can't do this!"

Judd grabs the door to keep me from slamming it in his face as I slip the key in the ignition.

"Goodbye, Judd. Just let me go . . ." I look into his eyes, pleadingly. *I can't . . . I just can't do this; not now. I can't take any more pain.*

As if reading my thoughts, his hand falls away slowly.

"Lyssa, please . . ." is the last thing I hear before jerking it closed.

Throwing the car in drive, I pull forward onto the road with tears flowing down my face and dampening my sweatshirt.

"Alyssa, what happened? Did he . . ." Abby stops mid sentence and places her hand over mine.

I can't talk. I can barely breathe and all I can think about, besides getting to my dad as my apartment fades into the distance, is the words that are on constant repeat in my head: *don't look back, don't look back;* and this time, I don't.

Hope in my heart

AFTER WE GET A SHORT distance away from my apartment, I am forced to the shoulder of the road and decide to let Abby drive. She doesn't ask any more questions, knowing I will talk when I am ready.

I lay my head against the cold glass of the window and watch trees and cars fly by in a blur, all the while forcing down an ocean of tears that are threatening to spill over. *My heart is being pulled in a million different directions.*

Pondering over Judd's words from a while back, *"Have you ever thought that maybe it is happening that way for a reason; kind of balancing the scale,"* I wonder, *so if falling in love with him and facing saying goodbye to Dad is a source of balancing, then what would losing them both at the same time be considered? What, a way to ultimately crush my entire soul and leave me drowning in hopelessness?*

My chest heaves up and down and a few tears escape my grasp. I can't hold it back but I'm afraid that if I surrender to the pain now, I may never stop crying. For now, I will force my grief down deep, because I know it is just a matter of time before there will be too much pain to hold back.

We pull into the hospital parking lot and waste no time rushing through the sliding glass doors to the front desk.

After getting directions to Dad's room, we skip the elevator and take the stairwell. There were too many people waiting to hop on, so we figure the stairs might be a less stressful method of transportation. Besides, neither of us can stand still at the moment.

We take them two at a time until a sign notating the fourth floor comes into view. Once we fly through the heavy metal door into the quiet hallway, we slow our pace and continue on into a huge pod. The large circular shaped room has patients rooms arranged side-by-side around a massive nurses station located at its center. I look up ahead and see Mom standing outside of room 407, talking to a doctor.

One glance and she runs to our side, throwing her arms around us both. Trickles of moisture hit my bare neck where she buries her face and I know this isn't going to be good news.

Andrea arrives shortly after us and the doctor gathers us all in a small white room with a table and chairs. He sits on one side while we all huddle closely together on the other side.

When the doctor opens his mouth and says "I'm just going to give it to you straight . . ." I know there is no way to prepare ourselves for this.

All four of us remain completely silent as the doctor explains Dad's condition in medical terms that I don't understand. Sitting in a complete daze, I barely register his words, only catching clips of the discussion.

" . . . due to his weakened immune system and of course, the progression of the cancer being in his bloodstream now means a simple cold can easily turn to pneumonia." I look over at Mom, who has tears in her eyes as the doctor speaks.

Only Mom has seen Dad so far; my sisters and I are growing more anxious to be by his side.

"But he'll be ok, right?" Andrea asks in a panic.

"We are doing everything we can so I cannot speculate on anything. All I can tell you is that he is in good hands."

The doctor reaches across the table and squeezes Mom's hands, which are tightly clasped together and turning bright red from the amount of pressure her hold has on them. The doctor goes on and on until all I want to do is turn and run away.

"Only family is allowed in the ICU, one at a time, so I'll leave you all to discuss a suitable visiting plan," he adds before leaving the room.

The door clicks shut and Abby immediately turns to question

Mom, "What happened last night?"

"And what did the doctor mean the cancer is in his blood stream? He talked like you already knew this." Andrea adds about information we weren't aware of until just now.

Mom lets out a solemn sigh and meets each of our eyes one at a time, before speaking.

"Ok, one thing at a time." She blows out another sigh and I can tell she is mustering up a truck load of courage. "Your father was ok all through the afternoon, weak but in relatively good spirits. He still had a little cough, but into the evening he started having some shortness of breath. He insisted sleep would help, so I stayed up and read for a bit while he slept. An hour later, he had a severe coughing episode and he couldn't catch his breath. I dialed 911 and an ambulance rushed him in. They have him on oxygen and he is stable now."

Mom looks down again, kneading her hands together as if she holds a ball of dough that she is determined to flatten. Abby's muffled sobs reach my ears and it's everything I can do to not cry myself.

"And yes, honey, it has reached his bloodstream. We found out on his last visit, but we didn't want to add more to your worry. The truth is . . ." Moms voice quivers and her eyes brim with tears. "We know your Dad may not beat this so we just want to live these last few weeks or months as normal as possible. He wants every day to be filled with life without a dark cloud looming over a time that should be filled with happiness and love. He knows death will come soon enough and with it, our tears and heartbreak, so he just wants to enjoy the time he has left. I'm sorry if you all feel we kept it from you, but would it really have changed the situation or made you face each day differently if you had known two weeks ago?" She explains it as if Dad had said it all himself and afterwards all I could do is agree with their decision.

Streams finally fall from Mom's eyes and mine soon follow. We've had months of preparing and knowing something like this could happen and yet, we are all completely and utterly ill-equipped to deal with this now.

My heart aches for Dad but it also hurts for Mom. I look up through foggy eyes and see her crumpled face shedding a river of tears.

She stares blankly at her hands and I wonder to myself how many times those hands have held onto my dad's while they were falling in love; how many times they have held on in sadness and happiness; how they held on while she was bringing each of us into this world and, at that moment, my heart shatters for them.

I have always adored the relationship my mom and dad have. It has always been something I hope to find someday. I guess that is just the romantic in me.

Just now, I realize that however hard this is for me and my sisters that this must be a hundred times worse for Mom. I think back to the bottom block of the tower I made when I was five and how Dad wrote Alex loves Angela like they were two sixteen year olds writing their declarations of love on the front of a notebook. They had a whole life before me and my sisters.

I stand up and walk over to Mom, wrapping my arms around her in hopes that I can steal away some of her pain. I know I can't, but at least she knows she will not be alone through this. And like a ghost sneaking up on me, I think of Judd and how badly I wish I had his arms around me right now. I push that thought away quickly and soon feel the warmth of Andrea and Abby's arms surround me and Mom.

We stay huddled together for a while before we come up with a rotation plan so that one of us will be with him at all times.

Through the day, none of us find the courage to leave the hospital. Abby, Mom and I sit in the waiting area on the fourth floor while Andrea takes her shift in with Dad. Abby has her feet kicked up into the chair next to me frantically texting someone while Mom and me sit quietly across from each other.

I catch Mom scrolling through her phone and every once in a while a brief smile touches her face. I assume she is looking through pictures.

Me . . . I'm sitting quietly trying not to think; trying not to feel and trying my best to stay sane. I guess we are all dealing with it differently.

"Hey guys." I look up at the sound of Andrea's voice and panic sets in.

My hands grip the arms of my chair in fear right as my ears tune into the familiar squealing of two rambunctious little boys. My nephews both run to Mom, wrapping her in tiny bear hugs.

"Greg came by for a bit so he could sit with Dad and we both thought the boys would be a nice distraction for you." Relief drowns out my panic as soon as I know my brother in law is with Dad. *I really would rather one of us always be present.*

"We can't stay long, because I need to give the kids baths and get them to bed, but I'll be back in the morning sometime," Andrea goes on and then takes a seat by Mom.

She ended up being right, too; my nephews offer a nice diversion for our minds and give us a reason to laugh and smile.

Hours later, I stare vacantly at the clock on the wall as it strikes 5:00 in the evening and, right on schedule, Abby comes into the waiting room.

"Alyssa, you're up." Abby drags herself past me to sit with Mom while I quietly walk into the ICU.

I stop at the entrance and follow the rules posted on a sign to scrub down your hands and arms to the elbow with the antibacterial soap provided for you at two wide sinks. After drying my hands, I make my way to Dad's room.

Once the sliding glass door is open, I peek in, careful to not make any noise in case Dad is resting.

He is lying on his back with cords hanging off to all sides and a clear, fogged up mask stretched over his mouth and nose. All the color is drained from his thin face and he looks so frail and weak. *How did I miss him going downhill so fast these past few weeks?* I knew he had been getting weaker, thinner and losing his appetite, but for some reason I still viewed him as the same strong, healthy, happy go lucky man I have seen for years. Now I get why he didn't want us to know how bad the cancer had gotten. I guess knowing someone is sick or sicker can somehow alter your perception of the situation.

Letting the door snap shut behind me, I sneak over to the chair sitting beside the bed.

As soon as I am comfortably seated, I reach up and grasp Dad's hand. I lower my forehead down and rest it against the back of his hand and say a silent prayer. *Please don't let my father be in pain. Please give us all the strength we need to face this and please, please let me know when I need to say goodbye.*

My eyes well up with tears as I think over what I really want to pray or more like beg. *Please let my dad get better! Please send me a miracle and please don't take my Daddy away from me!* As bad as I want to shout those words up into the heavens, I know Dad would not want me to pray for that. He has told me on several occasions that he has made peace with this.

I turn my face and rub the back of his hand across my cheek, feeling the strong hands that have guided me through life since I was born.

"I love you, Daddy." I whisper as I look up at his ghostly white face.

I sit silently for a long while and watch him. I watch as his oxygen mask fogs up with each breath. I watch as his chest rises and falls as I squeeze his hand in mine. The whole time, I force my mind to not think of the present, but to remember the past.

Finally, I open my mouth and decide to speak.

"Remember that big snow we got back when I was about seven. You took us up to that hill behind our house and we spent the entire day sledding. You hopped on the sleigh behind each of us, shielding us from falling off." My mind replays the memory and I can nearly feel the wind zipping across my face as we blazed down the hill.

I revisit my first day of eighth grade when I had finally taken shop class and I brought home my first project, so proud to show him. It was just a simple flat piece of wood that I had etched my name into with a scroll saw, but I was super pumped to brag about it. The memory of his praise over my work makes me laugh and as if the echoes of my laughter breaks through the fortress of his sickness, at that moment Dad's hand squeezes mine in return. His eyes flutter, but remain closed and the corners of his mouth twitch as though he's trying to smile.

I go on with story after story, knowing Dad is listening and reliving each moment right along with me. I don't talk about his pneumonia or his cancer. I don't ask if he is in pain and I don't tell him I'm scared, but I do tell him many times how much I love him and how much he means to me, because even if he wasn't sick those are things I always want him to know.

It doesn't take long for three hours to speed by and a nurse comes in to check on Dad. This signals me that it is time for Mom to take my place.

I walk down the hallway to the waiting area, feeling as though Dad and I had just gone on an adventure. It's as if we just spent hours sledding, laughing, working in his shop, talking, fishing and being together from the images that played in my mind as I told him story after story.

My heart still aches, but the weight somehow feels a bit lighter.

When I reach the waiting area, Mom stands and embraces me in a hug.

"Are you ok?"

All this is happening to her as well, yet she is so concerned about all of us. I have no idea how my mom has the strength to worry about us and deal with this at the same time.

I smile at her and nod my head. "I'm good. I told him stories and he even squeezed my hand."

She smiles back at me and brushes my hair out of my face.

"You go home and rest. You look exhausted."

We had all agreed that it would be best for Mom to take the entire evening shifts so that if something would happen she would be with him. It scares the heck out of me to not be in there for this long, but I know that is Mom's place; by his side.

I can't help but think of Judd's drunken words from last night, saying he wants me in his arms when he draws his last breath in this world. I know that is no longer likely, but I want that for my mom and dad, even though it causes a deep pain in my heart to even think it.

I plop down in one of the stiff chairs and see that Abby hasn't went home. Mom had offered for her to take her car, but I guess Abby refuses to leave as well. *No way am I leaving tonight.* They may have to force me to go at some point, but right now, this is where my bed will be.

Abby looks up from her phone and sighs. "Can I ask you what happened now?"

She knows better than to ask if I am ok, because neither of us are, so to discuss it would be useless. Discussing my issues with Judd would probably get both our minds off the current situation, but for me, it will only make it sting more. For one, I want him here; I want him holding my hand through this like he promised he would. I also want him to be able to say goodbye to my dad. Most of all, I want this whole morning to just go away. I want to rewind and start new, so I can be back in his arms, listening to him whisper how he wants me his whole life.

"I don't know if I can talk about it yet," I tell her as calmly as possible without breaking into tears.

Honestly, I really don't know what to say; I don't know what to believe. I saw it with my own eyes, but it just doesn't add up.

"When you're ready, I'm here. I couldn't help but hear a little of what is going on and I know it is still fresh, but right now you don't need to be shouldering all this on your own. I think it might help if you talk about it," Abby looks at me with complete understanding in her eyes.

"I'll talk when I'm ready, but just give me at least a day to let it all sink in. I'm still trying to figure it out myself. Actually, no, I'm just trying to not think about it."

I know she is right and I may very well explode if I don't talk about it, soon, but it is all just too much right now.

She nods with a soft smile. "Ok, I'm here though." Grabbing her belly, she looks around with a scrunched up face. "Come on, let's go get some food."

Deciding that the waiting room is a tad bit chillier than we'd like, we walk out to my car to get a blanket from the trunk then back inside to the café, grabbing two cups of coffee, some yogurt and two huge blueberry muffins. Given everything that is weighing on my mind, you would think I would not have an appetite at all, but I am actually starving.

The waiting room is vacant except for a nurse sitting at a reception area in the corner. We find a small couch near the back of the room, under a wall of windows and we snuggle up close together with the blanket draped over both our legs. I devour my muffin and yogurt in no time, savoring the combination of sweet and tangy, mixed with the creamy flavor of mocha flavored coffee.

"So, I start interning in January. I'm excited but a little nervous," Abby makes small talk to steer our thoughts in a different direction. "Oh, hey, did I tell you that Hayden asked me on a date for this Friday?"

I smile, letting her know I'm listening, because right now, focusing on chewing my muffin is the only thing keeping me from falling to pieces.

"I doubt I'll go, though," she adds with a shaky voice.

I know what she is thinking and I do not even want to go there right now. I refuse to think it.

"You should call him tomorrow. Let him know what is going on and then reschedule for when Dad is released." I flash an encouraging smile that is doubtfully going to convince either of us that everything is going to end well.

The next few days go similar to the first with not much of a change in Dad's health. Mom gave the doctors the ok to administer antibiotics for the pneumonia and pain meds for the cancer. At this point, the doctors feel the best they can do is keep him comfortable.

On day two, Dad is more coherent. He is able to nod his head when we ask him questions, smile and squeeze our hands, although he gets worn down quickly.

They move him out of ICU and into a room on the third floor in a wing reserved for advanced cancer patients. That should be comforting, but it makes me sadder. If Dad could walk around this wing, I think it would upset him that his last moments might be here. I still keep hope in my heart that he will be able to come back home, where he would be happier, but as the days pass by with little change, it takes a small chunk of that hope along with it.

Help me forget

DAD GETS SETTLED INTO HIS room late Tuesday night and finally, all of us are able to visit him at one time. We were initially going to keep our arrangements of Mom staying with him for the night, but Abby and I just couldn't make ourselves go home. Wandering into the room later that evening, we curl up in a worn out looking recliner side by side and fall fast asleep from complete and utter exhaustion.

This morning marks the fourth day since Dad has been in the hospital. It depresses me being here, so I can only imagine what this is doing to his spirits. I've sat through three full days of listening to monitors go off, three full days of nurses coming and going, three full days of watching Dad get weaker, and three whole days since I have felt the comfort of Judd's arms.

Sitting up, I bow my back and extend my arms, trying desperately to work out the kink in my back from sleeping all night wedged between the arm of the recliner and Abby's bony hips. As I look around, I notice Mom lying on the bed beside Dad.

The clock above the door reads a little past midnight, so I get up and sneak into the hall, careful not to make any noise.

After I take the elevator to the first floor, I make my way outside and get in my car.

When we got to the hospital on Sunday morning, I made it a point to leave my cell phone in my car. Everyone that I want to talk to is already here with me, and everyone that isn't here with me, are the ones that I don't care to talk to right now.

I definitely don't want to ever talk to Bethany again. What she did, not once, but twice, is unforgivable. I have no desire to talk to Kyle, given he never mentioned that my best friend, the girl I decided to room with, was the one he cheated on me with. If I had known, the decision to room with her would have gone a hell of a lot differently.

Then, there is Judd. As much as I would love to hear his voice and have him hold me, I know I can't. I don't understand how he could tell me he loves me so much and then sleep with someone else. I don't care how it happened; he should have known she was not me.

I'm beginning to think being drunk is a scapegoat for people that want to explore different options. No, I can't even group Judd into a category like that, because I truly do not understand what happened. Maybe I do need to talk to Abby about the whole thing. I guess it would be one less thing weighing on my mind, plus it would give me a different perspective on the matter. I wonder if he has even tried to call me or wondered where I am.

Once I am settled into the driver's side of my car, I pick up my phone from the console between my seats. I push the button to bring it up, but the screen stays black. *Shoot! It must have died.*

I pull my charger out of the glove box, plug my phone in and wait. It doesn't take long for my screen to light up and a couple of chirps to sound off, letting me know I have missed calls and texts. Not nearly the astounding amount that I had received when Kyle and I broke up, but then again, Judd is nothing like Kyle. *Well, I thought he wasn't.*

There are six missed calls and twelve missed texts. Only three of the calls are from Judd along with three of the texts. My heart drops. I guess I have been hoping he would be fighting and begging and pleading with me not to leave him. Two of the calls are from Bethany and eight text messages, with the remaining call and text from Kyle. *I don't even care to hear what Bethany has to say.*

I decide to start easy and listen to Kyle's voicemail first.

"Alyssa, hey . . . it's me. I ran into Piper this morning on the way over to pick up the keg from your apartment and she said your Dad is in the hospital. Give me a call or text and let me know how he is doing and how you're doing. Let me know if your family needs anything at all."

The message is dated from Sunday at noon so he definitely hasn't been brought up to speed on all the drama.

Piper must have slept through the entire morning blowup or she would have filled him in.

I move on to the first voicemail from Judd. Closing my eyes, I take a deep breath before hitting the play button.

"Lyssa . . . I know you're not going to pick up and I know you need time, but please know that I am so confused about all of this. I have no memory of anything and I have no idea how this could've happened. I know you are hurt and you have every right, but please call me back. Please don't end it like this! Let's talk about it all and try to figure it out together. I . . . I know saying sorry isn't good enough, but I will do anything and everything to fix this. You have to . . ."

My voicemail beeps, cutting him off. My grip tightens on my phone as I push play on the next message.

"Sorry. I guess I better make this a little shorter. Please call me, Lyssa. I love you. You have to know that! I know you need time and I know you are hurt so I will wait as long as I have to, but please call me. I can't lose you. I love you. Bye."

A tear slides down my cheek and I take in a quivering breath as I look down at the time stamp: *Sunday 7:42am.* This message was left not even an hour after I drove off.

I look down and click on the last voicemail from him, time-stamped for yesterday at 7:55am. He must have left this before he went to his Monday morning class.

"It's me. I know I said I would give you time to think, but I just wanted to call and say I love you and I'm here . . . you know, if you need me. I know it has only been two days since we've seen each other, but it seems like so much longer. I don't even remember the last time we went more than a day without saying I love you to each other, so . . . I love you, Alyssa."

He hangs up abruptly and my heart climbs into my throat with the pain I hear in his voice. *Does he even know how miserable I am, too?*

I brush through all the text messages from Bethany pleading with me to call her and apologizing. I hit delete as fast as I can, not even bothering to read each message through.

I get to Kyle's message and it is clear that he must have talked to Bethany when he picked up the keg.

Kyle: I'm sure you are probably pretty pissed at me now, but I hope you know how bad I wanted to tell you the truth. I was so ashamed that it was her and then after so long it just seemed it would be like throwing salt on a healing wound by telling you. I am so sorry and I understand if you're mad. Just don't stay mad forever . . . Please! I'm worried about you and your family. Call me if you need anything, please!!

Kyle definitely is relentless, but I'm just glad he didn't feel the need to blow up my phone again.

I click on Judd's name and scroll down to his three text messages.

Judd: Just wanted to say I wish I was holding you right now!

My eyes fall to the next message as my heartbeat picks up.

I'm getting ready for bed and I wanted to say that I am thinking of you! I can't stop thinking about you! I love you!

Slowly sliding my fingertips across the words I love you, my heart aches with the need to feel him say those words against my skin. I squeeze my eyes shut for a minute and take a breath before looking at the final message from him.

Another day without you and you're all I think about! I'm here if you need me, I hope you know that! I love you!

I look over the times of each text, the first stamped on Sunday at 9:22pm, the next on Monday at 10:01pm and the last only hours ago at 9:19pm. It makes my heart hurt, imagining him lying in bed each night thinking about me.

As I close my eyes, I release all the air from my lungs on a heavy sigh and push my head against the stiff, cold leather headrest. All his messages and words twirl around in my head like a tornado and a part of me just wishes I could get pulled away with the storm. *He has no idea how his words hit home. I do need him. I wish he was holding me, too.*

The passenger door creaks open and I look over to see Abby getting in. She gives me a weak smile and I automatically sweep my hand under my eyes to make sure my face isn't streaked with tears.

"You want to talk about it?" she asks in a sympathetic tone that finally breaks through the wall around my heart that I have constructed for the last three days.

We sit in the car for what seems like forever as I go over every detail of what I walked in on and all the words that were said. Abby is quiet the whole time, giving me her undivided attention.

" . . . I mean he was still drunk and I realize he may have mistaken her bed for mine, because he did do that from time to time, but still . . ." I realize I am trying to make excuses for him.

Once I stop talking, I stare at her hoping she can shed some light on how something like this could happen.

"Are you sure he slept with her?"

This is all that comes out of her mouth and it frustrates me even more.

"Abby, I walked in on them!"

She holds up her hand to stop me, "Wait, you didn't exactly walk in on the act. Are you sure Bethany wasn't just throwing herself at him while he was asleep? Maybe you walked in right in the nick of time before she could get that far."

I ponder on that for a moment and then look over at Abby, "I guess that makes sense, after all I wasn't gone that long, but Bethany confirmed it herself. She said they did have . . ." I cannot even get the words out.

"Alyssa, Bethany seems manipulative enough to lie about it. I mean she did tell you that she slept with Kyle and she has managed to keep that from you this whole time."

What Abby says is completely true; I know it's true, but something about hearing it again from someone else makes my heart sting like ripping a bandage off of a gaping wound. *How could my own best friend be so deceitful and cruel?* Tumbling her words around in my head leaves me in an even bigger state of confusion and wondering, *what if Judd did absolutely nothing wrong?*

Realizing we have been sitting in the car for a good hour or so, I decide it's enough talk for now. "You want to go back in and check on Dad?"

Abby nods her head and we both slide out into the chilly night and head back inside.

Halfway to Dad's room, an intense, unsettling sensation takes root in the pit of my stomach and I suddenly get a strong sense of urgency to get up to his room. *Come on, come on,* I chant in my head as I watch a green light flash above the door with each of the floor numbers.

The elevator dings and I rush out in front of Abby only to be met with complete pandemonium. Nurses flood the hallway by Dad's door, we hear alarms going off and a Code Blue is announced over the loud speaker. Mom stands in the hall, sobbing hysterically with her arms wrapped around herself. *Oh God, no! Not my daddy!*

My mouth twists open in pain and my body shakes as I run to the room, praying I can get in. A nurse grabs my arms and pulls me back.

"Sweetie, you have to stay out here," she says in a soothing tone.

Abby races up behind me, slamming into my back. "That's our dad," she pleads with the nurse.

Mom's arms instantly wrap around us both and we fall to our knees on the floor, together, each of our hearts shattering.

"What's happening?" I say through quivering breaths as I look into Dad's room and see his bed surrounded with doctors and nurses.

Mom squeezes me harder and I hear Abby's voice boom over the mass hysteria, "Mom, what's happening to Dad?!"

Mom takes a deep breath and calms her sobs long enough to speak.

"The doctor thinks he is having a stroke or a heart attack. I'm not sure. He was fine then all of a sudden his monitor went off and nurses came in. I begged to stay with him, but . . ." her voice trails off and is replaced with gasping breaths as she tries to keep her composure.

My chest shakes and I bury my face in Mom's shoulders. *Please don't take him, please don't take him!!* I know Dad would not want me to pray for him to stay while he is in so much pain but I can't help it. *Don't take my daddy!* I look up at the ceiling and continue to say the same line over and over.

All three of us huddle together, shaking and shuddering; tear after tear racing down our faces. Out of nowhere, a gentle wispy feeling moves across my back and up into my hair, but when I look around I find nothing. Turning my attention back to Mom and Abby, I see them looking around.

"Did you feel that?" I whisper.

Mom gasps in shock and then her face crumples into pain. Abby shakes her head, looking bewildered; almost startled. It's at that moment that I know I wasn't the only one that felt my dad's presence as he swept through the room. My heart jumps and I want to scream out, "No, not my dad," as all our heads linger back to his room.

Nurses begin to file out with remorseful glances our way. The one that held me back from going in gives me a sad, apologetic smile as the doctor walks up and crouches down beside us. He pulls the white mask down to his neck and his expression says everything that we feared is true.

"I'm so sorry. We did everything we could."

My heart is torn from my chest with his words and I fight to catch my breath. I urgently search for something to hold onto as the world spins out of control, taking a never ending river of tears with it. *I can't breathe, I can't breathe! No, please!*

Mom and Abby's bodies quake and tremble against my own.

The doctor places his hand on Mom's shoulder and gives her a reassuring squeeze and then goes on in the most sympathetic tone I've ever heard , but it does nothing to ease the pain.

"It looks like it was a stroke. We'll know more later, but it seems that he never woke up so he went peacefully in his sleep," he assures us.

"Was he in pain?" Abby's trembling voice cries out.

"No. Aside from the pain from the cancer, which he was being administered pain meds for . . . No, I don't think he felt a thing." The doctor pauses for a moment and dips his head, unable to look us all in the eye. "I am truly sorry for your loss. You all are welcome to go in and say goodbye. Take as long as you need."

My mouth gapes open at the thought of seeing my father's lifeless body. *I don't know if I can do it.* I shake my head as the doctor gives me a pat on the back and then stands to walk away.

Mom rises to her feet and reaches her hands out to me and Abby. I look at my sister's tear streaked face and then up to Mom. She pulls me up along with Abby and then we all face the door to the room.

"You girls don't have to do this if you don't want to," she states as she inches forward.

"Mom, are you going in?" She doesn't take her eyes off the door, but I see a new river of tears forming in her eyes as she gently smiles. "Yes. I want to tell him goodbye and hold his hand one last time."

I squeeze my eyes shut with her words; the gaping hole in my heart aching as I watch her walk into the room. From the doorway I can see Dad's feet lying motionless on the bed, but I cannot make myself go any further into the room.

Abby rushes to the door and then turns to me.

"Alyssa, come in with us, please; I need you with me," she barely gets out through her quivering sobs.

I shake my head uncontrollably, backing away from the room.

"I can't! I can't!"

It's the only thing I can think or say as I turn and take off running down the hall, down the stairwell and out to my car, not even knowing where I will go from here. *I can't! I can't! I can't stay there! I can't look at Dad like that!* He wouldn't want me to remember him that way. I want to remember him full of life with a smile on his face.

Once I reach my car, I fumble around in my purse until my fingers land on the cold metal of my keys. With trembling hands, I drop them to the ground half a dozen times before I can even get the door unlocked, but at last I tear the door open and climb in. I quickly seize the steering wheel with such force that my muscles instantly ache and throb, but I welcome the sensation, hoping it will redirect my mind from the pain in my heart.

Through hazy, tear filled eyes, I throw the car into gear and peel out of the parking lot, having absolutely no clue where I am going. *I don't care, I just want to forget. I don't want to think of his sickness and his feet sitting so still on the bed. I don't want to think about how I'm a coward for not joining my mom and sister.*

Not even a few yards away from the hospital and with tears still rapidly flowing down my face, I frantically reach to my lap and shuffle my hand through my purse again, in search of my phone. *I need to call someone. I don't want to think about anything or talk about anything, but I don't want to be alone either.* My heart is on the verge of exploding.

My hand slides around inside my bag until a cold, pointy object jabs into the flesh between my index finger and thumb. I pull it out and head for the interstate. Roughly gripping the steering wheel, I weave in and out of what little traffic there is on the road at 2:00 in the morning until I pull up to the building.

I don't think over whether this is a bad idea or not. I don't question what I will feel tomorrow when he is no longer by my side. I don't even worry about what happened only days ago. I just hold onto the key as if it is my last hope in this world and rush inside to his door.

Looking at the shiny metallic gift I was given only days ago, I take a deep breath then unlock the door. I fly across the living room with only one focal point in the dark room; his bedroom door.

I'm not sure what I will be met with and really do not care, as I open the door.

Judd is sitting up in bed, staring at me. His bare chest is bathed in the street lights that filter through his blinds. He slowly places his phone down on his nightstand and although, I should care who he was talking to at this time in the morning, I honestly can't think about that now.

His eyes stare compassionately at me as he very carefully and gently flips his comforter and sheets back beside him, as if summoning me into his arms. I practically leap across the room, sliding into the bed beside him and letting the warmth of his body ease a bit of the ache in my heart. His arms naturally fall around me and I mold myself to his body with his hands sweeping back and forth across my back and the hammering tempo of his heart filling my ears.

Nothing can take this pain away from me, but the feeling of Judd so close ignites something inside of me and all I want to do is be closer to him;

to feel him beside me;

against me;

around me;

inside me;

all over me.

I want that hole in my heart to be filled with the passion only Judd creates within me. I just want to forget for a moment.

"Alyssa, I wish I could take your pain away. I would do anything to shoulder this instead of you." He pulls me even closer to him and I know he can tell what has happened. "Oh baby, I wish I could make this go away. I wish I could stop the pain," he whispers with so much pain in his voice. "What can I do to make this hurt less?" he says hoarsely as his hands make circles across my back and up into my hair.

I grab his shoulders and pull my body up onto his so that I am level with his face. His gorgeous hazel eyes search mine and without a word I gently press my lips to his. A dam of emotion breaks open inside of me, flooding my heart with pain and pushing me to the brink of falling apart. He carefully grabs my face, pulling me away from his mouth and looks into my eyes to question my intentions.

"Judd, just for a moment . . . help me forget," I say in a barely audible tone before descending on his lips again.

Goodbye

JUDD SOFTLY CARESSES MY SKIN, looking at me tenderly.

"Baby, I don't think that is a good idea. Trust me, I know. All that pain and heartache will just be waiting for you afterwards and I don't want you regretting it later," he says softly while stroking his thumb across my cheek.

I let out a quivering breath at his rejection. *Does he not want me anymore?*

"Please, I need you," I beg him inching my face closer until our breaths are merged as one.

He tilts his head to the side and knits his eyebrows together in agony.

"Lyssa, we really need to talk about things if we are going to . . ."

I place my fingertips on his lips to silence him. He closes his mouth and I can see the torture on his face, but all I can focus on is forgetting.

"I don't want to talk. I need you. Please," I whisper softly into his mouth, feeling him nod once before the moistness of his lips move onto mine.

His hands run the length of my torso with such care and precision you would think I was a glass doll on the verge of breaking. He effortlessly slides me onto my back and hovers above me, inching my shirt up over my head, never once breaking eye contact. Once my shirt is abandoned on the edge of the bed, he moves his head down to my stomach, tasting and kissing just above my panty line up to the hem of my bra while his hands flow along my curves.

I moan and arch my back as waves of pleasure course through my body, from his touch alone. The fire from his fingertips continues to make me slither and writhe beneath him as he slides my bra and panties off. His mouth scorches my skin on a fiery trail back to my lips. I open my mouth for a deeper kiss and he begins to pull away.

"Are you sure? I'll hold you all night. I'll never let go . . . I promise," he asks me in a pleading tone and I should agree, but I just need that euphoric feeling to swallow me whole and let me escape my reality for a while.

"I need you; I want you." My words come out as a desperate plea as I tug him down on top of me.

The heat of his body melts into mine as he looks me in the eyes and slowly shifts to unite us. My head instantly falls back into the plush softness of the pillow and I let out a strangled breath from the sparks that swirl up into my belly and down to my toes.

He takes his time with slow steady strokes, looking longingly into my eyes just as he always has. I can't look away; only Judd can make me feel this way. I am whole when we are together; I am complete and I feel absolutely loved and cherished.

Waves of pleasure start to build in my core and I grab onto his shoulders pulling him deeper into me. I want him closer; I need him closer.

He holds onto me tightly, yet gently as if I will break, nipping at my neck and jaw between thrusts.

"I love you, Alyssa. I love you so much," he breathes out and it is all I can do to hold on.

Gravity has been sucked away and I am shooting off to another solar system; spiraling through space. Fire bolts through my entire body hitting every nerve and cell. I whimper from the sensation as a loud moan escapes his lips.

His movements slow and his whisper moves softly over my ear, "Tell me you love me, please."

I squeeze my eyes shut knowing what this must be doing to him, not knowing where we stand.

While still breathing heavily, he rises up and my hands are instinctively drawn to his face. I run my fingers down his right cheek to where

289

his dimple usually is as he continues to look at me. *He knows what I want; I want so badly to see his smile.* Still staring at me intently, he presses his lips together and the skin on his cheek dips in barely, highlighting his most adorable feature. I trace my fingertip over it and look up at him with a small smile that isn't forced at all.

Even with the crushing pain of losing my father, the only place I can find peace is within his arms. We have so much to figure out and work through if it is possible, but I don't even have to think about it.

"I love you, Judd," I say back to him with a small teardrop sliding down my cheek.

He slides off of me and half sits up against the bed frame, nudging me along with him.

"Come here. I want to hold you," he says as I lay my chest and head against his body, drinking in every drop of warmth it puts off.

I listen to the heavy thuds of his heartbeat and let myself rise and fall with each breath he takes, but as soon as the exhilaration from us being together dies down, the hurt comes back full force. He runs his hand through my hair, carefully sweeping each strand back behind my head.

"Shhh, I'm here, baby. I'm not going to let you go," he murmurs as I weep against his chest.

It feels as though someone is ripping my heart out with their bare hands; like they are crumpling and destroying it along the way.

Rising up, I hungrily press my lips onto his, needing more. *I just want to feel him. I want all the pain to fade away until I can handle it; until I'm prepared.*

I don't take my time. I sit up, straddle him and forcefully pull him against me.

Judd grabs my hips, breathing heavily and holding me still.

"Alyssa, baby, no. You can't run from this. You can't hide. You have to face this. I know it's hard, baby . . . believe me I know," he pleads with me while holding me motionless with one hand and gently stroking my cheek with the other. "We'll face this together. If you will let me, I will hold your hand through it all, I promise, but you have to face this. Otherwise, all that pain and hurt is going to come crashing down on you. You have to figure out a way to cope with it now while it's fresh."

He looks into my eyes with the same understanding that I saw on the lake when I told him about my dad. The same look he gave me that made me first fall in love with him.

"I don't know if I can," I cry, my heart slowly breaking wide open. *If I let all the pain in, it will kill me.*

"You can," he pleads with me as I stare into his eyes. "I know you can and I'll be right here."

My heart weights down as I give in and slowly slide my body down, settling into the mattress with my head on his chest. He scoots up to rest his head on his pillow and pulls my body tightly to his side with not a single gap between us.

Clinging to his body, I let out a breath and let the pain engulf me like a thick blanket. I shake and cry and scream in agony over losing my dad until my heart is a shattered, broken mess. Each time I think my tears may dry, a new wave of pain washes over me and has me clasping at Judd so fiercely that I swear I may leave bruises.

Through it all, Judd shushes me with whispered words of love and how he won't leave me. He holds me so tightly that it feels as his body is mine and mine is his. And as promised, he never leaves my side. Eventually, my eyes grow heavy and I cannot keep them open any longer.

Trickles of sunlight bleeding through the shades wake me that morning along with the clanking of dishes in the next room. I shift my bare body which is still tightly held against Judd's chest. Looking up, I see his handsome face slumped to the side of his pillow as if he tried to stay awake as long as possible, but eventually surrendered to a deep sleep.

I move just a bit to test if he will wake up, but as usual his arms grasp for me. For a moment, I consider crawling back under the covers with him, but then I decide against it. My family needs me today. Slowly sliding my hands up to his other pillow, I move it to the other side of him as a stand in for me and draw back as his hands wander to find me, again. That's when I quickly slide the pillow within his hold. He surrounds the pillow in his arms and pulls it firmly to him.

I stare down into his peaceful face, smiling for a second before I run the pad of my index finger along his bottom lip and place a barely there peck against his lips. As I move away, his tongue slides over his lips, moistening them as if he is craving my kisses.

My heart skips a beat as I think about how much I love him and just how hard it is going to be to say goodbye. *I just can't do this now! I can't deal with anything else! He's right, I have to face this! I have to figure out how to cope with this now and I know I have to do it on my own.*

I glide my body silently off the bed and quietly get dressed.

After I am done, I grab his phone from the nightstand and immediately see a missed text from Abby.

Abby: Is Alyssa still there?

No wonder he knew before I even stepped foot into his room last night. Abby must have called him. I don't think or worry about that, I just bring up an empty text screen and type a simple message that will make this as easy as possible for both of us.

I look over my message and read it word for word to make sure it is everything I need to say for now, even though it is not nearly all that I want to say or should say.

Judd . . . I'm sorry I came here last night. I really shouldn't have, but thank you for being here when I needed you most. I know there is so much that needs to be said, but I just need time. I can't deal with everything right now. I love you.

After reading it, I slowly tap on the delete button over and over, correcting my message before sitting it back on his nightstand, without hitting the send button. Glancing back at him one last time, I decide to whisper the words I just deleted, "I love you. Goodbye, Judd," and then I walk out the door.

I pull his door shut as quiet as possible, praying he doesn't wake.

If he wakes up, I know he will try to stop me and at this point, he would have no trouble convincing me to stay. Honestly, all I want to do is curl up in his arms and hide from the world forever.

The sound of dishes clanking together behind me makes me jump and I snap my head around. Evan stands at the island with his typical bowl of cereal in front of him. He folds his arms across his chest in a defiant stance and levels me with a serious glare that I've only seen on his face once before.

"Isn't sneaking out usually typical of the man?" he says in a bland tone and he isn't being his normal joking self.

I don't say anything, but instead make a bee-line for the front door. I can't deal with any confrontations right now and clearly Evan isn't up to speed on the latest events.

Reaching for the knob, I have every intention on racing out before he can say another word but when Evan speaks again, I stop dead in my tracks.

"Just for the record, I think your roommate is a lying bitch! You have to know he wouldn't have slept with her! He's dying over this!" he spits out and I realize how angry he is with me.

I also realize after I have come to terms with everything, I may in fact, have to speak to Bethany after all.

"I'm sorry," I whisper as I look down at the door, desperately wanting to be on the other side.

I don't know what I'm sorry for, but I feel like I should apologize.

Evan's tone softens as he adds, "Are you even going to say good-bye to him?"

I straighten my back; raise my chin and turn to answer him before leaving. "I did . . ." I take a deep breath, " . . . and now I am going to say goodbye to my dad."

All the blood drains from Evan's face as he looks at me with pity and sorrow.

I don't wait for an apology or an 'I'm sorry for your loss' comment, I just turn and leave.

One Day at a Time

By the time I left Judd's, Mom and Abby were already home with Andrea and her family. The hours pass by slowly and we are all complete zombies, each in our own world.

By night's end, the only sound that registers in my dark room, aside from Abby's sobs in the next room, is my phone chirping with a new message. Picking up my phone, my eyes quickly zone in to Judd's name. All day long I kept expecting to hear from him, even though I said I needed time, but he never called or texted, until now.

Judd: I know you said you need time, but I just want you to know you have been on my mind all day. You all have been. Alyssa, I love you so much!

My heart tenses with each word I read and I want so badly to text him back; to hear his voice and to beg him to come over right this minute, but I don't. Instead, I curl up under my sheets, bringing my knees into my chest and pressing the back of my hand into my pillow, still clutching onto my phone. I stare at my now black screen, feeling comfort that Judd was the last one to send me a message. I focus on his words, repeating them over and over in my mind until I fall asleep.

I love you . . . I love you . . . I love you . . .

The next day goes much the same; however, I finally question Abby about the text to Judd. She admits that she had been texting and talking to him each day to fill him in on Dad's condition. She even said that he had visited Dad in the ICU that first day. I can't even admit to myself the level of emotion that stirred within me to know that he got to see him before he passed.

Dad and Judd grew fairly close during our month together. They were like two college buddies, always retreating to the backyard and enjoying one of their guy talks. I'm so grateful that they had one last chance to see each other.

Later in the day, Abby, Andrea and I tag along with Mom to meet with the monument designer. We soon realize that Dad and Mom were way ahead of us all, already having picked out a headstone. *Of course Dad would have thought of that. He wouldn't have wanted to leave us with that chore.*

After showing us the beautiful granite stone Mom and Dad picked out, we sit down in a small conference room and put our heads together to come up with something worthy of Dad to be scripted on it.

Dad had always been the spirit of the family, our positive influence when things aren't going the right way, so nothing less than perfect will do. Mom stays strong the whole time while Abby, Andrea and I continuously break down and have to leave the room. I know Mom is putting on her brave face, but I also have no doubt that she crashes to her bed each evening and cries herself to sleep; I do.

On the way home and later that night, she busies herself with telling little stories of Dad and making us feel as though he is still here.

I can't help but wonder when I felt that brush of wind across my back in the hallway the night he passed, if a part of Dad's spirit united with Mom. I guess I'll never know, but it's a good thought.

After that, we stay home, taking each day as it comes and dealing with the pain in our own separate ways.

My means of handling Dad's death is probably not the best idea, but I read Judd's texts over and over. I haven't talked to him since the night I showed up at his apartment, but after the second message I received from him reading:

Judd: You're all I'm thinking of. I'm still here and I love you.

I noticed a pattern.

He sends me a text each night before bed so I know he is thinking of me; so I know I am not alone and so he can keep his promise of being here for me. Last night my text visit from him read:

Judd: ( ) This is me holding you! I wish you were in my arms right now! I love you!

No matter how heartsick I am at that particular moment, I always feel a bit of comfort when I read his texts. I find myself anxiously awaiting his messages each evening.

I know it would be so easy to pick up the phone and just say "I love you" and "Let's get back together," but in the end I know I have to deal with this first before I can straighten out the mess from last weekend.

Abby has been dealing with the loss by sitting for hours out in Dad's workshop.

I always thought that is what I would do since most of the memories I have of him were sitting at that old beat up worktable. Funny how the way you think you may react to a tragedy is usually the opposite of how you actually act when it happens.

Mom, on the other hand, spends most afternoons in their bedroom with photos scattered all over the bed. She has been clipping, cutting, pasting, and sticking photos in albums. So far, I haven't managed to be able to look at a single picture of Dad for very long without bursting into tears.

Right now, I sit on the floor of my parent's old bedroom and stare at the tower that I made for Dad. I study every swoop and line of his hand writing, where he wrote his and mom's names. *I can barely handle being without Judd, so I have no idea how Mom can do this. How can she live without him?*

My eyes well up with tears for the ache that I know she must be storing inside her heart everyday; the emptiness she must feel without his arms to hold her.

I look down at my phone and click it on to see last night's text from Judd. I gaze at the parentheses and run my fingertips over them before my phone screen can go to sleep mode again.

How can she live without him, is all I keep wondering. The respect I have for Mom swells with that thought and I realize just how proud I am to call her my mom.

A tear falls down my cheek and I wipe it away quickly, afraid to smear my makeup or mess up my appearance in any way. I am dressed in an a-line black dress with my hair carefully woven into a braid and make-up caked on, courtesy of Abby.

My father's viewing starts in a little over an hour and I have no idea how I am going to do this. Mom opted for an open casket and urged me to say my goodbyes this time. I promised I would say good-bye, but made no promises to face him when I do.

I'm afraid that if I see him lying there with all the life drained out of him; that is the image that will stick with me. I don't want to remember that. I want to remember his smile, his laughter, the way he wore a baseball cap like he was still a kid and the way he smoothed over any drama with carefully orchestrated words so effortlessly. That is what I do remember; all of it is meticulously cataloged in my mind and heart.

I may not look through photos like Mom does or sit at that work bench imagining Dad building something magnificent, but I take a stroll down memory lane about every other minute of the day. I revisit our fishing trips, movie marathons we had, woodworking adventures, laughing with him till my stomach hurt and I remember everything; every second. So I guess in a way, I am learning to cope, because sometimes when I think about him, I smile instead of cry.

I don't really believe the saying that time heals all wounds or will ease your pain, but I do believe that as time goes on, you tend to dwell on their life more than their death. That ultimately makes it easier. I think losing him will always hurt the same, though.

As I focus on all of the handmade treasures that line the shelf, I straighten my dress to keep it from getting wrinkled when the door creaks open behind me.

Andrea walks in looking absolutely stunning in a dark navy blue skirt and a white lace top. She and I have never been close. Considering she was starting middle school before I began to walk has always put a bit of an age gap in our sisterly bond, but just like when Dad was first diagnosed and how it made me and Abby grow closer, I see the same thing happening with us all through this catastrophe. I think that would make Dad proud.

She takes a seat beside me and stares at the shelf. Bending forward, she grabs the wooden box that she made Dad so many years ago.

"Oh my gosh, he kept this?" she says in disbelief and then smiles as she sits it back down.

I smile along with her, leaning my head against her shoulder as she pulls me into a gentle hug.

"Are you ready for this?" Her voice cracks when she says it and even though she's not expecting a reply, I answer anyway.

"No . . ." I mumble.

"Come on kiddo. We need to get there early. I need you to keep the kids away from the front. I don't want them to see Dad like that. I want them to remember silly grandpa sticking his tongue out or crossing his eyes. You know all those goofy faces he made." She waves her hand in the air with a smile and I see the unshed tears in her eyes.

I hug her back before we all make our way to the car.

The viewing is supposed to last four hours, but by hour two my feet are killing me and I am exhausted. I honestly haven't even had time for a single tear between all the hugs, condolences and offers of prayers. I float from one person to the next as body after body falls into me whispering their apologies for my loss. *Frankly, I'm sick of hearing that.* I don't go up to the casket, I refuse to, but I do look from afar. I can see a man that resembles my dad through the fog of people lined up to get a glimpse, but it's not my dad.

My hands fidget and I look around, not for anything or anyone in particular, but then I see exactly who I convinced myself I wasn't looking for. A tall figure stands in front of Abby with shaggy brown hair that is combed back and a black suit jacket and black slacks. His back is to me, but I know it has to be him.

I don't know what comes over me, but I fly through the funeral home, pushing people out of the way when Kyle blocks my path.

"Hey, I'm so sorry. You know if you need anything, I'm here, ok?" he leans towards me for a hug, but I lean to look around him. "Listen, I am so sorry, Alyssa."

I don't say a word; I just wander past him as he tries to apologize for past mistakes. All I want is to get into the other room where Abby is, where he is. *I need to see his face. I need to be wrapped in his arms so that the pain does not drown me.*

Once I get away from Kyle, I continue on my path into the next room until I see Abby standing alone and him nowhere in sight. *He didn't even come find me.*

I drop into a pew with an added sadness in my heart and decide to spend the rest of the viewing in this very spot. I don't have the energy to be hugged or questioned on how I am holding up by anyone else. Right then, Kyle scoots in beside me.

"Hey, how about I just sit quietly and keep you company . . . so you're not alone."

I smile at his suggestion; feeling defeated and beat down, but grateful for the distraction.

After the viewing, I head back out to the car with Mom and Abby when my phone chirps notifying me that I have a new text message. I slide the message open to view it and see it's from Judd.

Judd: Just Breathe! Close your eyes and feel my arms around you! I'm here if you need me. I love you! ( )

I do as he instructs and keep my eyes closed for the whole ride back home.

The next day is a haze of hurt, fear and denial.

I stand there, motionless, as the preacher speaks kind words over my father. I bow my head when he prays and I step up to throw a rose in as they lower Dad down into the ground. Mom finally breaks down as the casket descends further and further away from the surface of the earth.

As everyone staggers away from the gravesite, she falls to her knees and Abby and Andrea are immediately at her side.

I stand two feet behind them and sway back and forth, losing touch with gravity. A part of me feels as if he is being set free today, another part of me is screaming out in anguish from seeing him locked away in the ground. I guess reality is hitting us all, that we will never hug him again or feel his hands sweep away our tears. *Daddy, where are you? You promised you would still be here!*

Right then, my legs begin to give out and a pair of arms surround my waist to pull me back. I look over my shoulder and Judd's hazel eyes are looking back at me.

"I've got you," he says so easily, like he has never left my side.

And just like his text messages have done the last few days and just like having him so close the night my dad died, he restores my strength so that I can face this moment.

"Let's help your mom," he says and then pulls me forward with him.

I huddle down with my sisters and Mom on the ground as the grounds keeper finishes lowering Dad into the earth. Judd and Greg stand back behind us, giving us time to mourn and grieve as a family. We let it all out, frantically grasping onto each other for support.

Eventually, Greg folds Andrea into his arms and Judd's arms find me as well. I gladly accept his comfort, melting to his chest and soaking his shirt with my tears.

After my sisters' and I slow our sobs, we all stand quietly waiting for Mom to recover. My heart breaks for her as I look up into Judd's eyes and see the love he feels for me.

He links his hand with mine and I stay as close as I can to him. For now, all thoughts are put away. Today, I am not a girl in love with a boy who broke my heart. Today, I am simply a girl who desperately needs someone to hold me together before I crumble to pieces.

Andrea and Greg end up leaving first and soon Abby and Mom gather the strength to walk away, not far behind us. He offers to drive me home and I accept, knowing it will be hard to leave. After waving goodbye to my family, Judd takes his keys out of his pocket, but hesitates on unlocking the doors.

"You feel up to taking a walk with me?"

As soon as the words leave his mouth, I regret not going home with Mom. I really had thought that he would not push me to talk about what is going on between us today. In fact, I had counted on just a peaceful quiet ride with him back home. It's on the tip of my tongue to say no, but somehow he senses my inner conflict.

"Don't worry. I know today has nothing to do with us. I don't want to talk. I just want to show you something. Will you come with me?"

He easily places his hand out to his side for me to take in my own; and I do. I thread my fingers through his and then huddle my body against his for support as we walk back through the cemetery, heading away from my father's grave. I sneak glances in my dad's direction, hoping to feel his presence or see the exact moment that his soul ascends to heaven.

We come to a stop at the edge of the cemetery and I can still see the mound of dirt alongside Dad's resting place peeking out from between headstones in the distance. A deep sigh from Judd grabs my attention and I turn to where we have stopped.

There in front of me is a smooth, gray stone with a picture of an angel etched deep within it and below that, in elegant script writing is engraved:

Hailey Anne Michaels
March 25, 1976—April 29, 2011
Beloved Mother
The sunshine was brighter because you were here.
Always in our hearts: Tristan, Judd & Jake.

Drawing my eyebrows together, I feel the anguish that Judd must have felt right in this exact spot. His hand tightens around mine and I finally look over at him. He stares ahead at his mother's headstone, not bothering to explain why he brought me here. No words are necessary. I realize that only three short years ago he walked down the same path that I am walking today. He grieved for the loss of a parent just like me, only he didn't have any one to fall back on for support and to hear stories of their life from. He and his brothers were on their own in the moment they stood here.

I stare over at Judd, realizing how grateful I am for having someone that understands and that knows how my heart hurts.

As much as I wish he and I had never took this turn in life, I know that he was placed in it for a reason. What he had told me about fate intervening at precisely the right time when we met holds so much truth to me now.

He knows exactly what I am feeling, because standing here today and seeing the pain in his eyes, I know that loss is just as fresh for him as it was the day he lost her.

He knows there are no healing words.

He knows there is no hug big enough to steal away the pain.

He knows showing me this will help me to understand that I am not alone and that I will survive this, which means more than anyone else could ever know.

We stand there surrounded in complete silence for a while longer before he nudges me to walk with him further away from his truck.

For a moment, my heart stops out of fear that I may finally find out the whole story about where his Dad is as well, but then he leads me away from the cemetery.

We make our way past the last of the headstones, walking with soft footsteps as if we may wake someone, until we come to a rickety chain link fence at the corner of the property. Judd wastes no time jumping the fence and then turns to help me over.

I look back at his truck, a little baffled by where we are going. My lips part to ask him what is on his mind, but when his eyes meet mine and a soft smile reaches his lips, all questions drift away. Placing his hand on the small of my back, he carefully guides me across to a wooded area.

We walk for only a few minutes before a familiarity starts to register in my mind. Once we walk out from beneath the seclusion of the trees and a kiddie park rises up before us, I understand so much. We walk across the park still hand in hand, down a weedy path that I've walked before and end up at the sanctuary that is only his and his brothers.' In this moment, a part of me feels as though he is giving me a part of the peace he feels when he is here; giving me a part of his soul; sharing with me more than words could possibly relay.

Both our grips tighten on each other's hands as we sit on the bench above the tribute to his mother and I can't help but see three boys sitting silently together with so much pain in their hearts while they piece together a beautiful work of art.

I imagine their mother floating above them as they work, softly showering her love down over them to help ease their broken hearts.

My eyes seal shut in an attempt to stop the tears from escaping as I grab onto Judd's arm and pull myself against his side. *He knows my pain. He has been in the same place as me and I take comfort in that.*

After a long while spent within the solitude of his mother's wishing well, we both slowly walk back to his truck with a shared heaviness in our hearts.

Nestling my head into the comfort of his lap, we let complete silence surround us the entire ride home. From the corner of my eye I see one of Judd's hands steadily holding onto the wheel as he steers, but his other hand softly weaves through each strand of my hair in between shifting gears.

As soon as we pull into my driveway, I sit up, expecting to go inside. The instant Judd's hand reaches out to stop me, I tense up with worry that now he may want to talk about us. I know it has to come at some point, but today I really cannot rehash the night I walked in and found him with her. I can't deal with that too, no matter how much being apart is killing me. If we get back together for the sake of my grief, then when we least expect it, all the tension and anger from that morning will come crashing down on us. There is a lot of trust to be earned back and just simply acting like it didn't happen will have consequences down the road.

He pulls me back to him while shutting off the engine.

"I thought we could just stay like this for a bit," he says softly, gently nudging me back to rest against him.

Realizing he doesn't want to talk, I do as he requests and don't fight my desire to be near him for just a bit longer. It used to be Daddy's arms that helped me feel strong, but I have found that Judd's hold has the same effect on me, if not more so. He makes me feel as if everything will be ok, especially today.

We remain in the driveway into the dark hours of the evening. My eyes grow heavy as Judd continues to tangle his fingers through my hair and down my back. His touch soothes and calms me from the outside in and with each caress I'm able to breathe a little easier.

I slowly ease myself up to sit and give him a weak smile. His hand falls to the seat between us and he looks alarmed from my sudden movement.

It seems as if we have been sitting here for an hour or two, just listening to soft music from the radio and lost in our own thoughts. Not once has he tried getting me to talk or discuss anything and that means everything to me. *I should leave before I end up falling asleep.* The longer I'm with him, the harder it is to leave though.

"I really better go." I give him a strained smile and pull the door open.

Judd softly grabs my hand in his to stop me again.

My heart aches even more as I look down at our joined hands and fear what he might say.

"Alyssa, please let me be with you through this. I know we need to talk about what happened, but can't we cross that bridge later?"

I look him in the eyes and he looks away as if he is afraid of what my answer might be.

"Judd, thank you for today and please understand that I just need time," I tell him as gently as possible.

No other words are needed. He squeezes my hand and gives me a heartfelt smile that tells me he does understand.

One foot after the other, my feet find the ground as I step out of the truck and then walk to the front door of my house. The further I get from his truck, the more my heart aches and pleads with me to run back to him. My phone chirping and the sound of his engine pulling away from my house rise into my ears, making me want to turn and yell "Wait, don't go." Instead, I look down and slide my text message open.

Judd: Every second I'm without you only makes me fall more in love with you! I love you more than you will ever know! When you are ready, I will be here! I'm not going anywhere! I love you, Alyssa!

Spinning around, I press my phone against my heart and for the hundredth time today my eyes fill with tears as I watch his headlights dim out of sight.

It almost seems as if coping with not being with him is going to be harder than coping with what I walked in on a week ago. I let out a heavy sigh and tell myself, *one day at a time, Alyssa. Just take it one day at a time.*

Forgive me

I SPEND THE NEXT FEW days helping Mom keep her mind busy. She has a ton of phone calls to make and Abby and I try our best to lighten the load.

I called my school and arranged to finish up my classes via online. I may go back at the change of semester, but right now I am needed here. My work gave me eight days of family leave, so I go back to work on Thursday. I'm not looking forward to it, but at least it will keep me occupied. The hospital gave Abby two weeks off so she still has the rest of the week to help Mom out. That gives me some comfort. Abby and I discussed working our schedules out so that one of us would always be home, but I really think Mom could use some time alone. I just wish I could ease her pain some.

Judd still keeps up his nightly texts, but other than that I have not seen or heard from him. My heart aches for his comfort, but I am managing without him and learning to handle most things.

I try not to look at pictures just yet, plus there are a few possessions of my dad's laying around the house here and there that none of us dare move. He has an old button down shirt draped over the recliner in the living room and a pair of his socks that are rolled into balls at the foot of Mom and Dad's bed. I think they will stay there for a while.

A couple of mornings I have even woke up to Mom asleep on the couch. It's got to be hard lying in their bed all by herself without the warmth of him beside her. I know my heart aches each night, wanting

Judd beside me and to feel his arms around me.

This morning I wake up and try my best to paint on a semi-upbeat expression so that I can head off for work. Since I am no longer staying at my apartment, I get to enjoy a thirty minute commute in rush hour traffic, alone with my thoughts. *That should be fun.*

After work, I plan on swinging by the apartment and gathering all of my belongings.

Abby and I made a run to the grocery store yesterday and collected a couple of boxes that I can use for my move. I don't have that much stuff, mainly clothes; the rest I am not too concerned with.

My pictures will definitely be finding a place in the box. I have a framed picture that I printed off of my phone of Judd and me out at the lake, a picture of my family and another of just Judd. I am hoping that Bethany has not hijacked any pictures of him since she is hell bent on stealing away any guy I am interested in. If I so much as see that the picture of him has been inched in her direction, she will have a fight on her hands.

In the kitchen, I pour a cup of coffee and sit at the table so that I have a good view of the yard through the sliding glass door. All the leaves have fallen to the ground, layering the backyard in shades of red, orange and yellow. I smile, envisioning myself as a child jumping into piles of leaves that Dad would rake up.

Mom wanders into the room, grabs herself a cup of coffee and joins me at the table. I smile at her, studying her face. She looks so drained and disconnected.

"Mom, how are you doing?"

I know it is a stupid question and normally a question like this would get met with total sarcasm in our family, but instead she just smiles at me. The smile is weak, but it is a welcoming sight and it makes me happy.

"I'm good. Actually, I am doing better than I thought I would," she says confidently and I take this time to reevaluate her appearance.

Her hair is neatly pinned back in a barrette, she is wearing a light, lavender top that looks like it has been ironed and her face is pale, but all in all, maybe she is doing better than I thought.

"I am going through some more pictures today," she says before taking a sip of her coffee and gazing out at the yard.

I'm sure there is a mountain of memories that she sees when she looks out there.

"Mom, maybe you should give the pictures a rest for a while. That has to be hard looking at them each day."

She offers me a genuine smile before replying to my comment about how she has been coping with this. *I probably should not have said that.* It's not my place to tell her how to deal with this, but I worry that it is holding her back from accepting he is gone.

"Looking at the pictures isn't hard. Not seeing him every day would be hard. I don't think I could handle that. Looking at the pictures keeps my heart beating every single day. As the days go by and the years pass, I am sure I will look at the pictures less and less, but for now they keep me going."

My eyes fill with tears at her explanation, as hers do too.

I think about how badly I have wanted Judd beside me, despite what he did behind my back and I understand perfectly what she means.

"Maybe you should look at some pictures once in a while yourself."

This surprises me and I snap my face up to see my mother grabbing my phone off the table and shuffling through it. She lays the phone back down on the table and flips it around to face me.

I look down and my heart slams into my chest as I see the picture taken in the back of Judd's truck of him staring over at me as I happily look into the camera lens.

"You want to tell me what happened between you two? I know I have been preoccupied, but I'm not blind. I know it's none of my business, but I can see that you are miserable without him, honey," she says calmly.

"It isn't something I really want to talk about," I tell her honestly.

"Sweetie . . ." She reaches across the table and places her hand over mine. "I hope you are not shutting him out because you are hurting. People do that and sometimes they end up losing that person in the end. I'm sure this is hurting him, too."

I push the tears back that are threatening to spill over and take a deep breath.

"It's not that, Mom," I say and get up to put my mug in the sink.

"You know he came to visit your dad in the hospital."

I stop at the counter and look at her.

"I know. Abby told me that he came the first day that Dad was in the ICU. She said that she snuck him in and let him take a little of her shift."

"Well then I suppose he must have visited twice then. He visited the night your Dad passed away, too." I gasp at this new information and stand completely still, ready to hear everything she has to say.

Her eyes glaze over with tears and she looks back out to the yard. "You and Abby were asleep in the waiting room while I got him situated in his new room and Judd walked in. I wanted to give him some time with your dad, but I also didn't want to leave his side, so I stayed in the room and arranged all your Dad's balloons, cards and flowers while Judd talked to him." She smiles out at the yard and goes on, "Your father told me a couple weeks ago that Judd had told him about how his mother died and how he had to watch her get sicker and sicker each day. I guess in a way seeing your Dad sick, really hit home for him."

I barely breathe as Mom goes on about Judd's visit with Dad in the hospital. *He never even told me about how his mother died. I didn't know she was sick. I've never known anything about how she died really.*

I could not even see through my selfishness to see that Dad's passing away probably took a toll on him too. He has already lived through losing a parent, if not two. Then, he manages to fill a bit of that void with the bond he built with my dad and I don't even ask him to come to the visitation or the funeral.

Mom's voice and quiet sniffles break into my thoughts, "Your dad said that when he would talk to Judd, it was like looking at himself as a nineteen year old again. He really liked him. I know you may be dealing with an issue that you think is beyond my understanding, but I know for a fact that that boy loves you. He promised your Dad that he would take care of you and always love you as much as your father loves me." Mom giggles as she tells me this and I can't help but smile even though my heart is aching. "They both caught onto my eavesdropping as soon as I laughed at that comment, but it managed to get a small laugh out of your dad."

Mom looks up to the ceiling in deep thought and draws her brows together in a frown.

"You know, I think that was the only time your dad laughed in that hospital. It was the last time he laughed before he passed at least." She smiles through a few escaped tears.

"I will forever be thankful to Judd for that." Turning back towards me, she wipes the back of her hand across her cheek and gives me a sympathetic look. "Whatever the issue is with you and him, don't shut him out. If you truly love him, do everything in your power to hold onto him."

I am speechless at her words. Quickly clearing my throat, I offer her a nod and give her a huge hug before I leave.

My emotionally drained, worn out and about-to-burst-into-a-million-pieces body drags out to my car, in no way prepared for the long day ahead, while I ponder over everything Mom said. I'm praying this day will fly by so I can get to my apartment, but the fact that I want it to go fast is a sure bet that it will more than likely crawl by.

Luckily for me, the dentist's office is jam packed with appointments, leaving me little time for a lunch, potty breaks or even time to glance at the clock.

At three o-clock sharp, I hit the time clock and punch out.

Running on pure adrenaline, I race out to my car, throw it into drive and speed to my apartment. I'm not sure what I am excited or anxious for, but my mood is lighter than it has been in nearly two weeks. It's as though I am about to discover a treasure at the end of a rainbow. Maybe it is the thought of finally having my stuff back home or having my pictures to display on my dresser in my own room or maybe it's knowing I don't have to pay rent for the next few months, who knows, but I am going to just roll with it.

I rush up to my apartment door, lugging a large box with me and unlock it quietly, hoping Bethany is not here. The apartment is quiet and whoa, it is a mess. *Wow!* Well, it's not my problem anymore. I throw the box onto my bed and start tossing clothes out of my closet into it.

After I have all my clothing emptied from the closet, I carry the now full box out and stuff it into my trunk only to return with another empty one. I hope I can fit my entire dresser and under the bed belongings into this last box, because I really would prefer to not have to come back.

First thing I look at upon returning is my pictures on my dresser. They are still there and facing my bed. *She's lucky.*

I start emptying drawer after drawer into one box and then place all my shoes from under the bed onto the top. Just as I am laying the last of my things on the pile of my belongings, the bedroom door scrapes against the carpet, alerting me that I have company.

I turn and Bethany's troubled eyes look back at me. Completely fed up with her conniving, vindictive and unremorseful ways, I lean against the dresser and fix her with my best glare. *We may have been friends a little over a week ago, but I have no desire to have a friend like her.*

"Alyssa, I am so sorry for everything. I heard about your dad. I am so sorry for your loss!"

For considering herself my best friend for this long, you would think she could come up with something more original than that.

I fold my arms across my chest and wait. That's when it dawns on me why I was so amped to get here. I'm ready to listen now, ready for answers, ready to find out the truth and ready for closure.

I tap my foot on the floor impatiently as she sits on her bed. I'd rather her not sit there, because the last image I had from that bed was not something I would like to rekindle in my mind.

"Listen, I feel awful for what has gone on the last two weeks. I know you are hurting and the last thing I want is to create more pain for you. I tried calling and explaining, but you never called me back." She pauses.

"And?!" I urge her in the snippiest tone I can bite out.

"I made it all up!" she snaps out sharply while looking down at her fidgeting hands.

My eyes widen and my mouth drops open.

"You made up what?!" I spit out, moving forward towards her.

She rises up to face me with her face twisted in panic.

"I'm so sorry . . . you have to believe me. It just got out of hand."

Her words are not registering in my mind anymore. I'm still stuck on the "I made it all up" comment.

"What did you make up, Bethany?!" I say with my lip curled in disgust and fully ready to pounce on her.

"Ok, calm down and let me explain."

I take a deep breath and back off just an inch or two, folding my hands in front of me as I wait for her to explain.

"It all started our junior year . . ."

I blow out a huff of air and roll my eyes. *Geez, how many hours of my life is she going to waste telling me what she means?*

She looks at me frustrated before going on, "I had a crush on Kyle since sophomore year and everyone in school knew it. Everyone! I swore you knew but then the end of our junior year, when I asked if you were going out with him it was like a slap in the face. I thought you were just rubbing it in. We became friends and although I didn't even think I would like you at first, you truly became my best friend."

My blood is boiling in my veins the deeper she goes with this story and I wonder if she realizes what kind of a hole she is digging for herself. *This isn't saying you're sorry! This is throwing salt on a wound!* But I stay put, drumming my fingertips on my arm as she goes on.

"I didn't intend on sleeping with Kyle that night at the party. I really didn't! But he went up to his bed to crash and the drunker I got, the more inviting his room looked and the more jealous I got over you."

She looks up at me with a look of shame and I flinch.

I hope she feels as sleazy and cheap as she is, but she still hasn't answered my question.

I stand taller like an animal intent on intimidating its prey and ask her again. "What did you make up?"

She looks back up and her eyes are watery, but I don't feel even a hint of remorse for her.

"The morning you got up, I was in the living room and I was still pissed about you taking them both from me."

My eyes widen with those words and I want to scream out that I found Judd first, like a kid claiming a toy for themselves.

"I had been trying to flirt with him for a while. I even tried to kiss him just to see if he would kiss me back. I was just hoping that maybe he wasn't as serious about you as it seemed."

I let out a shocked breath, wanting to laugh. *Is she for real?*

"It's just most guys want me, but it just didn't seem fair that the two I wanted the most didn't want me at all. I was just eaten up with jealousy and I am so sorry. That morning, I thought you were leaving with your sister, so I went in my room. When I saw Judd asleep in my bed, I crawled in and figured he wanted me and not you. When he started saying your name in his sleep, I just went crazy with envy and just wanted him to forget you and want me. I didn't think. I just acted and took advantage of the situation. I know it was wrong of me now! I wanted to clear the air. Nothing ever happened. As soon as he felt me near him, he shoved me off and that is when you walked in. After you left, I convinced him that he slept with me hoping you guys would break up and he would want me. I'm so sorry."

Tears stream down Bethany's face, but I don't move; I am paralyzed from this new information.

He never did anything with her. I punished him this whole time; I shut him out from a time when I truly needed him near, a time when my family needed him there and he never did anything wrong. She lied!

"Alyssa, I am sooo sooo sorry! Please forgive me!" she cries out standing in front of me.

She raises her arms as if to hug me and I instantly clinch my jaw to fight the anger and emotion that is consuming me. *She lied this whole time! She was never my friend! She hurt me not once but twice!*

"Alyssa, please . . . I was honest about everything. That has to count for something, right?"

Looking at her, my blood suddenly turns to molten lava from the rage that is building inside of me and I know I can no longer hold back.

"Evan was right about you!" I spit out right before my fist makes contact with her left cheek.

She falls back onto the bed, instantly covering her face with her hand as a fresh set of tears fall from her eyes. I don't think twice and I don't feel bad for knocking her on her ass. I grab my box and walk out.

"I am sorry, Alyssa! I know I deserved that, but please . . ."

I keep walking as her voice fades into the back ground. *I am done with her!*

Overwhelmed with grief, yet now having a small sense of closure, I shove the last box in my back seat and get in, not wanting to go home.

I should go to Judd's and apologize for not trusting in him or our relationship enough, but I can't. *How do I face him and tell him that I made an assumption about him even when he swore to me that he would never have done that?* He knows that I thought he cheated on me. Even Evan and Abby didn't believe it, but I did. I believed the worst and even though, she also told him that he cheated on me, he still never believed it.

He could have been sitting with me in the hospital that whole time. Instead of going out to my car to listen to my voicemails the morning Dad left this world, I would have been there when he took his last breath and Judd would have been, too. Her lies stole all that from me. I should have believed him.

I pushed him away and now I have to explain to him that he did nothing wrong. *How could he ever trust me again, knowing I had no faith in him?*

Now that everything is out in the open and I know all the details of that morning, I am the one that should be ashamed of my actions. I turned my back on him and walked away. *He will never forgive me; how could he?*

Take my Breath Away

AFTER DRIVING AND DRIVING, I reach my destination and park my car half in the grass off to the side of the single lane road. As I push my door open, I slowly take in the surroundings. The sun shines bright in the sky and a gentle breeze whips through the air, making the trees appear to be dancing. I tread carefully along the path, stepping over twigs and leaves, afraid that the sound may alert someone to my presence.

I don't know why I am compelled to come here, but I feel like I should explain things to her first. It's almost as if maybe she or my dad can guide my way and possibly let me know what to do.

Once the sounds of running water hit my ears and the sparkling path catches my eye, a part of me relaxes. I can totally see what Judd's mom saw in this place. It does seem magical with its tranquil beauty and seclusion from everything else. It's as if I've climbed through a doorway to another dimension; another time.

I settle myself down beside the carefully laid stones and stare down at the magnificent angel with flowing brown hair and dazzling jade eyes.

Judd had told me that when he had gotten out of the hospital, the first thing he did was come here and tell his mom all about me. *I guess now it's my turn.*

Although I have been here on two different occasions with him, I almost feel it is necessary for me to introduce myself now. I clear my throat, a bit nervous, but mostly silly for talking to a pathway.

"Hi . . . ummm . . . Hailey." I remember reading her name on the headstone in the cemetery. "I'm Alyssa. I think Judd told you about me."

I crinkle my brows and look up to the sky wondering what the hell I am doing. Closing my eyes, I silently count to ten and push away the tears that are building behind my eyes. *I feel so lost! What do I do? If only I could rewind my life,* I think to myself as I take a deep, calming breath. I keep my eyes focused on the clouds above, but feel as though I am looking beyond them to something deeper that is invisible to the naked eye.

"I don't know where to go from here. I'm not sure what to do."

I sit there in the solitude of the woods, listening to the trickling of water and the rustling of leaves as I pour my heart out to Judd's mom.

"I'm . . ." My eyes fill with tears as I gulp down the lump in my throat. "I'm in love with your son."

I take a deep breath and go on, confessing the depths of my heart, "I never stopped loving him, but I didn't have enough faith in him. I should have never questioned him."

I talk and cry sharing everything I feel for him with her until I have nothing left. Running my hands along the smooth, icy stones, I can't help but wish that I could have met her. I wish death would have never come for my dad and his mom. *Will there ever be a day that I don't look at another father and daughter and think, why me? Why not them? Does it mean that our parents were needed more or does it possibly mean that we are strong enough to handle this and maybe others aren't?*

I ponder on so many questions that I will never get the answers to and ones I shouldn't even be asking, but I still do. After I have sat there in silence a while longer, I say my goodbyes and trail down the path towards my next destination.

Once I hop the fence and come to the cemetery, I wind my way along the path, passing grave after grave of someone else's loved ones. I skim over the inscriptions on each headstone, wondering what the story is behind each death; behind each life. I even brush leaves, dirt and debris from some of the older graves that look as if there is no one around to come visit them any longer. *I'm in no hurry.* I have nowhere to go at the moment and it brings me a sense of comfort being here; knowing Dad is so close.

At last I reach him. His headstone has already been put in place and the mound of dirt has been weathered down, nearly level with the grass. Fresh grass seeds lie on top as if they had been sprinkled just hours before.

I crouch down to the side of where Dad's body rests and stare at the heart-shaped granite stone.

ALEXANDER JAMES MASON
MAY 19, 1969—OCTOBER 29, 2014

BELOVED HUSBAND, FATHER AND GRANDPA
LIVE LIFE TO THE FULLEST AND LEAVE NO WORDS UNSPOKEN
TILL WE SHALL MEET AND NEVER PART
ANGELA, ANDREA, ABBY AND ALYSSA

"Hi, Daddy." I burst into tears and wish so badly he was here to hug me.

I really need to have one of our heart to heart talks. I need his advice. I need some of his words of wisdom of how I am supposed to handle this. I need to hear him tell me I am not a bad person for not trusting the one person that I say I am completely and wholly in love with.

"I need you Daddy. I need to see you. You promised you would be with me; that you would find me. Where are you?"

I look up to the sky as if he may appear with wings and a halo to wisp away all this crushing heartache. Gulping down breath after breath, I try to talk through the tears that rain down my face.

"I told you I couldn't breathe if you left me. I told you I didn't think I could do it and I can't. I can't do this without you, Daddy. I need you . . . I need you here with me . . . with all of us."

My body shakes uncontrollably and I don't think my sobs will ever cease. Plopping down on the ground with a thud, my hand feels its way across the cold granite. *This is nothing like my dad. He was so warm and full of life.*

My eyes focus in on the writing on the stone then down to the heap of dirt above where my dad now rests. Slowly inching my hand out from my body, my fingers dig into the soft crumbly dirt and I grab a handful. Holding my palm out in front of me as if I am offering it to the sky, I slowly let each grain slip through my fingers and back to the ground. I blink my eyes rapidly and a river of tears roll down my face. *Will they ever stop?*

I sit there as the minutes click by, pleading with my dad to come back for one last hug, one last 'I love you,' one last kiss on the cheek. *He promised.* He promised he would watch over me; that he would find me during every moment of my life. *I can't breathe!* I told him I wouldn't be able to breathe if he was gone and he said he would be here, but I still cannot feel him near. I lift my chin gradually to look up hoping and praying that I wake up from this nightmare. *Where are you Daddy? I need you.*

And just like an answer to a prayer, I see Judd standing only steps away.

Seconds pass as we stare at one another. I have so many things that I want to say to him, yet I can't seem to form a single syllable.

Words swirl around in my head, but when I finally find my voice, I can only croak out one sentence, "How did you find me?" I ask in a shaky voice.

He walks closer; close enough to touch, but still too far away. My heart beats rapidly, longing for his arms to be around me. Raising his arm, his fingertips come to rest under my chin and he gently guides my face up so that I am looking him in the eyes. It's there that I see so much warmth and love that it nearly melts my heart.

Then he answers, "I'll always find you."

He stops talking long enough to swipe his thumb across my cheek to wipe away all the tears. I blink my eyes and look back up at him, completely speechless.

"I know nothing happened that morning and I know for a fact that you know that now, too," he says with absolutely not a hint of anger or regret or blame in his voice; just love.

My chest heaves up and down, knowing that he knows that I blamed him for something he never did.

"I didn't trust you. I'm so sorry I didn't believe you. How can you still want me when I was able to believe her instead of you?" I gasp out between the tears, my heart beating a mile a minute when it really seems as though it shouldn't be beating at all.

His mouth lifts into a small crooked grin and I see his dimple appear.

"Of course I want you. Didn't you hear me? I'll always want you. Alyssa, you take my breath away. When we are together, I have to remind myself to breathe, because you make my heart beat so fast. When we're apart, I'm constantly trying to catch my breath, because I can't breathe without you. You're my life, my air, my whole world. You're it for me, Alyssa. I love you and I can't live without you. I'm lost without you, baby," he says as his voice cracks.

There is no stopping the tears now.

I close the distance between us in an instant and wrap my arms around his neck. He lifts me up into his arms, with my feet dangling above the ground. Tear after tear streams down my face as my lips crash into his. He drinks me in and kisses me with an equal amount of love, vigor and passion that I show him. My heart pounds fiercely in my chest and I can feel his drumming along with mine.

He sits me down and gently places his hands on my cheeks.

"I'll always find you, I promise . . . because you found me," he whispers, looking deeply into my eyes.

Quivering breaths pour from my mouth and I cry tears of happiness for the first time in the last two weeks. I know he didn't sleep with Bethany; he was always true to me and every time I have been lost he has found me, even the first day I met him. Every time I am crumbling, he manages to be the only one that can put me back together.

A heart to heart Dad and I had months ago rings in my ears and I swear I can hear his beautiful voice whispering in the wind, "Oh honey, you will know!" *And I do know.* I know Judd loves me without a shadow of a doubt. He is the only one for me and I am also lost without him.

I stretch up onto my tiptoes and kiss him with all the love I have in my heart. He kisses me back; pulling me into his arms like I am his home.

When we finally come up for air minutes later, Judd looks at me sweetly with his gorgeous hazel eyes sparkling under the sunlight.

"Let me take you to your mom and dad's house?"

I love that he said Dad as if he is still here, because I know for a fact he is. Dad told me he would be there at every breathtaking moment of my life and I know this is one of many I will have with Judd.

"I'd like that." I look up into his eyes and see all my love reflected back to me.

"I'm not much of a cook, but I was hoping I could make these for you girls."

He reaches down to the ground and grabs a small paper sack that he was holding in his hands just moments ago. He opens the sack and I peer inside and see a box of fudge brownie mix. I cover my mouth and laugh for the first time since Dad died.

"I think we would all really like that." I say as a single tear slips down my cheek.

This is not a tear of pain or loss, though; this is a tear of pure happiness and love. Judd wipes it away and grabs my waist to lead me to his truck.

As we walk through the cemetery, I turn one last time to Dad's grave.

"Thank you, Daddy," I whisper to him and I know he can hear me.

I know because he promised me that when I'm lost, if he can't get to me he would make sure he sent someone to find me, and he did. I smile up into the heavens and realize my dad isn't gone at all. He's here and he will always be here watching over all of these moments in my life that sneak up on me and take my breath away.

Keep a look out for:

Catch My Breath
Book Two in **The Breathe Series**

Judd's POV

Here's a sneak peek

FOR YEARS I'VE FELT LIKE I was stumbling from one life altering event after another. Just as my life finds some sense of normality, disaster strikes and I'm back to dealing with some bullshit that leaves me wondering why.

It wasn't always like this. Some of my first memories are of Mom and Dad playing with us in the backyard, taking us to the water park in the summers, big Christmas's at my Grandma and Grandpa's house, Easter egg hunts at church and all those typical family functions that you learn to love as a kid.

However, the one thing that those moments have taught me is that all good things come to an end, and it did, starting with the night my dad made it clear to us that we were simply a mistake. That's definitely not something a kid dreams of hearing.

I was nine the night it happened. Funny thing is that my parents didn't even know we were in the room.

Jake, who is a year younger than me, shared a bedroom with me while Tristan, the oldest of us three, was fortunate enough to have his own room. Jake and I also shared a fear of the dark. Mix that with our childhood love of television and it was a recipe for two sleepless boys.

After Mom would put us to bed, we'd bounce back up and sneak into the living room, crawling down the hall in complete stealth mode. Slithering along the floor with nothing but the quiet sound of our stomachs scraping the carpet, we would settle in behind a recliner against the wall at the entrance of the living room.

The sounds of the TV greeted us along with soft laughter from Mom and Dad who was as usual, all wrapped up with one another on our fluffy brown couch. We figured out pretty quickly that once we were all tucked away in bed, they would fire up the movie channels after carefully typing in their secret parental code.

Once we got to our rendezvous point, Jake and I would lie on our bellies, feet kicked up behind us while we watched along with movies that my parents deemed unsuitable for young eyes. Some of the films would leave me dragging my brother back to our bedroom before either of us saw too much.

That night, however, they were watching one that we had seen a couple of times already. It was still like sneaking into a movie theater without paying, so we basically did it for the excitement and the thrill of getting caught. We would laugh and talk about it for days like we had just gotten away with breaking the law.

This particular time, we ended up breaking the one rule we had set for ourselves during operation 'Crawl in Movie'; we fell asleep. Not just Jake; not just me; nope, we both fell flat-on-our-faces-passed-out-sawing-logs asleep.

I'm not sure how long we had laid there wisped away in dreamland and I'm not even sure what transpired between movie time and us waking up, but I do know I woke up to all hell breaking loose.

My head bolts up from the carpet to the sound of glass shattering and a piercing scream. Pushing up to my hands and knees in a hurry, I look around the recliner to get a view of what is happening; that's when Dad's voice begins to boom, like cracks of thunder.

"I can't do this! I can't! I won't!"

Mom pulls herself up off the floor by latching onto the arm of the couch. Dad has a crazed look in his eyes while impatiently pacing back and forth a few feet away in front of her. *Why doesn't he help her?* I can't even pinpoint everything I see, but to me, they both look scared; frightened.

"Scott, I'm sorry. I don't know what to say," she pleads, tears streaming down her face.

"Hailey, do you know what this is doing to me? Do you even care?!" he shouts out.

Looking around, I survey the situation and see a turned over lamp with shards of thick, amber glass littered across the floor. Mom is finally standing, but seems unstable, leaning some of her weight onto the coffee table which used to house the lamp.

"I just don't think I can do this. I've questioned this for years." He places his hands to his side and looks down with Mom staring at him in confusion.

"What do you mean?" she barely gets out between the tears as she lowers herself onto the edge of the couch.

He snaps his head back up and squints his eyes in an angry glare.

"I mean I can't do this anymore," he motions between her and him. "You know what? I never wanted this in the first place. We got stuck together when you got pregnant . . . you know that." He sighs and Mom dumps her head into her lap, sobbing uncontrollably.

"Wait, I don't understand. I thought . . ." Mom manages to get out in a quivering voice.

I have no clue what Dad is talking about either, but I want so badly to go hug mom. I hate seeing her hurt. He knows she's been getting clumsier lately, she's been to the doctor several times, but I just don't understand why Dad doesn't go over to tell her it's alright.

They assume I don't notice little things like her losing her balance and the way her legs don't seem to cooperate as they once did. Another thing I haven't missed sight of is how Dad prefers to keep us all at a distance lately. He watches her when she cries, he even looks sad for her, but he doesn't hug her like me and my brothers do. I don't understand it and it bothers me more than they see.

The other day, out of the blue, Mom ran to her room after one of her spells. Tristan was loading the dishwasher and Jake was taking out the trash, but she ran right past me in the hall as I went to help my brothers with our chores. Once her quiet sobs filtered through the air, I sneaked back and peeked through the crack in her door. She sat on the bed with her face buried in the pillow crying. Dad sat on the floor in front of her with a sad expression on his face, just watching as she shouldered the pain alone. A little while later she came out pretending like nothing was wrong with a painted on smile.

"God, I have been trying to make this work. That's why we had Judd, but then you got pregnant again, and it just seems like too much. You know, I never even wanted kids, Hailey. Did you know that? Do you even think we would have stayed together if you wouldn't have gotten pregnant with Tristan?"

Watching the entire scene unfold, what he is saying finally starts to sink in. *Is he saying we are a mistake?*

Looking up through tear streaked eyes her voice comes out shaky and confused, "Where is this coming from? I don't understand where all this is coming from. You could have left years ago, if that were true. You're just scared and I am, too," she huffs out. "It doesn't have to be like this, Scott."

I look back over to Mom and see that she has stood up and is inching closer to Dad, her hands out as if she is trying to tame a wild stallion.

"Hailey, no, please! I just realized I never wanted this and now with you being sick . . . I'm just . . . I'm out!"

Mom runs to Dad, tripping over her feet in the process and grabs onto his arms before she tumbles to the floor again.

"You don't mean that . . . you don't! I know you're just scared, but I know you can do this. I know you can," Mom's voice softens and I crane my neck to watch. "We'll face this together."

She has her arms against his chest and for a moment I think everything is better; that the fight is over, but it isn't.

Grabbing her by the arms, he shoves her away, yelling with more anger than I've ever heard; the sound of a stranger's voice, not my dad's.

"It's over! This is over!" He points his fingers towards the hall where all our rooms are located and then lowers his voice; almost too quiet for me to make out. "This was a mistake . . . they were a mistake and this is not the future I want."

Confusion and disbelief fill my mind and I begin to rise up to make my presence known. *I need to defend my mother,* but suddenly hands grip the back of my shirt and pull me back into the hall. Tilting my head, I see Tristan's face above me, crumpled into a scowl.

"Get back to bed, now," he says in an angry tone.

My first instinct is to protest, but one look into his eyes and I know I better let this go. Something about the way he continues to look over the edge of the recliner I'm hiding behind and the storm of rage in his eyes tells me I better listen.

After I am within the safety of my bedroom, he rushes back out and down the hall without another word. What had been only the raised voice of my father with a background melody of my mother's hurtful sobs is soon joined by Tristan's amplified hollers. His furious tone rises over Dad's and immediately muffles out Mom's cries.

"Don't you ever . . . ever touch her or shove her! Get the hell out of here! We don't want you anymore than you want us! We don't need you!" The anger in his voice sends chills down my spine. "Leave, just Leave!" his voice blares out.

"Tristan . . ." Mom's voice calls out as I lean in the doorway of my room, trying to strain to see what all is going on. "Honey, you don't under . . ."

"Get out I said," Tristan's shrill tone vibrates through me, bringing tears to my eyes.

What's going on? Why is everyone yelling at each other?

Something crashes in the other room and I flinch against the door frame, fear gripping every corner of my soul.

"Get the hell out of here," he yells out again, his voice laced in rage.

Turning my body, I slowly slide down the wall beside my door much like the tears that now drip down my face. With my body planted into a ball on the floor, I think over everything that I heard, feeling lifeless and drained of emotion. Pushing my palms over my ears as more noise ignites from the living room, I look up at the ceiling not understanding, yet not sure that I want to.

A few minutes later, a muffled slamming noise penetrates the protection of my hands over my ears and then all goes quiet. Assuming it was the front door, I race to my window; watching just as Dad climbs into his car and speeds out of the driveway.

My heart hammers in my throat and I wonder when he will be back. *Maybe he is leaving to cool off.* With that single thought, his words come back to me, "I'm done . . . I'm out," "I never wanted this," "It's over," "They are a mistake." *He didn't want us . . . he doesn't want us? He's not coming back?* Rejection, grief and sorrow engulf my heart as my mind spins out of control in a tornado of questions and doubt.

The door eases open behind me and I watch as Tristan carries Jake in. Folded in his arms like a big baby, I realize that somehow he managed to stay asleep.

I remain quiet, holding back a river of tears as Tristan lays Jake into the bottom mattress of the bunk bed. His jaw is tense and his eyes are red as if he had rubbed them raw before coming into the room.

"Tristan, is Dad coming back?" I ask quietly, not wanting to wake Jake and involve him in this daunting catastrophe.

Tristan pulls his arms out from beneath Jake's back, stands straight and levels me with a firm glare that I've never seen on his face before. Suddenly my brother looks older; bitter and angry.

"Judd, go to bed. You're up way too late and you should not have been out of bed anyways," he says calmly and then slowly walks to the door, shutting it without another look my way.

I turn back to the window and touch my hand to the cold glass, my crushed heart pleading that this whole night is only a dream. It's at that moment . . . that solitary second, that I recognize the significance of what just happened. *This is the last time I will ever see my dad. We're on our own.*

And it was.

After that night it was one thing after another; jumping around from apartment to apartment trying to make ends meet, scrambling to find any odd job to help Mom put food on the table and then losing my grandparents. All the while, Mom was getting sicker and sicker. Just when it seemed like life was getting back on track and we settled into a nice house, one of which me and my brothers still question how on earth we were able to afford, that's when it hit rock bottom. With only a few months until I turned sixteen, I found myself in a whirlwind of responsibility that ended with us laying Mom to rest.

Immediately following her death, life spiraled out of control for me. Through an endless stampede of casseroles and baked goods being brought to our door, Tristan, Jake and I, who had always been close growing up, went in three different directions. That first day, there was no hugging or comforting words spoken between us; just silence and solitude until finally, I couldn't take it anymore.

I always envisioned myself staying strong for the sake of my little brother when Mom died, but I completely went in the opposite direction. It wasn't Tristan that ran off and got plastered drunk and ended up sleeping with some random girl he had never met. No it wasn't him; it was me.

I woke up the next morning in someone else's bed, in a strange house, with a pounding sensation in my head, foggy memories of the night before and some mystery girl draped over me.

A couple used condom wrappers, our bare bodies and her clinging to me was all I needed to realize I had given away something in my drunken stupor that I couldn't ever get back. It wasn't that I was hoping to hold onto my virginity forever or anything, but I expected it to be with someone I cared about and I sure didn't think it would be before I even finished going through puberty. *How could I be so irresponsible; so stupid?!*

That's part of the reason why I didn't let myself get all hung up on high school romances, partying and messing around. I made myself a promise that night to never be so reckless and foolish in the heat of the moment. That one evening was enough carelessness for me to last a lifetime.

From that point on, I stayed busy with football, kept my grades up, worked and continued to try to catch my breath from a sequence of events the led to me being one of three brothers trying to raise ourselves.

I'd catch my breath between being a positive role model and supportive friend to my younger brother.

I'd catch my breath from struggling with nonstop training and studying to ensure a scholarship, along with working every available second to help make ends meet, that it left me with very little time to enjoy being a teenager.

I'd catch my breath between remembering every moment that I had watched Mom's ALS get crueler and harsher until eventually her worn out body had to give up the fight.

Now, catching my breath has become second nature, along with having to pick up the pieces of Tristan's life.

Every minute felt as though I was drowning, sinking, being buried alive; until I saw her.

That's when catching my breath no longer felt like a struggle; it no longer felt painful. It reminded me that I was alive and I was finally able to look at my life and realize that every turn, every crook in the road and every road block had led me to this moment . . .

It had led me to *her.*

Acknowledgements

I have to give a huge thanks to my husband. He has endured countless hours and nights of me reading page after page to him, asking for his opinion a hundred times a day, listening to my stressed-out rants and stood there by me, believing in me the whole way. Thank you, babe, for everything! I wish I could say that now you can get some sleep, but we have too many more books to go.

Thank you to my mom, which has been my biggest fan. You have been my positive reinforcement along the way and I could not have done this without you. Talk about a Breathe Series, I think I actually held my breath until you told me you loved the book.

To some wonderful supporters: Cori Wray, Brandy Kirn and Jen Martin. You all kept me going from pep talks and lunch dates with Cori to hour-long phone calls with Brandy and long walks while I vented with Jen. Your faith in me has been unyielding and in times that my stress and frustration got the best of me each of you were able lift me back up. Thank you. A special thanks to my best friend, Cori Wray, who was the first person to ever read this book. Thank you for helping me believe that I can do this.

To my editor, Jeremy Thompson, thank you for all your wonderful advise from purple skinny jeans to colorful phrases like "flick of the tongue" and "knee him in the buttons"! This book leaped hurdles and bounds with your help! Where would I be without you?! Writing a book comprised of one big paragraph, that's where! Btw, did you notice all the exclamation marks; just for you!!

A big thanks to Karen as well, for follow up edits.

Thank you to a great group of Beta Readers: Carrie Travillion, Tara Dameron, Brandi Ackerman, Karrie Zschille, Brooke Reynolds, Kelly Smith, Sara Kiplinger, Jaclyn Keller, Zack Koeller, Jason Wray, Darla Her, Ashley Shoen, Cori Wray and Heather Pope. You all helped me so much with fabulous input, keen eyes, advice, opinions and support. You truly helped breathe life into this book. A special thanks to

Karrie Zschille, who went above and beyond with late night proofreading, advice and words of encouragement. You rock, girl!

Thank you to Kari for a stunning cover design, Mandy for gorgeous photos and for pulling double duty to be the perfect Alyssa and Julio for being the perfect Judd. You all truly brought my characters to life.

Also thank you to Ashleigh Pettis for taking some great author photos . . . beautiful work as always.

Most importantly, thank you Lord for giving me the courage, capability, determination, mindset, confidence and talent to put into words, what I can only see as signs from you that I need to finally take a risk and write a book.

Last but not least, I'd like to pre-thank everyone who takes a chance on this book. I hope that you all love it, enjoy it and fall in love with the characters like I have. They are truly in my heart and I think everyone should take the time to get to know them. There's more to come, so stay tuned.

About the author

Wendy Wilson is an independent author. As a little girl on through adulthood, she has dreamt of writing and has finally put that dream into action with the release of her first book in a series of novels called *The Breathe Series.* She enjoys spending time with her family, hanging with her friends and reading. She also has a passion for running and has found it is the perfect time to create and think up more exciting plots and characters to add into her books. She currently lives in Chaffee, Missouri with her husband, two adorable sons and two cats.

Visit my website at:
www.wendylwilsonauthor.com and
FaceBook: https://www.facebook.com/wendylwilsonauthor

www.ingramcontent.com/pod-product-compliance
Lightning Source LLC
Chambersburg PA
CBHW021304250626
47155CB00002B/367